FEB 16

W9-AUK-590

# The Female Complaint

# Praise for *The Female Complaint*

"Spellbinding stories about the active, spirited lives of women. ...Throughout each is the common denominator of an active female character who embarks on her own hero's journey....With prose that ranges from the humorous to the lyric and forms that range from the real to the magical, here is a vital addition to contemporary literature."

—*Kirkus*

"This is more than women being unruly: this is women being courageous, outrageous, brutally honest, and more than anything, talented. The stories sing off the page— and then turn into a howl of rage, delight and hope."

— Rene Denfeld, author of *The Enchanted*

"Forty years ago when women blazed literary trails, they were paths through the woods where no one heard the trees falling. This time... women are still throwing themselves and their lives out into new thematic territory."

—Cris Mazza, author of *Various Men Who Knew Us as Girls*
and co-editor of *Chick-Lit: Postfeminist Fiction*

"Often unsettling in the best sense, these stories cross cultures and mental states....Compelling and ambitious stories dedicated to honoring the more turbulent desires."

—Lee Upton, author of *The Tao of Humiliation: Stories*
and *Bottle the Bottles the Bottles the Bottles: Poems*

"These fictions are aggressively spirited, wild, winking, sexy and funny, and it's inspiring to watch the lead female protagonists take the kind of provocative, hard-to-predict agency they wrestle from their less intelligent enemies—made up of self and other."

—Betsy Boyd, literary editor, *Baltimore Fishbowl*

# The Female Complaint

## Tales of Unruly Women

Edited by Rosalie Morales Kearns

Shade Mountain Press
Albany, New York

Shade Mountain Press
P.O. Box 11393
Albany, NY 12211
www.shademountainpress.com

The female complaint: tales of unruly women / edited by
Rosalie Morales Kearns

ISBN 978-0-9913555-5-6 (pbk.)

1. Feminist fiction. 2. Short stories—21st century. 3. Short stories—Women
   authors. 4. Women—Social life and customs—Fiction.

Printed in the United States of America
17 16 15    1 2 3

Cover art: Detail from *Copper Vessel*, by Elsa Muñoz, copyright © 2012 by Elsa
Muñoz.

Shade Mountain Press is committed to publishing literature by women.

# CONTENTS

## PART IV. MOTHER FIGURES

## PART V. TRANSFORMATION

# INTRODUCTION

There are so many stories behind these stories.

First, the anthology's title phrase, with its multiple meanings that can't be pinned down. The term "female complaint" evokes nineteenth-century patent medicines. It hints that femaleness itself is some kind of malady. It speaks to the patriarchal tendency to dismiss outspoken women as complainers.

Then there's the story of why I chose this theme, which is connected to the story of why the pieces are all by women writers, and that's connected to the story of why I started Shade Mountain Press.

Some readers may remember a glorious wave of women's anthologies in the 1980s and early '90s, titles like *Midnight Birds: Stories by Contemporary Black Women Writers; Dreams in a Minor Key: Tales of Magic Realism by Women;* and *What Did Miss Darrington See? An Anthology of Feminist Supernatural Fiction.* I was in my twenties at the time, and I devoured these books; I was starved for them. The canon was skewed male; most of the work I was assigned or encouraged to read had been by male authors. Now it seemed that just over the horizon was an era when this exclusion of women would be a thing of the past.

Fast-forwarding to 2015, the literary landscape has not changed much. Celebrated male authors make disparaging statements about books written by women, their styles, subject matters, tones. According to systematic research by organizations like VIDA: Women in Literary Arts, the ratios of men to women in literary publishing are still horribly skewed. In many book review venues, 75 percent or more of the titles reviewed are by men. Literary journals and publishing companies have shown similar rates of acceptance of male authors: two-thirds, three-quarters, even nine-tenths. At some presses, a season's entire list of new and forthcoming literary fiction consists of works by men.

Literature, it seems, is still a territory women need to claim. We're being told it isn't truly ours, that we have no full right to be there.

That was my impetus for founding Shade Mountain Press, publishing literary fiction by women. Our first two titles appeared in 2014. As a publisher, I had a chance to compile an anthology like the feminist collections that had meant so much to me. I was tempted to put together something in the fabulist mode (or call it magic realist, slipstream, speculative), but rather than specify a genre, I decided to focus on a theme. And what better theme, for women transgressing onto hostile territory, than formidable, convention-defying women?

There are many ways to describe the women in these stories: feisty, unruly, indomitable. Above all, they take action. They make change. They stand up for themselves, for each other, for their beliefs. These are stories of solidarity, resistance, transformation, connection, joy. There is a lot of humor here, a bit of violence. I can't promise that no one gets killed, but the death toll isn't very high. The stories navigate that fine line between anger and laughter; they hint at visions of something better.

⚜

As I've struggled through the learning process involved in starting a press, and then in compiling an anthology, I've come to rely more and more on Shade Mountain's first authors, Robin Parks and Lynn Kanter. They have been patient sounding boards, wise counselors, and models of writerly generosity. I will always be grateful.

Rosalie Morales Kearns
Albany, New York

# Part I

# Resistance

# Ironing

## *Sarah Marian Seltzer*

E sther watched Tennis Boy amble across the hotel lobby, racket slung
across his back, and decided on the spot he'd be her first boyfriend. He
wasn't noticeably handsome, but he was noticeably normal, and to Esther's
twelve-year-old eyes, that was everything.

The mirrors on the wall created four of him, no, six, each more polished
than the last. Esther's own family needed no multiplying, boisterous and
too many already; they monopolized the desk as they checked in for their
reunion in Puerto Rico, her uncle passing out room keys like prizes.

Given that Tennis Boy would be gallivanting past at regular intervals, he
was an obvious choice. He would fall for Esther's wholesome looks, a contrast
to the gussied-up falseness of his friends back home. He and she would dive
beneath the same surging wave. Impressed by her courage when she rose in
the surf's wake, he'd compliment her. Then as the sun sent light skittering
across the turquoise waters, he'd kiss her. She would soon be transported by
a momentous passion, leaving behind her squabbling clan, the impending
double doom of braces and bat mitzvah, the fact that her best friend, Lin,
had a date to the winter formal, and the terror that underlay it all: a sense
that each day since seventh grade began had colluded with the day before it
to shove Esther into a shackled crouch, to render her one day less free.

Unfortunately for Esther's plans, the hotel's private beach was lake-like:
no waves. Even worse, the air above it was what the girls at school called "bad

hair day humid." Though she'd ignored her cousins' request to build a sand fort so she might recline beneath the umbrella and alternate reading a *Star Trek* novelization with conjuring Tennis Boy's lips brushing hers, her curls still bloated.

Her cousins gave her a new nickname, after the expanding animals on TV infomercials, those hideously mushrooming balls of greenery. "You know what Estie looks like? A Chia pet!"

They sat at dinner at the resort's mediocre Italian restaurant, all in polo shirts. She'd already lathered in gobs of her brother's gel, so much that her scalp itched. But LA Style 100 Extra Hold had failed.

"Ch-ch-chia pet!" Her brother's shoulders churned up and down with mirth, like engine parts. The adults gulped their amusement back, their throats constricting. Esther's mother, whose hair was cut close to her skull, ran a hand through the girl's massy locks, but was halted by thick, gel-caked snarls.

"Like me," she said softly.

"Like *your whole* family!" Esther's aunts, not Jewish, denied involvement in the travesty. "Esther, honey, don't butter the bread. You're not getting taller."

"Well, she's certainly sprouting," said her uncle, and everyone tittered because Esther was a noticeable B-cup, which was something for a twelve-year-old, *not that it sent the boys running in her direction yet*, she had heard her father telling her aunt on the tarmac this morning, adding, *Thank God*.

Esther, who had been attempting to be a good sport at dinner, wondered suddenly what kept the boys from running. Did she want them to run? She squeezed a spongy curl, felt it rebound, and fantasized about impaling her family with a butter knife, then stabbing herself in the heart.

Tennis Boy and his family emerged from a corner table. Esther thrust her shoulders back and offered him a bold natural gaze, which he neither noticed nor returned. Yet he beckoned her into a better daydream; her T-shirt morphed into an evening dress, her hair softened and spread like wings and together they danced until dawn to Caribbean drums. She buttered her bread and floated away.

Esther's best friend, Lin, had met a boy on vacation in Mexico and gotten to second base, a relief because what else did you even *need* before high school? Esther could achieve this too, she knew, if she applied herself, sat still, laughed at the right times, and didn't say anything dumb about *Star Trek*.

The next morning Esther swam with her cousins at a more distant beach with waves, though she knew the salty water would not help her hair situation. She joined them building a new fort, soon smashed and flattened by the surf.

"You're way more fun today," she was told. She snorted and splashed; somehow she had the idea that while she bobbed, Tennis Boy might be gazing at them, wondering who these people were, these people who acted so carefree.

Through the window of the cab home, she noticed a Walgreen's. A hair iron waited in those aisles; the girls at school, if in her predicament, would buy it. Surely Esther's mom would never approve the idea: "What a waste," she'd say. "We're in a beautiful place and you want to go to a drugstore?" Yet the iron floated before Esther's eyes, a sacred object.

Later, Esther's brother and cousins embarked on a video game tournament. Esther sat alone, picturing Tennis Boy coming to visit her on her block at home, a red rose in his hands, and Lin's jaw dropping at the idea that a boy *like that* would go for *Esther*. In the vision, her hair was straight. Ironed straight.

She opened her eyes to the sunlight and there stood the real thing, with his racket, talking to her cousins at the entrance to the arcade. His shirt was off; his shorts slung below his waist revealed a trapezoid of fine-cut muscles. Esther draped a towel around herself, covering his indecency by proxy, and sauntered toward them, hearing phrases like "high score" and "next level."

"Hey, Estie," the youngest cousin called.

"Hey, Chia Pet! Ch-ch-chia!" the cousin added as Esther struggled to formulate a socially acceptable way of saying hi back.

"Chia?" Tennis Boy said. He looked right at her and laughed like it was the best joke he'd ever heard. He quaked with it as her brother had, each peal a knife entering between her ribs and perforating her heart.

They began to talk about a tennis tournament but Esther couldn't pretend to care: she fled into the bathroom to weep pitifully into her resort-issue towel. What a loser she saw in the mirror there, too preoccupied with the rooms of her mind to tackle the halo of frizz that crowned them. She craved a friend, a girl to hand her tissues or coo. Instead, the shrieks of children on the waterslide battered her ears.

A thumping drumbeat began in her chest and spread down to her stomach. She had to act. Esther dashed upstairs to the room she shared with her brother, shivering from the hotel's air conditioning. Ignoring the wet stains spreading over her T-shirt from her thick hair, she pulled on the handle of the adjoining room and saw her mother asleep, her head framed by a pure white pillow.

Esther had never lied or stolen a thing. And her mother was so peaceful, so tired, as if the family's teasing, the tugging, had caused her to retreat just as it caused Esther to venture out.

Esther pushed back her pity: the moment demanded something harder. She grimaced, reached into her mom's purse and pulled out a wad of cash. Before she could reconsider her descent into petty thievery, she exited: out through the lobby with the slot machines blinking and bleeping and the sad old people throwing their money away, as her family described it.

She stood still on the sultry street. On their tour of the giant fort on the first day here, they had learned about how horribly the Europeans and then Americans had treated the island. Oppression, poverty, just like the creepy Borg on *Star Trek*, traveling to different planets, assimilating people into slavery. Her father had gripped her shoulder on the way back and said, "Hey, stay close to the Hilton, Estie." She had said, "I ride the bus into Boston all the time."

"Hey you. Hey, Chia!" She looked up and saw Tennis Boy, lounging in front of the hotel with a drink in his hand. "Tennis later? Your cousins are coming. Ask them for deets. What's your name again?"

"Esther," she squeaked out.

"Okay cutie," he said. "Bring your racket."

She nodded and watched him glide away, "cutie" reverberating in the air. A window had opened with that word; a real one, not imaginary. She might puke with excitement. Now she *had* to see this mission through.

She walked toward Condado. Her thighs rubbed together and her shorts rode up inside them, about a centimeter. Her aunt said she wasn't growing taller. True, a small puddle of belly now spilled out over her bikini shorts. She should do sit-ups. Yes: she had to iron herself out from top to bottom. Sweat gathered behind her neck and beneath her breasts.

She stopped halfway across the causeway for a breath. The tide flowed beneath her feet from the wild Atlantic into the lagoon. Her hotel looked like a dollhouse. She felt dizzy but kept on down an avenue lined with shops whose windows held the little frogs, dolls, and seashells that her family called *tchotchkes*, always in a singsong voice—chach-kees!

She passed two homeless men asleep on the sidewalk, one cop with a machine gun, dozens of tourists, and six elderly people awaiting the bus. Where did the bus take them, and wouldn't it be nice to just sit on it until the end of the line? Esther imagined the ride, the bumpy road, the sea views, the small houses growing smaller and smaller as they left San Juan's center behind. Perhaps there was a perfect pink house for her and Tennis Boy, with laundry in the yard and some chickens.

Next to the bus stop she saw a group of teenagers, American boys. They reminded her of her cousins, but older. Like Tennis Boy, too. Their laughter was harsh; they barely saw her pass.

Esther hurried toward Walgreen's and shoved the door open, standing still in an oasis of air conditioning and discount beauty products.

"You get them!" "No, you do!" a pair of teenagers giggled in the condom aisle.

Esther hid her face, sidestepped them on the way to the hair section. She had enough cash to buy the iron and for added kicks the cheapest eyeshadow, mascara, and lipstick she could find.

At the register the woman gave her everything in a plastic bag.

"*Gracias*," Esther blurted out.

"That iron works good on curls," the cashier said in approval—or was it disapproval?

Tremors traveled through Esther's limbs: what if her mom woke up and missed her? But she was bursting with the need of it, to use her new purchases, to rip open the plastic and erase her face, tame her tangles. She slipped into the lobby of the Condado Plaza hotel and followed the signs to the ladies' lounge.

Once there, she savagely attacked the box with the iron in it, unsheathed it and plugged it in. While it began to heat up, she fell upon the makeup, hurling the pieces of packaging in the trash. She stood at the mirror: shadow, stroke, fill. She didn't know what she was doing but she was doing *something*: dab, line, stroke. Her eyes became encircled by big dark patches.

The iron radiated heat. Esther inhaled, then ran it down each curl, pressing it against the strands, stopping when she felt the singe, the crackle on the ends of her hair.

Oh, the sick smell of it. She had a friend who cut herself. Another friend who had stopped eating anything but balled-up pieces of white bread. Esther kept going: lock by lock, kink by kink, she conquered the flyaways until a woman who reminded her of her mother barged in.

"Ugh! It smells like burning! Why are you doing this down here, honey?"

"My mom's sleeping." No lie. Still, she ought to return. Tonight they were going to Old San Juan for dinner.

"Giving yourself a makeover?" the lady asked.

"Sort of."

"You're gorgeous. Don't change—you're too young." The woman went into a stall.

*Shut up, old woman*, Esther wanted to say. Usually, she never even *thought* things like that. The woman began to pee. Esther looked at herself in the mirror and she couldn't help it; she grinned. She had done it; she was finally beautiful.

Esther held her head up high on the way home and let her hips sway, slightly, like Lin's did. She smiled to herself. *She had done it.* She noticed the American boys in college sweatshirts and backwards caps on the sidewalk, milling, and stared at them: frank, natural, bold.

This time they noticed her too.

"Yo. What're you looking at?" one asked. She froze.

They swarmed, like the bench spilling over after a school basketball game. They were fourteen or older; it couldn't be *her* they were lurching toward. She instinctively crossed her arms across her chest, looked down, walked on.

"Why is she not answering?" she heard. "Raccoon eyes."

"You were checking us *out*, girl. J, she likes you."

"Her tits are big!"

"Where's she going? So rude!"

"Hey, chica!" They were tourists like her. Maybe they even went to her school, and she'd have to see them in January. Esther walked faster, engulfed by blasts of hot shame. Why had she looked their way? Why had she been excited when they looked back? Her face perspired; her eye makeup was running down the sides of her nose.

"Why won't you talk to us?"

"Ugh, fuck her!"

"Would you, though?"

"I'd hit it."

She lost them on the causeway, hearing over the din her raggedy breath."Leave me alone!" she told the air.

Evening was arriving on the lagoon; she watched the white scrim of the waves hit the breakers. Salt settled on her tongue; air moved across her damp neck.

Esther lifted up her hand, weakly, and spent her last five dollars on a cab ride that took her eight hundred feet.

She looked at her selves, all eight of them, in the mirrors of her hotel lobby. Gone was the frizzy hair, yes, but she saw now that the effect looked off, as if her head were straining against a leash. The tendrils near her face remained fuzzy: sweat.

Yes, her eyes looked like a raccoon's, her lips lurid, a cheap imitation of Lin or the girls at school. A *tchotchke*.

Tennis Boy, dressed in black shiny fabric, blocked her way to the elevator.

"I kicked your cousin's ass in tennis," he said cheerfully. "Your mascara's running," he added, as if it were obvious that she would wear mascara.

She put a hand to her face.

"Well see ya, Chia!" he said, finding her mute. "Hey, that rhymes."

Esther slid down the side of the elevator and sat on the floor as it climbed. She was Chia Pet, yes, but he wasn't Tennis Boy. He was Andrew, Josh, Evan, or Jake. Of course he had a girlfriend; boys like that just did. She saw Tennis Boy raising his racket and sending an ace over the net, leaving her relatives speechless.

Her mother paced the hallway, growing frantic. She pulled Esther by her arm and then wrapped her in a smothering hug—an act that led Esther to spill the details of her subterfuge and a few more tears.

In the taxi to dinner, Esther learned *there would be consequences* for her actions. She heard the words "chores" and "grounded." But her mom wished it were easier, she did. She believed she had raised Esther to be herself, not underhanded. Esther, wretched, wished her mom would hug her again or go back to sleep.

The trees in the old city's plazas were festooned with lights that slid up and down like drops of illuminated water. Kids set off firecrackers and pigeons swooped, then hobbled around eating the clusters of crumbs.

"Whoa, you look different," said Esther's brother. "I miss your Jewfro."

"She looks good," said the older cousin.

"I see you're putting more into your appearance," her aunt whispered. "It's about time. Easier on the eye makeup, easier on the dessert."

"Your aunt has a problem," said her mother. "Don't listen, Estie."

Tunes engulfed the plaza, but Esther heard only the replay of the day: the rough talk of the boys, laughter from her would-be lover, her aunt's fretting.

Esther sought refuge in her mind, but imagined only the high balcony of her room and herself climbing the railing. She felt herself overtaken by a wave. She dodged a car swerving toward her on the causeway.

She sensed in a thousand ways her visibility, her invisibility. Maybe she even sensed a future of being overlooked, leered at, always wanting: objects packaged as salvation that never were, promised approval that never came.

The trees rained light. Somewhere close by, waves swept in against the rocks, the soft sand. Her cousins tossed a tennis ball in a circle. The moist breeze with its fingers began lifting each tendril of her hair and lacing it in a spiral, undoing her work.

Her journey to Walgreen's felt filthy: a betrayal, a waste. But she felt she'd have to make it again, to flatten and press things down until they burned at the edges. How endless, how exhausting this would be, like the tide coming in each morning for years, wearing down the sandcastles the children built.

Esther squeezed her eyelids shut, then opened them. But wait—what if there was still a chance? She craned her neck, strained to get a glimpse of Tennis Boy walking the street toward her, hoping still for a rescuer, hoping still for a story that wasn't hers.

# Diversion

## *Joanna Lesher*

———⁂———

Okay, now answer me this," said the man seated behind me. "Why do they all wear pantyhose to work?"

It was another curious line in a conversation full of them. The speaker, I'd learned through twenty minutes of continuous eavesdropping, was a thirty-two-year-old sales manager named Jake with a new apartment, a small-breasted girlfriend, and two dogs who liked to hump each other. His seatmate and captive audience, Gunnar, was a truck driver with a penchant for pithy *mots juste*.

"Dunno," said Gunnar.

Jake continued, ignoring the laconic response: "Japanese girls, man. They go to the office, they gotta have every square inch of skin covered, all prim and proper. They go out at night, though, and they're slutting it up in thigh-high boots, tops cut down to here, those big fake eyelashes, and enough makeup to supply an entire troop of clowns. It's like, what kind of message are they trying to send?"

"Dunno," said Gunnar.

"I don't either. My brother says it's just mind games, is all."

Jake's brother was a resident of the Marine base in Iwakuni. Hence Jake and Gunnar's presence on an IBEX commuter flight from Tokyo to Hiroshima.

The plane was a twenty-seat turboprop. Seventeen of those seats were occupied by Japanese people. Jake and Gunnar had evidently elected to proceed as if no one on the plane spoke English, which would have been a good assumption had I not been there. My blonde hair and five-foot-eight frame clearly marked me as a Westerner, yet they seemed not to notice me. I wasn't surprised. Men like them tended to overlook plain girls, their blank gazes skittering past us as if we didn't exist. It bothered me only so far as it exposed me to a lot of uncensored male posturing.

Case in point: Jake was about to start tormenting the flight attendant again.

"*Okyakusama, ogenki desu ka?*" the woman said, smoothing her loose red pencil skirt. She was in her early forties, short-haired, with fidgeting fingers and a nervous smile.

Jake snickered at her under his breath. "Oh, great. Here's some more instructions we can't fucking understand."

The flight attendant held a Dixie cup aloft. She explained that it contained nuts and dried berries—our mid-flight snack. She would now distribute a cup to each passenger. There would probably be enough for seconds, if anybody wanted them.

"Nice fucking cup," said Jake, far too loudly. "Now take your top off."

Gunnar gave a huff of amusement. I watched as the flight attendant's smile faltered. She seemed to suspect the American passengers were mocking her, but didn't have enough English to prove it. Visibly steeling herself, she made her way down the aisle with a plastic tray of cups.

"In France, they knew English," Jake said. "In Germany, they knew English. In Nogales, hell, everybody knew English. But not here. What do you think, Gunnar? Why the Japanese no rikey English?"

"Dunno," said Gunnar.

Jake grunted when the attendant handed him his cup. Then, as she straightened to leave, he said, "I've got some nuts for you too, darling."

The attendant tittered anxiously, recognizing the tone if not the words. A sympathetic burst of bile erupted in my throat.

There were a few precious moments of silence as my fellow Americans downed their snacks. The attendant finished her rounds, then disappeared behind a curtain at the head of the cabin. Whether she had duties to see to or was simply hiding, I didn't know. I wouldn't have blamed her either way.

"Hey," said Gunnar, after the lull. "You think your brother will beat the charges?"

I raised an eyebrow. The plot was thickening.

"He better," said Jake. "Dumb bitch is just trying to get her name into the papers. The local press busts a nut at the smallest whiff of sexual assault. It's their obsession over here: *the Marines rape, get rid of the Marines.* It's all political, man."

"Hm," said Gunnar.

My skin began to crawl. I didn't like where this was headed.

"Granted," Jake went on, "it's sort of an international thing. I've had loads of girls in the States—"

Gunnar interrupted with a "Hm?" The note of disbelief in his voice had me giggling into my elbow despite my mounting sense of dread.

"Shut up," Jake said. "My point is, white girls do it too, sometimes. But not like the Japanese girls. Steven says they come up to you in clubs, bat their eyes at you, grind all up on you, bust out a few suggestive phrases: 'Hey, you rike Japanese girl? Hey, ret's go.' You get them home, you get them undressed, suddenly they're crying: 'Prease, no. Prease, ret me reave.' They change their minds like *that*." He snapped his fingers. "It's like, on the one hand, they're gagging for American meat. On the other hand, they're ashamed. Such a repressed fucking country. If you're a Marine looking for a good time, you can't win."

"Hm," Gunnar mused, philosophically.

"What it comes down to is, if you don't want it, don't ask for it. It's not a difficult concept."

My stomach roiled. I was struck by the almost irresistible urge to reveal myself, to announce that I had heard it all, had understood it all, and that they should be ashamed. Whether it would have done any good, I don't know—I suspect not.

Fortunately, the flight attendant chose that moment to provide me with a much more enticing opportunity.

"Our apologies, everyone," she said in Japanese, having sneaked out from behind the curtain and positioned herself once again at the head of the cabin. "We'll be passing through some rough skies in a minute or two. The captain would like to remind you to fasten your seat belts, return your trays to the upright position, and remain calm as we navigate through the turbulence. Thank you."

The other passengers set about fastening their belts immediately, prompting Jake to ask, "What just happened? What the hell did she just say?"

Suddenly, I knew what I had to do.

I began to pant audibly. "Oh no," I groaned. "Oh God, oh no, oh please, not this again."

I could hear the sharp click of Jake's jaw slamming shut. A moment later, he tapped me on the shoulder. I turned to look at him for the first time. His face was square and tan, framed by a receding hairline at the top and a sad, scraggly soul patch down below. His eyes were yellow with cirrhosis and contorted with apprehension.

I allowed my lower lip to quiver. "I swore I'd never fly IBEX again," I told him. "Not after the last time. How can they keep doing this?"

His hand tightened where it gripped my armrest, causing his knuckles to blanch. "Doing what?" he said. It pleased me to hear the rough edge in his voice. He may not have noticed me before, but I certainly had his full attention now.

"We're diverting," I said, after a conspicuous moment of hesitation. "The cloud layer over Kobe is too thick. We have to fly around it, which means we'll be passing over..." I swallowed. "Over..."

"Over *where?*"

I lowered my voice and whispered, "North Korea."

Jake reeled back as if I'd clocked him in the face.

"*North Korea!*"

Seventeen heads—eighteen, if you counted Gunnar's flabby, grizzled noggin—turned to look at him.

He clutched at his chest, his features rearranging themselves in a convulsion of terror as he repeated, "*North Korea? North* fucking *Korea?*"

"What about North Korea?" said Gunnar.

"We're flying over it!" Jake said.

"Oh." Gunnar thought for a moment. "Is North Korea the bad Korea, or the good Korea?"

"The *bad* Korea."

"Oh." Another thoughtful pause. "Shit."

"It'll be okay," I said, like I was trying to convince myself. "I mean, probably. These turboprop planes are really zippy. Last time we out-maneuvered like, five surface-to-air missiles."

"They shot *missiles* at you?" Jake was well on his way to a coronary event. His voice had been rising steadily in pitch; it now resembled a helium balloon rubbing vigorously against a pleather couch.

Before I had a chance to respond, the first rumblings of turbulence shuddered down the hull of the plane. I gasped and ducked my head. The woman seated next to me eyed me curiously, but I offered no explanation, secure in the knowledge that she would thank me if she had any idea what I was up to.

Following one last reminder to fasten our seat belts, the flight attendant rushed behind the curtain to fasten her own. A smaller bump caused her to stumble along the way. She kept her footing. The two men behind me, meanwhile, lost their composure.

"Shit!" shouted Jake. "They're shooting at us!"

"They don't like people entering their airspace," I said.

"Are we going to die?" said Gunnar, his nostrils widening almost imperceptibly. It was the most emotion I'd seen him display during our short acquaintance.

The cabin address clicked on. "Attention, passengers," the captain intoned in no-nonsense Japanese. "The worst of the turbulence is up ahead. Please remain seated, and secure any loose items. We should be through it in approximately ten minutes."

Wide-eyed, I turned to Jake and translated: "The North Korean military has been signaling the plane, but the captain refuses to respond. He says he's feeling lucky."

"Jesus Christ."

The plane shimmied to the left, then dropped twenty feet. Listing jerkily to one side, it squeaked and thumped and writhed in the throes of some mechanical St. Vitus's dance. It was buffeted from the right, then from the left, then from directly below. A child started crying. Jake did the same.

"Jesus *Christ*," he repeated. "This can't be—I mean, you've got to be..."

The plane dropped again, belly-flopping through a sixty-foot free fall. Its nose dipped as the pilot attempted to fly under the choppy spots.

"We're going down," I whispered, just loud enough for my fellow Americans to hear me.

In response, Jake turned his head and manfully vomited into the aisle.

The child who had been crying stopped to give an appreciate shout. "*Wa!*" he said. "*Gebo gebo shita.*"

"I think that kid called you gay," Gunnar said, but Jake was too busy heaving.

The cabin address clicked on again. "Attention, passengers," said the captain. "We are in the clear."

"They took out one of our engines," I explained, "but the other's still running."

"Repeat: we are in the clear. Please remain in your seats with your seat belts fastened. We should begin our descent into Hiroshima Airport in about twenty minutes."

"A day may come when IBEX Airlines cowers before the communist scourge," I translated, "but it is not this day. This day, we have struck a blow for freedom. We will continue to fight until the breath is driven from our bodies, until our hearts cease to beat, until the last syllable of recorded time."

Jake raised his head and blinked at me, tears in his eyes and vomit around his mouth. Rattled, sickened, and dumbstruck, he shook his head.

"These people," he said, "are fucking *crazy*."

In the end, a fellow passenger with a gentle nature and a bachelor's degree in English laughingly let Jake and Gunnar in on the joke. I wasn't there at the time, having already deplaned and made my way to the baggage carousel. Not until Jake seized me from behind did I realize that I had been exposed.

"You fucking bitch," he said, grabbing and twisting my wrist. "What the hell is wrong with you? You like messing with people? Are you some kind of sociopath?"

I whirled around and tore my wrist free. There was something deeply satisfying about the resulting ache in my metacarpals.

I locked eyes with Jake. He wasn't especially tall, but he was much broader than I was—and, at the moment, much angrier. The cords in his neck stood out in sharp relief. His brows clashed violently over his rectangular slab of a nose. Spit pitter-pattered against my cheeks as he leaned forward to hiss in my face:

"Who the hell do you think you are? Say something, bitch."

There was really only one thing to say. Raising my chin, I mirrored his menacing lean.

"If you don't want it," I said, "don't ask for it. It's not a difficult concept."

His fist came up a second too late—I had already danced away.

# Your Giraffe Is Burning

## *E. A. Fow*

———⊶⊷⊶———

I stood there exposed, but my sister stood with me. After everything, we two remained, monumental, "selfish and unkind." Structured by frameworks of family and tradition, the bones of our ancestors propped us up, like cervical rods piercing the spaces between our vertebrae. They held us erect, like dinosaur skeletons in a museum. We stood in the plain, under the sky blue with emotion but not possibility.

We had agreed to go to psychoanalysis together, surely a bad idea when there are so many more family members invested in remaining the same. It would be two against the many, and we did not like their odds.

*Your giraffe is burning! Your giraffe is burning!*
    The girl shouted "Your giraffe is burning" again and again and again, as if the words themselves were water to extinguish the flames, or perhaps the words were the flames themselves and they would consume the giraffe.

While driving to the office, we laid a bet on how long it would take the analyst to ask about our mother. How long would it be until he insinuated she had been cold, or distant, or perhaps entirely absent. It's so very easy but so wrong to lay the blame at the feet of women who had so few choices except to be impregnated and to raise the fruit of their husbands' loins, as if their lives were lived in paradisal orchards, and they longed for nothing but tending the trees. All those psychoanalysts and their unloving mothers, but our mother was warm and loving and so was our father. We were a happy family, one of Tolstoy's happy families that are all alike, except our family complaint lay in commitment, stability, and warmth, not its absence.

*Your giraffe is on fire!* she called out, and no one heard, or everyone heard but no one would turn around.

We sat in the analyst's reception room. There were prints on the wall of real art, not pink flowers or sunsets with boats. Magritte's homesick angel stood looking over the railing, and a lion lay at his feet facing another direction. He would not be eaten, but would the angel jump? I wondered if it was an appropriate painting for this room. When I pointed it out to my sister, she shrugged and pointed at Picasso's *Weeping Woman*.

"Not very comforting," she said.

Behind the receptionist were melting clocks, and I began to feel as if my time was elastic and expanding then snapping back; waiting was interminable, but the thought of meeting the analyst was worse. I considered leaving, but I could feel my sister's determination without even looking at her. I knew she'd be sitting up straight with her perfect posture, and I had promised her.

Once inside we were awkward and we were embarrassed, and when we were asked why we were there, I practically shouted, "It's not our mother!"

The analyst and my sister both looked at me like I'd vomited on the carpet, and normally that would have flung me into a pained self-conscious state, but instead I felt something move inside me. It was as if some sort of mechanism had been activated. I barely heard the other questions asked, as I was so distracted by the shifting and scraping that I first felt under my skin. After a few moments, I realized these were the faint, telegraphed perceptions of bigger movements deeper inside, perhaps in my stomach cavity, or emanating from my organs, but then it seemed to be happening in my legs, too.

I barely heard my sister talking about our family. Her voice sounded faint and distorted, as if she was talking but the wind was carrying her voice away and sometimes back. I knew she would be explaining about the generations of stable, committed, religious folk, who made up our bones, our infrastructure, and whom we rejected wholesale by staying childless.

"Ungrateful daughters, selfish, and unkind" floated over to me, but I could not hear any more as the sensations inside me grew stronger, then suddenly pushed outwards and through my skin, and the drawers inside me opened.

Everything I had tried to keep hidden was exposed to the light, the drawers tilting open, hanging there, and I couldn't move, I couldn't walk forward for fear the seven drawers in my leg would spill out and fall down, their precious contents would be scattered for all to see, dispersing, and I'd never be able to gather them back up again. Obviously the drawer beneath my breasts held the most important documents, the secrets, not of my heart, but of my lungs and spleen. That drawer, so much bigger than the rest, was half out, revealing the void behind it, with only the skin of my back stopping anyone from seeing completely through me.

Why did I ever go to therapy? I would never have known about the drawers, and they certainly could never have been opened.

"Oh for God's sake," said my never-to-be-born daughter, and I bent to tell her, "No, no, you cannot say that," but she ran from me, and the drawers fell further open, and I had to stop again. I wanted to reach down and push the drawers closed, but I did not want to touch them with my hands. I knew if I looked down, I could see inside some of them, and just knowing I could was more than uncomfortable; it felt unnatural, much like seeing inside my own layers of skin after cutting myself in the kitchen. I did not want to look, not at all convinced by our five minutes so far in analysis that one should see and know the things inside oneself. I was so afraid of the putrid, painful things that would be crouching in my drawers or lying decaying, but really, not looking took so much effort that it was exhausting me.

Finally, it was too much, and out of weariness more than fascination I looked down into the drawers, steeling myself, hardly breathing, and then horrified because there was nothing there—the drawers were empty. I looked in all of them; empty, empty, empty, all the way down my leg. I looked up at my sister and the analyst and gestured to them to come and look, too, and they were completely taken aback.

"I've never seen this before," said the analyst. He pointed to my sister, who stood there holding a large piece of meat, almost a whole ribcage, perhaps of a sheep. "That, I'm used to," he said. He glanced once more into the empty drawers, then shone a tiny flashlight from his key chain into the smallest one, right above my knee. "But this," he exclaimed, "this is truly extraordinary!" My knee quivered, delighted.

*Your giraffe is burning*, she said softly this time, and everyone turned and looked, not at the giraffe, but at her. Now the alarm was gone from her voice, they could hear her words and they were curious, so curious that they did not notice the giraffe, its neck engulfed by fire, walk across the road. It didn't bay; it didn't show any sign that anything unusual was happening. It just walked, the flames roaring upwards, and everyone looked at the girl even though she was pointing at the giraffe.

I looked over to my sister, but she was looking away from me, intent on the slab of meat she held up in front of her face. Behind her I could see a vast plain, stretching all the way to the mountains; the office seemed to have lost its walls. The furniture was still there, and the analyst was still seated, but the ceiling had dissolved into sky. There was no sun and the light was dull. The sky was a saturated blue as if night was falling or perhaps the day was beginning; it was hard to tell, but it was lighter at the horizon just beyond the mountains. Were they mountains? Perhaps they were hills. They looked smaller somehow. They did not tower over the red earth of the plain; we did. We were suddenly so tall, so incredibly tall, my sister and I.

From the corner of my eye, I could see flames in the distance, and I could hear someone crying out, not panicked, but amazed. With monumental effort, I turned to look, the bones of my ancestors creaking with the effort, and I saw something on fire in the distance, a giraffe. Its neck and back were ablaze, the flames hot orange and billowing smoke, but the giraffe did not appear to notice. It did not move or bay; it just stood there. In front of it stood a figure, the girl who had cried out, but she was quiet now. The giraffe continued to burn, and it remained perfectly still as the blue sky above and surrounding us grew darker and grainier with smoke. The giraffe was burning, I thought, and it did not know.

# Break

## Gina Ochsner

———⊷⊱❀⊰⊶———

Afternoons and weekends Avis worked at Suomi Heights, a three-story care home for men. It was perched on a cliff facing the mouth of the Columbia, where the river current collided with the ocean tides and the larger ships were known to founder on the shifting sandbars. Those who could walk lived on the third floor, where Mr. Kreder, the director, had an office. Those who were sick beyond help were kept in the infirmary on the first floor. Avis divided her time between these first-floor men and those on the second floor, an entire fleet of stove-in, broken-up men, most of whom had lost their powers of control. Loggers and fishers, most of them. Finns, all of them. Sometimes they asked for Nora, but more often than not, they asked for Avis in the wee hours of the night, for always it seemed that was when they'd founder. They'd push their call buttons, the men on the first and second floors, and ask for Avis. It was her strong hands they'd want holding theirs.

Not her first choice in jobs, but women like her, whose men had left them—or in her David's case, had literally vanished from sight—had to take what they could. Twenty years ago, when Kreder first hired her, Avis was a hot little rip, her hair hanging to the small of her back. It was so dark, so shiny, that the men could see their own faces reflected in it. During her first shift at Suomi, old Niska covered his eyes and moaned in Finnish. Jirka, who even then had weak eyes, but a keen ear, translated, his voice hushed with gentle reproach.

"It's bad—to see yourself as you are—old and getting older."

As he spoke, Jirka did not look at her hair, or her face, or even at her backside.

"Put that hair up," he said finally, his voice breaking. "We're old men, for God's sake."

Now her hair was streaked gray and dull as charcoal. Any one of those men could have looked as long as they liked, and wouldn't have seen a thing. Worse, she was becoming more and more like them every day, her skin thinning in places, the lines on her forehead deepening. Only her hands hadn't changed. She had thick fingers and strong wrists, hands built for work and lots of it. Early every Saturday and Sunday morning she pulled linens. She lifted their skinny, tired legs, rolled them to their sides, and whisked their soiled bedding out from under them. She steadied their arms at their elbows and lowered them into wheelchairs. And she listened to them talk. About the fire at Cathlemet, about the men burned, about the war—the second one—and the regiment from Astoria, their brothers and cousins—lost down to the man in Iwo Jima. She listened to them call up and clarify their memories, sharpening one recollection against another. They'd wear themselves out talking this way until mugs-up, the time when Nora, her shift manager and only friend in the world, came with the coffee and fattig mand, a sugar pastry the men liked, though Avis didn't care for the greasy crumbs and flakes she had to clean up afterward.

If it were a Sunday, like today, the men listened to the Finnish Lutheran services piped over the PA. They murmured the prayers in that soft language that seemed to Avis more vowel than consonant, more water than rock. And because Nora flatly refused, Avis groomed the men. She clipped finger and toenails, shaved necks and trimmed mustaches and beards. Everything on the north coast smelled of mold, even the men—particularly the men, which is why Avis took it upon herself to wash and groom them as thoroughly as they could all tolerate it. It was, after all, the right Finnish way.

She did this for everyone on the second floor: Kalle and Simon in 2B, Toivo and Onnie in 2C, Lasse and Bernhard in 2D, and now in 2E, Jirka who had lost his sight. Only Niska, who shared the room with Jirka, wouldn't let her near him. Twenty years he'd been here, always bucking the air whenever she entered the room, thrashing like a shark on the hook.

Jirka, from his chair by the window, whispered the translation: "Bad luck to have a woman at sea."

"He's not at sea. He's in a nursing home," Avis said.

Jirka turned his gaze on her, his eyes a calm of white cloud. "He feels the pitch and roll all the same. He's on the water day and night. He's sailing to the far shore." Jirka fastened his milky gaze to the windows.

The crows fly through the open leaded glass windows of the library. Through the stacks of periodicals and over the blank pages of the newspapers hanging like skins on the wooden racks. From the hollow tips of their wings comes the black ink, come the words, sentences and headlines dropping into place until the world dries right and the day can begin, everyone knowing all they need, if only they would stop and take a look.

This was the story Avis told the older students at Lewis and Clark Elementary during their Library Orientation. She used to talk about the miraculous journey that went into making a book, which started as a mere seed of an idea inside someone's head and somehow became sentences that took on ink and ran across pages and pages that tucked together to become a book. She talked about the sacrifice of trees, what a gift each book was. But in the last few years the Oregon timber industry had turned bare-knuckle sore. Kids didn't want to be reminded of sacrifice. Nor did they want to be in her library, entertained by her stories.

The fourth and fifth graders sitting before her now made faces. Bored by her words, by the dark birds bobbing their heads like the dark nibs of retractable pens, the students rocked onto the hind legs of the mustard yellow plastic chairs. They yawned, burped, and passed gas. A few of them, always boys, trained their gaze on her face, eyes shining with a challenge. What will she do? What can she do? Her job always was and is to simply acquaint the children with the resources at hand. To inspire in them a love for reading. Not to teach, never to teach.

The lunch bell clanged. The children rushed for the door, their chairs colliding in their push for the hallway. Never had Avis witnessed a group so eager to get away from her. Avis bent for a chair and set it on its fours.

"We liked your story." A boy, eyes ringed red, nose snuffling, reached for a chair and set it on its legs.

Avis squinted at his face, his hair, both the color of burnt copper. Already he had the rough-hewn look of a life spent working out of doors.

His forearms were raw from hauling and stacking cord after cord of wood, Avis guessed. Behind him stood a girl, thin and small, the kind of smallness that invites quick sympathy. Her black hair reflected squares of overhead lighting. "Which ones are you?"

"Dozier. And this here is my sister, Odessa."

"What kind of a name is Dozier?"

The boy wrinkled his nose. "My name."

Avis smiled. Schooling hadn't stomped the will out of him—not yet.

Avis unlocked a door behind her desk and retrieved a tall wooden ladder. Together she and Dozier and Odessa carried it to the aisle closest to the far wall.

"I hide the really good books," Avis confided as she climbed the ladder. "Now what do you two like reading about?" Avis directed her question to the girl, but she'd drifted to the windows, where the crows studded the sills.

Dozier worked one hand in the other. "Rocks. Thundereggs."

Avis's fingers danced over the spines of the books.

Dozier nodded. "Outside they're dull, but inside they're dazzling and beautiful." Dozier paused and bit his lip. "People are like that, too."

Avis peered down at the boy. "Is that so?"

Dozier nodded solemnly. "Oh, yes ma'am. But it takes something hard and heavy to break them. But that's the only way their beauty can be seen."

Avis turned and studied Dozier more closely, taking in the cuts on his knuckles and his arms, and mentally placed Dozier's parents on her list of parents she did not like. Her fingers resumed their dance and she reached for a book.

"In that case I have something here with a big section on geodes." Avis clutched the book to her chest. The ladder wobbled and bucked. Quick as a shot, Dozier steadied the ladder.

He looked at her balefully. "Miss Crewes, you should be more careful."

Mornings Avis rubbed down the library windows with vinegar and newspaper, erasing a week's worth of mistakes. Then she'd sit at the new microfiche machine, a glowing box dark as the ocean. If she had caught up shelving the returned books then, as per the PTA's request, she was to type into the machine all the newspaper articles from the local newspaper from the last twenty years. A slow-going task, especially since Avis felt compelled to read each article, scanning for the names of people she knew. Whenever Miss

Riffle or Mrs. Bolt sent a student her way, a yellow hall pass clutched in hand, Avis was to stop typing and help the student with his or her reading skills. Tutoring was a duty not traditionally assigned to librarians, a point Avis was quick to make when Principal Marks had called her into his office the week before school had started. It was only his second year at Lewis and Clark Elementary, and Avis felt her seniority entitled her to a token protest.

Marks cautiously ran his fingers through his thinning hair, every blond strand carefully accounted for. "I know you don't have special training, but you're a natural. Anyone can see how the kids like you." Marks made to touch her hand, then thought better of it.

"Kids used to like me," Avis said. The truth was she'd lost her temper once or twice in the past and had been reprimanded for it. All this was in her permanent file, and it surprised Avis that Marks didn't appear to know this, or if he did, didn't care.

Marks grimaced. "Either way, we're short-handed. All you have to do is listen to them. Easy."

But now that her first student, Ike Sorenson, stood glaring at her from under his shaggy white hair, Avis wasn't so sure. She remembered him from last year—a chair tipper and a burper. The kind of kid who licked his fingers before turning pages. In his pudgy hands and pale eyes she could read about him everything there was to know: big pancake breakfasts and plenty of sugared lefse during the holidays. She also knew that the Sorensons came from a long line of electricians, which made Ike part of the coastal upper class. Ike's father had steady work year-round, had heat and light when others didn't.

Ike dropped his book bag on the wooden table. He sat and glared at Avis. "Now what?"

"Now we read." Avis slid the bright red Level Two reader toward Ike.

He studied the cover, then opened the book, pressing his elbow over the spine. "I'm not stupid." Ike pushed the reader back across the table. "I know how to read."

"Of course you do. This is a Level Two—intermediate. Consider it extra practice."

"You can't make me read out of this baby book." Ike stood and hooked his book bag over his shoulder. "My mom's in charge of the PTA."

"Of course she is," Avis said, mentally adding Ike's mom to the list of problem parents. Avis stood as well and crooked her finger. "Follow me." Avis moved toward the microfiche and the bank of file cabinets. She withdrew a thick red file of newspaper clippings—all the articles yet to be transferred. Through the windows the east hills were visible. The dark lines of turned and raised earth met in V-shaped sheths. Overhead the geese cut that same pattern from the cloth of sky, white and silver chevrons gliding beneath the clouds.

Avis nodded to the windows, to the sky beyond the windows, to the birds. "Strange news flies up and down some days." She turned to Ike, who had followed in spite of himself. She would scare him, just a little. With these clips, she would startle him into a respect for stories, for her library. Avis's fingers ticked over the articles, all of them tragic and strange. The one about the storm at sea, about Kalle and Jirka's trawler, the *Toveri*, about her fiancé. David gone overboard—that one her finger paused at, then skipped over.

"Listen to this." Avis plucked at a clip so old the print had smudged and the paper had yellowed. "January 17, 1934. Two pickle weed harvesters tied their wives and children to the rigging of their boats." Avis turned to Ike. "At high tide they sailed their families beyond the bars, past the nets, past the float lines." Avis's mother had gone to school with one of the children.

"They're all gone now," Ike said. "What does this have to do with us?"

Avis took a breath, held it, then exhaled slowly. "It's good to know what badness is out there. To reconcile yourself with it. Knowledge is power, you know." Avis nodded at the reader.

A bird bigger than any crow Avis had ever seen tapped its beak against the window. The spell broken, Ike looked down at the reader in his hand, let it drop into his open bag. "No, it ain't. It's just more weight to carry." Ike hoisted his book bag onto his shoulder and hauled for the door, knocking two chairs over on the way out.

At the Heights that following evening, the men were restless. The rain pounded the roof and siding so steadily, it was as if water were not falling from the sky, but rising from the ground, fist by fist. In a few hours the tide would be at the year high. Crossing the bar would be even more treacherous than usual. Likely a boat would call in distress. Likely it would go down. Those who could wheel or walk themselves had gathered in the great room, calling to each other in a lively exchange of Finnish.

Avis wheeled her linen cart past the great room and down the hallway. Outside 2B she took a big breath through her nose, held it. What she liked best about this job: that moment when she pushed through a door. Before her eyes could adjust to the dimness of the room, she imagined David was there. Because he wasn't dead. He had just disappeared. And people disappear all the time only to later reappear. And if David were to return to her, it would be here in this place of broken-up working men. He'd be here, in a bed waiting for her, his betrothed, to nurse him back to health.

Avis pushed the cart and the door swung wide on the hinges. A man lay in the bed. Not David. Just Kalle. 2B. Always Kalle. He turned and smiled at her.

"Storm coming. Big one," Kalle said. Outside, the storm had driven the gulls inland and now only the crows remained, cutting into the wind. Avis unfolded the fitted sheet. Of all the men, Kalle was Avis's favorite. He made her job easier, first rolling to the left of the bed while she tucked the upper and lower right corners, then rolling to the other side of the bed so that she could secure the left corners. They repeated this dance for the flat sheet, a series of choreographed moves perfected over fifteen years of practice. And for a Finn, he seemed uncommonly extroverted, even going so far as to look at Avis's hands instead of his own when he talked to her.

"I'll bet you've seen rougher seas than this." Avis glanced at Simon. He stirred, then resumed his snoring, burring like a Briggs and Stratton running lean. "Remember the big storm we talked about the other day—when you were caught past Peacock Spit?"

Kalle's gaze traveled from her hands to her shoulder and then to the window. He suffered from lapses, Avis knew. Some days he could remember lines from the *Kalevala* and knew who had won the most recent wife-carrying contest back in the homeland. Other days, like this one, he was like a child: in need of firm prodding.

Jirka scuffled through the hallway, his fingers tracing an invisible line along the wall. He shuffled past the open door, stopped, then shuffled back, and stood there, listening.

"Remember David?" Avis asked, leaning in so Jirka wouldn't hear. "He was on the boat with you."

"No." Kalle observed the crows that had settled on the broad windowsill.

"You worked together on the trawler for over two years."

"No."

"And then there was the storm. He went over. Over, but not under—isn't that right?"

"No."

Avis bent near to Kalle's face. "You were there. Tell me what you saw."

Kalle looked at her for a long time and Avis thought perhaps she had gotten through, perhaps she would finally hear what she so badly needed to know.

"Never stack cans upside down in the hold," Kalle said solemnly. "It will cause the boat to roll."

Jirka shuffled on. Avis stood abruptly and pulled at the blanket, tucking it tight over Kalle's thighs. Then she shoved the cart hard through the door and stomped through the hallway for the laundry room.

Even though she cared for Kalle, for all of them in ways no one else ever would, they would never let her forget that she was, for all her efforts, still a trespasser in this territory of men. They wore their history on their bodies, each mark on thinning parchment of skin a reminder of old lessons. Every crease on their faces and necks was evidence of hard wisdom come from working in weather. She knew about the snapped choker that had lashed Kalle's ribs; she'd seen that thick pink arc of raised skin around his torso. She knew about Simon's sixty-foot fall from the top of a Douglas fir; she'd seen his bandy legs, bowed from having been broken and poorly set afterward. She had undressed them, given them sponge baths, re-dressed them. But when she asked them questions—Where were their women who had touched their necks and knees before her? Who had put them in this place and forgotten them?—they pretended they couldn't hear her, or couldn't remember. And when she pressed for details about the *Toveri*, about the storm that pulled her David over and out? Nothing.

In the kitchen Nora sat at the galley table, raking her fingers through her hair, a reddish fluff she had to whip up then spray into place because her hair was even thinner than Avis's. Avis sat next to her, lit a cigarette, and watched the water lash the windows.

Avis reached for Niska's mug. It was the only mug he'd drink out of. It said *Sisu* in bold blue letters. It meant intestinal fortitude, in Finnish. She'd taken it from his room, to clean it. Now she was taking her time returning it, knowing that nothing else she could do would exasperate the man more.

Nora reached for the coffee pot and filled Niska's mug. "Go easy on Kalle. He's old and forgetful. Besides, you and I both know that men who go over don't come back."

Avis sipped at the coffee. It was bitter and an oily sheen slicked the surface.

"It's been twenty years," Nora said. "You gotta let go."

Nora's husband, a pilot and one of the best at navigating the sandbars, had also been lost in a storm, twenty years ago or more. It was why they could sit together and drink coffee. It was why Nora was the only friend Avis could have and keep. They had lost their men, they had this in common. But Nora had given up and Avis hadn't. Wouldn't.

The plan: he'd fish and she'd work at Hanthorn's cold storage, packing tuna. For two seasons, maybe three. Only until they could get enough together to get out of town. "Let's just go. Now," Avis had said. The most impulsive words she'd ever uttered. But David had merely smiled his goofy lopsided grin. "Bide a wee." His way of saying *wait*. He was the sensible one in those days. She'd always thought so then. The sockeyes—fat as cows—were running. The smart thing to do was to keep fishing. And that was the last she saw of him, twenty years ago.

"You could date," Nora suggested, breaking the silence.

Avis snorted.

"You've got to have a life outside of this one." Nora turned her gaze, warm and wet, on Avis.

"I do have a life." Avis wiped her hands on her uniform. "I have the library."

The library. Her library. Her haven. A sanctuary of muddled noise and muted light. All the edges blurred to shadow, and she could hide in that refuge, in the shade of the long bays of catalogues, the tall stacks. In rare moments of sunshine, light flooded the east windows, illuminating galaxies of dust. And yet, even in all this movement, the library was a place of consummate order, a place that, like Avis, depended upon and thrived upon systematic arrangement. She loved how her fingers knew before her eyes did where to find what she wanted to know. That was the beauty of the Dewey decimal system: it provided numeric geography for her books that exhaled the musty smell of binder's cloth and glue and all that is good and reliable and familiar. And she appreciated the patterns, particularly took comfort that in much of the fiction, formulas reigned supreme: endings almost always worked out tidily. Old maids married late and love found the unlovable. Children got up to mischief but never got punished or hurt for it. Criminals were caught and brought to justice. And if there were any surprises she did not care for, a chapter she did not like, she could simply stop reading.

Her library followed patterns, too. There were rhythms to the seasons Avis could identify, could plan for. September was the golden month for the library. The kids behaved themselves. During the first four weeks of school they could be coaxed into goodness. They wanted to be liked by their teachers, whose opinions of them hadn't yet set up firm for the year. But by October, by the time they learned the hierarchy of power within the school, understood that Avis held no real authority, not even to revoke library privileges without the principal's approval, the true nature and interests of the kids emerged.

Ike, Avis quickly observed, was a predictable reader, always heading to the 940.00s, the second to the last stack, where all the World War II books were kept. Dozier borrowed every book she had on geology. And Odessa, more shadow than substance, never talked above a whisper, never checked anything out. Just ran her fingers along the spines of as many as she could or looked at the pictures in the encyclopedias.

Every day after lunch, Mrs. Bolt sent Odessa to the library with simple notes: Review sight words: *the an a like love this that what where*. But after a few days it became clear to Avis that for Odessa, it was best to lower all expectations. Best to forget Mrs. Bolt's study guides completely. Together Avis and Odessa parsed through the alphabet, sifting forward and back, never making it past *Q* and *R*. For Odessa, Avis found birding magazines, and together they traced pictures of birds to correspond with each letter of the alphabet: D for dove, E for egret, L for loon.

And though Avis still helped the other students, she wasn't as attentive to them as she was to Dozier and Odessa. Why should she be? The others didn't need her like Dozier and Odessa. They were smaller versions of Avis, wounded and overlooked. They were another Hansel and Gretel whose mothers and fathers wanted them lost, had lost them already. But she could show them that in time their wounds and their neglect would become their strength. They would be the stronger ones for it. But first they had to survive Lewis and Clark Elementary.

And they seemed to understand this. During recess she read Odessa the most outrageous clips she could find while Dozier rinsed out the chalk rags, watered her ink pads, stacked books in the go-back cart. She explained to him the Dewey system and showed him how to shelve the orphans and strays. For Dozier she kept the ladder out so that he could retrieve any book on the top shelf. What she wanted—and on this point her self-scrutiny had risen bright as a boil on the skin—was to be remembered by a child. To be regarded years later with fondness.

By Friday the storm still hadn't let up. The children spent their recesses in the multipurpose room, hurling rubber balls at one another. Odessa drifted in from the hallway and sat behind Avis's desk, working the alphabet, never moving past the quarrelsome letters *Q, R, S.*

Avis took in the girl's hair, dark as wet soil. Her fingers, long and thin, tapped impatiently at the letters. She had good hands, she'd make a good librarian, with those nimble fingers. If only she could read.

Odessa pushed the heels of her palms into her eye sockets.

"These letters just swirl around on the page."

When Odessa talked, it sounded like someone had just kicked her hard in the chest. Hushed and strangled at the same time.

Avis slipped a hard candy into Odessa's hand. "You've got to try, Odessa, really try. You can't let ink on paper get the best of you."

Odessa's eyes watered.

Avis rapidly handed over more candy and led the girl to 598.00, where the winged vertebrates occupied one solid shelf. Together they leaned toward the stacks, taking in the intoxicating scent of aging paper, cardboard, and glue. Avis put her arm around Odessa's bony shoulders.

"One day, and soon, these books will be your best friends," Avis whispered in Odessa's ear. "You'll take care of them and they'll take care of you."

"Oh, like how them birds look after the library." Odessa lifted her chin to the windows.

"No, Odessa," Avis gently corrected. "I take care of the library."

Odessa silently regarded Avis with somber dark eyes and crunched the hard candy between her molars.

The bell rang and Mrs. Bolt's third and fourth graders burst into the library, all noise and bustle and smelling of sweat. The girls pretended to be horses, snorting and pawing in the aisles.

Dozier maneuvered the go-back cart to the aisle furthest from where Ike and his friends sat, their hands and feet anxious to hurt. They punched each other, played a game called raining hammers and nails, delivered random karate chops. And boredom having overtaken them, they turned their attention to Odessa.

"Is it true your mother is really your sister?" one of the boys jeered.

"Odessa, say 'She sells seashells by the sea shore.' C'mon. Odessa."

Avis recognized the cruel banter. In her fifteen years at the library the biting intent of children changed so little. And she knew it wasn't entirely their fault. They had listened to and housed every harsh comment they heard at home. They had learned to mimic such talk, tone true, until it became their own.

Ike pinched his nose between forefinger and thumb. "Odessa, do you ever run a comb through that dirty Dago hair?" The other boys hooted and brayed, their voices straining in their necks. Outside the windows, the crows shrieked.

Avis watched until she couldn't take anymore. She grabbed a remedial reader, the Level One with the childish yellow duck on the cover, held it high over her head and approached Ike.

"You still haven't returned the reader I lent you last week." In her own ears her voice blared like a foghorn. "You'll not be allowed to take out new books until you've returned it." Avis made sure that all the kids could hear her. Made sure the boys at Ike's table saw the yellow duck on the cover.

Ike lowered his head. She'd humiliated him, and she marveled at her quick capacity for it. Marveled at the pounding in her chest, the heat in her face, how pleased she'd felt, how easy it was.

The crows scolded outside the window. Avis clapped her hands and the birds lifted in a solid veil of black that wrinkled the sky to the tree line.

At the nursing home, Kalle and Simon watched a public broadcast on TV, a ballet.

Simon squinted at the way the girls traipsed on tiptoe. "I don't understand." He turned to Kalle. "Why don't they just get taller girls?"

It was mugs-up, and in a gesture of small generosity, Avis decided she should return Niska's *Sisu* mug. She shouldn't be so petty. So what if the man didn't like her? No reason to punish him.

Avis backed through the door with the cart, her thick-soled nurse's shoes gumming to the floor. The door swung open and a warm wet odor, a smell so thick and rank it could only come from the human body, forced her throat to close. Then her knees buckled. If she hadn't been hanging on to the cart handles, she would have gone right down.

Jirka lifted his chin. "Niska needed help getting to the bathroom. We pushed the call button. Twice."

Avis made her way over to Niska's bed. "No, no." Niska waved his hands in front of his face. Avis folded an arm to his side and began rolling his body and pulling at the linens. "No!" Niska thrashed and the mess in his sheets splattered against the cart, soiling the clean set of sheets and the blanket she'd brought.

"Lie still!" Avis instructed, leaning her weight onto Niska's shoulders. "You need a bath." Avis turned to Jirka. "Tell him I'm trying to help. He stinks."

"He's upset," Jirka said.

Avis pressed her elbow into Niska's chest and rolled the linens from under him. His feet caught the cart and his *Sisu* mug fell to the floor with a solid thud, then skittered to pieces.

"No, no," Niska, on his side now, moaned.

Avis pulled the cart through the doors and stormed down the hallway for the service elevator that took her to the laundry room. There she loaded the empty washer with the soiled linens, measured the detergent and punched the start button. Above the washers, the dryers hummed, the oversized drums rolling. Avis pulled a hatch open and—quick—yanked the hot linens. She buried her nose in the sheets, her face in the burning clean smell of scorched fabric.

When she returned to Niska's room, Nora was changing Jirka's bed. Jirka was asleep and Niska lay snoring on his mattress pad, a blue bathrobe over his body.

With quick flips at the sheets, Nora hooked the corners around the mattress. She'd been at Suomi Heights two years longer than Avis, and she could change a bed seven seconds faster. It was, Avis decided, because Nora bent her body right over the bed, her face so close to Jirka's she might have been kissing him. Avis shuddered.

"Be careful with Niska," Nora called over her shoulder.

"I'm always careful with Niska." Avis rolled him to his side and dressed the bed.

"I'm not telling you how to do things, but I've noticed bruises."

"He's old. He's got bad blood and bad circulation."

"Not these bruises." Nora patted Jirka's bed down, then crossed for Niska's. She lifted Niska's arm and Avis saw them for herself: four fingertip-shaped bruises on the outside of his bicep, a larger single thumbprint on the underside. "Just take it easy with them. Kreder's got his knickers in a knot.

Some families sue, you know." Nora patted Avis's wrist, then vanished through the doorway. Avis stood beside Niska's bed and watched the old man breathe. Then she held her hands up and looked at them with utter astonishment.

The next morning Avis sat behind her desk mentally preparing for Mrs. Bolt's fourth graders. Mrs. Bolt, a permanent fixture at Lewis and Clark Elementary, fulfilled every inch of her name. Steadfast and singular, her lesson plans had not changed one iota over the fifteen years that Avis had known the woman. September: library orientation. October: living history report. Avis had promised Mrs. Bolt that she would teach the children how to use the microfiche to find newspaper articles. This involved photocopying a set of instructions, which Avis distributed to each of the students. Then she appointed the tallest fourth grader—always a girl—to supervise the machine. The fact was, Avis did not want to be bothered with the living history reports. Not today. Niska's bruises were troubling her. Also, she had a huge stack of newly returned books to process.

Principal Marks materialized beside her desk. "How's progress?" Marks hooked his chin toward Odessa, who sat at a nearby table. She had borrowed Avis's oversized stapler and was now punching bird-shaped designs with staples on a piece of black construction paper.

"Well, she tries hard," Avis said.

Marks nodded at Dozier, who sat poring over the massive *Webster's*. The ladder, its hinges bolstered now with duct tape, blocked an aisle.

"Why is that ladder out?"

Avis felt her cheeks burn. "I only let my aide use it now and then, and he's no more than sixty pounds."

"I don't think it's wise. And it's not a good idea to have favorites. God knows we all do. But it's best not to let on." Marks winced. It was the closest he could get to a smile, Avis realized. But what, really, did he know about children? He was the third principal in almost as many years at Lewis and Clark. What did he know about *Sisu*, about wearing people down, about weathering hard times?

Avis pulled a book from her stack and opened the back cover. "I don't play favorites. But if they want to spend their free time in the library, I don't turn them away. Some days I need the help." Strong and light and furious, her hands flew over the pages of books, feeling for damage, feeling for the back page stiffened with the pocket and the green ruled due-date reminder. She would not slow down, not for Marks.

"I know we don't have the resources other schools do." Principal Marks rubbed his hands over his face. "But we have some things they don't."

"Card catalogues. We have those," Avis said. "And leaded glass windows. And crows."

Marks manufactured another wince. "We have closeness. I like to think all of us here are a family."

Avis pulled another book.

"And you know as well as I that sometimes not everyone in a family gets along."

"I know that," Avis said.

"You're a"—Marks pulled in his breath—"strong woman. And the PTA is a strong supporter of this school. Don't put me in the middle."

Avis felt a weight drop to her stomach and settle over her thighs. "What are you talking about?"

"There's been some talk," Marks whispered. "Complaints."

"Who's complaining? What are they saying, exactly?"

Marks lifted his shoulders in a gesture of helplessness. "You have sick days. You should use them."

"No." Avis fixed her gaze on his. "I'm not sick. And I've got work to do." She pulled down a book.

"Just remember why and for whom you've been hired." Marks strolled out of the library, his gaze sweeping over the tops of the heads of the third and fourth graders streaming in.

As if on cue, Ike approached Avis, his head lowered, his bangs hanging in his eyes. "I need help."

*Don't we all*, she wanted to snap. Instead she forced a bright look to her eyes and followed Ike to the back of the stacks, to the 940s. The bucky ladder sprawled in the aisle. Ike pointed to the top shelf. The book he wanted: *Encyclopedia of War: History, Tactics, Weaponry*. A huge book. Heavy. Oversized, like him.

Avis folded her arms across her chest. The books belonged to the shelves, to this room, to people capable of loving and treasuring them. And because there are—and always would be—a million ways to deny a child, to hurt, Avis shook her head slightly. "I don't think so, Ike."

Ike gripped the rails of the ladder.

Avis tapped her finger against Ike's wrist. "The ladder is only for the librarian or her aides. For this assignment you're supposed to find newspaper articles. Use the microfiche like everybody else, Ike."

"But I need to check something. I know it's in that book and Mrs. Bolt said all of our facts have to be correct or we won't get full credit."

"Sorry," Avis said.

"But I have to pull my history grade up. You don't know what will happen if I don't." Ike tipped his chin, his eyes on the book. A shiner ringed his left eye. Scholastic motivation that came from the back of a hand—that she understood. "Use the microfiche," Avis said, feeling her heart slide into a hard country beyond compassion.

"Miss Crewes." Ike's voice fell to a whisper. "Why don't you like me?"

Avis blinked. "I like you heaps and buckets, Ike."

"But you won't help me."

Avis pressed her mouth into a hard line.

Ike lowered his head and brushed past her for the machine.

Ten minutes passed. Twenty. She had made good progress through the returned books, had managed to forget entirely Ike's question. And the children, they were busy and relatively quiet—just the way she liked them. But the crows outside screeched at one another, knocked against the panes as they bit each other's wings. It was how they showed affection, she'd read somewhere. It was the only way some creatures know how, by picking and nettling and drawing blood.

Ike bolted to his feet. "Miss Crewes! Look what I found!" He waved a newspaper article overhead. The top drawer of her file cabinet was open and her red folder of instructive disasters lay on a nearby desk. "Does this count as a living history artifact?" Ike's eyes were unnaturally bright. There was something too steadfast about his gaze, something in his posture that set her teeth on edge. But she wouldn't let a fourth grader cow her.

"Why don't you read it," Avis said.

Ike wiped his mouth on his sleeve and began reading. "Tragedy on the High Seas: Tuesday while trawling ten miles off shore the fishing boat *Toveri* was caught in the storm of the decade. Deck hand David Roys went overboard."

Avis felt the blood drying inside her veins. She knew this clip well—had the words up by heart. She should stop Ike, she knew, but his words gathered and rose like those waves of the storm. The other children, sensing the change of air inside the library, fell silent and turned to listen to Ike.

"The swells measured over forty feet high, according to Captain Jirka Hililla. The captain and first mate Kalle Jorgers lost sight of Roys immediately. Though rescue efforts continued through the night, 24-year-old David Roys is presumed dead. Survivors include his mother and father, Anders and Karen Roys, and his fiancée Avis Crewes."

Ike folded the paper into squares. "Gee, Miss Crewes. You're a part of living history. I guess that means I could do my report on you. "

Avis closed her eyes, imagined her strong hands pushing the anger down. She imagined her pain was a freshly starched sheet or a single piece of paper she could fold in halves, then quarters, then fold again into eighths until she couldn't fold it any more. Avis snapped open her eyes. She wanted to say something neutral and breezy, like "Thank you, Ike. That is quite enough." Instead Avis raised a shaky finger at Ike and pure scorching rage broke open. "Get out of my library. Get out!"

The children stood absolutely still.

"All of you—go!" Avis bellowed.

In a panic, the children rushed for the door, knocking over every chair and even an ornamental spider fern and the standing world globe.

Outside the library, on the windowsill, a row of crows sat preening their feathers. "Go away, go away," Avis moaned at the birds. "Please go away."

"They can't go away." Odessa's voice floated from behind the stacks.

"What are you talking about?"

Now Odessa appeared beside the fallen globe. She set it upright and dusted the continents with her hand. "They're not done here yet," Odessa answered. "You said it yourself, the birds bring in all we need to know and it's not all come in yet."

That evening, Avis sat in her bedroom, smoking one cigarette after another and waiting for Marks to call and reprimand in flinty tones or flat-out fire her. And she was reconciling herself, too, with the other, harder thing. David was gone. All these years of pushing doors, flinging them wide open like hope on a hinge, thinking every man could be him, she'd known. Known it in her bones because you can't live on the water and not know what water does. Can't help but know the law of water: for every haul, something must be given in return, somebody. And Kalle and Jirka and Niska, they'd known it, too. Had been telling her in their turned shoulders and set jaws, telling her in the way men answered such questions from women.

An hour before her shift was to start, the phone rang.

"Kreder says don't come in today," Nora said. "Everyone's sick. It's just one kidney basin after another to clean." Nora paused. "Also, some bad news. Niska's died."

So that was it, then. That was the bad thing waiting to happen. Avis's shoulders slumped. She was sorry the old man died. Sorry his mug had been broken. Sorry that in such petty ways she'd aggravated his misery.

"He liked you a little," Nora offered.

Avis winced. "No, he didn't," she said, sliding the phone into the cradle. Though her hands still shook, her rage had calmed to a simple anger. And something like relief. The badness would stop now. Her world would keel up steady and balance. The birds would fly away.

Avis stretched her body over the thin mattress. The trees and the hills leaked black ink onto the water, into her room. The storm had broken. She studied the darkness at her window, hoping for a scrap of moon. She only wanted to take a spoonful, just enough to walk by, just enough to find her footing.

By morning the clouds had stacked to the east, their swollen bellies snagging on the hills. Though the wind was still up, Avis felt calmer than she had in moths, years even. She unlocked the library, stood in the center of the room among the round study tables where the light gathered. She could hear the birds calling to one another, but so far not a single one had lighted at the sills.

Avis turned for the far stacks, walking through the aisles, her hands touching the spines. Near the far wall, at the stack of oversized and rare books, the ladder still stood open in the aisle. She supposed she should put it away. It was a hazard, after all. But first she would straighten the top row. The military book, the one Ike had wanted, jutted over the shelf like a bucktooth. Avis gripped the ladder rails and climbed. She did not like Ike, did not like his mean-spirited bullying. But it was not her job to punish him for it. She was to help him. And where she had failed with Niska, Avis determined as she reached for the military book, she would not fail with Ike.

She would leave the book perched on the fourth shelf, eye-level to Ike, where he could not possibly miss seeing it.

Avis pulled the book, cradled it to her chest. A heavy volume, so much heavier than she reckoned. It was good the boy hadn't attempted it. Avis shifted her weight, felt with her foot for the step. A thud at the window, two crows fighting, startled her. Her grasp on the book slipped. Avis scrambled to catch it, but the book slid from chest to hip, hip to thigh. The book dropped, the ladder bucked. Avis clawed at the shelves of the stack. For one glorious second she clung to the shelving. And then she went over, pulling the stack as she fell. With a tremendous thud the stack collided with the wall above her head and the books slid on top and all around Avis.

The morning bell rang. The noise of children filled the hall outside the library. Children laughing. Shrieking. Carrying on. Avis closed her eyes. She felt herself drifting in that sound, in that darkness that was ink and wing and storm. Somewhere beyond these windows the tide was rising and she could rise out with it, if she let herself. Silly. Get a hold of yourself, Avis scolded. You've taken a knock to the head, you're buried to your armpits in these damn books you love so much. This is funny. So laugh. And she wanted to, the whole thing was so stupid. *Breathe*. She wanted to. A sound—it could not possibly be her—rattled in her throat. *Move*. She wanted to. But the weight of the books on her stomach pushed her, held her down.

"Help," Avis moved her mouth. Silly, she knew. The many books in the many stacks dampened all human noise. The only sounds now were the birds at the windows. They'd come back, that much she could see through the gap between the stack and the avalanche of books. From the sills the crows pecked at the window, folded and unfolded their wings, took the light from the room. They were so many of them, it was as if they'd become one giant bird, one giant set of wings.

A pair of boots moved within her line of sight. Now she could see hands, blue jeans, Ike's face, rowanberry-red. And then more feet in muddy shoes, Dozier with his frayed laces and the other boys. With a groan the stack swung upright.

Light, book-end–shaped blocks of it at a time, emerged. And air, then breath.

Ike gripped her forearms and pulled hard. A good boy, and strong. He and Dozier guided her to a chair. Ike patted her hand. "Don't worry Miss Crewes."

"We'll fix everything," Dozier said.

From her chair she watched the children with their quick hands gathering up the books. They worked in teams, sorting and stacking the books, the taller children putting them up on the higher shelves, the smaller ones the lower. Unflustered by this colossal upset, they knew exactly what to do in her library. And they were such hard workers, quiet and busy and strong and useful. Only Odessa strayed to the windows, where the birds sat with their heads tucked under their wings against the wind.

"Miss Crewes?" Marks appeared in the doorway. "What happened here?"

"I took a spill. So did the books." Avis touched the knot on the back of her head.

Marks clicked his tongue, inventoried Avis with a quick glance. "First that ladder. Now this."

Avis looked past Marks to the children. "Some of those call numbers are tricky. I should help." Avis rose slowly.

"Wait." Marks laid a finger on her wrist. "What if it had been a student who'd fallen?" Marks raised his voice, as if he were talking to a child.

"It wasn't my fault. These stacks aren't bolted down."

"It's not just that. I've been getting phone calls. From parents. The things you say to the kids and your unorthodox methodology—frankly, some of the students are afraid of you."

"What?" Hollow and raspy, Avis's voice sounded just like Odessa's.

"Miss Crewes, I don't think Lewis and Clark Elementary is the right place for you any longer."

Avis stared at Marks. His eyes were of such a pale blue they were like skim milk, like shallow water. Like nothing. She knew her way through the stacks well enough. She would have thought that after all these years she'd have learned how to navigate among the treacherous ways of new principals and PTA parents.

Avis glanced at Odessa, still tapping in code on the panes.

"At least let me say goodbye to the kids."

Marks folded his arms across his chest. "I don't think so."

The wind outside pushed against her legs and back, drove her across the school playground toward the care home. She could feel the knot throbbing at the back of her head. Not wisdom, just tender soreness that comes from failure. The thing was, and this she could tell Dozier, brokenness might be beautiful, but usually when it was happening to somebody else.

Avis ducked her head and turned for the cliffs. She'd never been so foolish as to really think she was indispensable. But she'd never imagined being sent away. And the sloppy injustice of Marks so willfully misunderstanding her—Marks who didn't know a thing about her world or ways—it made her angry. That's what she was. Brimming with it. Her hands tingled with righteous indignation. She supposed she'd have to thrust them into the dryers—her face too—and remind herself that the bright white heat and scorch was her only comfort, her only source of warmth. Avis clenched her jaw, fixing her game heart, trying to conjure the proper ending for her disaster, some way to make it useful and instructive. No doubt she'd have to explain to Nora her failure, why she was at the care home hours before her shift. Why it was necessary to beg, yes, beg—Kreder would see to it—for more hours. She had a good idea how it would go: he wouldn't give her the good hours, day hours or afternoon mugs-up hours with Nora. They would be the long, first-floor night hours, filled with soiled laundry and the wet sounds of the men, unmoored in their oceans of old-man dreams. The storms would roll in and Avis would sit there, telling them her stories. She'd hold their frail hands in her strong ones, while those on the threshold drifted away.

# The High Priestess Never Marries

## *Sharanya Manivannan*

My old flame, the Lucky Bastard, he of the nefarious intentions and the devastating lines, jets back into town on a borrowed Scooty, reeking of pleasant aftershave and profound desperation. He lifts his sunglasses with cinematic somnolence to the top of his curly head, sighs, and says,

"The tides were high and the moon was just rising. If you had come when I called you the other night, we could have had epic sex."

"We've already had epic sex."

He looks at me. I look at him. He crosses his arms and poses against the bike. He's an archangel but only in profile. He's a cenotaph. Whenever he bit my nose, the diamonds pinned to it disappeared into his mouth.

"Ever heard the story about the chick who would ride between Pondy and Madras every weekend?" I say as he starts the engine.

"No."

"So every weekend she could be seen taking the ECR on a Bullet. Up to Madras on Friday, back to Pondy on Sunday. And the highway cops couldn't figure out what the deal was, what it was she was smuggling. They stopped her many times, stripped the bike, never found anything."

"Maybe she was visiting her boyfriend?"

"Much later, they worked it out—she had been smuggling Bullets."

It takes a second too long for him to get it, but he laughs. I roll my eyes behind his back. Under my hands, his shoulders are supple and capable of jeopardizing anyone's common sense.

But that isn't going to happen. We are meeting today in the interest of civility and skullduggery, both in the service of parties other than ourselves. His former roommate, the edentulate Swede, needs the vouching of respectable people in order to convince his landlady to extend his lease. He says he doesn't know any respectable people. For the sake of a little booze and a little bribery, I am riding sidesaddle in a saree, pretending to be married to this knave, this rapscallion, my former predilection and current accomplice, the Lucky Bastard.

I am, as the Lucky Bastard knows only far too well, alarmingly easy to persuade.

At a traffic light, I shout, "I'm only doing this because you are a family friend and I am a loyal person."

"Honor-bound as always," he says, still looking straight ahead. "Where would the Tamil kalaacharam be without you?"

"Married to you for reals, probably."

"Did you remember to wear the metti?"

"Metti, kolusu, kaapu, pottu, podavai. What more do you want? I draw the line at thali." I am a woman who wears altogether too much metal, on the interior as much as on the outside. I jangle like a poltergeist. Kavacakundalam ain't got nothing on a girl like a kuthu vilaku.

"Good girl," he says. "Such a sweetheart."

"Always."

When Erik sees us his eyes go large. "You are both looking very very nice," he says.

I thank him sincerely. The Lucky Bastard is too vain to acknowledge compliments; I am vain enough to assume they are actually only meant for me.

I adjust my saree (a chartreuse green with a red print, paired on this occasion with a high-backed Naidu Hall readymade) a little more than necessary and try to appear demure. The Lucky Bastard cocks an eyebrow, but only after an adorable, inadvertent grin.

The three of us take the stairs to the second floor and ring the doorbell. The woman who answers it is as dour-faced as cautioned, with a permanent wrinkle between her brows that divides her kunguma pottu in almost perfect halves. Her house keys are hooked to her waistband, as is the end of her saree. She gives off the distinct impression that we have interrupted some prayer that could have prevented the apocalypse.

"Maami," Erik begins, and it's impossible to tell if she has bristled or blushed at the honorific. "These are my friends, Mr. and Mrs. Kumar. I used to live with them before I came here."

"Where?"

"K.K. Nagar," says the Lucky Bastard.

"Family house?"

"Umm, no, it's a flat. Two bedrooms. We rented one to Erik."

"Why?"

I keep my eyes firmly focused on the metti on my timid and wifely toes.

"Uh, for some time we thought the rent was high and so…" He's trailing off already. I can sense the panic. All Indian men are secretly terrified of women. It's the state of the nation.

"Your wife works?"

"No…"

"Child?"

"No, no."

I sneak a look at the boys' faces. The Lucky Bastard's expression is that of an emoticon. Erik wears the archetypal beam of all polite, linguistically impaired white people in India.

"Why?"

"Sorry?"

"Why no children? How long have you been married?"

"Just two years."

"Immediately after marriage you rented out room-a?" She looks perplexed. I resist the temptation to tell her that my sex life is hardly in detriment. And neither is the Lucky Bastard's, I'm sure.

"Y-yes. Then Erik moved to your other apartment after one year."

"And your spare room?"

I interject as quickly as I can. "For our parents, when they visit. They are in Coimbatore."

Her face softens for a split second. And then she turns all her attention on me. "Have you seen a gynecologist, ma? Maybe you are doing something wrong. You are taking any breast enhancement hormones?"

In the end, after a long and painful conversation about everything but his lease, Erik's landlady drops the news that her son is moving back to Chennai from abroad and would be taking up that apartment upon his return. We trudge down four flights of stairs, dejected, embarrassed, and thoroughly pissed.

"Bitch," snarls the Lucky Bastard. Erik nods gravely.

"She talks," I say, "like her tongue is all scratched up from drinking too much pineapple juice to induce a Tamil padam abortion."

The Lucky Bastard snorts appreciatively. The cockles of my cold black heart warm slightly.

"Well, I still owe you guys drinks," Erik says. "And you look too nice to waste on going home. Unless, umm..." His eyes shift quickly, suggestively.

"No," we both say at once. I look at the Lucky Bastard and am not sure if I'm relieved or offended.

"We'll do drinks," I concede. "No sense wasting this saree, after all."

And I make a show of asking for Erik's hand to climb into the high seats of his Endeavour, while the Lucky Bastard, smoldering behind his sexbomb sunglasses, remains perfectly unreadable. Like a Sphinx. Like Tamil letters on a billboard when I'm on a bike that's moving too fast.

The waiter wears a nametag that says "7 Hills." "Elumalai!" I screech in comprehension, and understand, at the same instant the boys do, that this has to be my final drink of the night.

"When are you going back to Coimbatore?" I ask the Lucky Bastard, most needlessly.

"Next week, maybe."

"Why are you even here?"

"Some work."

"Did you come all the way here to help Erik?"

"No. I came for other reasons."

"You break my heart when you're cryptic."

'You break my heart all the time."

I am dangerously happy. Something erupts at the next table, a woman shouting at a man, a spilled drink, a shattered glass.

"Okay, guys," Erik snaps, "it's time to call it a night."

"Yes yes," says the Lucky Bastard, in Tamil. "Watch him now as he forgets he's supposed to pay the bill."

"I don't have any money, do you?"

"Why should we? We did him a favor."

"I'm sure he'll pay. Don't embarrass him."

"This son of a whore really embarrassed us today. How quickly you forget."

"Okay, you guys have to stop speaking a language I don't understand. It's rude. Good night." Erik swiftly takes out his wallet, removes three crisp thousand-rupee notes, places the edge of an empty martini glass over them, stands up, pushes his chair back in tidily, and walks toward the door.

"What the fuck was that?" exclaims the Lucky Bastard.

"Nordic anger," I say with a sigh. "Whatte cool."

He shakes his head in the direction of the door and watches it for a few moments, as though he expects an indignant return. Then he summons Mr. 7 Hills for the check, places the cash into the folder, and smiles at me almost—almost—sadly. And then something happens.

"So it's just you and me, kannamma."

It's like someone aimed a rubber band at my heart and didn't miss. I have waited my whole fucking life for someone to call me kannamma.

"I have waited my whole fucking life for someone to call me kannamma," I say.

He looks at me. I look at him.

"I'll take you home."

"Just put me in an auto, please."

"No chance." And then he takes my hands, both of them, and kisses them.

I like my fights dirty, my vodka neat, and my romance anachronistic. He carries my shoes when I decide I can't walk in high heels, gets a plastic bag for them, and hangs it on the handlebar. I rest my head on his back and watch the city as it zips by sideways. And then, of course, it starts to rain.

We take shelter under the flyover and share a cigarette.

"You're not coming home with me." It isn't a question.

"No," I say.

"You and I could be the culmination of centuries of human longing."

"Don't tell me about longing."

A strong gust of wind sends the tops of the trees at the park and the American consulate circling. How beautiful this city, or perhaps any in the world, is to a woman who knows her own bed awaits her even as she lingers, barefoot in the rain at midnight, pretending for just a few minutes that she doesn't know everything she already knows.

A part of me wishes I could still burst into tears at will, overflow with arsonist passion, say all the things I would say if I hadn't already come such a long way, such a long, long way.

And because I have nothing else to say and neither does he, he treats me to one of his signature moves—throwing back his hair, looking pensively into the middle distance, then training that heartbreak of a face right at mine only when he's sure he has me hooked. He has raindrops on his lips.

My cellphone rings. It's someone from far away. "I'll see you on gTalk in an hour," I say. "I'm just coming home from Zara. So I will be delightful."

"You always are." She laughs and hangs up.

The Lucky Bastard is waiting for me to finish what I started. Even Gemini Circle is as empty as a morning after at this hour, and I remember one night when we had hit every petrol bunk between Adyar and Nungambakkam, looking for one that was still open, kissing like fools all the way down Uthamar Gandhi Salai. Everything closes so quickly, before you know it, before you've even had a chance.

And then he gives up. "Why are you always so damn cool and mysterious? Like an oracle. Like a high priestess."

"The high priestess," I start—and then I have to take a breath because I have said this line so many times but never have I said it this way, and I want to do it right, do it the way the Lucky Bastard does it—stylish as cinema, sexy as smoke, unforgettable as trauma.

I look him dead in the eyes. "The high priestess never marries."

And then his chest heaves in something I recognize as pain but can no longer empathize with. He pulls me into a hug and before I know it, I feel him sob into my neck.

"I know, baby," I say, and I hold him tight. "I know."

# Accident

## *Tracy Gold*

———

I'd completely forgotten I had a paper due today. I realized it as soon as I sat down in my uncomfortable plastic chair in English class, and everyone else started shuffling through their bags to take out their neatly typed papers. I totally could have done it last night, but instead, I'd stayed up late working on a drawing for art class that wasn't even due until next week. If I could, I would quit school and just take art classes, be an artist. But no one understood that about me, and there I was, practically handcuffed into my chair, wishing I could be home sketching instead.

We'd just finished reading *Lord of the Flies* and Mr. Drake wanted us to write three pages about the id, the superego, and the ego, but I didn't buy that psychoanalysis bull. You didn't need to be stranded on an island with a group of them to know that teenage boys were animals.

But I still needed to write that paper, and I'd be damned if I couldn't at least get two pages done during class. So Mr. Drake kept on rambling in his mental-masturbation way about how the boys raped some pig on the island when really they just killed it, and I scribbled until my hand hurt. "The id is the true soul of the human male," I wrote, "because the id is the same thing as the penis." Mr. Drake would like that. It was wonderful, what I could come up with while my classmates sucked in Mr. Drake's words as if each phoneme were some ecstasy-laced lollipop.

I glanced up, to make Mr. Drake think I was actually paying attention, and Alan was looking straight at me. I looked back at him and he put his hand up to his mouth and stuck his tongue into his cheek on the other side, that pantomime blowjob crap that used to make me laugh but now made me want to vomit. I didn't even know what a blowjob was before I met Alan, but he was really cute, and asked me to Homecoming, and we danced all night, and, afterwards, you know, I gave him one. I guess it was pretty bad, or at least, that's what he told the whole school. He didn't tell me anything, though. My friend Emily told me she'd heard it from her friend Katrina. And damn, if I'd known this was going to happen, I would have bit the whole thing off when I had the chance.

It took a good amount of reserve not to jump out of my seat and just bite it off right now. How dare he not talk to me for weeks, spread rumors about me to the whole school, and then freaking sign-language blowjob in the middle of English class? I could feel the heat in my cheeks. I looked down and kept working on my essay, scratching my pen on the paper so hard I ripped the page in a few places. And that was my big mistake.

"Olivia," Mr. Drake said, "what are you working on over there?"

I had just finished a few very personal sentences, and I hoped Mr. Drake wouldn't read them aloud, which would be even worse than him knowing I was writing my essay in class. And I was just angry, angry at Alan, angry at Mr. Drake.

"A haiku about Alan's tiny penis," I said. Alan's face turned bright red, and there was this silence in the room. I could tell half of the class wanted to laugh, and the other half was waiting to see if Mr. Drake was going to blast my skinny ass to the principal's office.

"Apologize," said Mr. Drake, all glasses and floppy blond hair and argyle sweater. He walked up to the table and grabbed my paper. His face was red too.

"Sorry," I said, looking at Alan, but I had my middle finger up underneath the table where no one could see it.

Alan didn't say anything, didn't even nod. He looked down as his Adam's apple wobbled with a gulp.

"You watch what you say in my class," said Mr. Drake. He hadn't looked at my paper yet.

"Yes sir," I said. Why couldn't Mr. Drake have looked at Alan five seconds earlier, when he was doing his blowjob hand signal? Alan was the one who deserved to get in trouble.

Mr. Drake looked down at my paper. In my head, I paraphrased my last sentences, which, given the chance, I probably would have crossed out before handing the paper in: "The superego is just the id in disguise, because the only reason humans pretend to be moral is because it's in our own self-interest. That's why my parents got married, after they had me by accident: self-interest, not morality."

Mr. Drake looked up from the paper, and gave me this look, which was part pity, part disappointment, or maybe that's just what I felt, looking at him, and it was all inside me.

"I see you completed your paper well ahead of time," he said. Even though the man wasn't smart enough to collect papers at the beginning of class, like our older teachers, you had to give him credit for finding out what I was up to.

"Uh-huh," I said, middle finger still up under the table, but now pointing at Mr. Drake.

"Well then, you must be ready to hand it in," he said. "Shame, it's only one page." He walked to his desk and put the paper down on the table. Damn it. I shouldn't have written so loudly.

Mrs. Glassman was holding my charcoal drawing out in front of her as if it was going to give her the super flu or something. Woman didn't get me, but hell if I was going to change my art because of it.

"Olivia," she said, "I'm very disappointed in you."

My heart dropped in my stomach. I actually heard it. It went *thunk*, and then *thunkety-thunkety-thunk*, and suddenly I thought I was going to have diarrhea right there in the art classroom. I focused on Mrs. Glassman's face, which was oily and wrinkled at the same time, and the feeling passed.

Okay, so this was just some failed artist who was teaching high school art, but still, I'd come to this school because they were supposed to have a good art program, and my teacher already hated me. Great.

She held out my drawing. I thought it was amazing. It was Alan, right, except you weren't *really* supposed to know it was Alan. Anyway, he was just staring straight ahead in the drawing like Frida Kahlo does in her self-portraits. I gave Alan a unibrow and all, so seriously, he should have been unrecognizable. In one of my favorite paintings—okay, favorite in a horrifying way—Frida drew her husband on her forehead, like some tyrannical alien implanted, or incubated, there. But instead of a creepy guy, on Alan, I drew a penis with two tiny brains for balls. And I mean, the detail was fantastic. I gave the penis hair, and the brain-balls had little pimples.

"What were you thinking?" said Mrs. Glassman.

"That men think with their dicks," I said, looking straight into Mrs. Glassman's eyes, those beady little black eyes that twinkled when she talked about making your art "appropriate" for your age. She'd given us this whole big lecture on the first day. I'd chosen to ignore it.

"Well, I'm afraid I'm going to have to tell your parents," said Mrs. Glassman, "and I'll have to confiscate this for now."

"Fine," I said. I hoped she would give the drawing back, but my parents wouldn't care. Dad lived in Hong Kong making shitloads of money, enough money that we could use dollar bills to wipe our asses if we wanted to. Yet Mom still didn't think it was okay for her to come home from work before nine at night. It wasn't like she was saving the world, for Christ's sake. She worked in marketing for a mega law firm, not one of those environmental firms or even a criminal defense firm. Her firm had recently saved poor, poor Mason Oil from paying up after one of its tanks leaked and ruined almost all of the wells in a nearby neighborhood. And night after night, that's what she's chosen over spending time with me.

Still, Mom and I were supposed to get dinner tonight, as she was going to come home from work at a luxuriously early seven. I'd actually have something different from pizza and Chinese food to eat, though it would probably just be burnt chicken, knowing my mother's cooking skills, or lack thereof.

I hoped Mrs. Glassman would wait until tomorrow to tell my mom about the drawing. I was looking forward to just being with my mom and just talking about things, whatever girls and their moms talk about, I wouldn't know. But my mom would be mad I'd upset my teacher and she wouldn't understand my art any more than Mrs. Glassman did. Before my parents split up, my dad had all these awesome nude paintings he'd collected over the years. He'd always spent money on art, and I think seeing that art was part of why I started drawing seriously. But when they split up, and Dad moved out, my mom systematically went through the house getting rid of all those exquisite nudes. Maybe she blamed the paintings for my dad's affair.

Thought his promiscuity was encouraged by the perfectly painted titties hanging all over the house. Or maybe she was trying not to admit that he left because he'd never wanted to marry Mom in the first place. He'd only done it because of me. Of course, he never told me this. But you didn't need to be a rocket scientist to pick up on it.

Anyways, Mrs. Glassman walked away with the drawing, and I kept working on what I was doing—drawing Alan, naked. I had planned to draw a teeny tiny penis, but since Mrs. Glassman didn't seem to like the peen, I thought I'd just leave it off. It would make the same point. You get the best revenge through life, my dad had always said when I was upset, and art was my life, or at least, the only part I cared about.

When the bell rang, I felt my phone buzz in my pocket. Mrs. Glassman was preoccupied setting up the classroom for the seniors, who came in next, so I looked at my phone. It was from Mom.

*Held up at work. Can we resched dinner?*

I shouldn't have been surprised, but it hurt anyways. She did this all the time, but today, this was the one thing I had to look forward to, you know. I typed my response:

*Fuck you.*

I probably shouldn't have texted that, but when was the woman going to get it? She couldn't keep doing this to me. She could always make time for work, but not for me. I was fed up with pretending not to care.

I stared at my phone for a minute as the rest of my class left, but she didn't text me back. Figures. I shoved my phone into my backpack and hurried to my next class.

I was walking out of school after last period, finally headed home to where I'd have peace and quiet for the whole night. I'd order some pizza and eat about five chocolate bars. I'd started to see some cellulite on my thighs but I was basically skinny, so I'd be fine. More cushion for the pushing, Alan used to say, when we were still talking.

I turned the corner, and there he was, walking along right in front of me. I still felt angry from English that morning, and Mrs. Glassman, and my mom. I felt like a dog whose hair was rising on the back of its neck. Seriously, I had long hair. If I could get it to rise up like I was attached to some sort of adrenaline Tesla coil, I would gel the craziness until I had a head full of spikes, electrified knives. I could just spear Alan through the heart by head-butting him, like some killer goat.

"Hey asshole," I said, and Alan turned around. Worked every time. "So you know your name?"

"Bitch," he said, and put his hand down by his crotch and tossed out his fingers, like they were sperm, "leave me the hell alone." I guess he hadn't appreciated my tiny dick comment in English class that morning.

Well, I walked right up to him, and got in his face, and I could see him kind of sniff, like I hadn't showered or something. I had showered, but I sniffed too, and he smiled. It took all the control I had not to slap him right then.

"Why did you tell everyone?" I said. I hadn't confronted him about this before. In general, I was not a confrontational person. Today was an aberration. It's hard to build people skills when it's just you in your house, alone. But today—well, you know, everyone has limits.

"I consider it a service," Alan said, "to warn my fellow men of sluts who don't know how to swallow."

And that was it. I swung back and brought my fist into Alan's face, and I felt this satisfying crunch. It was so surprising—I thought I was going to miss and just hit the lockers behind him instead. I couldn't believe I'd made contact. I drew my hand back from his face, and at first, I thought, damn, my hand hurts, and second, I thought, oh my god, I hurt Alan. He was holding his right hand over his nose and there was blood dripping out of the cracks between his fingers.

He didn't say anything, just balled up his left fist like he'd like to hit me back, but I backed away and he turned around and stomped off toward the nurse's office—which was right next to the principal's office—holding his face. A low chorus of "ooohs" rose up from the other kids in the hallway. Their faces swirled around me in a blur.

I was in for it. But I thought I might as well try to make it home, so I set off toward the lobby exit, almost jogging but not quite, so I wouldn't draw too much attention.

I had almost busted out of the lobby doors when I heard my name. "Olivia Morgan!" It was Vice Principal McIntyre. "Come with me."

I froze. I was a bad liar and there was no way I was going to get out of this. I would just have to go. So I turned back into the lobby and walked toward the hallway, kids brushing against me on their way out of school.

The ones who hadn't seen me hit Alan probably thought McIntyre found my hat in the Lost and Found or that I'd been caught with pot, depending on their innocence level. But scrawny Olivia Morgan hitting hot Alan Fisher? Smashing that gorgeous nose into his brains? No, no way they'd be thinking that.

"Sit down," said McIntyre, when we got into his office. Judging by his red eyes, he probably drank a little, maybe in the morning, maybe at his lunch break. Or maybe it was just that his eyes reflected the red from his hair.

"We're sending Alan to the hospital," he said, and my stomach did that *thunking* thing again, and again I thought I was going to have to go to the bathroom, but I just focused on McIntyre's squinty freckled face. I started sweating, even though it was cold in here, and the swirling in my stomach stabilized into this low pain.

"Is he going to be okay?" I said. I had never punched anyone before. How was I supposed to know I was going to hurt him?

"Looks like you broke his nose," said McIntrye. "This is extremely serious." He let his words hang, and I imagined that we were standing in a gorge, and that there was this echoing *serious, serious, serious*, and I felt like laughing, but I held it in. McIntyre continued: "But as you haven't gotten in much trouble otherwise"—so Mrs. Glassman and Mr. Drake at least hadn't gotten to McIntyre yet—"we might be able to make it so you just get suspended."

*Just* suspended? What, like they were going to expel me for practically punching a guy by accident? Okay, it hadn't been totally by accident, but still, breaking his nose? I hadn't meant to do that.

"I didn't mean to hurt him," I said, looking down. Part of me really, really wanted to do the middle finger thing under the table and flick McIntyre off because he just didn't get it. Alan had hurt me way worse than a broken nose. But another part of me, maybe the smarter part, maybe not, kept myself from doing that.

"You need to learn self-control, Olivia," said McIntyre, and I didn't know what he was talking about. How did he know what I needed to learn? He'd hardly even spoken a word to me since he'd come and given his silly little student handbook talk at the beginning of the year.

The door of McIntyre's office creaked open, and this older lady who worked in the office came in. She was dressed in way too tight of an outfit for someone her age, leggings and one of those dress-shirt things the preppy girls loved to wear.

"Mrs. Morgan is on her way," she said. I looked down at my watch. It was 3:00 p.m. They'd actually convinced my mom to take off from work and come get me? When she'd already cancelled dinner on me? I was so shocked I didn't bother to correct the older lady. My mother was now going by "Stephens," her maiden name, as if "Morgan" were some disgusting schizophrenic alter ego.

"Thanks, Margaret," said McIntyre, and even though this woman was probably sixty years old, I saw him watch her ass as she left the room. I wanted to break his nose, too, at that moment, but I restrained myself. See, I had plenty of self-control.

So Vice Principal McIntyre and I just kind of sat there in silence for a while, and McIntyre filled out some paperwork.

Finally, once it seemed that all the noise had left from the school building—it was eerie, really, I'd never been there after everyone had cleared out before—I heard my mother's high-heeled footsteps coming down the hall.

"Oh, Olivia," she said, and she put her hand on my shoulder. It felt weird—when was the last time she had touched me?

"Your daughter punched another student this afternoon," said McIntyre, from his throne behind his desk.

"I heard," said my mother, giving me a stern look. But behind the sternness, there was—I could just see it—guilt. Let her feel guilty. Let her think I'd done this because she'd cancelled dinner on me. But that wasn't it. It was mostly an accident.

"We may have to suspend her," said McIntrye. "We'll have her hearing tomorrow at ten o'clock, and you should keep her at home until then."

"All right," said my mother. I just knew she was thinking about all these meetings she'd have to miss at the fancy law firm. La-di-da.

We walked out together to the car. I hadn't spent time with my mother outside when it was daylight in a long time. And it was a whopper of a fall day. Not too cool, not too hot. Just perfect. Figured. A storm would have been much more fitting.

When we were in the car, I took out my sketchbook and started drawing. We lived really close by, but I just felt like I had to sketch or I'd do something crazy, like grab the wheel, or break my mother's nose too. I would never actually do that, but then again, I'd done a lot of things today that I would normally never do. Also, I could feel my stomach clenching, and I knew I'd better get to the bathroom at home quick. In the meantime, I put my feet up on the seat and balanced the sketchbook on my knees so the movement of the car wouldn't affect my drawing too much.

"Olivia, I just, I don't know what to do with you," my mom said. "I got an email from your art teacher, too. She said you were drawing penises?" When she said the word *penises*, in this high voice that made me want to laugh, she turned to look at me instead of looking at the road. She wanted to talk with me so badly that she didn't care if we crashed on the way home.

I thought about telling her about Alan. The blowjob, the whole thing. Maybe this was our chance for mother-daughter bonding and all that crap. She'd tell me some disgusting story about her sex life, back when she had one, and I'd make puking noises, and we'd both laugh, and the pain in my gut would dissolve with every word.

But she would never understand. She'd said it herself. She didn't know what to do with me, as if I were some piece of software from work she wasn't trained to use. I just focused on my drawing, and my stomach settled a little. I was sketching my mom. She was looking back over her shoulder, but in her right hand, she was holding a pistol. She was pointing it straight off the page, pointing it at me.

# Grave to Cradle

*Catherine Haustein*

When she got the message, she was surprised. Celeste, a maiden lady, a scientist, who lived with and supported her elderly parents in the midsized town of Cedar Rapids, had forgotten all about the prize, a meeting with Isaac Newton—brought back to life by HiGenTek. Her mother had died that spring and the speed at which the undertaker whisked away the still warm body in a zippered bag woke her to the possibility that she was running out of time.

After the mortician had taken the body to be cremated, her father turned to her and said, "Now that it's all over, I'll have a hot fudge sundae with cashews. Go fix it for me. I've got some laundry piling up as well." She understood why her mother hadn't fought death, just commented that it didn't hurt much and felt kind of creepy. Celeste, however, wasn't her mother. And the thing about your mother dying is this: you'll never be more alone or more free. She would be free now, come what may.

Following the funeral, her brother, Acer, took most of the family furniture and the funeral flowers back to Forth Worth, a distance of 869 miles. Trying to find a spark of beauty on an overcast April day, Celeste bought a pot of blue pansies and put them on a yellow tablecloth in the kitchen—the table and three chairs had been left. Her father said, "Those flowers look dry. Could you get me a beer? Can't you match your clothes better? You look damn homeless." When you're a working chemist there are two things you don't do no matter how tempting: make illegal drugs and poison someone. She texted her brother to and come get Dad. He didn't.

Celeste was the analytical chemistry department head at HiChemTek, a company that made breakfast cereals and pet foods. Because she liked her job, she didn't poison her father or sedate him beyond annoyance. She moved from the house she'd shared with her parents to an apartment. For a while the morning sun in her own kitchen was enough to tell her she'd made progress. The mirror had different ideas, however, and in time revealed the Enlightenment notion of always moving forward, building on the past, standing on the shoulders of giants, to be flawed. A wyvern, the totem animal of Entropy, had walked all over her. She looked like hell. So much for progress and dreams of children. For solace, Celeste turned to what she'd tried to leave behind as foolish, the fine art of alchemy. She called upon Venus by lighting a red candle with the wick pressed down in the wax.

The prize—a day with an alchemist—was a welcome diversion and hinted that life still had unexpected delights to offer. Now here he was—Newton—looking a bit lost around the eyes and resembling Kurt Vonnegut, but shorter and plumper, with a smaller head. Escorted by Mr. Altotus and accompanied by a film crew consisting of well-coiffed women on teetering heels, he'd come to her laboratory at HiChemTek. Newton was glum, little more than a trick pony in the stables of HiGenTek along with Paracelsus, Miriam sister of Moses, and Gerber. Resurrection hadn't been cheap, and the company marketed the alchemists and exploited them for profit. A scientist might do something out of curiosity, but why would a company do anything but make money? HiGenTek wasn't a person, after all. It could expand and progress like something not alive. The family who owned it, the Cochtons, meant to live forever or close to it. Resurrecting the alchemists was just a trial run. Such ambition wasn't cheap.

To be honest, Celeste had hoped for Gerber, the Arabian who put chemistry in its cradle. They could talk about distillation or sublimation. Or with Paracelsus she could discuss measuring and *Primun Ens Melissa* — similar extracts were in the pet food and cereals. But the marketers didn't understand the difference between chemistry and physics and had matched the lottery selected winners with their alchemists according to personality types. It was a publicity stunt for HiUTek, a company perfecting personality analysis tests for employers. The public was eager to see who was as devotedly divine as Miriam, as flamingly fun as Paracelsus, as clever and good with gadgets as Gerber, or as unfriendly and hostile as Newton. At least Celeste knew now why she hadn't married and had rarely dated since college, when looks mattered more than personality.

A nicely dressed older fellow straight out of 1705, the year he was knighted, Newton stood in her lab looking more like the guy who prosecuted coin clippers than the genius who'd penned *Principia*. No surprise that he looked fatigued and a bit crazy. He'd been overworked. She'd seen him in advertisements for anything associated with force or gravity, products ranging from cologne to mufflers. The poor man's eyes drooped and so did his mouth, as if he had a neural lesion. His hair still looked good, though, lush and snowy, and he had that cute dimple on his chin. Celeste handed him a pair of safety glasses. He didn't take them, so she put them on him, her hand brushing the soft, thin skin of his face. He smelled like old books. He tilted his head to stare at the ceiling and then the floor.

"Optics," he said. "How I love to see through a glass. Warm thanks to you from your humble servant, Isaac Newton." He bowed stiffly and wobbled in a way she found charming. Celeste came up with another way to delight this innocent father of science. She fished some diffraction grating glasses from a drawer of science novelties she kept for student tours.

"Try these," she said, replacing the safety goggles with this party trick that made white light into rainbows. The film crew tittered as he wagged his head and examined the fluorescents overhead.

"Wondrously lit," he said as he gazed about and clapped his hands like a child.

*Here's a problem with modern science and the employment of scientists*, she thought. *Wonder is expected, demanded, paid for. We're expected to roll out wonder as if it were a product and to hand it to the marketers to whisk away and make even more magnificent, but in a false way.* The film crew was giggling as if he were a buffoon.

"You may keep them," she said. "But they aren't safe for the lab. Here, change them out for now." She put them in the pocket of his waistcoat, and with her hand so close to the groin of a great man, she felt a surge of new life within.

"That which is above," she said with the force of an eruption but quietly, to him alone.

"Is as that which is below," he replied to her alone.

The film crew zeroed in on his brightening countenance. Altotus poked her. "Unnecessary display of alchemical secrets. No passwords in front of the common people." Altotus was a slight man with crooked teeth. He was either old or old before his time. He was correct. They'd exchanged the sacred words of alchemy. Celeste took Isaac's hand and led him through her laboratory with Altotus scurrying behind.

The tour of the lab cheered Isaac, particularly the monochromator display, where light was dispersed through a grating and fell upon a black metal plate in a perfectly separated rainbow. Isaac liked all things spectroscopic, which was fine with Celeste. She'd done phosphorescence in graduate school. He bounced on his buckled shoes as they walked through the halls. Replications of art from the nineteenth-century West covered the walls. The founders of HiChemTek, the Cochtons, saw themselves as cowboys and patriots—the true owners of the land and everything on it, and of the secrets their scientists uncovered too.

Shortly after they visited the animal lab, in which Isaac showed great interest, while Celeste was explaining an x-ray fluorescence (XRF) gun, an alarm went off and the building was evacuated. The production crew, Isaac, and Altotus were lost in the chaos. So many people outside the lab drew a crowd, and within that crowd would be the pickpockets and identity thieves who made up the loose band of robbers and unemployed craftsmen known as Counter Force. Celeste was sympathetic to Counter Force and their refusal to buy from, sell to, or work for the Cochtons, but who could live without technology in the rural outskirts as they did? They were just asking for their idealistic hearts to be crushed and their children to starve. Crops grew best on rooftops and required fertilizer and filtered water.

Celeste was still holding the XRF gun. Nobody would know it shot x-rays and was meant for metal analysis and not bullets. She swung it about and tried to look dangerous, although she was on the small side. Celeste spotted Isaac in the parking lot watching the swirling police lights through his diffraction glasses. She took his arm and led him to her car.

"It's not safe out here. Too many people." She unlocked the passenger door.

"A fine chariot." He bowed.

"Get in. And hurry."

Isaac's jacket was bulging and moving. The black face of a hooded rat peeped out of a flapped pocket, followed by an albino rat with twitching whiskers.

"Did you steal those?" she said.

"Yes, I've sinned." He pointed to the XRF gun under her arm. "You pilfered a piece. We're co-conspirators."

Celeste put the gun on the dashboard. "Where's Altotus?"

"He left with one of the ladies, saying I was where I needed to be. He likes the ladies."

Not sure what to do with Isaac and with emergency vehicles all around, she drove to her apartment. No doubt he could tell by her sparse furnishings that she'd moved there in haste.

"Are you hungry?" she asked, putting her lab coat on the back of her chair. She was wearing Capri pants and, like him, a ruffled blouse.

"Yes. Is it teatime?" He was trembling. Could he still have mercury poisoning after all these years? It isn't as if the element would go anywhere. She put two mugs in the microwave. Celeste wasn't sure what to say. Surely he would be bored with hero worship.

"Here we are," she said with a smile, handing him a mug.

"Yes. Kind of a surprise. You're making it pleasant. I feel more kindly than I did before. As if I finally had a good night's sleep."

"How did they do it?" she asked. "Did they just yank you from the grave?"

"Yes. I was peacefully at rest. Preserved in the method of the alchemists. I'd given instructions to my niece, Catherine. She was both dutiful and beautiful. This new time is filled with wonders, but I didn't know that death would bring such rest, and that rest would be so pleasant. I was happy not making progress. I expected to be resurrected by other alchemists. Who are these heathens who did this to me?"

"They're rich. The noble lords of our day."

"The rich have been charitable to me, but I found better friends with the Whigs," he said, watching steam rise from the mugs. They stood together at the counter and dipped tea bags in the hot water.

"Water is one of my favorite elements. This steam could be harnessed for energy," he said.

"Over two hundred years ago. And water isn't an element. It has two parts, hydrogen and oxygen."

"You're teaching me something and opening my heart. Only my dear professor did this for me. The rest just took."

"How about some pasta?" She put her hand on his to stop the tremors. He still had his cognitive functions. It couldn't be mercury.

"I don't know what that is but it sounds enjoyable."

She retrieved a pack of crackers from the cupboard, put a pot of water on to boil, and they sat across from each other at the cheap table watching the rats eat crackers and drink from a saucer.

"I love learning. It's all I had," he said. "I lived for knowledge."

"I understand."

"My mother abandoned me as a child. My father was dead and she wed another. I was born misunderstood."

"You must forgive her. It's hard to be a woman."

"Are you a woman? Your love of science and manner of dress and hair confuses me."

"Yes, of course. Do I resemble a man to you?"

"A bit. Not that it bothers me. I've avoided women as I have avoided being shot through the knee with an arrow, but I find you affable."

"The same for you." His irascibility was legendary, but she was seeing none of it. "What happens to you after today?"

"Paraded around like a spectacle, I imagine. Here, Diamond." The white rat crawled up his arm. "She's friendly."

The door rattled and opened. Two police officers with drawn guns approached Celeste.

"Identification."

She held up her wrist and the fat officer scanned it.

"We're taking you in. You got the cuffs, Barnabus?"

"Don't take her! I came willingly," Newton said. "It's not a kidnapping."

"Calm down, Hair Boy. It's not about you. It's elder abuse," the thin one said. He looked at Celeste. "Your father was found abandoned and covered in feces. He's been taken to a facility. Your bank account will be tapped to cover the costs. Once you sign the papers and pay the fine, you'll be released."

"Way to tell her, Ace," said Barnabus. He pointed his gun at Diamond. "Is that a rat?"

The pot of water boiled over and splashed on the stove. The noise distracted them and in that second Celeste grabbed the boiling water and tossed it on the officers. Newton fell upon them as they writhed on the floor and beat them unconscious. Celeste took his hand and pulled him through the apartment hallway and into her car in the garage below. They drove to her parents' house. She still had the key. The place had an earthy stink, and dirty dishes were everywhere. Rummaging through her mother's closet, Celeste tossed a flowered dress at Isaac.

"Change into this. We mustn't be recognized. It will look good with your white stockings."

He did as she instructed. He had a nice physique for an older man, well, a bit of a fat belly, but agreeable to her and strangely marked near the navel with what looked like a blue four—the sign of Jupiter and the element tin. Celeste stripped to her bra and unisex briefs. Newton had been right about how ambivalent she'd always been about womanhood.

Newton put his hand on the tattoo on her belly—light through a prism and on the prism the sign of Venus, the looking glass. It hadn't suited her but that was her element, copper, the metal of Venus. She'd drawn a copper strip from the bag at the ceremony long ago.

Their bodies brushed together as she pulled up his hair and covered it with one of her Mom's chemo wigs, something with red spikes. She put on the one that was black and curly. They each selected a large purse, suitable for the XRF gun, rats, crackers, and diffraction glasses. Celeste slipped on a black dress and low-heeled pumps.

They took her father's car this time. Night was creeping up on them. Isaac fed the rats bits of cracker and watched the lights through his diffraction glasses.

"We shouldn't have done that," Celeste said. "I just hate to be messed with." Her heart beat in her mouth. She'd been stupid.

"I agree. I had a man hanged, drawn, and quartered for less. But we've mucked things up now. Where are we going?" He adjusted his glasses.

"Out of town," Celeste said. "Watch the lamps on the chariots. If you see lines of violet, indigo, blue, green, yellow, and red, lots of red, tell me and we'll turn off on a side road. It's the constables. They have special headlights with strontium. The Cochtons have friends who own strontium mines."

"Strontium?"

"An element. Just keep your eyes peeled."

"Wouldn't I have to take off these optics to do that?"

"Observe. Can you do that?"

"Of course. It's part of my profession." He looked into the night at the spectra of the headlamps.

Celeste drove to the suburbs and parked in a Cochmart lot in a bad neighborhood. She set the keys and her phone next to a man sleeping on the sidewalk. She didn't want to be traced. Isaac went into the store and came back with candy.

"At times like this, I turn to mathematics and sweets," Isaac said, offering her some chocolate.

"Me too. You always know what you're getting with mathematics. Did you steal this?"

"Yes. I have sinned."

No one came from the store to confront them. This happens when wages are low.

"Hold out that purse now," she said.

"But Diamond and Bronze are in it."

"They won't be hurt. I'm surrendering to Counter Force. This will be faster than searching for them. Hold it out and when someone comes to steal it, we'll grab him. Good chocolate." Celeste receded into a shadow.

"And then we'll be stolen?"

"Yes. You're a smart man."

Isaac stood dangling his purse and gazing through the spectral glasses. Holiday lights flickered in the window of the bar across the street. It was May, hot, with storms rising. Moisture collected on their faces. Celeste was used to filtered air and a controlled environment. It kept her equipment functioning at top capacity.

Newton wiped his forehead. "The world is so warm now. Best to not be fat these days. I sweated much before I died that last time. It was painful. Tell me again why we are out in the night like this. Is it the constables? I'm sure they can be bribed. Most men can be."

"We're on the wrong side of the law and my life savings are going to the upkeep of my father. I'm leaving society. Certainly there's use for science everywhere. Perhaps it could even be used for the good of the people."

"I honestly believe that bribes are the better option. Of course, I haven't any money. It all went to my heirs."

"You don't have to come with me. You're valuable property. Take the car. The keys are still right there on the curb. Go back to those who resurrected you. They'll live forever soon, and perhaps so will you."

His mouth drooped, but it might have been a lesion.

"You are telling me that these lords look for science without benefice?"

"I am."

"Will you embrace me once before you go?" he said. He looked like an abandoned scarecrow with his red wig, shaky limbs, and blowing dress.

Celeste wrapped her arms around him. He was warm, so warm, and yielding, and alive. She put her lips to his. They were chocolaty, hard, and dry. It was a terrible kiss, but her heart leapt into it.

"We might need to work on that," she said, stepping back. He'd asked for just one embrace and she was precise.

He said, "Gravity is a weak force, unlike loneliness. That last life I had—I squandered part of it. I have things to learn."

"Matter draws itself together. You said this yourself."

He put one hand on his chest. "There are places where the mass is thin. In my previous life, my affection was tossed to the fire."

Celeste put her hand on his heart. "Work. Love. It all takes time. Time is a finite dimension. You said that yourself. We've spent time on important things, forsaking love. Our sacrifice was not in vain. Natural philosophy, science, was a freeing force once. I still believe that it will set us free. But all must own it together, not just these few. And we must open ourselves to the possibility of magic. Not all can be explained."

"*A man might imagine things that are false, but he can only understand things that are true.*" He put his hand over hers. "I'll allow myself to become embroiled. This escapade makes me feel as giddy as the day I took over the Royal Society." He smiled. He was missing a tooth.

Celeste straightened his wig. "Are there more than balls in your cradle?"

"Perhaps. Newton men have been historically fertile."

Celeste leaned on the window of the store. "That's what I need. When the time comes, don't fight it."

"What do you mean by that?"

"You'll see. Be aware that things have changed. I won't be waiting on you and there are no servants where we're going."

"I also have progressed and I have always wished for the love of an equal."

In time, a person came to steal the purse. The look of a madman upon him, Isaac grabbed the thief and Celeste held the XRF gun to his neck.

"Take us to your leader lest we be laid by the heels," said Isaac, swinging the squeaking purse.

"Asylum," said Celeste.

For a time, HiGenTek looked for Isaac. The surveillance cameras showed nothing of his departure from HiChemTek, and the film crew swore Isaac had never made it to the facility. Ace and Barnabus remembered slipping on a wet floor in an empty apartment. It was assumed that Celeste had finally run off with a man. At least that part was true.

Counter Force was skeptical until Isaac built rat-powered generators and a windmill to demonstrate his utility to them. With the aid of her XRF, Celeste sorted scrap metal and melted it into tools and ploughshares for the gardens. Isaac learned to love tomatoes, and their little house had an east-facing window where Celeste could greet the sun.

Eventually the other alchemists, repelled by greed, joined them. For, as everybody knows, science is an attempt to touch the divine, and greed drives divinity away. Gerber set up a distillery. Paracelsus formulated medicines. Miriam's burning bushes kept all intruders away and one swipe with a rock from her pocket erased Celeste's identification chip.

Yes, the time came when Celeste and Isaac had children—just three, but all were handy with tools and figures. On clear nights you could see them out together, their hands filled with gadgets, their eyes filled with stars, their hearts with the optimism that conceived them. With science as with alchemy there is always hope, nothing is impossible, and what is possible is still filled with wonder.

# Stony Limits

## *Enid Shomer*

———◦⁂◦———

When I wheeled through the door of Room 12A at the Heloise Gumm High School for Exceptional Children, the first thing I saw was a shiny red football helmet looming over a blond wooden desk. Well, I thought, at least the dress code is lenient. The last school I attended was pretty strict: no denims or T-shirts, no high heels, no more makeup than Jackie Kennedy wore.

Mrs. Page motioned me toward the front of the room. "Class," she began officially, "this is our new student, Maggie Freer. I'm sure that you'll all make her feel at home." I hate being reduced to third-person, so I stared at my little toe, which was wiggling. It's the only part of me from the waist down that moves. When I'm nervous it gets going on its own.

Mrs. Page asked all the kids to state their name and handicap. "It saves a lot of time and questions later," she explained.

"I had polio when I was ten," I said when my turn came. "Six months before the vaccine came out." There was a little awed hush in the room. This was familiar to me—I call it the Prestige of Polio. When it comes to wheelchair disabilities, it's the top of the heap. Maybe because a U.S. president had it. I don't know. But for six years now people have always been impressed when I mention my disease.

The football helmet was called Julio, and there was a kid with real bad cerebral palsy named Carl. And I was wrong about the dress code: Julio had hydrocephalus and wore the helmet day and night for protection. What would it take to get him to remove it for me?

Mrs. Page was teaching geography. She pulled a glossy map of the world down in front of the chalkboard. Lots of pink, yellow, green, and blue blotches. I noticed that Thailand was still called Siam. The bell rang, but no one left. They wheeled their chairs back from the desks and huddled, chatting, in small groups. Only Julio stood, tall and lean, without a chair. Then, in about ten minutes, the bell rang again and Mrs. Page began English. I had gone to regular schools all my life, and I missed being carried along with the crush of students changing classes at a regular school—the commotion, the sly remarks and quick digs.

"*Romeo and Juliet* is a tragedy," Mrs. Page started, "of doomed love, of a love which tries to go against tradition and the weight of social custom." I detected a faint snicker behind me. "But there are many other important messages in this play, as in all of Shakespeare." She quoted: "'He that is strucken blind cannot forget the precious treasure of his eyesight lost,'" then paused respectfully. "But mainly," she went on, "we could sum it up with these words: 'Alas that love, so gentle in his view, should be so tyrannous and rough in proof...violent delights have violent ends.'" Having read the play aloud with my dad many times after my spinal fusion, I quoted to myself the apt, "She speaks, yet she says nothing," while I doodled a cartoon of Julio on the inside of my notebook.

At lunch the kids were real friendly. First everybody in chairs went through the line, then Julio, then the born deaf kids from the second floor, who talked rapidly with their hands in miniature karate chops. The only sign language I knew was the international screw you finger, so I smiled a lot at them but didn't try to join in. I showed Julio my sketch of him, thinking he'd be flattered.

"Someday I won't need this," he said, adjusting his chin strap. "Otherwise, I'm completely normal."

"That's good."

"What about you?" he asked, looking at my small legs.

"This is it," I answered.

"Yeah, well, at least you're not in a potty chair like some of them."

"I'll remember that next time I say my prayers."

"You wanna take a walk?" He didn't hurry to rephrase his question, which was a good sign. I was tired of people adjusting their vocabularies to accommodate my wheels.

We headed out the door onto the playground, a dismal paved area surrounded by very tall fences. Across the alley was a body shop and an envelope warehouse. I remembered the photograph on the school brochure. It showed the front with its wide, spanking white double doors and closely cropped shrubs. Julio twined his fingers in the chain link and was silent. I felt like a parked car with all the glare and concrete. My wheels were hot to the touch, and my foot pedals were starting to burn. Then we saw Carl motioning us and returned to the lunchroom.

"She's going to announce it after lunch," Carl said, fighting for each word.

"You sure?" Julio asked. I watched Carl struggle to maintain control of his movements. He nodded, then rested against his chairback.

"What?" I asked.

"Another field trip," Julio said. He tore open a pack of Tom's Peanut Butter Crackers, dropped the wrapper, and crushed it under his foot. The cellophane unfolded spastically, just like Carl.

"I saw a cow in person once," Carl managed to say.

"Oh yeah," Julio said, "we've had some stellar field trips."

"Now I'm going to get to see God," Carl continued.

"Like one time they loaded all of us into a bus." Julio crunched down on the whole bundle of crackers at once. "You know how *long* that takes? And then they drove us over to the rich end of town to—get this—see the azaleas in bloom." At that moment his front teeth were blooming with orange flecks of cracker and peanut butter.

"And music," Carl said, touching my hand.

"Yeah." Julio explained for him. "We go to the symphony four times a year. They have to take out the whole first row of seats for us."

"I like music," I said. "It makes me feel like I'm flying."

"Me too," Julio conceded. "The music part is great. It's the way they talk to us that gets me. You know, like we're retarded, too."

"*Bolero* was good," Carl said. "Have you heard *Bolero*?"

The deaf kids were returning their trays through the cafeteria pass through. They were a rough and tumble group—punching each other on the arm, banging the trays around. It never occurred to me that deaf people would be so noisy. "What about them?" I asked. "Do they go to the concerts?"

"Course not," Julio answered.

The deaf kids lined up at the bottom of the stairs. It was a steep metal staircase with one landing and rivet-like pockmarks all over it, like something salvaged from a battleship. The noise was tremendous as they stampeded up. Julio pointed out their teacher, Miss Simons, who brought up the end of the line—a powerful looking woman with meaty arms and legs and a long chestnut colored ponytail. She looked about forty but bounded up the steps energetically, her arms extended as if to catch all of them if the tide turned.

After lunch we had a rest period in the physical therapy room. Everyone got out of their chairs and lay down on thick leatherette mats. Mrs. Page brought me an upholstered cube and placed it at the end of my mat. I got into Fowler's antigravity position—my knees crooked as if I were seated in a chair that had been tilted back onto the floor. Mrs. Page put on a recording of *Swan Lake*, and my mind began to drift.

The next thing I knew a little dog was licking my face, a toy poodle with pink skin and eyes streaked like marbles.

"Oh my poor, darling, sweet thing," a voice behind me said. I twisted my head around to see two heavy brown walking shoes and thick support hose. Then a hand brushed my face. "Lamar! How rude of you." She scooped the dog up, then touched my face again. "You precious little thing," she crooned. I realized, then, that she was talking not to the dog but to me.

"Who are you?" I asked, raising up on both elbows and reaching for my chair parked alongside.

"Let me help you, dear," she said, going for my armpits.

"No!"

Mrs. Page lunged between us. "Maggie, this is Mrs. *Gumm*." Suddenly I made the connection—she was Heloise Gumm, the benefactor and founder of the school.

"Pleased to meet you." I hoisted myself into my chair.

We arranged ourselves in rows for Mrs. Gumm. Then the deaf kids torpedoed through the doorway, laughing and poking each other.

Mrs. Gumm beamed. "My dear silent angels," she said. They ignored her. Miss Simons settled them in and joined her at the front to translate into sign language.

"My dear children," said Mrs. Gumm. "It's all been arranged for two weeks from Friday. A big field trip." She looked to Miss Simons for help, then mimicked the sign for "big." "Pilgrims and tourists from all over the country come to Withlahatchee Springs, Florida. The radioactive waters are said to be healing."

Carl, seated next to me, raised his hand jerkily.

"Yes?" Mrs. Gumm noticed.

"Are we spending the night?"

"No, dear. But we'll have lunch and dinner on the road, and the park has refreshment stands. Won't that be fun?"

I quickly scrawled a note to Carl: OH GOD, JUNK FOOD AT LAST. He smiled.

"Where was I?" Mrs. Gumm asked Lamar, whose head peeked out from her arm. "Yes. Christ of the Orange Grove. A magnificent statue. A holy shrine without the great expense and danger of traveling to the Holy Land. A modern wonder of the world."

I looked over at Miss Simons, trying to verify what I'd heard. She jabbed the palm of her left hand with her right index finger, then punched a similar "hole" in the right hand. Then she tapped her way up one arm, like someone playing "this little piggy." She kept repeating these gestures. A fat tear slid down Carl's cheek. Taking my pen hand in his own, he made me circle the word GOD on my notepad.

Mrs. Gumm visited our classroom every morning to give an inspirational message. "I was without shoes," she began on Wednesday in an ominous tone, "and wanting the pity of the world until I saw a man without feet." I knew it was supposed to make me feel better, but all I could see the rest of that day were stumps.

After her pep talk, she went upstairs to her silent angels. Rumor had it that the deaf room was a scientific wonder, with state of the art earphones and oscilloscopes. Kids said it was brightly painted and wallpapered and had shag carpeting. Amanda Frank's mother had told her there were all kinds of posters—polar bears with "real" fur and photographs of castles that Mrs. Gumm had visited on her yearly European vacations. I itched to see it. Could it really be so much nicer than our shabby room, with its green chalkboard overhung with the cursive alphabet? Mrs. Page often brought flowers from home for her desk, but otherwise the room was a dull beige designed to hide dirt for years.

Thursday at lunch I convinced Julio to eat with the deaf kids. Carl tagged along. We waved hello as we pulled up to the table where they were bent over their macaroni casseroles and milk. A few returned the wave, then ignored us.

"I told you," Julio said, grabbing hold of Carl's chair handles to return him to our side of the lunchroom.

"Wait," I said, throwing on the brake lever of Carl's chair. He lurched slightly forward.

"They don't want us," Julio said, his foot tapping in annoyance.

I looked at the ten or so faces at the table. Most of them seemed relaxed as sleepers but with open eyes. They sat much closer together than hearing people and leaned and rubbed against each other. I decided to go for it and put my arm against the thin arm of a girl with reddish hair. She turned to acknowledge me and kept on drinking her milk. I felt a slight pressure back from her warm, smooth flesh. Then, as if someone had lowered a curtain, she turned away and began gesturing to the boy on her right.

"They don't like us," Carl said.

"No. They just like each other better," I said. Julio's face brightened. He moved his hands from Carl's chair to my shoulders.

"I like you," he said, and began to massage my neck. Out of the corner of my eye, I saw Carl blush furiously, then move his wavering hand to touch Julio's leg. We froze for a moment. Then Julio released his gentle grip and pushed Carl to the wheelchair side of the cafeteria.

"The Christ is seven stories tall," Carl said, his face returned to its usual pale color.

"All I want to know is do they sell cotton candy," I told him.

"I heard the Christ is so white. When you touch him your hands come away all silvery. And beautiful. Like moonlight."

"Or chalk," Julio said.

"They have a big Bible," Carl continued. "I heard the pages are made of steel."

"I heard they have lots of natural springs, and Mrs. Gumm wants us all to get baptized." Julio fiddled with the straw in his milk.

"Oh no!" I lamented. In the two years I spent at Warm Springs, clergymen of every faith had visited me, not to mention the evangelists I attracted on weekend family outings who tried to talk me into attending tent revivals.

"On the other hand," Julio said, "maybe they have rides."

"Oh sure," I said, "like the Tunnel of Sodom and Gomorrah."

Julio cracked up.

"I could get cured," Carl said, staring out the window at the body shop, where blue fire flared from an acetylene torch.

Back in the PT room, Mrs. Page arranged us on our mats, put on Beethoven at low level, and left the room to join Miss Simons and the rest of the staff in the faculty lounge. Beethoven always reminds me of someone having a temper tantrum, so for the first time I stayed awake. I looked at the other kids lying on the floor, some with knees bent and legs elevated like mine, others on their sides, and some curled up like unborn babies. Julio's red helmet stood out like a Christmas ornament three mats away. He was reading *Battle Cry*. It looked like a steamy sex novel from the cover, which showed a couple kissing, the man's uniformed body pressed hard against the woman.

"Hey, Julio," I whispered, "are you getting ready for *Romeo and Juliet*?" We were going to read parts of it aloud in class for the next few days. Julio shushed me and kept reading. A moment later he said, "I'll turn down the pages with good parts for you."

"Thanks." Just then I heard thumping from the ceiling. Nothing so loud as to startle, and not that creepy groaning that makes you think the roof will collapse. This sounded like people batting tom toms.

"What is that?"

Julio came over and sat down beside me. "I don't know. Maybe it's some kind of vibration therapy. Or dancing."

"Have you ever been upstairs?"

"No. But they do it just about every day." He suspended the book in front of my eyes. "Read this," he said.

"So what?" I said, after speeding through it.

"I thought only babies sucked women's tits," he admitted.

"Well, that just shows how much you know," I said, trying to sound cool.

Mrs. Page had turned off the classroom lights and lowered the window shades to simulate night. She was posted by the switch to bring the dreaded dawn on cue to Romeo and Juliet. Amanda was reading the part of Juliet, and Julio was Romeo.

"It was the nightingale," Amanda insisted, trying to get Romeo to stick around even though he'd been banished.

"It was the lark," Julio argued. I waited for my lines, but it took forever. Besides, Juliet's nurse didn't have a lot to say in this scene.

"Yond light is not daylight," Amanda said. "It is some meteor that the sun exhales." She sounded like someone reading the ingredients on a cereal box.

But Julio was really getting into his role. "Let me be put to death," he screamed, clutching his chest. "Come death and welcome! Juliet wills it so."

This startled Amanda, but she continued to read flatly. "Now be gone," she told him with equal emphasis on each word.

Mrs. Page flipped the light switch. Julio looked at the ceiling as if he were seeing it for the first time. "More light and light. More dark and dark our woes!" he wailed.

I quickly wheeled over to the couple. "Madame!" I reprimanded Juliet. "The day is broke, be wary, look about."

Julio planted a wet one on Amanda's hand and retreated to the back of the room. By then Amanda was very interested in her part, and her "Oh think'st thou we shall ever meet again?" was passionate.

From the doorway Julio's voice boomed in an astounding stage whisper that gave me goose bumps. "I doubt it not," he reassured Amanda, "and all these woes shall serve for sweet discourses in our time to come."

Amanda just sat there, a lovesick expression on her face.

"Cut!" Mrs. Page ordered, returning to her desk. "That was good. Would anyone like to talk about the meaning of this scene? I mean, how we might apply it in our own lives?"

"Can we rehearse it again?" Amanda blurted.

"We won't have time today, I'm afraid," Mrs. Page said.

Carl was thoughtful. "You just know they aren't going to live happily ever after," he said. "I don't know how, but you do."

"That's true," Mrs. Page agreed.

"But you want them to so bad, like wanting to believe in miracles."

Four days before our trip Mrs. Gumm delivered an orientation lecture to the whole school. I took plenty of notes, figuring that a studious, attentive attitude might come in handy if I had to bargain for taffy apples and chili dogs.

"Gethsemane Sinkhole," she intoned. "Even the name is magical." She paused while Miss Simons signed for the deaf kids. Julio passed me *Battle Cry* with a juicy passage set off by blue ink brackets. I read it as I continued to take notes about our destination. It was a strange combination of facts and word pictures:

Harold J. Wilson whose money had built the Christ and whose features it supposedly bore.

*A dressing gown, sheer, white—it flowed like a billow to the floor.*

From a distance the outstretched arms (sixty-five feet across) give the appearance of a mammoth cross surrounded by twenty thousand orange trees.

*Across the room each heard the other's deep breath. He could see the nipples of her breasts through the film of silk net.*

Three automobiles can be suspended from either wrist without affecting the statue. Free juice samples.

*Their bodies seemed to melt together. She sank her fingernails into his flesh. "Oh God, God, God," she said.*

Seventy feet tall. White cement.

"Bring your cameras," Mrs. Gumm suggested, "and some mad money. The Christ Only Art Gallery has lovely crucifixions." She pulled a large crocheted handkerchief from her purse and stretched it taut against her black dress. The familiar gossipy groupings of *The Last Supper* emerged in incredible detail. "Handmade," she crowed, pivoting so that everyone could see the sacred scene displayed on her chest.

On my notepad I wrote Julio a message: I NEED TO TALK TO YOU.

Rest hour was the obvious time to get a look at the deaf room. Julio and I sneaked out of PT together. The other kids were asleep as usual and the teachers safely out of earshot in their lounge.

"This is perfect timing," I reassured Julio, as we contemplated the steep staircase to the second floor.

"I'm not worried about getting caught." He shoved his shirttails into his trousers with abrupt pecking motions. "Maybe I should bring you up in your chair?"

"The chair would make an awful racket against the metal."

He kicked the bottom tread, and a slight ringing filled the stairwell. "You're right," he said.

"I'm strong," I told him. "I can pull myself up by my arms. Come on, Julio, I'm dying to see that room."

"Me too. Mrs. Gumm's 'heaven on earth' for her little angels! And we can see what the noise is, too."

"Yeah." Actually, I hadn't thought about the thumping since that first day I heard it, but now I noticed again random thuds right over my head. I slid onto the second step. "Only seventeen more to go," I said cheerfully.

"I can help you," Julio said, as I began my slow ascent. "Tell me what to do."

I have been called "fiercely independent" so many times that I practically answer to it as my name. I looked at Julio's pale cheeks against the red of his helmet and his hands outstretched vaguely in my direction. "Stand on each stair as I climb. That way I won't get scared looking at the spaces between the steps."

He stood above me, backward, on the stairway, his arms extended straight from the shoulder to grip the iron railings on either side. It was comforting to see his legs firmly planted in front of me instead of the floor receding below as I hoisted myself along. His black trousers were neatly cuffed and his sweatsocks nice and clean. Soon I began to use his ankles to grab onto as I climbed.

I stopped at the landing to catch my breath. "Let me pull you the rest of the way," he whispered. "We can practice here first. I'll drag you along a little bit, and you can see how you like it."

In my mind a big neon sign began flashing BREASTS BREASTS HANDS HANDS. I knew that for him to get a good grip he'd have to touch me there, but I told myself it would be like a doctor doing it. "Okay," I muttered.

Very gently he put his arms around me and, locking his hands together, slowly pulled me six inches closer to the steps.

"Try to relax and just let it happen," he said.

I recognized this as the line that the soldier in *Battle Cry* used to seduce his girlfriend, but said nothing.

I couldn't completely relax as he pulled me or my bottom would have been bruised blue as a berry. His helmet frequently grazed my cheek, and more than ever I wished he'd take it off. I knew the bones of his skull hadn't joined together, but I was sure I wouldn't be shocked by the sight of his head.

Finally we reached the top of the stairs, outside Room 22. Julio straightened up, turned the doorknob slowly, opened the door a crack, and peeked in with one eye. "Oh!" he gasped, and closed the door.

"What is it?"

"Oh boy," he said, his face a deep pink, the color your hand turns when you shine a flashlight through it.

"I can't reach the doorknob, Julio. Open the door!"

Wordlessly he turned the knob, pulled the door ajar, then flattened himself against the wall. I squirmed to the door and Julio goosenecked around me. We looked in. My throat closed and my eyes popped open like umbrellas. There they were, the silent angels, partly undressed, some of them doing it. Julio slumped down beside me. I eased the door shut. We sat there for what seemed like an eternity. Finally he said, "I don't feel sorry for them anymore."

"Right," I said.

Julio took my hand in slow motion and placed it inside his helmet against his cheek, kissing it as it passed his mouth. I felt all my blood flow into that hand, as if the rest of me had gone to sleep. My fingertips tingled.

"Oh, Julio," I said, moved beyond the point of trying to sound original, "that feels so nice."

We snuggled closer. I squinted my eyes shut and kissed him on the mouth. The air around me felt thick as cotton batting, and for the first time in my life all I could do was feel pleasure, a sensation of floating. After a while, he unbuttoned my blouse and very gently placed his hand over my heart. I felt the blood throbbing in his neck with my fingers. Then suddenly I felt his body stiffen. He yanked his hand from my blouse, squeezed my shoulder, and cried out, "Maggie!" From the corner of my eye I saw the bronze legs of Mrs. Gumm.

"What is going on here?"

I buttoned my blouse.

"How dare you! How dare you do this in *my* school?"

Julio kept holding my hand on his thigh.

Mrs. Gumm leaned into my face. "Maybe they allowed such goings on where you came from," she hissed, "but not here. I won't have it. I won't have any tramps in my school."

"Open the door," I said.

"Girls like you have no—what door?" Mrs. Gumm was confused.

"Open the door," Julio said quietly. "Please, just open the door."

As if moving through someone else's nightmare, Mrs. Gumm complied. Though we couldn't see the kids from where we sat, we had a clear view of Mrs. Gumm's face as she beheld her angels caught in the act. Her mouth opened slowly, forming the shape a mouth makes before it howls in pain. "*Miss Simons!*" she yelled over her shoulder. "Come here immediately!" Then she froze. The deaf kids must have noticed her in the doorway, because I heard a scurrying inside like kitchen mice at night. Miss Simons came clanging up the steps. Mrs. Gumm turned to me again. "However you got up here, you get back down," she ordered. Then the two women strode into the room and slammed the door shut.

A special assembly was called that afternoon, right before school let out. By then, of course, everybody knew what had happened. I regretted having left my wheelchair in such plain view. If I had asked Julio to fold it up and hide it behind the stairs, Mrs. Gumm might never have discovered us or the deaf kids. Other than that, I felt no regret whatsoever. Julio had already told Carl he was madly in love with me, and Carl had already told me that Julio had told him.

The buses waited in the parking lot like big yellow slickers waiting for rain. Mrs. Gumm and Miss Simons joined forces at the front of the room. "I have always thought of the deaf," Mrs. Gumm began, "as children who are seen but not heard by anyone...except God." Was she going to cry? I looked at the deaf kids. They were as relaxed as usual. "His real sheep," she went on. "And I am shocked and appalled." She sniffed. "I don't know how these perversities began, but they will not be tolerated."

The deaf girl with reddish hair nudged my shoulder and smiled. Carl, sitting on my left, was as expressionless as a juror.

"If I cannot trust my children here in school, I cannot take responsibility for them out there"—her arm swept up—"in the real world."

Carl looked at his wristwatch. Julio circled something in his English book and passed it to me: *Rom: For stony limits cannot hold love out.*

"Therefore I have canceled our field trip," Mrs. Gumm announced. There was a low groan from the room. "You are not deserving of it, particularly considering the nature of your"—she searched for a word—"waywardness." Miss Simons's rendition seemed much more to the point: she jammed her finger in and out of a fisted hand.

Carl's voice cracked. "Not all of us were bad," he said, holding back tears.

"I cannot single anyone out for favors," Mrs. Gumm answered, making me hate her at last. I'M SORRY, I wrote to Carl. Julio underlined it in blue and passed it to him, giving my hand a quick squeeze. Carl read it and pushed the notepad to the floor. I wanted to tell him it wasn't the end of the world, that maybe it was better in some mysterious way that he wasn't going to see Christ of the Orange Grove. But when I turned to tell him, the bell rang, and he rolled past me through the door.

# Our Lady of the Artichokes
## *Katherine Vaz*

e need to invent us a virgin," said my Tia Connie.

She came up with her scheme to fight the landlord while I was lying on the sofa muffled in its original plastic so that I crinkled every time I breathed. He had doubled our rent. She'd already remarked a dozen times, *May he die with his mouth twisted*, and I should have been fascinated that we were weeks from being thrown into the street, but all I wanted was for her to keep crocheting, watch her *Jeopardy* to learn better English (she also watched it in the hope that one night there'd be a category about the Azores and she could pretend to win thousands of dollars), and leave me to sharpening my fantasy that a banker (I'd named him Noland) would carry me away in his Jaguar. He was built like a cornstalk, with a tuft of yellow silk hair, and when I held him too fiercely, he'd say, *Ouch, you'll snap me in two*. Tia would be grateful for the checks we'd send. I'd write letters to her from Noland's greenhouse, among the irises. He'd share my passion for menthol cigarettes.

I sat up to make sure her plan was entering my ears right: We would issue a scream heavenward—it would ricochet back to earth—that we'd beheld an apparition of the Virgin Mary outside this very apartment building— Estudillo Gardens—on East 14th Street in San Leandro. I asked why Mary would think of blazing a path here, and Tia Connie looked hurt and said, "I tend so nice those artichokes in the patch in front. She'll visit and be Our Lady of the Artichokes, perch on the thorns, and she'll cry and cry, then disappear. People will say, 'Come back to me, water me with your tears.' The landlord son of a bitch gets trampled, maybe to death. That part I cannot help."

The richly piquant part of this miracle was that I, Isabel Serpa, seventeen-year-old smoker, a roller of my eyes at Mass to convey that I believed nothing, would report the sighting; my infidel status gave me more credibility. Estudillo Gardens would be declared a shrine, and just try and lock out women and children where the Madonna had burned her outline in the exterior paint the shade of "sand dune," one of those timid California earth tones when mauve or chartreuse would be sunnier to come home to. Tia hadn't dreamt clear to the end of the story, but God could pick up the thread, seeing as He hadn't done much so far, but OK, He had all those baseball players crossing themselves, demanding the downfall of their millionaire enemies. I was beginning to suspect that all prayers were requests for immediate action, and no one was willing to sit inside any mystery— which seemed the point behind even a simple Our Father...a release of the will into a timeless thing I couldn't name.

"Don't be crazy," I said. "I'll get a job after school to help pay the rent."

"No! No! You save your energies, study, sneak cigarettes and talk big make-believe with friends, be a big saint or big cheese or somebody some day, my job is to worry, what the hell else do I have to do, answer me that."

"I've got worries too."

"No, you no got you no worries. What you got now is a homework that you tell everyone Our Lady she talk with you."

She kissed the picture of Jesus in Gethsemane, snapped off the light illuminating him, and covered him with his brocade square, which she hand-brushed twice a week. She draped a baby's blanket over Senhor Zé, her canary the color of limes, before tucking me into bed under my crazy quilt my mother left behind when she ran off with a dentist from New Orleans, and I itched to burn the quilt and mix in sulfur and find out where she was hiding solely to mail the bitch the ashes, but Tia said that a crazy quilt was good for leeching madness out of your bones. My quilt she dry-cleaned whenever she sensed the cloth swollen, as if with a blue yeast, saturated with the panic and want and what-have-you that I failed to contain within me.

I heard Tia fitful in her room. Normally she was a goddess of sorts of equilibrium. Though she ate as she pleased, she was thin; she was fifty but her hair was pure black and she did not dye it. Her skin was perfect, soft as an eggplant, which is why once when I had acne boiling on my cheek, she dragged me to a lamp, pointed at my face, and said, What is that? as if she were a creature from another planet, and I yelled with shame and slapped her, but instead of hitting me back, she punched the lamp.

When I heard her slip out the front door, I put on my robe and snuck to the kitchen curtains to watch her waving around the pastry torch I'd given her for Christmas. Her family in Fontinhas had owned a bakery, and she liked blasting sugar into amber glass on the tops of puddings or wielding the fire to form hearts with arrows, or bows with split, snake-tongued endings. She was using the torch to brand the outline of a veiled woman near the strip of garden at the front of our building, and my only prayer was that no one else was watching. The last thing we needed was a bill for repainting where a lady of bright light had burned, in toast colors, the nimbus of her body to announce the blank of her white heat.

I am not without my talents as a liar, and I own the raw stuff to have sounded the first note of hysteria—but I couldn't. Tia Connie had to enlist a chorus of widows. After her day's labor at Snow Drift, a Laundromat, she joined the prayer group kneeling with their rosary beads near the stain. The landlord must have figured it would create a bigger stir to have them hauled off for vandalism. My auntie's full name was Maria Conceição Amparo Serpa because she was born on the Feast of the Immaculate Conception, so the widows whispered that she and the Virgin were *just like this* —and they'd open two fingers into a wide scissors and then slam the scissors shut.

Clutching my schoolbooks, I walked past this display of the hardening that visits female solitude. The women were old frights, like the progeny of birds of prey and boulders; a guy's thing had rattled their privates for decades before dying, and it gave me a crawly feeling of pythons in crevices. Those penciled brows, hairs stiff enough to pry open locks, those wounded, glassy stares. I feared the widows would climb onto me in bed and suck my desires out through my eyeballs. *Blessed is the fruit of thy womb ... blessed art thou amongst women.*

My friend Lily told people at school about the vigil, and I stared at my white shoes when Mark, the boy I liked, walked past. He always pretended I wasn't there. My shoes looked like lozenges of stale cream.

It was my youth that might have saved Tia and her friends from the howls of laughter: Old women! Biddies, *beatas*, here's-Christ-in-a-tortilla, sex-starved fools, the snickers barely containable in a two-inch column on page 10, Metro section of the *San Francisco Chronicle*. I waited for her reproach, but instead, at the dining room table, under the framed picture of JFK festooned with a black ribbon—almost thirty years past his death—I heard her extending the rhythm of nonstop praying, *Oh, come to us, Oh, come to us*.

Late one night I caught her wrapping a noose of clothesline around the neck of her statue of Saint Anthony. "What's the poor guy done now, or is it me?" I said. If I found him head-down in the laundry basket, it warned me that I'd upset her and therefore he wasn't doing his job as the patron saint of love.

"Nothing, he does nothing and I'm sick to death of nothing." "You're not going to win him over if you hang him again," I said. "He won't learn I mean business elsewhere. I'll sew him a new cape if he behaves." "You're being gruesome, Titia." She held him up. "Isabel, Izzy. This is a statue. Not a man." "You never quit fighting with him. How's he supposed to like you?" "Well, OK, you and I always are fighting too," she said, and dangled him by his neck in her clothes closet.

Smothered laughter brushed up and down us when we arrived at the Holy Ghost Festival. We were ten days from our eviction notice. I'd listened to Tia's chants of *Make my girl the next queen, please, Sant' Antão*, but this year the honor had been granted to Lúcia Texeira, a pretty girl with a bum leg. Her crown was like a wedding cake invisible except for its sparkling trim. I was assigned to traipse behind her, and I swear she was leaning on her cane and going extra slowly in an excess of piety and injury designed to make me a crazy woman, and so half by accident and half on purpose I kept stepping on her cape...and Lúcia countered with half-turns and half-smiles of forbearance, *Ah, yes, you live in those shitty apartments with the nut who sprayed her wall with a blow-torch*, and I lost my mind and kicked her in the back of the knee of her crippled leg.

Ten witnesses reported—to the police and the bishop—that they'd seen me kick Lúcia, who dropped her cane and flexed her stupid leg in both hands and screamed. And then—simply walked. The way everyone backed away from me I could have been a drop of acid.

Do not mess with the Holy Ghost, the faceless fire, Tia used to say. For Easter there's the eggs, Christmas we got the tree...what outward sign exists for Pentecost? In the early Church, doves were released in a basilica to provide a usable symbol, and they crapped on the heads of the faithful. Tia and I roared ourselves sick whenever she reveled in this story; "little dove" in Portuguese can also mean vagina.

I told anyone who'd listen that Lúcia liked infirmity, claimed it as a special mark, and I'd merely done what some doctor should have forced upon her long ago. Her kneecap needed realigning; I'd happily, freakishly reset her leg and ruined her act. But that night in front of Estudillo Gardens, the old ladies were joined by mothers bringing their children, and a few men, and I heightened the call in my brain for Noland, my made-up boyfriend, to spirit me away. I fell into a chant that filled the air of his Jag with a thorny calligraphy: *Save me. Save me. Save me.* Then suddenly I was alone, wearing an apricot-colored slip while standing at a window in Paris, with Noland due to arrive and take me out—somewhere. He was off on international banking business. He sat on sacks of silver coins, their metallic edges bulging ridges in the cloth. We'd drink burgundy and eat little game birds cooked with their bones. He'd show me where the knife should go to cut them. When he finally entered our room, I turned to him—oh, the horns, cars, iron lace, melted-caramel light—and said, "I was afraid you wouldn't come to me."

I heard a wail from the women outside calling for the Virgin, and I summoned my courage; miracles do not come to those who wait, God helps those who help themselves, etc., do not dream your life away, etc., and I lit a cigarette and called Mark and exhaled smoke when he answered. "We're awaiting our visitor from heaven," I said sunnily. "Why don't you come by and watch with me?"

"You're as wacked as your father was," he said.

I stumbled outside, past the ladies. They didn't see me. I lived with Tia across the way from a diner called Zinger's, with a revolving sign of a chicken brandishing a revolver and wearing chaps and spurs. This Great God Chicken of the West faced the outdoor cage of canaries that Tia housed on the side of Estudillo Gardens. They were vivid and tart-colored as jawbreakers, yellow, green, and orange, and one little peach fellow who'd doom me to sobbing when he died, and one I'd swear was blue and of a size that made him like a darting eye.

I walked to the movies so I could be alone in the dark. *Celine and Julie Go Boating* was playing at the foreign-film place. Celine and Julie dissolved a hard candy on their tongues and the sugar transported them to a distant scene, where they solved a murder mystery. I'm not sure how tears seeped through my head, but my scalp was sopping when the movie ended.

A light was shining in our kitchen. The crowd gazing at the stain of the Virgin had dwindled, but Zinger's was filled with the sheen of pilgrims, ions sparking other ions, metal filings in search of a magnet. I wasn't ready to face my aunt. I rested my head on my knees and cried for my father. He'd stumble home from the dairy immaculate in his white uniform and fall onto the couch with arms open, legs splayed as if broken, as if he'd been dropped from a height. White is rigor, white is melancholy. The method he chose was pills. An envelope addressed to me said: "Love is tender. Nothing is forever. Goodbye, my darling." He was especially proud of how well he'd learned English. My mother vanished. Conceição, his oldest sister, took me home with her. I was fourteen. That first night she cooked three pork chops and gave me two and a half of them while saying, We have us a deal, sugar-pie, yes? You have a car, you take me where I need to go, here, there, store, church, Laundromat. I'll never go to the graveyard to visit my brother; he'll stay here now, some in your blood and some in mine."

The car she'd been referring to had been my father's, and I used to steal and drive it even though I was underage. Now it would be mine, until the DMV caught up with us. It was a Chevrolet with grillwork that gave it a frog's face. It grinned whenever it broke down on me. Tia named it "Mister Better Late Than Never."

The canary Senhor Zé was trilling like mad, and I walked in to find my aunt sprawled on the kitchen floor. "Jesus!" I said.

"Naw, only me, I polished the floor, thinking the people to see Our Lady will want to use the bathroom, drink a glass of water, my house needs cleaning, and I slipped. I take good care, bang, I get punished. Life. My neck is not so good."

I started screeching as I grabbed for the phone. "I'm calling an ambulance!"

"No! I am not a peasant! I have to change first into a good dress."

I told her to lie still, but she stood, her head tilted to one side. "I think maybe the floral one with the tie-bow because my neck, Isabel, my neck asks for a little cheering up."

The doctor said, "Mrs. Serpa? Are you aware that you've broken the bone the hangman tries to snap in the condemned?"

"Huh," she said, "so what."

She was fitted with a metal contraption to keep her head immobile for two weeks. Her skull was stuck in this silver birdcage of open slats with screws I had to tighten. I put her to bed and asked if it hurt. She said, "I'm alive. But what is wrong with my child?" I whispered I was fine, just worried sick about her. "Come here to me." I climbed next to her and curled up. With only one hand she could reach into my hair and form a loose braid. "What I know about boys is not so much, Izzy, but mostly it is air and attraction, and you cannot study how to make them want you." She said she'd been a lover of parties in her young days, but no one had dazzled her; she'd never slept with a man; it seemed that a girl must not pretend there's a dazzling when it's only hope churning a bit, or fear of loneliness churning a lot.

Like a comet forced into a chute, the world poured hard down our street and to our door, and my palm, on the door's inside, throbbed from the heat of the mob. Tia's surviving a broken neck was the second miracle. Even those who'd figured my kicking Lúcia resulted in a fluke cure were willing to rethink the violent, inexplicable ways of wonder. While I brought Tia her soup, sponge-bathed her, adjusted her metal cage, read her favorite tales from *A Thousand and One Nights*, we heard desperate believers tapping at our windows, groaning, all that heaving, sagging longing pawing at the stucco. The single-paned windows rattled in their casings, and noses and mouths left a smear of fog from peering through the slit partings of the curtains to catch a sighting of the young saint and the old saint. Such tormented desire, such a willingness to whip and beat and shout the ordinary into sanctity. I would have laughed to the point of collapse if it hadn't been so scary. I no longer went to school.

I called Mark, thinking I'd ask what to do. I'd never been to his house, but I pictured it soothed with beige and lemon paints, with chrome that wore starbursts flung down from the track lighting. His mother would favor whimsical refrigerator magnets, strawberries with protruding seeds that would drive Tia and me to get up at night to pick at with our fingernails. Their cupboards would have cranberry waffle mixes, and Caribbean spice pouches, and stuffed green olives, and twisty metal with signature beads to wrap around your very own martini glass so no one would by mistake wash down what was yours. I howled in pain. "Mark!"

"What? Who is this?"

I hung up on him.

When I thought it was safe to sneak out to the grocery store, I was set upon with a shrieking that swallowed my own shrieking as hanks of my hair were ripped out by the follicles and my clothing got torn. Someone's nails gouged my bare breast.

A man pulled people off me and marched me to the door, but my eyes were shut tight and I only had the feel of his hands, which seemed to have the weight of wood, but pliable, on me, guiding me back home. When he'd delivered me to the door, waves surged against his back but he wasn't knocked aside, and when I opened my eyes and turned to say thank you, he was already on his way. He wore a blue uniform. His back was a large square, like the picture of a swimming pool. An orange bus waited at the curb.

I tried to joke with Tia that the third miracle was that I was able to get back inside owing to the kindness of a stranger. I'd observed that rivulets of blood now obscured the torch's stain, from people trying to scratch the shadow of the Virgin. On the television, we saw the lame, the blind, the deformed, the arms with angry sores and the legs with ulcers, the women who'd pulverized their lifelines into raw meat from clutching rosary beads. Tia and I, starving, gnawed an ancient salami and stale Ritz crackers. Senhor Zé loosed an aria about being low on birdseed.

Our landlord—a single day before the notice was to have been posted—announced that he was a deeply moral man and, given the surprise events, he would postpone a rent hike. We listened to boots circling the house, stamping out a moat, and then—television was still our best way of fathoming what was going on right outside—the hawkers came, the vendors of Our Lady of Fátima and Guadalupe; the scapular- and candle-waving brigade, the dealers in aromatic oils and talismans, the fortunetellers with card tables and the police scrambling to arrest them; not long after the bullhorns ordered everyone to disperse, a woman rammed her head against the thin membrane of Tia's bedroom window, broke it, got hoisted in, sliced her forehead on the cut glass, came staggering forth with red cataracts over her eyes and shouted, "Kiss me," and Tia sat up in bed and said, "The truth is it was all my invention," but she blew a kiss in the direction of the bleeding woman. The people following the first invader through the window knocked the last fangs of glass out of the frame and ground it underfoot on the carpet so that no one else pouring in got injured, and from the inside of her metal halo Tia leaned forward to give each of them her best version of a kiss, saying, "The truth is it was all my invention, forgive me," and to a person they answered, "Please, I'm dying for your kiss," and into the night I directed the parade of strangers through the bedroom and out the front as if our apartment had turned into a stomach, and they asked the same of me too, "Kiss me, dear, kick me if you like," and I'd offer my lips. My arms deepened to a midnight bruising from the grip of believers needing to touch me, my nose and half my face were abraded red. The flying glass had come to rest after being jagged little shears, pinking a touch the threads of the carpet.

I waited for the man in his blue uniform, but he did not show up for me to thank him right before I begged him to rescue us again.

Of course no third miracle occurred, and we were called charlatans. The blood was fresh as new kill on the outside wall, and in place of the artichokes was a trench six feet deep, from everyone making souvenirs of the roots and any dirt that might have brushed against the roots and any second-degree dirt that had brushed against that dirt. My Chevy's frog snout was smashed, his hood dented, his feet stripped. Tia said, "My lips are a ring of fire from kissing that much, forgive me."

The taunts returned, and the landlord sent out a notice that in one month, per the previous plan, the rent would double, but out of the kindness of his soul he'd pay for a repainting and replanting—some zinnias? mums?—instead of bringing certain overwrought women and children up on charges.

Tia forced me to accompany her to a special bingo night at St. Joseph's in Alameda. Her metal headpiece had been removed and replaced with a cloth neck brace. My car wouldn't start, and she was frightened of traveling on the buses alone at night. The bingo ladies liked to carry bleach bottles they'd sawed in two, ringed with punch holes, and fitted with a drawstring knit top, like a purse, to carry their individual markers. "You can be so embarrassing," I said, refusing to carry it.

In the hall, with the other ladies with their bleach-bottle purses and the din of *N-17, O-42,* she made me help her cover the four cards she was working at once. "My luck she gotta change," she said. "Going to." "Huh?" "*Going* to change. You get in with all these Portuguese ladies, you start losing your English." "No, I do not." "Yes, you do, and as you recall, you keep asking me to bring such matters to your attention." A lady next to her shouted, "*Mexe!*" because the barker had taken a fifteen-second break. "*Mexe!*" yelled Tia. "See?" I said. "Oh, excuse me, I mean… *Mix!* Oh, my, that is a huge difference." "I should break your neck for real, Tia." "Go ahead, you do me a favor, I no have to live with you no more." "Let's go home." "I think you should buy a nice card, maybe win some money, fix your car, forget boys who they no good." "What boys? I can't get a date." "Because the boys they no good, otherwise they ask you out." "What do you know. You just keep me around for that stupid piece of shit car." "Yes, good, that is right. For your excellent car that is the reason we take the bus tonight." "I want to go home." "Aw, Madonna! I lose again!" She dumped her markers back into her bleach bottle; a new round began. "Are we going to be here all night, Tia?" "Until I win." "You've lost thirty dollars. This is a dumb way of paying the extra rent." "My luck she gonna change." "My luck is *going* to change." "I just say that." "Tia, please! Remember when you threw your back out working the slots in Vegas? I had to take you to the hospital then, too. I'm going to sign you up for Gamblers Anonymous." "I am not anonymous. Don't call me that. One time I pull one muscle in my back, you no let me forget nothing."

She was near tears when we left at midnight. She'd lost fifty dollars. We weren't speaking at the bus stop, except for me to hiss that it was likely we'd missed the last one of the night. The haze around the streetlights made it seem we'd been swimming in a heavily chlorinated pool for hours. "Aw, looka," she said. A bus picked us up. We were the only riders.

"Good evening, ladies," said the driver, and I stormed down the aisle to hurl myself into a seat, but she stood dropping the coins for our fares in the slot, one by one, chink, chink, chink, and I said, "Tia?" Because from the back, where I was, he looked like the man who'd ushered me home during the Our Lady of the Artichokes riot. "Sir?" I said. But he was staring at my aunt.

She said, "Where are you from, Senhor?" His name was Rui Alves, from Angra do Heroísmo, the capital city of the island of her birth. She adjusted her neck brace. He was driving a bus, he said, owing to his desire to be different, sort of a city fellow, not in the dairy business or on the ranch like the other Azorean men who came to California. He was strangely tall, with a rock-hewn face, black eyes; a widower, forty-eight. *A younger man*, said Tia. It came out like a breath.

"Hold on," he said, spinning the large round wheel pressed to his midsection. "You're that lady the Virgin she talk to."

"You were there," I said. "You showed up."

"I hadda go see, yes," he said. "It was big stuff on the news."

"And you saved me from the crowd," I said.

He turned around in his seat and grinned at me. "Naw," he said, "the Virgin she rescue you."

"The truth is she was a girl I dreamed her alive," said Tia. "The miracle, well—I invent her."

"I'm sure she's grateful you did that," he said. He seemed to switch between knowing English well and knowing it halfway.

She sat in one of the pews reserved for the infirmed, holding the silver pole and smiling at him while he drove. No one else boarded the bus; it was the last run until morning, and he knew right where to take us, if we were ready to call it a night.

They married a week later, and he moved into Estudillo Gardens with us and paid the rent.

While they were on their three-day honeymoon in Monterey, Mark appeared. He took my hand and said he'd never seen the genuine spot where that fuss had erupted about Mary and the vegetables, could I show him? He looked pale, but the bones in his face stuck out; it seemed to hurt him to have a skeleton bent on announcing itself every minute. The Zinger's chicken in its cowboy hat spun around, *bang*, spun around, *bang*. I led him to where the blood had been scrubbed off and the wall recoated. The burn mark was gone now, I said, as if he couldn't see for himself. We leaned there, and he kissed me. When I asked why this sudden change, why the interest, he said the caper I'd pulled with my aunt made me almost a famous person and famous people were hot.

"Almost—hot?" I said.

"Yeah."

"Then I need to tell you a story right now," I said. "Let's say you go over to that cage of canaries and touch one. She'll lose her oils where your fingers went. The world gets in at those spots, and the canary dies."

"What are you going on about? You're famous but still crazy, I guess."

"It might be tonight or the next night or the next, but she won't survive. Haven't you ever learned that animals can flat-out die if someone touches them? In part they die of fright."

"Speak English."

"Go away, please. Please, before I change my mind."

Rui wasn't sure why I was moping, but he quickly had enough of it. One Saturday the three of us piled into my car and he drove us down the coast to the Mystery Spot near Santa Cruz, a point where a magnetic crossfire throws off everyone's balance. Balls roll up ramps. A person standing still seems to be tilting to the point of falling. A whisper disappears and pops out a corridor of air away. Water swirls in the wrong direction beneath a grove of redwoods, their stiff branches converting them into red candelabra. I held out my arms and my aunt and new father laughed and said I looked to be a mile off. At the point where the confluence was supposed to be strongest, Rui asked Tia, "What does it feel like?" Waves of her hair cupped gold, from the afternoon ladling out reductions of its own light. She was wearing silver pumps like a runaway bride because beauty should cause a little pain. He'd started her on the habit of putting lanolin into gloves to wear at night after working all day at the Laundromat, and her veins had stopped bulging at the knuckles. She said something along the lines of it feeling like him, like somebody had changed him into an actual place, as far as she could see.

Tia got out her Singer machine at home. I hadn't known about her keenness for sewing. Rui came from a family of dairymen, but some of his neighbors back home had been fishermen, and as a boy he'd liked repairing the nets. He stitched on our missing buttons and instead of just tacking them on, he added the winding shank beneath, and he darned our socks, and one afternoon he and Tia outfitted the canaries in capes and bonnets. "Is Easter almost," she said. "They put on the new bird."

He took both of us to my senior prom at San Leandro High School and borrowed a bus from A.C. Transit; my car was in the shop again. With our orchid corsages we appeared like time travelers from the fifties at a party whose theme was "Punk Carnival," with glitter-clotted streamers from the ceiling of the gym to the floor. Rui found the music unbearable, so we each danced two waltzes with him and prepared for an early exit. He was good at weaving us clear of the gyrating bodies. He held my hand as if we were stepping even farther back, to the seventeenth century, as he said, left foot, right; good; now right, left. In the dark, he dissolved, with that accent born close to my father's village, into lost male tones in waves breaking over the scene, the loud music, our silence: *Forget your heartbreak; put on your pretty dress; if you won't go to the party yourself, I'll take you, step here, now there, like this.*

He parked the bus on the grounds of the Dunsmir Estate, and we drank wine out of Dixie cups. I was thrilled that my blood might get tinged purple. Our faces were greasy from being up late. Tia had packed small round cheesecakes, and they were so pleasantly laced with the smell of diesel fumes that they tasted like travel.

Rui was with us for three years before he was diagnosed with leukemia. A fine white powder settled on his papery skin when he was finally in bed at home. Within his reach I propped a snapshot of him with Tia at the kitchen table, grinning; they'd just downed two glasses of buttermilk, the old live-wires; and the drained insides were coated white, like the drippings caught off ghosts. The outdoor canaries were allowed in, uncaged; sometimes death will seize a tiny animal and leave a sick person in peace. But the birds were wily and flew so fast in the air of our rooms that they were beyond capturing, as if their bodies were melting, painting streaks in the air—lemon, orange, emerald, and a tartan cross-hatch—and the colors solidified back into birds, and then again melted. The three of us were bound in the bright weave of these ribbons, and the birds pulled it tighter and tighter. "Put that tray down. Look at me," said Rui. I'd been fussing at his bedside. Death runs a scalpel through the gel surrounding us and says, Come out.

I sat down. I fell into his sights.

Good night, Father. Oh, what if prayer is really surrender? What if it is up to each of us to love in a way that gives birth into the dreamed-up realm of the world?

We did not mention that the notice had come that Estudillo Gardens was slated to be torn down for luxury condos. Checks would be forthcoming as an aid to relocation for tenants. All of us would find it utterly impossible to buy even a closet in the deluxe new building.

Rui said he regretted that he would not hold the baby I'd have some day.

I laughed and took one of his hands in my own. "Baby!"

"Sure, just you wait and then you see," he said. Could we indulge him this once, he wondered, with a fantasy of him being a grandpa?

I might own a canary named Senhora Xica, in tones of marmalade, who screeches *joy joy joy* when I find out I'm to be a mother.

"Is it a girl? Or a boy?" said Rui, shutting his eyes.

"A girl," I said.

"And her name?" asked Tia, clutching Rui's other hand. Soon she would kiss his lips as the last moth rose from inside him; perhaps she'd want to swallow it so that she could follow him, but the moth would move at phantom speed and spiral into the air to be eaten by the birds.

"Clara," I said. It means light, gap or opening, egg white, clarity. "She's stunning. She's dazzling."

"Clara!" shouted Tia Connie. "Beautiful! It's Portuguese and English! She'll be us from that other world, and you from this one! Heavens!"

"I send her my love," said Rui. "Teach her everything you know."

Come along now, Clara. Where shall we begin? This is how to eat an artichoke: Cut off the thorns. The stem is called the leg, and it's an extension of the heart; don't throw it away. Toss the inner protective junk. The green pan of the heart is delicate; lots of work for small reward. Life is tender. There's a smile on you! A picture of you is burning through me forever. The leaves carry tips of the heart. Pull them hard between your teeth, my darling. Again. Again.

# Part II

# Solidarity

# The Last Man on Earth

## *Karen Stromberg*

S he heard the plane long before it came into view, its small engine sputtering and whining. The jungle fell silent as the plane climbed into the sky and died. It hung weightless before spiraling into the ocean. A moment later, a parachute opened—one small blot in a pristine sky.

She was impressed by the way the man worked the lines of his chute, swinging in his harness, moving toward land. Once he hit water, the white silk settled over him and floated on the surface like a large jellyfish.

Well, that's that, she thought, watching the slow current carry the whole mess around the south end of the island.

Later, just as the trio of black-crested gibbons were finishing their evening song, a yoo-hooing voice moved toward her.

"Thank God for your signal fire." A young, haggard man sank to his knees. "It led me right to you."

Men, she thought, taking the single fish from the spit and offering it to him on a banana leaf.

"Do you speak English?" he said a moment later, as he returned the leaf with its small nest of bones.

"Yes, I do. English major. Virginia Woolf." Her eyes followed the scalloped moonlight of the shoreline. "I thought I'd done her one better."

"Well, Virginia," the man said, laying out a large knife and a small folding saw, "your troubles are over. Tomorrow, I'll start whipping this place into shape."

At sunrise, he lashed the knife with its thick leather handle to a bamboo pole. "Any predators here? Large ones?" he said, as he waded waist-deep into the lagoon.

"Just us," she called. She watched as he brought up the first fish, a small grouper, a huge hole in its pink side, its gill covers flaring wildly.

"There's no refrigeration," she said, watching the fish slam its tail against the sand. She stunned it with a stone.

"Well done," he said, anointing her with a smile as he dropped a black bass beside the grouper.

"We can't eat all these." She inspected the wound on the bass. "They won't keep." She raised her stone.

"I'm taking an inventory. It's good to know what you have." He grinned and trotted into the water, the spear glistening overhead.

She dispatched the bass and walked to the next lagoon. As she bathed in the pristine water, small fish nibbled her fingers and toes. He was a nice-looking man, she thought, good facial symmetry, adequate cranial circumference, and he had blue eyes. So did she. It tickled her to think that a recessive gene suddenly stood a small chance, not only of surviving, but of becoming dominant.

"We may be," he had said, the night before, "the last two people on earth."

A momentary gleam ignited in his exhausted eyes as he spread out the parachute like a silken sheet and fell asleep.

"Very likely we are," she'd murmured, as she curled her body against his and felt him pull her snug against his side. She had not told him about her surveyor's cabin with its small stove, cot, and fourteen months' worth of ecological diaries.

The line of dead and dying fish had tripled by the time she returned. The man stood thigh-deep in water maneuvering a sea turtle toward land.

"That's an olive ridley," she said, recognizing its heart-shaped shell. "They're critically endangered."

"Soup," he said, pinning the turtle to the beach with one foot. "And there's monkeys here too." He freed the knife from the pole.

She looked deep into his blue eyes. "I've got something much better. Much, much better and just for you," she whispered as he turned toward her and the turtle slid back into the water.

She selected a puffer fish from the row of bodies on the beach, and taking the knife from his hand, she filleted it, liver and all.

# Bringing Down the Clouds
## Kathleen Alcalá

Estela sat in the courtyard of La Escuela fanning herself against the hot night. The city groaned and grumbled around her like an unhappy giant, and she was afraid to go home, afraid to leave the women of La Paciencia to their own devices on an evil night such as this. The city was in the third year of a terrible drought, and most of the city subsisted on pulque, but even this was beginning to run out as the maguey plants themselves began to die of thirst, the water tables dropping below the reach of their deep, enduring roots.

She wasn't sure what she thought might happen. Both Hermelinda and the Profesór had been missing for three days, and she suspected that they were together. She was both furious at them—for neglecting their duties to the school—and worried that misfortune had befallen them. Several of the women had not yet returned from their jobs, long overdue, and Estela was loathe to lock them out as midnight approached.

One woman came up to the gate, and waited resentfully as it was unlocked.

"Where have you been?" said Estela. "You should have been back ages ago."

"Are you my mother?" the woman shot back, before making her way to her room. She might have been inebriated.

More and more, the women who had collapsed gratefully at the gates of La Escuela came to resent the restrictions imposed on them. Mindful of the protection provided by the strictures, they had come with their children to escape abusive husbands and lovers, to see their children fed and clothed. Some had come with sores and contusions, with infections that required the attention of a doctor. Their children limp with malnutrition, the women had surrendered them to the ministrations of Estela and her helpers.

Yet some of the women had been mistresses of their own time, unused to the rigorous schedule at La Escuela. A few left immediately upon regaining their strength. Others left when it was made clear that they were expected to work in some capacity—either within the school, or at a respectable occupation outside of it. Some had come and gone several times. Estela, per La Señorita's instructions, never turned them away, as long as they were sober within the gates of the school, and did not fight with the other residents. Some moved on, but left their children. Sunday afternoons were reserved for visits between these families, and Estela was able to see the hopes and fears of these families played out—children waiting impatiently for the impending visits, or for the mother who never returned.

Estela could hear the dogs barking from the city dump, a horrible, wild noise of fear and gluttony. Somewhere, a donkey brayed, vehemently, and stopped short, or was stopped, never drawing its next breath. It made her shudder and pull her shawl, which had fallen down around her elbows, a little closer.

The stars above the courtyard were hard and bright, and Estela could hear the creak and clop of a carriage coming through the streets long before it came to a halt before the school. Even before the gatekeeper had let her in, Estela recognized the small, black bundle as La Señorita.

"Why are you staying here?" she asked, motioning at the women sitting and dozing, or talking in small groups around them.

"I...don't know. I'm worried. Hermelinda is gone."

"And the Profesór?"

"Yes."

"Well then," said La Señorita with a dismissive wave of her hand, "let them be gone. They'll come back."

"Is Noé asleep?" asked Estela. She had sent him home earlier with Josefina.

"Yes, he is fine. But you must not preoccupy yourself all the time with these weak women," said La Señorita. "Leave it. Come with me. I have something to show you."

"Oh, no," said Estela. "I'm too tired to go anywhere."

"This will take no energy," said La Señorita, taking Estela by the arm and steering her toward the carriage. "This will give you reason to carry on."

The carriage dropped them at the train station, and, without a further word passing between them, the driver tipped his hat to La Señorita and drove off.

La Señorita boarded the southbound train with Estela, greeting the conductor as though she knew him well.

"Where are we going at this hour?" asked Estela. "I have no hat. I'm not at all presentable."

"It doesn't matter," said La Señorita, as ever elegant in black, as she settled herself on the leather banquette.

Estela could not tell if it did not matter where they were going, or that she did not have a hat. By now, she knew that La Señorita had made up her mind about what was to happen that night, and that she, Estela, had no choice but to be swept along in her wake.

As the train pulled away from the station, the moon shone like hard coconut candy in the sky, brittle and white, casting the buildings, as they passed, into sharp relief and shadow. The men in their white straw hats and trousers looked like paper cutouts in a Nativity scene. The houses became farther and farther apart, and the train picked up speed as they left the city. La Señorita was strangely quiet, the glowing tip of her cigarillo occasionally moving in the darkened train compartment. Estela must have dozed.

In what seemed like a moment, the train began to slow. Estela started awake to see La Señorita gathering her skirts around her. The conductor came to their car and stood by the door.

"Ready?" asked La Señorita. "We are going to disembark here."

"But the train hasn't stopped," said Estela, trying to peer into the night to see where they were.

"No matter," said La Señorita as the conductor opened the door.

As the train slowed, a small platform came into view, pale in the moonlight. With a firm grip, the conductor lifted first La Señorita, then Estela out the open door into the capable hands of a strong youth. The train, which never did actually stop, picked up speed with a whistle and disappeared into the night.

Again, La Señorita greeted the youth familiarly. He bowed and escorted them a few steps to a doorway, through which they stepped down into a room hot and bright with voices.

Estela looked about herself with astonishment. She was in a large, well-appointed room filled with tables. On each table stood a bottle of tequila or rum and a candle, and around each table was gathered a small group of women—talking, smoking, or playing cards. There was not one man in the room. The women were dressed in every manner imaginable, from traditional village dress to evening gowns to trousers with pistolas on each hip, boots on the table. Estela could barely keep herself from staring. As La Señorita had assured Estela, it did not matter that she was not wearing a hat.

The women greeted La Señorita noisily, and she stepped forward into the crowd, waving and kissing and calling out names. A tall, striking woman stepped into the room from a doorway at the far end. She was dark and of exceptional beauty, dressed in a traditional white embroidered dress. She and La Señorita greeted each other with abrazos.

"This," said La Señorita to Estela, "is our hostess, the incomparable Doña Cata."

Estela greeted her shyly, but recognition was beginning to dawn. She was in the famous mansion that Don Porfirio had built for his mistress, La Doña, one of the most powerful women in Mexico. She ruled her village like a man, and owned vast holdings of farmland and factories—much like La Señorita.

When they were seated at a table, Estela leaned forward and asked, "How can these women be out at this hour without their husbands?"

La Señorita threw back her head and laughed. Estela had never seen her like this.

"These women answer to no men," said La Señorita. "These are the mistresses of power. The men have their Congress, but the women have Doña Cata's." La Señorita looked around the room. "This is the only reason there are health checks for the working women on the streets," she said, "and any schools at all that accept girl students. Don't think for a minute that the men would have thought of these things on their own, or approved of them. Still," she said, sighing, "there is so much left to do."

Estela tried to look around discreetly. Some of the faces looked familiar, but most of them were unknown to her. This did not surprise her, since most of these women were never seen in public, at least not officially. Estela tried to imagine which woman was with which prominent man in the government. La Señorita tried to help her out.

"That's Doña Reina, who goes with Senator Gonzalvo-Bilboa," she whispered, "and that's the proprietress of one of the most expensive houses in the District, Doña Carmela."

The men would take their wives, if any woman at all, to official functions, including those held by La Señorita to raise money for the school. Still, as La Señorita introduced Estela to them, a few said, "Oh, yes," as though they knew who she was, and some even said, "The Woman in Grey," as though it were her title. She wondered if, in their minds, she was associated with Victor Carranza.

Estela could hear conversations about banking and transportation, about the best colleges in Europe, the best sea routes to get there, and who had just acquired a prized painting for her collection. The finest hand-rolled cigarettes were offered to each table, the best rum and tequila and even sherry. Someone in a corner strummed a guitar that was almost impossible to hear beneath the shrill and hearty voices. As the noise and laughter swirled around them, Estela managed to choke down a glass of sherry. She was also served cool water, a commodity more precious in the Capital, right now, than liquor.

The voices seemed to grow louder as time passed, until Estela could not tell one from the other. She nodded and smiled dumbly when she thought she had been addressed, but really, Estela could not understand a thing. All around her, the women laughed and talked familiarly, calling each other "cara" and "maja"—dear and queen. In a farther corner, two of them embraced and kissed in a rather intimate manner, oblivious, it seemed, to the crowd around them. Estela was beginning to understand what La Señorita meant by the phrase, "women who answer to no men."

After about an hour, as far as Estela could tell, the guitarist put down her instrument and clapped her hands sharply, several times. The room stilled, and the claps were answered by claps from the doorway in the same staccato pattern. The guitarist continued to clap in rhythm as several women in traditional dress entered the room, stepping and stopping in unison. Reaching the center of the room, the four of them stood facing each other, two facing two in a square, and began a dance accompanied only by the percussive clapping of hands and the surprisingly forceful stomping of bare feet. Their faces were serious, their eyes shining.

Soon, others joined them from the tables, in all manner of dress, until there were two lines of eight facing each other. The sound and motion, repeated over and over, yet too complex a pattern to remember the first time heard and watched, were intoxicating.

At some point they stopped, and one of the women sang a mournful song in a language Estela did not recognize. The original four exited the way they had come, stepping and stopping, stepping and stopping, while the others returned to their seats.

La Señorita had disappeared at some point during this dance, and Estela looked about the room to see where she might be. Then she heard that laugh again, the one La Señorita had uttered upon their arrival, and Estela saw her coming in the door arm-in-arm with La Cata. La Cata was smiling and shaking her head no, no, as several women entreated her, then seemed to relent with a shrug and a smile as a chair was pulled out for her at a table.

La Doña Cata was said, by some, to be a sorceress, a diviner. Bottles and glasses were cleared away from the table, and she spread a deck of playing cards. As she turned them face up, one by one, the other women, now standing and gathered around, murmured and exclaimed.

The sixth card La Cata turned up was the King of Diamonds. The seventh was the Jack of Hearts. As she craned her neck to see, there was something about the Jack that looked different to Estela. She couldn't quite place her finger on it. Something about the length of the hair or the curl of the lip that made the figure look both masculine and feminine.

La Cata surveyed the cards and took a long draw on her cigarette. "The drought will end," she said, placing her hands flat on the table over the cards, "when the fathers acknowledge their daughters."

This was met by cheering and gritos, and La Cata swept up the cards into a compact bundle and left the room.

"But what does she mean?" murmured Estela. "How can she know that?" No one answered her.

When La Señorita could see that Estela was about to wilt, she stood up, and along with several other women, took leave of the assembly. As she did so, La Señorita brushed Doña Cata's lips with a cool kiss, and Estela felt an ugly thrill in her stomach, as though she could not tell if she had wanted to see that or not. They stepped out into the cool night air as a train light became visible in the distance. With the same agility with which they had disembarked, the women boarded the train north and took their seats in the otherwise empty train. In Mexico City, the familiar carriage was there to greet them, and Estela fell into it and did not remember getting into her bed before hearing the cock crow. All she noted was the thin mustache of cloud that passed before the face of the moon.

Elsewhere, deep in the night, after the priests had gone to bed, the Virgin of Guadalupe left alone with her candles and her baby Jesus, young girls came out to dance. They were dressed in white chemises—stitched by their mothers of purest cotton—and they danced under the clear night sky to bring down the clouds, to bring down the old men on horseback to kiss the young girls and graze the earth with their cloudy horses. As the drought had deepened, more and more girls came out each night—arms and heads bare, bodies visible beneath the white gossamer dresses—and danced for the sky. Ancient songs went up, songs that hadn't been heard out loud for a long time, rising up into the dry darkness to entreat the old chaacs to come down and visit the daughters of the bat-faced Coyolxauhqui. Children of the moon, the girls danced and danced, first in random motions, then in faster, circular motions, raising their arms in an ecstasy of trance and sleep deprivation. For every morning in the quiet before dawn, these same girls put on their skirts and huipiles and rebozos and carried what potable water remained to their masters and mistresses, ground the corn, kneaded the masa, and cooked the tortillas for a million souls.

Floors went unscrubbed, however, and the streets unwashed, so that the reek of the city changed from its odiferous, tropical smell to the ripeness and stench of death. Dogs and horses were dropping in the streets. Wails of mourning rose from the barrios, the roadside, the dirt lane, as babies died of diarrhea from the contaminated liquids fed to them, or from no liquids at all.

In the secret convents, the nuns were praying. Don Porfirio, indirectly of course, through his young second wife, asked that there be no raids on their illegal convents by the civil police during this time, so that they might pray for rain uninterrupted. In a certain part of the Capital, not too far from Chapultepec Park, old men were bowing and praying. Was this a sign? Had the corrupt government of Porfirio Díaz, built on the backs of the poor, been struck by plagues like Pharaoh's army?

The earth had become so dry that the snakes had crawled out of their holes in disgust. There were grinding, cracking noises from deep beneath the ancient buildings as the normally damp soil contracted and compacted under their weight.

And the young girls danced, round and round, faces turned up, tempting the old water gods to come down, come down, and taste the curve of their young lips, caress the taut flesh of their young bodies, and leave their horses in the thirsty fields to graze.

# Noelia and Amparo

## Glendaliz Camacho

———◦❀❀◦———

Amparo met him on a Friday night, when the brothel was resurrected by the women's laughter (too high-pitched to be sincere), tobacco smoke, and dimmed lights winking off chipped glasses of rum. She strode into the bedroom, where he was sitting with the posture of a war hero's statue in the plaza.

Amparo introduced herself by offering her back so he could unzip her dress. His hands were smooth and weighty like rocks worn flat by constant water, unlike the callused sugarcane cutters who sometimes held her by the throat, as if she were a goddamn reed herself. Amparo removed his fedora, somber gray suit, tie, shirt, shoes, socks, and underwear, hanging up and folding as necessary. She was as thorough the rest of the night, so that the scar on her right index finger, the faded burns on her left forearm, or her pendulous breasts that hung like a wet nurse's did not matter. He finished not with a grunt but with an anguished pant in her ear as if he had bitten into food that was too hot. Amparo poured him a glass of water from a jug on the nightstand.

"When can I see you again?"

She lit a cigarette, inhaled, and passed it to him, while he gulped down the water.

"Ask yourself." She pointed her chin toward his wallet, which she had placed conveniently within his reach on the nightstand. She would not remember his name until his fifth visit, when she wiped the sweat from his forehead with someone else's forgotten handkerchief and Fede told her he loved her.

Noelia had spent every year since her twenty-third tightening the habit of spinsterhood around herself so that now, at thirty-three, she found that men were wholly obscured from her sight. Men were something to be sifted through like the pots of uncooked pigeon peas that as a child she would watch the cook inspect for pebbles. Noelia had no shortage of suitors, but sooner or later—thankfully always sooner rather than later—they revealed themselves as pebbles. Noelia saw no good reason to risk what was certain to be a cracked tooth.

Noelia's brother introduced her to Federico on a Sunday after Mass. He spoke to her for too long, too animatedly, about his work at the sugar refinery, the book of Pedro Mir poems he was reading, how the music young people listened to like that merengue sounded as if it barreled straight out of a bayou, his sonorous voice drawing curious glances. Noelia found him silly, especially for a man of forty-three, but there was something about his enthusiasm that made her smile as he spoke.

It was not until she was at the dining table, later that same Sunday, surrounded by her parents, brother, sister-in-law, sisters, brothers-in-law, nieces, and nephews, that Noelia allowed herself a moment to indulge in wondering what it would feel like to have a man seated next to her that she could look upon with tenderness, as he brought a forkful of food to his lips. To her surprise, she pictured the somewhat endearing laugh lines around Federico's mouth.

Noelia declined Federico's first invitation for coffee after Mass (since visiting London, she preferred tea) and a subsequent one for lunch (she ate with her family). His dinner invitation was far too intimate, but she finally acquiesced to a walk in the plaza. He was shorter than she would've preferred and his spicy cologne was so overpowering, she was grateful their proper walking positions—he on the outside, closest to the curb, and she on the inside, closest to the houses and shops—did not place her downwind. Yet she found herself wondering if his kiss would taste of his last meal, the mints that clattered against their tin prison in his suit jacket pocket, or nothing at all.

Their courtship was much like that first stroll—pleasant, unhurried, respectful. Saturday afternoons they enjoyed films at the local cinema— *The*

*Bridge on the River Kwai, An Affair to Remember, Tizoc.* They attended dances at the San Juan Social Club, established by the burgeoning community of Puerto Rican émigrés, thanks to the refinery. Noelia waited for him to lie, make a disparaging remark, or cross the line of propriety between a man and a woman, but the moment never arrived.

One evening, after the customary light dinner with Noelia's family— fish soup, white rice, toasted bread, and marble cake that night—Federico smoked his cigarette on the porch. Noelia sat beside him on the swinging bench that cupped them in the breeze. The full moon hung low and heavy like an expectant mother.

"How beautiful." Federico's exhaled smoke drifted up to the moon like an offering.

"If you like old rocks," Noelia teased.

"That old rock has been illuminating the darkness for millennia."

"Don't we have the sun for that?"

"The sun is a tyrant. The Earth is forced to revolve around it or die, but the moon orbits around us."

"That makes the moon nothing more than our slave."

"Not at all. Because as much as we pull the moon toward us, she also pulls back and rules a part of us. The ocean." Federico clasped Noelia's hand in his. She was no longer looking at the moon. Six months later, they were married.

Amparo had not seen Fede in a couple of months, but she only realized it when he reappeared seated at the foot of her rickety bed with a box in his hands. From the way Fede's eyes grew large behind his glasses and he cleared his throat, Amparo could tell he was not expecting to see her hand holding another's. I bet this will put out his fire, she thought. Her son peered at Fede from behind her thigh. She leaned down, whispered in his ear, and the boy slipped away.

"I noticed you have pierced ears, but never wear earrings." Fede handed her a red box tied with white ribbon. Inside was a pair of diamond earrings mounted on white gold. Amparo resisted the urge to bite them, but considered their utility in an emergency with a visit to the pawn shop.

"You have new jewelry too." She eyed his wedding band. Even in the caliginosity of her room, Amparo saw Fede's cheeks flush. She began to unzip her skirt, but he grasped her wrist and patted a threadbare patch of sheet next to him on the bed.

"I've been promoted. To civil engineer."

"Congratulations."

"I want you to stop working."

Amparo nodded as if she were indulging a child. "You don't say." She marched to her door and swung it open, fist planted on her hip. "You don't want me to stop working. You want me to work for you instead."

A panic rose inside her like a wave and crashed in her head. It was that same feeling that made her believe in a man once. Back then, she needed to believe in just one man's word. Because all the girls in her barrio did before getting married. Yet she was the only one in a whorehouse. She misstepped in her choice of man or how much of herself she gave. Her mother always said if two people are in a relationship, make sure you're not the one in love. Her heart still limped at the memory of her son's father, like an animal that manages to survive a trap, but not without broken limbs and missing patches of fur. She wondered, though, if it wasn't too late to get back to where she was supposed to be in her life.

"Get out," she whispered hoarsely, barely louder than the din in her head.

Fede extracted bills from his clip and placed them on the nightstand. "You owe me time, then. Or change."

Amparo cut her eyes from Fede to the money. She closed the door, but hovered in front of it, fingers wrapped around the broken doorknob. The door trembled against its ill-fitting frame every time the girl and customer in the neighboring room exerted themselves.

"What did you dream about when you were a girl?"

"If you're going to ask me stupid questions, I'd rather give you your change." Amparo lunged at the money.

"Wait. Just answer me. What kind of life did you want to have when you grew up?"

"The same shit all the girls wanted."

Amparo stopped riffling through the bills. A blanket of dust had long settled over her wants, and she was afraid she would regret this moment, disturbing it.

"I wanted more than what I had," she said. "A clean house. A handsome husband. Children. A dog. My mother said it would be cruel to make a dog go hungry with us."

Fede guided Amparo to sit next to him. "When I was a boy, I had a piglet. León. I fed him with one of my sister's old baby bottles. He slept with me every night until he grew too big.

"Oh, don't look at me that way. Pigs are intelligent animals. We've just limited them to being food. Anyway, one day, a hurricane ripped everything away. The only cow we had, the chickens, the two other pigs, the mango tree, the roof, and two of the walls. León was the only animal left. Until my father told me to fetch León.

"Look, there are things we want and things that ensure our survival. When they're one and the same, that's a blessing, but when they're not... Well, we are animals too, so we'll always guarantee our own survival above anything."

Amparo brushed invisible crumbs off her skirt and tested the truth of what Fede said against the misery of her twenty-five years. Survival was wrapped around her life like a plantain leaf around a *pastel*.

"Now, I may not be exactly what you dreamed of," Fede said as he lifted his fedora and ran his palm over his receding hairline, "but I can give you a better place to live. Your son can go to a private school. And I do love you. You and I are like two different fruits, but grown in the same *conuco*."

Amparo narrowed her eyes. "What about you? What do you get out of this?"

"I've already secured my survival. Now I'd like to have what I want."

Amparo did not receive another client—after Fede made arrangements with the madam, of course. Two weeks later Amparo had chosen the row house Fede would rent for them.

Fridays and Saturdays, Amparo and Fede expressed what they didn't have time for during the week. He, his ardor, through roses, Neruda poems whispered in the dark, and love letters left on the nightstand before Sunday dawns. Amparo, her cautious gratitude, with stuffed peppers, meatballs, and stewed codfish.

Amparo was very clear on her place and wasn't in love with Fede anyway. That didn't mean she was indifferent to his well-being or happiness; in fact she cared so much she was willing to be the reason for his. That was some kind of love, not the one he wished he would see in her eyes when he was on top of her, she was sure, and not the love that made her blood dance like her son's father did, but it was something, and it dug into her a little deeper each day.

Federico's absences did not go unnoticed by Noelia. She came close to asking him several times, fortifying herself through the night with the belief that truth was preferable to illusion and questioning what good principles of character were if they crumbled at the slightest pressure. Hadn't she considered herself a woman *hecha y derecha*? Well, here was an opportunity to distinguish herself as a woman who is, rather than a woman who thinks she is, but when Federico arrived Sunday mornings there was only enough time to get themselves ready for Mass. Then Sundays did not seem appropriate for anything but devotion to God. The rest of the week settled into a rhythm she was averse to disrupting on the distant hope it would continue through the weekend.

Noelia was certain, however, and she took that certainty and busied herself in the kitchen for fear the turmoil would devour her—which gave the cook heart palpitations about losing her job, but Noelia assured her this was just a whim and she would be needing her for the real work.

Noelia's fingers found peace in the repetitive chopping and stirring that quieted her mind so that only the dish mattered—not her charred ego or slices of jealousy. Cooking filled any holes that had eaten through her soul like moths, made them not quite whole but aromatic and vibrant. Noelia remembered how much she enjoyed the smell of onions and garlic sautéing, heralds of the good meal to come, before it became improper for her to spend her days as if she were the help. When her sisters were pregnant they craved her *rellenos*, bursting with pork seasoned with salt, pepper, garlic, and oregano, and only her hen soup would do when her father came down with a cold.

At first it was random things that she prepared—*ñoquis*, bread pudding, goat marinated in bitter orange and rum—until the first time Federico did not come home on a Thursday. She escaped the mocking of her empty bed before dawn and began a purposeful banquet, by the light of an oil lamp, so that her shadow on the wall resembled a witch hunched over a cauldron.

There was a knock at Amparo's door precisely as she was adding *auyama* and carrots to the simmering pot of *arvejas* for Fede's lunch. When she opened the door, a young black woman in a servant's uniform stood on the porch. Avoiding Amparo's eyes, she thrust a large basket in her arms. "*De parte de Doña Noelia.*" The girl scampered away before Amparo could say or do anything.

From Federico's car, Noelia thought Amparo looked more like a cook than a whore. She was a sturdy mulatta with coarse hair held away from her face by a red headband. She'd actually come to the door in a faded housecoat! Noelia couldn't decide whether to be relieved or offended. When her maid climbed back into the sky-blue Ford, Noelia asked the driver to take them home.

When Fede arrived at noon, he showered as he usually did. As he dried his glasses and sat at the head of the table—which Amparo liked to point out was square, so for all they knew the empty seats were the heads—Fede asked, with a pinch to Amparo's bottom, if they were having an indoor picnic.

Amparo unpacked the *ensalada de vainitas y repollo cocido, higado, pan, aguacate*, even *dulce de naranjas en almibar* for dessert. The lettuce, string bean, and cabbage salad glistened with olive oil and vinegar, reminding Amparo of the schoolgirls with shiny long hair who always chose to stand next to her and shake their tresses in her face.

*That bitch*, Amparo thought as she served the liver. The one thing that Amparo couldn't stand to eat—there was just not enough garlic and oregano in the world to make liver taste better than sucking on a handful of coins—and here it was reminding her of the things life would serve her whether she liked it or not. *You don't know who you're fucking with*, she fumed as she bit into a piece of crusty bread. She had never swallowed anything life threw at her—not her father's nighttime visits, not her son's father leaving soon after her menstruation stopped, and not this now.

"How is everything?" Amparo asked Fede as he chewed a mouthful of liver.

"Very good. As always."

When she told him the meal was courtesy of his own house, his wife, he turned a shade of yellow to match the center of the avocado slice on his plate and choked on that mouthful of liver as his food went cold. As did he.

Noelia arrived at her parents' house with two suitcases. Her parents looked at them as if they were stuffed with tapeworms instead of clothes. When Noelia confided to her mother that she had followed Federico, her mother shook her head. "Who told you to go snooping?"

Her father, the voice of reason, merely suggested finding a solution, because while allowing Noelia to stay unmarried for so long had only inspired a few whispers—which they tolerated out of love—this was more serious. Besides, they were getting older. Where would she run to when they were no longer there? Perhaps a child would keep Federico at home more. After all, the man had no family, no roots in the Dominican Republic.

Noelia did not bother to stay for dinner. As her father's driver took her home, she thought of Adam and Eve being expelled from Eden, except she could no longer agree that their sin was egregious enough to merit exile.

A child. Apparently, she was herself only a child whose life decisions were really only indulgences her parents had granted her. Her life was like the tea parties she had with her dolls as a girl—she controlled the proceedings, but only until she was called for dinner by the real adults. She was not a moon, a sun, the earth, or an ocean; she was a woman. Just a woman.

Back home again, Noelia's unpacking was interrupted by a knock at the door. She told the maid she would answer, relieved for the distraction and yes, despite everything, hoping it was Federico, but it was a boy. About five years old, with beautiful brown eyes that swept about nervously, he handed her a bag he could barely carry and ran off the steps, down the street.

She unpacked the bag on the mahogany dining room table and almost said "Touché" out loud. The smell of *sancocho de mondongo* made her insides lurch. It was accompanied by steaming white rice, avocado, and *dulce de coco con batata*. She hated when *mondongo* was cooked in her parents' house. Everyone was insane to even think of eating beef tripe. That was only a few degrees from eating entrails, and they might as well be savages if they ate that way.

*She didn't back down, and she expects me to.* Noelia forced a spoonful of *sancocho* into her mouth. *She's got nerve, but that doesn't only grow in barrios and campos.* Noelia continued to plunge her spoon into the food until it was all gone. There was another knock on the door, but Noelia could remember nothing but the sound of her own retching and the acrid taste of bile after the policemen gave her their condolences.

When her throat still burned the next morning and her stomach would not stop convulsing, her mother and sisters insisted it was the impact of such a terrible tragedy, but it occurred to Noelia that Amparo could have poisoned her. A visit from Dr. Linares proved them all wrong, though. Noelia was pregnant.

Amparo watched Noelia from the gate of the cemetery as mourners filed past her. Noelia's face was hidden behind large sunglasses and a hat with a veil, but the hair that peeked out against the nape of her long, ivory neck was fine and blond. Despite the balmy weather, her black dress, and gloves, she seemed encased in a block of ice, apart from all those people around her. She moved only to dab her cheeks with a white silk handkerchief.

At the end of the service, Noelia motioned to her family to walk ahead, that she needed a moment. She walked over to Amparo, lifted her veil, and removed her sunglasses. Neither woman spoke; they stood side by side, watching workers shovel dirt onto his coffin.

Noelia's hand rested on her stomach. "I'm pregnant," she said.

Amparo turned to face her. "You'll have to eat better."

Noelia was the first to pucker her lips to dam the laugh in her mouth, but it was no use. Both women burst into laughter behind their palms, until tears spilled over and all that was left at the end was a deep, simultaneous sigh. They drew more than a few stares and whispers from mourners walking to their waiting drivers. Both women regarded each other for a moment, curious but too spent to ask.

"Take care." Amparo turned and walked away, remembering her cravings for freshly baked French bread with butter when she was pregnant. She stopped at the bakery for a loaf. As she bit into the handfuls she broke off, her tears mixing into the butter, she wondered if Noelia's growing belly would eclipse the memory of them all. She whispered a blessing for that baby.

# Revenge on a Plate

## *Dawn Knox*

———⚬✤⚬———

The old lady hovered at the entrance to the railway station, studying the queue of taxis and the line of weary commuters. A woman in a smart, gray business suit climbed into the first taxi and it pulled away smoothly, allowing the next cab to glide into position.

This was the one. This was the taxi.

The old lady launched herself forward and staggered as if she'd tripped.

"Oh, oh!" she cried, in case anyone in the queue hadn't seen her. The bag of shopping fell to the pavement and a packet of biscuits rolled toward the curb. She clutched at her heart and moaned loudly.

A round-faced man dressed in paint-spattered overalls stepped from the back of the line and touched her elbow.

"You all right, love?" he asked, his face a picture of kindness and concern. But she needed to attract the attention of the smartly dressed man at the front of the queue, who so far had turned to look but had obviously decided his journey home was of greater importance than the drama unfolding behind him. The businessman stepped toward the door of the cab.

She stretched out her hand in appeal to him.

"I'm so sorry," she croaked "my medication is at home. I need to get it quickly, or…"

The man at her elbow called out to the businessman, who'd already opened the cab door and had one foot raised, ready to climb in.

"Oy, mate. This could be yer mother. Yer wouldn't want someone to leave 'er on the pavement, would yer? Can't yer get the next cab?"

The people in the queue nodded, craning their necks, to see how the businessman would respond.

Realizing he was now the center of attention, he stepped to one side and ushered her forward, as if he'd merely been opening the door for her with not the slightest intention of grabbing the first cab home and leaving her to fate. He sensed the disapproval of the file of people behind him, who'd recognized his earlier unwillingness to help. In an effort to win them over, he picked up the old lady's packet of biscuits and fussily tucked them into her shopping bag, as the man in overalls helped her into the cab.

She clutched at her heart and settled herself on the back seat, waving feebly to the people in the queue as the cab pulled forward.

"Rose Cottage, Elms Lane, please, driver," she called as he half turned to enquire where she wanted to go and she allowed herself the merest glimmer of a smile.

It was definitely *him*.

She'd worried that her eyesight might let her down and that the station entrance was too far away from the taxi rank to be able to recognize him with any certainty. But there was no other way of ensuring that she got into a cab driven by *this* driver. It was a shame she'd had to deceive the nice man in overalls, but if she'd queued at the taxi rank, she would've had to take the first cab that came along when she reached the front. She could hardly let people pass until *he* arrived.

Thankfully, the driver was silent until he turned into Elms Lane.

"Whereabouts?" he asked curtly.

"Just past the farm on the left," she replied weakly. "Second cottage."

The cab drew up outside the semi-detached cottages. The first appeared to be derelict, with a wild, overgrown front garden. The second cottage was neat and well-cared-for, and the driver drew up at the gate.

"I'm so sorry, driver, I seem to have mislaid my purse. I wonder if you'd mind accompanying me to the house, and I'll get some money out of the savings jar. Perhaps you'd be so kind as to carry my shopping."

In the rearview mirror, she saw his eyes roll upward with irritation. Without replying, he got out of the cab, opened the door, and took her shopping bag. He probably wanted to get away before she had a heart attack, inconveniencing and delaying him further.

She hesitated at the door of the cab and, coughing pathetically, held out her arm for help. There was no mistaking his irritation, but he allowed her to lean on him until she was on the pavement.

The old lady deliberately walked as slowly as she could behind him, looking up at him pitifully whenever he turned to see how far she'd progressed up the garden path. Finally she arrived at the front door, puffing and panting and clutching her chest.

"You all right?" he asked.

His concern, she knew, stemmed not from any interest in her health but in the fear that if she died on the doorstep, he'd have to call the ambulance and the police and then he'd never get back to work that afternoon.

She took the door key out of her pocket and asked him if he'd mind opening the door for her while she leaned against the side of the porch, trying to catch her breath.

He snatched the key and tried to ease it into the lock. Obviously the sooner he could open the door and get rid of her, the sooner he'd be back in town picking up another fare.

She knew he wouldn't be able to unlock the door. It was her sister's front door key. But while he fumbled at the lock, she pulled a truncheon from her baggy handbag and with electrifying speed and all her strength, she felled him with one blow.

After tying him securely to a kitchen chair and taping his mouth, the woman took the driver's keys and drove the cab into her garage. It was unlikely anyone would've seen it parked outside the house, as very little traffic used this road since the bypass had been built, and the cottage next door had been empty since Mrs. Patterson died last year.

When he finally regained consciousness, the old lady was sitting opposite him sipping tea from a delicate china cup. He moved his head back and forth slightly as if trying to focus on her.

"I expect you're wondering what you're doing here," she said, settling her cup on the saucer. Gone was the frail edge to her voice, and she no longer stooped, nor had the appearance of the vulnerable old lady he'd conveyed home. He stopped rocking and she assumed he'd managed to focus, as his eyes now reflected shock and disbelief.

"You are invited to dinner," she said and laughed as if she'd made a joke.

He shook his head and tried to speak through the tape.

"It's not optional," she said, suddenly severe. "You *will* stay to dinner."

Knotted veins stood out on his neck as he strained against the bonds round his wrists and ankles, but she'd tied the cords securely. The kitchen chair bounced and rocked, sliding on the tiled floor while he struggled to break free. Finally he paused, chin on his chest, as if exhausted.

"Goodness me! Where are my manners?" she asked in mock consternation. "Would you like tea or coffee?"

His eyes swung about, looking for some means of escape.

"You look like a tea person. Am I right?"

He nodded, obviously humoring her, his eyes pleading.

She busied herself boiling water and filling a china teapot with loose tea, explaining as she did so how to make a good cup of tea without the use of those "newfangled" teabags.

"Sugar?"

He shook his head and watched as she set the cup before him on the lacy tablecloth.

He expected her to rip the tape from his mouth and braced himself in preparation, but she merely pulled it millimeter by millimeter, as if prolonging the pain.

He rubbed his lips together, attempting to alleviate the stinging and throbbing.

"Will you untie me, please? I can't drink the tea." His voice wobbled slightly, but he kept his tone courteous, much as one would speak to a willful child who'd unexpectedly gained a position of dominance over an adult.

"Mmm," she said thoughtfully, "I can see how that would be a problem for you. But *my* problem is that I don't believe I can trust you not to escape if I untie you. I suppose I could hold the cup to your lips if you like."

"Perhaps when it cools a bit, if you don't mind," he said, eyeing the steaming tea.

"As you like," she said and continued to sip her tea, studying him over the rim of the cup.

Her silent contemplation appeared to be unnerving him, and his eyes darted back and forth as if searching for some means of escape.

"Please," he begged, "please let me go. I've got money, if that's what you want."

"I just want you to stay to dinner," she replied indignantly. "I don't want your money."

"Okay, okay," he said quickly. "That would be nice, but perhaps I could just phone my wife to let her know that I'll be late. I hate to worry her—"

"You couldn't care less about your wife," she snapped.

"Yes, yes, I do," he said, his voice even and calm although his eyes were wide in alarm. "She'll be worried. You wouldn't want her to be worried, would you?"

"Young man," the woman said carefully placing her teacup on the saucer and drawing herself up to her full height, "do not talk to me as if I am a child. I understand that your wife may be worried, but as far as I'm concerned, she's better off without you. And as for you being worried about your wife, well, what nonsense! You weren't worried about her when you seduced my Maureen, were you?"

"Maureen?" he whispered.

"Yes, my daughter Maureen. You played with her affections for a week or two, got her pregnant, and then went back to your beloved wife."

"Preg—pregnant?" he stuttered.

"Yes. Pregnant. With child. Expecting. And then you left her."

"I didn't know. Really, I didn't know she was pregnant."

Trevor thought back over the last few months. He'd met a mousy girl in the pub one Friday evening after work sometime in September, but he couldn't remember her name. Or perhaps Maureen was the loud blonde who'd come on to him when he'd picked up a party of drunk women after a hen night in town. That had been in August. He blinked as sweat trickled down his forehead and ran into his eyes. The truth was there had been lots of women, but he didn't remember a Maureen.

How could he admit to this madwoman he didn't recall her daughter? One thing was for sure, he dare not deny he was the father. The woman was unhinged. He had to remain cool. He'd already offered her money but everyone had their price, right? If he made it sound like he was taking responsibility, she might untie him.

"So, how's the pregnancy going?" he asked. "Is Maureen well? Does she need money?"

"It's more than nine months ago since you callously cast her aside, but no, you don't have a child—not by my Maureen, anyway. Lucky for you, I used to be a nurse. I dealt with it."

"What d'you mean?"

"What d'you think I mean?"

He stared at her in disbelief. "You aborted your own daughter's baby?"

"Don't you get all righteous with me! I was merely clearing up your mess! You should have seen the fetus. So tiny. Hardly more than a mouthful." She licked her lips and allowed saliva to dribble down her chin.

For a second, his heart stopped beating.

It was just a phrase. She didn't mean...no, of course she couldn't have meant...It was just an unfortunate choice of words.

"What do you want with me?" he whimpered. "I'll pay—anything. What do you want?"

"I told you, I want you to stay for dinner." Slowly she wiped the drool from her chin with her sleeve as she stared fixedly into his eyes.

*Keep calm*, he told himself. *Don't let her see you're afraid. She can't keep me here forever. She'll have to let me go soon.*

The woman rose abruptly. Taking a large saucepan from the cupboard, she filled it with water and then returned for a frying pan, in which she placed a large lump of butter.

"Sweetbreads," she said. "We're having sweetbreads for dinner."

"I...I'm not sure I know what they are."

"Sweetbreads can be either thymus or pancreas. I'm not fussy. Perhaps we'll have both. Do you have any preference?"

"I'm really not hungry," he said. His eyes swept the room again for some help. She was obviously going to make him eat something disgusting. But once she'd got her own back, perhaps she'd let him go.

"I didn't ask if you were hungry. I asked if you have a preference. Thymus or pancreas?"

She took a felt tip pen from a drawer and advanced toward him.

"The thymus is just...here," she said as she unbuttoned his shirt and drew a blue circle high on his chest. "And the pancreas is about...here."

He looked down in horror at the blue circles on his body and pushed his feet against the floor, trying to propel himself away from her, but the chair wouldn't slide, it merely began to tip backwards.

"Don't—don't touch me."

"Or what?" she asked "You're in no position to threaten anyone."

The sound of the key turning in the lock brought fresh hope to his eyes. He swung round, hoping that the ordeal would be halted.

The door opened and a plump, plain woman entered, struggling with two supermarket carrier bags.

He remembered a brief fling last summer. No one special. She'd started talking about marriage and he'd dropped her immediately.

"I got the veg—," she began and abruptly stopped as she took in the scene in the kitchen.

"Maureen! Help me, please!"

She bent down and placed the carrier bags on the floor.

"Mum, you promised! You said after Raymond you wouldn't do this anymore."

"I know," the old woman whined, "but Raymond was so tasty and the freezer's nearly empty. Anyway, I don't know why you're bothered about this one, after the way he treated you. No one will miss him, and his wife'll be better off without him."

"Maureen, please help me! I'm sorry, I had no idea about the baby, I really didn't. I would have stood by you if I'd known. My wife and I don't get on. If you get me out of this, perhaps we could start seeing each other again. I miss you, honey."

Maureen lovingly traced the outline of his cheek with her fingers and stared deeply into his eyes.

"I'd like to believe you, Trevor, really I would, but I'm seeing someone else now and I really have no feelings left for you at all." She turned to her mother. "Well, I suppose it'll be all right just this once, but no more. After Trevor, it'll have to stop."

The old lady reluctantly nodded.

"I'll have the kidneys, if that's okay with you, Mum," added Maureen as she picked up the bags and placed them on the table.

Trevor screamed hysterically until the old lady cut a piece of tape and threatened to stick it over his mouth. His screams subsided to whimpers.

"Well, I'll leave you to it, Mum," Maureen said brightly. "What time will dinner be ready?"

"About seven."

"I don't like this bit," said Maureen confidentially to Trevor. "It gets a bit messy." She turned to her mother. "See you about seven, then."

Something snapped inside Trevor when he saw Maureen prepare to leave. She was his last chance. She couldn't leave him alone with this madwoman, surely? They'd shared a few intimate moments, that must count for something. But apparently not to Maureen, who was humming brightly as she closed the front door behind her.

As her footsteps echoed down the front path, Trevor erupted, screaming obscenities and insults at Maureen until the old lady slapped a piece of tape across his face, suppressing any further invective.

"Don't know what Maureen saw in you," she commented as she eased her head through a large, plastic disposable apron and tied it behind her back. She chattered cheerfully as she assembled the ingredients for the meal.

"These are my mother's recipes," she said, holding up an ancient, battered book. "I'll pass it on to Maureen when I'm gone, although she's not really interested in cooking. My mother could make a meal out of nothing, and she often had to do just that. Times were hard when I was a nipper. We had to use whatever was available. There was never enough meat, and my old mum was very…creative."

She chopped onions and carrots and placed them in the large, steaming saucepan, then moved the butter round in the frying pan until it sizzled, giving off a nutty, buttery aroma. The lacy tablecloth was whisked from the table and replaced by a plastic cover, which she liberally dusted with flour. "There's something very satisfying about making pastry," she observed as she got the rolling pin from a drawer and sprinkled flour on it.

"Just about ready for the sweetbreads now," she said, turning the heat down under the frying pan.

The old lady wrestled with a pair of heavy-duty gauntlets, extending and releasing each rubber finger with a thwack, until she was satisfied they were comfortable. Then she took an electric carving knife from the cupboard.

Trevor's eyes bulged and he screamed, although the tape effectively muffled the sound. After laying old sheets round his chair, the old lady plugged the carving knife into the socket, squeezed the trigger, and inspected the two vibrating, serrated blades.

"They'll do," she muttered. She advanced toward Trevor, who was straining at his bonds and scuffling at the floor, trying to propel himself backwards, away from the buzzing blades.

She lined the knife up with the blue circle and gently applied them to the flesh.

"Another piece, Maureen?" asked the old lady.

"Just a small bit, please."

The old lady cut into the golden crust of the meat pie and laid it carefully on her daughter's plate, then she spooned chunks of meat and gravy and arranged them next to it.

"Pity Trevor isn't around to enjoy this!" observed Maureen. She raised her wine glass and offered a toast.

Mother's and daughter's glasses clinked together.

"To Trevor!"

Maureen began to giggle.

"Mum, you are wicked!"

"Nothing less than he deserved," the old lady replied.

"It's a shame about wasting all that whiskey, though," said Maureen. "He spat a lot of it out when he choked. If he hadn't struggled so hard, the funnel would have gone down his throat quite easily. Stupid man!" She held the bottle up for inspection. "Look, it's almost empty now."

"Never mind," said the old lady. She held up a roll of banknotes. "Some loose change fell out of his pocket. We'll put that toward a new bottle."

Maureen giggled.

"Mum, you really are wicked! But I'd give every penny of that to see what happens when the police find him."

"Yes, he's going to find it hard to explain why he's drunk, in charge of a cab, and in the middle of a field. I expect the police have found him by now—I gave the exact location when I phoned them."

"He's bound to tell them about being here, Mum," said Maureen anxiously.

"Good," said the old lady. "I'll simply tell the police he forced his way into the house and tried to rob me. He stole the whiskey and some money and drove off and that's all we know. If he starts talking about sweetbreads and kidneys, I have the box from the frozen meat pie here, to prove what we ate for dinner. Don't worry, Maureen, I've thought of everything. And when he finally gets home, he'll be lucky if his wife doesn't kill him after reading what I wrote on his back in felt tip pen!"

"Mum! What did you write?"

The old lady blushed.

"It's not the sort of thing for your ears, my girl, but suffice it to say, she will be in no doubt about her husband's 'activities' with the ladies."

# The Conversion of Sister Terence
## *Liz Dougherty Dolan*

While Sister Terence rattles on, I am gazing at the white-suited worker on a swaying scaffold, steam cleaning the soot-covered walls of the Waldorf Astoria across the street. It seems to me that the man has been swaying on that scaffold since I entered high school and that he raises and lowers it each day, shadowing whatever classroom I'm in. When I hear my name called, I jerk my head in Sister's direction. "*Que quiere decir*, Isabel?" Sister says.

"*Que quiere decir?* What does it mean, Sister? Uh, *que*, Hermana?"

Sister sighs. "Pay attention, please; your parents are making sacrifices to send you here, my dear."

Not really, my dear, I want to say. I work on Saturdays to pay my ten bucks tuition.

I know the next part of her speech by heart; I always mimic her at lunch till I have my classmates splitting their sides laughing. Sister tells us once again about her sainted parents, who raised ten kids and sent them all to Catholic schools; half of them became priests and nuns, blah, blah, blah. Each night they prayed the family rosary on their knees glorifying God. Will she ever get back to the Spanish lesson?

I glance back at my buddy Colleen, hoping she will mouth the answer to the question Sister asked me. But five-foot, nine-inch Colleen is slowly rising from her seat without raising her hand, without a nod from Sister's

Mary Todd Lincoln black-bonneted head. Great, I think, Colleen's going to answer the question.

"Hermana," she says, with her rouged cheeks and Tangee-red lips already an affront to school rules, "the three oldest boys in a family of nine hang 'round my stoop till eleven every night smoking and drinking beer. They've already dropped out of Gompers Vocational. There isn't much glorifying of God going on in that Catholic family."

Because Colleen and I live across the street from each other, I know the Barry family she speaks about. One boiling Bronx summer afternoon the Barry boys organized a balloon fight. They filled cardboard boxes with water balloons, ascended five flights to their roof, and dropped the balloons on their enemies below. Things escalated; from nearby streets, hooligans showed up who tossed whole boxes of balloons and fiery newspaper torches into backyards, taking lines filled with laundry down with them. Then Vinnie Barry came careening up the street with a three-foot silver fire extinguisher, spraying all of the neighborhood kids with foam. What had started out as fun had turned into a melee. The cops nabbed all three of the Barry boys and charged them with theft and destruction of private property.

Of course, the fact that they smoke, drink, and get arrested only makes them more attractive. As a matter of fact, Colleen and I both have our eye on the oldest, Emmet, whose thick dark hair and long eyelashes make us salivate. He looks like Elvis, has the same cocky walk and crooked smile. But I know Emmet has an eye for Colleen.

Last Friday night at a parish dance, Colleen and he, his pack of butts rolled up in his shirt sleeve, melted into each other to the beat of "Earth Angel." After the dance, I walked home with them, not that either of them noticed. From my bedroom window I saw them making out under the eaves of the stoop. Then they walked toward Cypress Avenue. I waited for her to return until my head began to nod.

The next morning Colleen, puffy-eyed and pale as a scone, and I were on the subway heading to see a rock 'n' roll concert at the Brooklyn Paramount.

"Whose idea was this?" Colleen whined. "Are we in Australia yet?"

"Whose idea was this-s-s? We've been saving our money for weeks to buy the tickets."

Waiting on line in the rain for two hours didn't sweeten her sour mood either. Even Fats Domino and Jerry Lee Lewis didn't help much.

"What's up with you, Colleen, got your period or something?"

"Nothing's up with me," she said as we left the ornate theater, pulling up the hood of her trench coat.

"Maybe you're grouchy because you stayed out too late last night."

"What are you talking about?"

"I'm talking about I saw you and lover boy leave the stoop." I bent over to even the cuff of my jeans.

"Really, Miss Snoop? Well, you must have been dreaming. Don't accuse me of stuff just because you're jealous."

Colleen was right. I was jealous, but I still saw her walk off that stoop with El Gaucho.


Sister stiffens her back and closes her textbook as Colleen continues, "I think a little birth control might have helped that family out."

What the hell? I am gasping. Birth control? Is Colleen heading for Bellevue? I look back at her again and grimace, hoping she will shut up. I want to raise my hand and tell Sister that Colleen hasn't been herself for a while. I'm not sure who is more stricken by Colleen's rant, Sister, whose plump cheeks purple, or her thirty students, who turn their heads in unison toward Colleen standing tall near the back of the room. I can tell by the deep breath she is taking that she has only begun. She continues like she is Masters and Johnson. "I don't think every time a man and woman have intercourse they have to intend to make a baby."

Intercourse? She has actually said "intercourse" in front of a nun, in front of a Sister of Charity, a sober lot at best. Colleen might as well applaud Khrushchev's recent detonation of a fifty-eight-megaton hydrogen bomb. For some absurd reason, I begin making up Spanish words in my head for intercourse: *intercurso, mediocurso, mediocorrido*. Oh, my friend, I think, you will never see the inside of this classroom again. Sit down, sit down now, not while you are ahead but before you are so far behind you'll never see your diploma. You'll end up wearing a plaid peaked cap on your auburn D.A.; you'll end up serving nutted-cream cheese sandwiches at Chock Full o' Nuts across from the Forty-Second Street Library. Even the lions will weep for you.

"As a matter of fact, Hermana, I wish my own mother had had access to birth control. She has five kids, does all the washing, ironing, cooking, and then runs every night to clean offices in the Chanin Building so she can pay her kids' tuition. She rides home on the subway at two in the morning. I'm not sure when she sleeps."

"Really?" Sister says sweetly, her five feet of solid flesh rising, her pudgy hands gripping the back of her slatted chair. "Which one of her five kids do you wish your mother hadn't had? You, perhaps, you who blaspheme in a classroom where a statue of the Virgin Mother herself stands; you who in the month of May brought a garland of daisies you wove with your own fingers to crown her Queen of Heaven?"

Colleen, who stands taller than every girl in the class, squares her broad shoulders framing her huge breasts, the envy of each one of us, and stands her ground. I lower my head and pray for Colleen and for myself. I think about how after Colleen gets expelled I am going to have to ride in the morning rush alone. I think about how the mashers whom I always knew would have preferred targeting the voluptuous Colleen somehow always managed to choose skinny, flat-chested me. With every rumble of the train they would press against me. My left arm filled with textbooks, I would elbow them but that would only encourage their ardor, the sorry jerks. Holding on to the overhead leather strap, I will not be able to signal Colleen to bellow, "Get lost, you creep."

"Hermana," she continues, "did you ever question why you became a nun?"

I stretch my neck to see if Colleen looks glassy-eyed, having overdosed on caffeine or Midol.

"Maybe it's because you didn't want to become the slave your mother was."

My God, Colleen is on a roll.

"I bet *she* never had time to get a PhD from La Universidad de Madrid. Did she even graduate high school?"

Colleen and I often joke that Sister Terence is so pompous she'd soon be hanging her diploma under the crucifix in our classroom so we can bow our heads to that, too.

"Sit down," Sister says, tightening the black bow of her bonnet.

"I won't sit, Sister. I've listened to you for a whole year—in two languages. Why can't you listen to me for five minutes? You don't know anything about love, or God, for that matter. God is love. Right? Right. "

I glance over at the steam cleaner, who is completely unaware of the drama taking place across the street from him. I wish he could swing his scaffold into our classroom and whisk Colleen away to safety like Superman.

Like a train pulling into a station, Sister chugs down the aisle toward Colleen. Is Sister going to smack her with the force of twenty centuries of Roman Catholic authority behind her? I could picture the Pope on his Vatican balcony waving backwards, cheering her, "Vive Soror, vive Soror." Colleen, a head over Sister, stares down at her; they are close enough to hear each other breathe. I haven't seen anyone get walloped since our fifth grade nun smashed Bobbie Barrett for calling Angela Hurley a fat-assed liar, which was God's honest truth.

But instead of yelling at Colleen or smacking her, Sister looks up into Colleen's wide-set eyes and she begins to cry. I mean cry, cries that turn into sobs, sobs that well up from her toes, out of her mouth, and shake her whole body.

Some of our classmates start flipping through the pages of *El Camino Real*, probably hoping that someone, anyone, will continue the lesson with a simple *"Buenos días, clase."* Of course, Kiss-Up Laverne, sitting right in front of me, is weeping too. At any moment I expect her to rush toward Sister and throw her arms around her, ensuring her "A" for the year. Colleen almost smiles, the familiar whisper of a smile that tells me at this moment she feels powerful. She looks around at the stunned faces of her classmates, a college-bound class of sophomores, some of whom still think sex is Rock Hudson dry-smooching the helmet-haired Doris Day. Sister, her shoulders slumped, teeters out of the room. I can tell by the way Colleen's face softens that her feeling of power has dissipated into one of total defeat.

"My God," she says, looking at us as though she were next in the line of command, "they always win, don't they? They always win."

At that moment, the fire drill bell sounds. Even though Sister is absent, we file out in silence, fly down five flights of stairs out onto Lexington Avenue, walk to the corner of Fifty-First Street, and halt at our appointed spot, right next to the entrance to the IRT subway. Because we know each other so well, Colleen and I know exactly what we are going to do, something heretofore we never would have dared, never would have considered. Instead of filing back into school for eighth period, we slip off the line and dash down the subway steps.

On our daily subway rides, Colleen and I have always shared our feelings. What no one, except me, knows about Colleen is that she fell in love with Sister Purissima in second grade when on the first day in class she saw Snow White and the Seven Dwarfs in colored chalk on the blackboard. That day she decided to become a nun, but the sisters have never seen her as a likely prospect. Maybe it's her voluptuous look; maybe it's her outspoken nature.

On the way home, I look at Colleen staring at the Miss Rheingold poster over her head.

Maybe she's thinking about which gorgeous brunette she'll vote for, even though they all look alike.

"You know, Colleen, even though Sister is pompous and I'm sick of hearing about her magnificent family, I hated to see her cry."

"I was stunned, too, when she started to cry," Colleen says. "She's pompous sometimes, but she's a good teacher. *Me gusta mucho español.*"

I wish Colleen would explain why she mouthed off in class today, but maybe she doesn't know why herself. I believe she's sad about her mother's hysterectomy, but I think she's afraid to talk to her about it. Maybe she's afraid of what her mother might tell her. She says her parents have been arguing a lot lately. "So unlike them," she says wistfully. And I think I'm not going to pressure Colleen into talking, because I'm afraid of what she might tell me.

As the train ascends from the underground in Manhattan onto the elevated Bronx tracks, I am always surprised by the beauty of the sky, no matter how gray the day, no matter how sooty the windows. I can hear The Platters singing "Smoke Gets in Your Eyes" at the Friday night dance and I think about the man on the scaffold. I see him in my mind's eye, a can of Glass Wax in his hands, polishing the windows so Colleen and I can see the sky more clearly.

# A Big Girl Has a Good Time with Small Men
## *Heather Fowler*

They had to be 5'7" or shorter for Melinda to comfortably toss. This was the cut-off. Any taller and they bothered her wrists at the annual Man-Throw. She wasn't one of those true amazon-like women who chucked any man at will, even in common society. Only convicts and ne'er-do-wells received her services. Serial cheaters. Mamas' boys. Abusives. In short, those sent by the Board of Human Decency for retraining at Alganis, the remote desert island where she and the other mod women lived and worked.

On the mainland, in fact, as she'd protested lately, she could even be trusted to eat with or near any men in her vicinity and nary inflict so much as a derisive laugh. At work, however, it was a different story. The prisoners she tended were those for whom the system had hope enough to enact paid measures before terminating, those considered powerful or wealthy enough to be somewhat societally necessary with a change in their unacceptable behavior patterns.

Abducted in the middle of the night, half-dressed and sometimes without the permission of wives or significant others, they'd been subjected to humiliation for hours before Melinda met them. Sometimes days. Trainees handled orientations, the young girls not strong enough to throw.

Men arrived at Alganis with panties applied on their heads that truncated airflow, and bound wrists. They arrived with foppish flowers in their lapels or dandified pants of lilac silk, from which they'd soon be parted. They arrived unshaven or depilated and drenched with emollients, whichever seemed more damaging. They arrived and arrived, and, for a year of reprogramming, they could not leave.

In general, prisoners forwent the use of any nonpermitted language. Language use was earned. Melinda and thirty-seven other women participated with their formal retraining, having been bred and enlightened to do so. Equipped larger and stronger than normal women, she and her colleagues seemed mammoth compared with those seen in suburban homes, so most men perceived them as huge, which was a desired perception.

*Welcome to biological warfare of the largesse variety*, Melinda often thought. Her mods were kind of like that thing scientists do with grapefruit chromosomes that caused the final fruit to almost triple in size, only this experiment resulted in gargantuan warrior girls with wide thighs and sinewy bodies, free to roam. Melinda, at 8'10", was one of the smaller ladies, hence her short height requirement for men.

This is not to say she wasn't proud of her strength. Her muscle mass resembled a hippo's—so thick she could clench these small men between her thighs, either using their resistance as an added challenge or crushing them outright. This power turned some men on, but rarely changed them. Sometimes, since they slobbered with desire, she let them please her.

Her breasts, each one, could be brandished as a separate weapon, or she might clap men's heads between them in a scenario not unlike having both one's ears boxed. One swinging breast was large and solid enough to induce a non-mod concussion. The crook of one elbow could produce a more-than-adequate chokehold.

It was hard to be so powerful all the time, Melinda meditated now and again, on an island full of the similarly powerful. Still, she was known earlier as the kindest trainer. Of the women assembled, Melinda was the only one who ever truly tried to care for those she rehabilitated. At first, this was a good practice, a matter of hope. Kind were her head- or ass-pats to reward men's good behavior because they were required to learn to serve her, but when they liked to serve her, this made them better lovers.

She enjoyed her work. When more than one of them joined forces to create her physical pleasure, she could almost sense the illusion that there might be a whole man there, one her size, by putting the two participants to work as one entity, ignoring the awkward movements, and closing her eyes.

She gave the largest men who arrived to her larger sisters, and, for a time, all was well. But this was before the leadership exiled her to the island's far side, after she killed two prisoners. "It was necessary," she'd argued. "I knew they could not be rehabilitated. I was wasting my time!"

Granted, the killings were spaced months apart, but the occurrence of the second killing quite negated her plausible deniability. He was a senator's son or something. "You were supposed to retrain them," her boss, Rodan, said. "Why kill them instead?"

"The first was not fit for retraining because he was small-minded and cruel," Melinda replied. "He wouldn't have changed, no matter what."

"You didn't try to change him," Rodan rebutted. "You flung him up at such an arc that his neck cracked on the Man-Throw Court."

"Yes, that was excellent," Melinda said, with the audacity to smile. "I only chucked him once. He went down just as planned. And it had to be done. He was so undignified."

"And the second?" her boss asked. "What about him?"

"He looked at me funny. That was strictly a pleasure kill," Melinda said. "Did you read his file, see what he had done?"

"No pleasure killing!" Rodin admonished. "You should have used more redemption techniques."

"I didn't feel like it," Melinda said. "I need a vacation."

"You need an exile," Rodan replied.

"Alganis is good on the far side," Melinda said, acquiescing, but what she meant was: The training locations on this island are no good whatsoever. She'd begun to doubt the founding philosophies and practices. *We have retrained these men*, she thought, *by subjecting them to abuse until they lie and lie and lie again, repurposing mendacity to simulate the reactions of those with morals and hearts—but they do not get better.*

Humans without modified chromosomes are a loop of repetitive failure.

She had learned from a source that no tracking went on after prisoners were returned home, unless a man regressed to old habits and was caught in another debacle. Then he was labeled and returned to the island with extra restraints. The two she had killed were both returned specimens.

How many children will be molested before these are put down, she wondered? How many crimes will go undiscovered for years?

If the second Alganis attempt failed, there was the penal colony, which was no island. Still, they got a wire at Alganis in such instances. Few were the successful who'd already been trained twice. On the mainland, those men with less power and money, those with lesser crimes, were terminated without even so much as a lengthy trial. The ones to arrive at Alganis had already enjoyed too much lenience.

Yet she had a good time playing with them while they lasted, sometimes even cared enough to check in on various prisoners. But it was fun to be a big girl throwing small men around, she had to admit—not kind men, not the sort who frequented other islands with small women who catered to them on shared vacations—but the kind of men who must be sent somewhere completely different, some otherwhere twice removed as a punishment or redemptive measure, since their crimes were predominantly psychological, and standard jail or instant termination would not work to sufficiently address them.

Still, Melinda now believed, after much deliberation and a small amount of remorse, they all should be simply killed on arrival, happy accidents. Besides, she was not displeased in exile. There were bananas and coconuts and fish! It was only when she thought of the last man she killed, the one who had only grunted rather than speaking, for she'd never permitted his speech, that she wished she could return to her large sisters for comfort.

After viewing the pictures of what he had done to his wife, she recalled she'd initially juggled him a bit with her feet at the Man-Throw Court, tossing him up as if he were a malformed circus ball sealishly spun, but soon dropped him lightly and proceeded with the usual counseling and training routine.

She'd planned to do everything right, down to his eventual release—but she could not. She'd needed to crack his stupid little neck. The photos alone told a story more condemning than any lie of regret he might come up with later during punishment.

So, yes, in a certain respect, she hadn't much remaining faith in talking. She wished she could return to her sisters, but only for conversation, which was preciously rare in such exile, or could serve as a subversive influence to convince more of them that "accidental" eliminations were necessary, for she knew she would kill more men if she returned.

She began to understand them better now, those little men she could bounce on her much larger knees, those who appeared on the island again after wrongdoing—those she was superior enough to break and maim—

which was fine, though she'd grown tired of action with ambiguous results, so found some actions were better, quicker, cleaner, at solving problems.

Except, sometimes, she mused, sipping fresh coconut juice from a cracked shell broken in her own two hands, it was kinder to the element of chance and more effective for fate, to give the man a good toss at a nice, high angle and let his mode of landing make the life or death decision. Such high ascent. Such a fragile little neck…What chance!

"Please, please toss me nicely," she remembered they'd beg.

Of course, if fate's decision didn't match one's inclination the first time, at the Man-Throw, Melinda could always throw the man again, like chucking a sort of dirty dice. Or she could toy with him further, and then do so.

At play, if she juggled men on her feet, she could kick them straight up, thirty feet in the air, and then catch them on her toes.

Because small men, for Melinda, were light that way.

And with them landing upon her soles and squealing like pigs, as was the way of a smallish man or animal bounced on a larger woman's able feet, she always, before sending them soaring, had a riotous good time.

# Part III

# Entanglements

# Silted Castle Walls
## *Megan Rahija Bush*

*Italiam non sponte sequor.* (I follow Italy not by my own free will.)
—*Aeneid* 4.361

They were saying goodbye because it was time for her to leave, which had been true for twenty-four hours though she'd been so behind on packing that she'd called the ferry and paid the change fee to leave today instead of yesterday, which Sam thought funny and endearing, though he hadn't said so out loud. They were saying goodbye inside the bug canopy of his bed because it was 4:00 a.m. and she had only fifteen minutes, she probably should leave now, but in a small town you didn't *actually* have to show up when the Alaska Marine Highway asked you to, which was her argument every time. But, he thought, she would be twenty-four hours and fifteen minutes late: typical.

She was always late. Like when a few weeks prior they'd spent the weekend together in Haines, acted like a couple, Sam thought, and at the end of the day she wanted to see the adult puppet show, which foiled her plan to hitchhike to the ferry terminal. And they'd had to walk and shuffle-run the three-mile road to the terminal, like drenched Monty Python horses galloping with sleeping bags and tents on their backs—because anybody who could have given them a ride was already at the ferry, prompt, like he would have been had it been up to him. He clenched his teeth so hard he gave himself a headache, and even she stopped chatting as they walked.

But they made it, and everything worked out as she'd planned. He eyed her sideways as she hummed "The Lucky One," and made the I-don't-know-it-just-happened-face, and he couldn't help but laugh.

They were saying goodbye, which Katie had to initiate. Typical, she thought.

"So..." She prodded him awake. "Think we should talk about what next?"

He nodded solemnly, speaking with those eyes that made up for the mousiness of red whiskers. Though he already knew what she was about to say, she felt obligated to voice it anyways. "I...I guess it's over, right?" she said, looking at his mouth rather than his eyes. "We should leave with a wonderful memory, a relationship that worked, you know, before it gets messy." She brushed a stray hair or mosquito from her eyes, and started to cry.

Which was good, she thought. Tears were good.

She really *was* going to miss him, she realized. She was surprised.

She had met Sam, right as she moved to town. She had been sitting at a campfire talking about explosions and cabin restorations—work, the thing that consumes you in the seasonal job. He'd wandered over and perched stiffly on the edge of a log, not looking at them. Katie understood that he was local not from his gruff, halting manner, but from the way Patrice, who'd lived in Carthus for years, glanced, said, "Hey Sam," and turned back to her. Sam mumbled something, then sat as if he were waiting for something, his attention held by the flames almost licking his Xtratufs.

A loner, Katie thought. The fire spat embers as one of the kayak guides added damp driftwood to the flames and she shifted, torn because the fire's warmth was exactly in the current of spitting smoke. She pushed sand around with her hands and turned back to Patrice. She wasn't looking for anything, she told herself; she was in Carthus to understand, preserve, and explore nature, not people—and this job was just for the summer, and then she would leave.

They were saying goodbye because she was about to leave, had been about to leave since the moment he met her, and now it was time or she'd be late, though she wasn't working very hard to leave the crook between his bare chest and his arms because, he thought hesitantly, perhaps she didn't want to go.

Sam wondered if he should have said something earlier, let her know how much he appreciated her presence. Not so much as to change her going, but just—to say. That it was nice to have her here. But even in his head it sounded flat, he wasn't sure, and their relationship wasn't like that; they didn't talk about feelings.

He hadn't told her that he wanted her to stay. But he did want that. He remembered when he'd first seen her. She'd been building a sandcastle, he remembered, while she chatted to Patrice. Confidence overflowed like a crown woven into her blond hair.

That first day, he only noticed her because she exuded something so polar to his anxiety. Even here in Carthus, where he should feel like he belonged. Sam waited for a break in conversation to ask if he could bum a beer, which took way too long, and with every second he felt the old freezing feeling creep up, the bile in his throat; he needed a beer to make the anxiety recede but he couldn't ask. After five years of knowing some of these folks, they were his friends, but just asking Wesley or Patrice to toss a beer in his direction felt like too much, every time—to find the right pause in conversation, to put it right.

Finally, Wes noticed and took pity. "Lookin' for one of these, my friend?"

"Thanks, Wes," Sam said, released from panic as he cracked the can open. "Welcome back, happy summer."

"You been here the whole winter, Big Boy?" Wes asked.

"Yeah, been meaning to ask," Patrice chimed in. "I thought you were living in Juneau these days?" Sam had seen Patrice around town for months, but in the winter locals didn't ask: such questions felt like prying. Only in the company of this migratory crowd could Patrice ask the small-talk questions that she knew had more undercurrent than simple conversation.

"Went for a semester in the fall." Sam shrugged. "Don't like school so much."

"And so you came back? For good? I bet your dad likes that."

"Sure, he's glad. I'm taking classes online for a while." They weren't judging, but he couldn't help but feel defensive for coming home.

"I hear you're working on that new dock with Tony," another voice, another kayak guide, chimed in. And the conversation glided on to the new dock, and Carthus urbanizing, a conversation he'd heard his whole life, like a play performed every time people in this town shared a beer. Carthus, where people moved to be alone together. He'd heard his dad grumble about progress with each new tourist venture, the very ventures that had brought most of these folks to town. If they all wanted to be alone, why'd they build their cabins on land next to each other? He, for one, liked company as long as it didn't demand he think up words to contribute. He sat back, relaxing into his beer and the familiarity of these people. Their faces changed with each summer, some came back, some didn't, but somehow the feeling of them, the fire and the mountains and the beer, stayed the same.

The wind burrowed through his flannel, but that too was familiar. He watched Katie's hands as she paused on the castle she'd built in the silt; she eyed it contemplatively for a moment, for the first time conscious of what she'd made, then pushed the sand flat to start again. Her fingers busy, moving, as new castle walls formed effortlessly in her hands.

At first, she'd run into him at the Gallery at Four Corners; he'd be sitting in one of the hokey "homemade Alaska chairs" sold to tourists, sipping a smoothie and watching people come and go. She'd sometimes sit down for a minute between errands to say hi. After the second or third time she could see the slow smile tip his facial hair up when she biked over and the tenseness she sensed in him melt in the one-on-one.

"Moose in my garden this morning," she'd announce.

"Hmmm. Knows you're new, easy pickings when your veggies come up."

"I'll build a fence, then."

"You? Build a fence? You're new to town *and* you're a woman. I'll believe it when I see it." He smiled to signify the joke and she crossed her arms. His gruff misogynistic front amused her, but she wasn't going to let on.

"And I bet you learn all sorts of things lazing in that chair and playing video games on your phone, huh? Is that what it means to be an Alaskan mountain man these days?"

He smiled and shrugged, but she always had somewhere to be, couldn't stop moving, and she was always late, so no sooner than she'd sat down she popped up and biked away.

But by the third time she could see hope pool in his eyes when he'd run into her, a question he did not have the courage to ask, and she felt herself drawn and repelled, horrified that she was still chatting and—shit—flirting, leading him on if she wasn't going there. But while his eyes asked questions, he didn't push. Despite the "I'm a man" façade he so desperately cultivated, in the ways that mattered he wasn't doing the asshole-man-thing. That question didn't morph into greedy desire she'd seen in other men's eyes, when she could watch her reflection turn from human to a coveted possession with no life goals of her own. Instead, he asked the silent question and nothing more.

"You headed out now, Sam?" she asked, finally, one night as he stood up from a bonfire. "Me too."

She made conversation the whole walk back and didn't stop him when his step stuttered, unsure, when they passed the turn to his yurt. She let him walk her all the way home.

All summer he'd wondered why, exactly, she was dating him. When Katie was around he felt socially at ease, which was a fraud—he wasn't a social sort of person—and it was fun and disconcerting at the same time.

Beer, for example. When they arrived together to the bonfire she'd say, "For you!" and hand him two beers she'd swiped from Patrice's stash. "Open, please!"

Two, he thought. Like we're a couple. Which they weren't, not really, although they didn't talk about it.

And he snapped the caps with his lighter and handed one back.

And it became routine; she'd hand him a beer but ask him to open it—"I try that lighter trick and it just doesn't work, I'm hopeless"—so that the focus was on her deficiency, not his. She never acknowledged that if he tried to ask for a beer himself he'd freeze, and so he never had to grovel with gratitude.

Then, beer in hand, she'd flash him a grin and turn, pick her way away from him to the other side of the fire; she'd say something loud and conversational to the others—"Well hey there, Wes, I hear that last group tipped you *big* for that whopper of a king you sent home with them. How come it's not *your* beer we're drinking?"—effortlessly turn a quiet set of strangers into community.

He'd plunk down at the closest log and watch her. Once he had a beer, he could recede peacefully into the background. He liked it that way, each doing their own thing. He imagined they exuded an independent sort of couple-ness. If they were a couple, which he thought perhaps they were, for now, while she was here. And who knows, maybe she'd stay.

"Spending lots of time with Sam, aren't you now?" Patrice had probed. They were pushing back devil's club that had grown toward the light on this well-worn trail. Patrice, ten years Katie's senior, had come out here years ago and never left. They cut trails into the old growth, with chainsaws and noise, so that tourists could photograph what could better be heard or tasted. Destruction in one corridor so the rest could stay pristine, Katie thought. Personally, she preferred not to leave a mark, to slip away without hurting people or places, as if she'd never been there at all. She never could make herself stay, she felt compelled to push on, to follow some nebulous compass that told her she was destined to impact the world in some way. It was her destiny, her debt to the places she loved, and if it meant she had to move from place to place, she would.

"He's super easy to spend time with, Patrice."

"Mmmhmmm." Patrice stuck a piece of flavored chew in her mouth, offered one.

"No thanks," Katie said, rolling a freshly cut log down the trail. "It's like I've always known him."

"Sounds like you're married."

"We hardly know each other."

"Sounds perfect."

Katie sighed, disconcerted at the gash through the old growth in her wake. "Patrice, I'm not small-town enough for perfect."

The stump oozed sap from where Katie'd sawed it down. Thirty rings, she counted: that tree was five years her senior. Give the stump a couple years and it would decompose, rot, in the same place it'd been born. Katie shivered. How lovely to be tied only to your roots and not driven on by a nagging sense of purpose.

"Does Sam know this?" Patrice asked. She spat and Katie let her question linger.

There'd been a time when she'd been small-town. Small-town enough to think that perfect happened and that it was what she wanted. Jason had been older, but quiet, too, like Sam. He'd been sweet at first. She'd pursued him and so when he turned out to be vulnerable and lost, she was still rushing forward and hadn't realized what it meant. And then he became her sense of home, though unstable like a city under siege. Fights and insecurities were part of relationships, she'd told herself. Besides, he needed her. His raw emotion made her feel closer than she'd ever felt to anyone. And when he'd explode every few days, smashing walls in anger—that too became a part of it, intertwined with duty and part of it. If she loved him, she loved all of him, she thought. Plus she could mitigate his anger, and be facilitator to the outer world. It gave her purpose; Jason was home.

Their friends turned away, disgusted: "He's no good for you." But they didn't understand. Her grades dropped, and she rejected school because it was all just a joke anyhow and she had him. They turned internal, into themselves, and he kept smashing walls, and she was there for him, because there was meaning beyond happiness. But her faith in that relationship had been back-stabbing, her doubts had wiggled into their home, like a Trojan horse between the walls; she'd rolled it in herself. And he kept smashing walls.

And then he smashed her. And a voice like a goddess whispered that there was more to life than home, she was not made to nest. A curtain lifted and she could see what her life was: broken, burning, and lost. She made a pact that the only home she'd fight for was the natural world: never again would she hold on to another human being like that. She let go of her charred relationship, took her broken body and fled.

They were walking on the beach after work, he remembered, one of their first times hanging out, when she'd told him she was headed to law school. The sun hung in the sky, like an emblem to newfound love, still many hours from setting. It was one of those days when even in the daylight he could make out Venus winking just above the mountains.

"But I love school!" she'd said. "It feels so essential, you know?" She stopped to look up at the stretched ocean that sloshed in its mountainous bowl and sighed. "I love a lot of things, it's hard to choose. What I know is that Denver Law School expects me in the fall, so."

The rock beach sprawled dark next to the white-gray of the day. The seaweeds, brightest contrast on the beach, seemed vital, rich like gold, and he counted four eagles that eyed them from the towering roots of a downed log ahead.

"So?"

"So, I'm going, Sam. I've spent enough years doing nothing, and I can't explain it. I have to do something meaningful. I'm compelled to, it's almost not a choice, you know? We're killing this world and I have to do what I can to protect it. There's something bigger than me and you that I have to follow. So."

He had never seen her so passionate. She was collecting beach greens and goose tongue as they walked, stopping periodically to look at her *Southeast Alaskan Edibles Guide* ("because the *Local Boy* doesn't know edibles," she teased). He admired her energy. These edible plants, it seemed, were just one more thing she set her sights at understanding, and she would, he had no doubt.

"So even though this place feels like somewhere real, someplace I could dig into, like a home, the next step calls, you know?"

He didn't know. Carthus was home, but he'd had this conversation before with friends who'd left for college, left for Juneau or Portland or somewhere, saying they'd come back when they were ready to settle their bodies into the place they'd been born in; he imagined them like the stench of returned salmon, coming home in time to rot happily and spawn just before they died. And it always made him feel insufficient, broken; why wasn't he compelled to leave?

One of the eagles started as they approached and cackled angrily as it landed in a sprawling nest he hadn't noticed, far above their heads. Another white head protruded from the scraggly home, a nest they'd built together for years—but Katie was too busy with her edibles to notice.

Once you found that place that worked, he thought, why push it away? But the question was rhetorical, and he didn't ask it out loud.

"And who knows, maybe I'll be back." She shrugged, crouched like a child, absorbed in a tide pool of lime-green sea lettuce. She seemed encased in her own thoughts, guarded. "This place sure does make me want to settle in."

He imagined her hands building castles in the sand, big enough to live in. He bet settling in, finding home for her was effortless, and he wondered what effortless felt like.

She hadn't meant to go there, but at least she'd been clear that this was just for now. Even the broken condoms had been problems in the moment, intimacy in the moment, not anything lasting.

They'd shared pieces of themselves, sure. They sat, trolling in his boss's boat, separated by the vinyl of Grundens necessary against the wind and the steady drip from the sky, and talked, told each other the things that had hurt the other times they'd tried to love. She'd mentioned "control" but without the detail of what it had done. He told her about growing up in Carthus, but, she noted, without mentioning his anxiety. Which was fine, he didn't have to tell her. She cared about him; she wanted this relationship to feel real, otherwise what were they doing? But the Grundens jacket kept rain out and her feelings in and her eyes did not look up from under the fisherman's hood.

And when they'd be on the edge of sharing too much, diving too deep, the zzzzzzzztt of the line would pull them back together, hold them in the safety of the present moment and the task of a fish. Fishing would be her favorite memories with him. They'd take turns reeling the fish in, and then she'd whack it, hard, twice.

He loved that she wasn't afraid to kill; it was business-like, no nonsense. The same attitude as when she eased him into groups and didn't acknowledge that she'd done so. But he could never tell her he liked that she wasn't squeamish because she didn't open this up as a topic of conversation. There was no room for compliments. Their relationship wasn't like that; he understood. The slick sheen flashed silver in the light, scales that water could not permeate: dinner.

But they were saying goodbye now, that is what they were doing, and he was hugging her, encircling her and not crying. And after a bit, after thinking through what to say, he said,

"I guess, just like White Fang, I have to let you go." His voice in her ear was kind and mocking, and she laughed and snorted tears up her nose. He didn't cry, and she was glad that in the end they could leave both believing that he was the strong one.

"I like that," she said. "Thank you."

He wondered what she thanked him for. He'd never had any choice in the matter, he'd always been along for the ride and he'd always known that at the end he'd have to let go.

He remembered watching her fillet a coho, deft, as if she'd been doing it her whole life, and he admired and hated her for it. It was too effortless; her knife pressed hard between the dorsal fins to slice through the thick hide and she pushed through the animal's impermeable skin. She caught the female's eggs, pink-red like candy, as they slid off the cutting board. Two ravens cocked their heads and hopped toward her, brazen, wanting a share in the remains.

As they laid concrete on the new dock, Tony had asked Sam, "Are you guys dating, or what?" Tony'd been nudging Sam toward every girl that came through town; the whole goddamn town seemed to watch him.

"You meet anyone at the university?" Mr. Richards, who owned the Gallery, asked whenever Sam stopped in. A question that, if he were older, he wouldn't be asked. It was only their business because he was still young, which irked him.

"How *are* you?" the library volunteers asked, a concern that seemed linked to being single at his age. But also linked to his frozen moments. Those goddamn frozen moments, he thought, frustrated. But he'd gotten through them, he was an adult now, couldn't they see that? He was fine.

This town had watched him since he was small, worried by his anxiety. He'd be asking for a piece of pizza after school and he'd be hit: frozen. He knew what he looked like, he'd seen that look in the eye of a deer in the pause before you shoot, the frozen moment when eyes connect, full of life, terror and stillness. He could control the moments better now, especially in Carthus, where he was comfortable. He had fused those moments into a gruff and distant personality that worked for him. The freezes were barely discernible now, nobody but him even knew they still happened. Still, they looked at him like he was a child; he would never live down what they remembered of his childhood, and it was hard to defend something left unsaid.

Also, he wasn't hiding by moving home; he was living the way he wanted to. He'd bought land, someday he'd build a house. He had a job, a good job, he was building a life here, just like they had done years ago. And yet it wasn't enough, they seemed dead set that he should be nesting or partying; that at his age he should not live alone.

Now though, with a girl sharing the bug net canopy in his yurt, which the whole goddamn town seemed to know about, the questions had changed. What are you two? Everyone wanted to know.

"So, is she your girlfriend?" Tony asked again.

"Yeah…no, I don't know. Yeah." It wasn't confusing when they were together, only when the rest of this damn town wanted to know.

⟶❧⟵

On the porch of her cabin after work, the drizzle tinkled through the Sitka spruce and made Katie and Patrice feel cozy under the awning. They sat with a boxed wine from Jimmy's between them, their Xtratufs piled and stocking feet breathing for the first time all day. Katie whittled a spoon for her kitchen to keep her hands busy, one of many techniques for staying put.

Patrice stared her down. "He's your boyfriend."

"No he's not, we're just dating."

"How long has it been, Katie? Three months of sleeping together? And it's not about the sex; you said that. He's your boyfriend."

Katie fidgeted. Boyfriend implied control. Boyfriend implied owing him something.

"Okay. Boyfriend. But I'm not telling him I said it."

"Fine."

She started inviting him to her cabin after work. Patrice would be there, or Cassie, or anyone else she ran into at Sundrop or the Gallery, anyone she biked past at Four Corners; always people, always motion. Which he liked, actually, sitting in the corner, ignored but part of it all. She set up knitting circles, stir-fried seaweed, made salves and picture frames from things she found on the beach, and she let him be there, part of this community she'd fused so naturally in this place that was supposed to be his home.

But then he'd find out something new. "I didn't know you taught violin," he said, late in the summer after he stopped by and found a child scratching away under the awning, Katie giving lessons and knitting at the same time.

"Oh, yeah. Well enough." She brushed her skills aside. "Helps pay the bills when the Forest Service only pays that pitiful stipend."

He'd been embarrassed that he hadn't known this about her sooner, and it didn't seem to be something she wanted to discuss, so he didn't ask more.

In July, the first condom broke. Katie shrugged and walked into Sundrop for Plan B. At the counter, Sheryl asked her about work and how she liked Carthus, as she did every time Katie came in to grab food, and they both ignored the box Katie held out to purchase. Everyone knew Sam and her were together, and she wasn't ashamed of sex, just the irresponsibility of this accident. But she was a big girl, she could handle the awkwardness of it, and this was better than any of the alternatives; she wasn't about to go on the pill for any boy, that would imply permanence, and she wouldn't even let her mind go to what would happen without the emergency contraception.

But the second time the condom broke, she sighed. "Listen. You buy a pack of condoms that's not older than you are, and I'll get the Plan B again, okay?" And so she'd gone to see Sheryl, wondering how many town secrets Sheryl knew, unable even to hold up the pretenses of small talk as she paid for the contraception.

He went into Sundrop after work, and came out with a box of cookies. Sheryl had asked about his father even though they'd all seen each other at the Gallery for music last Saturday, and he'd said, "Oh, he's fine, great." And hadn't asked for the box of condoms behind her chair.

He'd gone in the next day and come out with a bag of chips and an energy drink. "How's the dock coming along?" Sheryl asked. "You guys gonna be done by the time summer's up?"

"Think so!" he'd said, impersonating the voice of his boss, the importance of it all. He was twenty-three, after all.

"Tony's selling you that company, isn't he? You gonna be a small business owner! That's good, Sam, that's good."

He'd nodded to Sheryl and walked out without asking, paused like a tin soldier at the door—don't freeze—and came back in. "Forgot—Katie asked me to get her some jam," he lied. No, all Katie had ever asked of him, all summer, the only *only* request, was for a set of condoms that wouldn't break on her. Sheryl smiled and rung him up for the jam. He could see how pleased Sheryl was that he'd acknowledged the girlfriend to her.

The old man's beard in the forest where he'd set his bike hung bedraggled like laundry in the rain and he hated that he lived in a place where you bought condoms from a person you met in diapers.

There had been a moment, just a brief moment, when she'd tried out the fantasy of *us*. "You want to help me pickle kelp?" she asked one day, before he even said hello.

"That sounds terrible!"

"I bought Rainier."

"Better. I'll drink beer and judge your housewifery abilities."

"I expect some quality judgments, I won't tolerate any niceties."

He'd showed up right when he said he would, predictable; she smiled, never even late to a casual evening. He'd taken off his raincoat and boots on the porch so the mud would not cross her entryway. She loved that kindness in action trumped his guarded silences and gruff front.

He leaned down, kissed her briefly before opening the fridge and sitting down.

"Hey, chop this, asshole," she said, throwing him some garlic. "You're not paid to look pretty."

He'd grimaced at her happily, but picked up the garlic as he sipped his beer.

"Sam, you ever thought about whether or not you want kids?" she asked. What was she saying?

Sam looked up, his eyes both kind and terrified; she could see his anxiety, the edge of frozen, but he managed to answer. "Sure. Have you?"

"Hypothetically, I guess. As long as it didn't interfere with my goals. As long as the right person is there to share the responsibilities."

Sam nodded, looking away. She knew how she sounded. Like he was the right guy. Katie changed the subject quickly.

"I'm sorry I'm always dragging you into these projects," she said, for once vulnerable. She suddenly wondered if she'd been nesting, when she hadn't come here to stay.

But then he told her he liked her in motion.

"You know, I kind of like it. I like you in motion."

Motion. He liked her in motion. He didn't just put up with it, he liked it. The past relationships had liked her, yet always after a while had tried to hold on, had tried to make her be still like a doll. He liked her in motion. It almost made her feel she could believe in small-town, believe in *us*.

The third time the condom broke he'd held her hair back as she puked in the garden.

"Well, now, you're fertilizing. Seaweed's good for the garden, and you eat so much roughage from low tide that it's the garden's lucky day!" he joked.

She stared at the mussel shells she'd used to frame her plot, even though this was the only summer the garden would be hers.

"Just as long as that fucking magic pill stays in my stomach." She tried her hardest to sound witty and strong between the dry heaves. She hated him seeing her like this. Scared. Sick. It wasn't how they operated. It wasn't who they were: she was the strong one. But he rubbed her back and for a second she let him ground her.

He wiped sweat or rain—she wasn't sure—from her brow with the back of his hand as she heaved into the yard.

"Gross," she said. "You don't have to touch me. I'm fine."

"Stop being so tough, Katie."

It had scared him, but for once he was able to hide his anxiety from her. What the hell, they weren't goddamn teenagers and here they were, three condoms broken in one month. This was the kind of shit couples had to deal with, real shit, shit that made it hard not to feel his body tense and freeze, shit that Katie's presence usually alleviated and here it was, this relationship, causing it. This relationship wasn't built on a sturdy foundation, it was built with silt; it was meant to erode. And here came this real shit to deal with, and it scared him.

And then, a couple days after the third time she took Plan B—the only time she let him see how physically her body reacted to their sex life—late one night as they'd been fooling around, now so afraid of condoms that they wouldn't go there, but kept touching each other because they couldn't help it, she looked him squarely in the eye: "You know, pull-out's almost as effective."

And that had scared him even more.

Today, they were saying goodbye. Katie, fully dressed, leaned over to kiss him one last time. "Goodbye! Going to be late if I don't get out of here!" she said jovially, and he managed to smile. Goodbye. She swung her summer belongings across her back, and didn't look at him again. And the last image he had was of the patch she'd cross-stitched into her backpack, an emblem of three women: one young, one middle-aged, one old, the mother and daughter holding hands, the grandmother perched on the shoulder of the middle-aged one like an ancient witch. When he had asked what it meant, she shrugged. "A family emblem. So I remember who I am." Which was evasive; an explanation slick like obsidian, and really no explanation at all.

She hated leaving; every time she left a place she wondered why she did it, but when she was there too long it never ceased to encase her in claustrophobia.

She stepped out his door, into the forest; her Xtratufs held the rain out and kept the sweat and emotions of her body tightly in. She was happy to be headed away to a big city for a change, ready to be dry and fresh, impersonal like baby powder and CFL bulbs.

The old growth smelled soft and deliciously decayed.

"Hey, stay out of trouble," she called as she left, "and don't drink too many beers. I want to hear from Patrice that you bought that business, okay?"

She regretted it as she said it. It was so impersonal, her final dictation in the relationship: Don't call me, I won't call you. Instead, she could have said, "Call me sometime. Just to say hi, okay?" Let it be a little messy, let just the smallest thread linger.

As she left, he replayed their conversation from yesterday in his head.

He'd told her she probably should pack up that cabin of hers and she'd said, "Fuck off, Sam, I'm savoring the forest."

"How exactly do you 'savor a forest'? You're not eating moss today, are you?"

"Is it edible?" she asked, laughing. She nibbled on the needles of a spruce tip and cocked her head in mocking question, like a blond raven with calculative black eyes.

"Please. I hunt protein; I leave plants to the womenfolk."

"And I hunt protein and harvest tides and leave nothing to any folk, asshole," she said, going back to her tree gazing or savoring or whatever hippie scheme it was she was up to. "It's called independence."

Katie slipped through the yurt entrance and into the rain. She'd figured out how to make social situations easy for him, she ruminated, but had not tried to learn why they'd been hard in the first place. She'd never met a boy so shy. He wasn't a child, even if the rest of this town still tiptoed around those strange moments when he went blank, when the blacks of his eyes dilated with panic as the rest of him went still. When it happened, someone would clap Sam on the shoulder and say, "Lookin' for Wes, Sam?" or "Sam! Did you come here for the Costco shipment from Juneau I told your dad I'd send over?"

And she followed suit, learned the technique for alleviating those moments, one step in front of frozen like a wind that nips at the clouds but never seems to make them go away. Why hadn't she probed at the source, why hadn't she undressed his fear?

She biked down the dirt path to the main road and turned right at Four Corners. The retro red paint of the gas station seemed too bright for the soft fertile green of this forest.

Fred, the purser, rolled his eyes at her as she scrambled to hand him her ticket.

"Boat was about to leave without you, missy," he said.

"Do you need me to dig out my ID, Fred?" she asked, ignoring his teasing.

"I know who you are, hon. That boy's going to miss you. This town's going to miss you."

"This town'll be fine," she said, trying not to cry. The morning mist seemed more pixilated in the dim light of dawn, and it smelled like spawned-out fish. An eagle cackled and picked at the eye of a chum, his beak not sharp enough to cut through the thick hide that encased the rotten meats from the elements. She watched the eagle, and thought that this place stank with the idea of the quiet small-town life, and she missed it already and she wasn't even gone. She wished loving a place was enough to fulfill her. Who knows, maybe she would come back.

Sam rolled over and fell back to sleep, so that when he woke she was all the way, utterly gone. He'd been dreaming what he'd been dreading, not that she'd go, he realized, but that he'd tied her to the bedpost so she couldn't, and she didn't fight it, she accepted it, her eyes empty, her body rounded and heavy and still. The same look she'd had when she puked in the garden.

But it'd been a dream, she had safely gone and he'd successfully let her go, which was the way it was supposed to be. He imagined her in her law school classroom, taking notes, knitting, always moving. He imagined her making a difference in the world. If she was pregnant—no, he wouldn't even go there. She couldn't be. He wished he knew she'd call him either way, let him share the burden of it, even if he knew already her decision. But he knew she wouldn't; she had said goodbye; she was gone.

A mosquito snuck through the netting and he could hear it buzz annoyingly in his ear, pregnant with his blood. He swiped it and it fell, rounded and heavy and still.

# Not a Through Street

## *Judy Juanita*

---

## Week 1

I need help. I can't write down my jokes and routines with all this pain in my arm. The doctor diagnosed a torn rotator cuff, but until I get an MRI, I get no relief, just pain pills, which I detest. But it hurts like hell, especially at night, until my doctor refers me to an Owen Schreib, RPT. Registered physical therapist. An herbalist, acupuncturist, and physiotherapist. When I call Owen Schreib I'm taken aback by an accent I can't place, but make an appointment. His brochure says physiotherapy is a professional, highly credible and natural medical treatment option offered to all Canadians to improve quality of life, and its primary focus is the restoration of function. So he's from Canada practicing in California.

I drive up to a ranch house on a quiet cul-de-sac in Kensington, a block from the Berkeley border. When he opens the door, I stumble. He's young and handsome, incredibly handsome. Why didn't he mention this over the phone? That would have been helpful. We sit down and I fill out the history. I'm not embarrassed about age because I look younger. Then he tells me his age. Rapid calculating means I began drinking legally about when he exited the womb. When he asks my occupation, I stumble again. If I say stand-up, I have to explain comedy clubs in San Francisco. He has killer eyes, gray and piercing, that demand an explanation.

"The underground comedy clubs in the city are so far underground they trigger plutonium." He laughs and then says what everyone says. "I got a friend who does that."

Physiotherapy, he explains, is more common outside the States, but he has additional training in acupuncture and as an RPT.

"You checked on the sheet that you have an abnormal amount of dreams?"

"Yes, I dream a lot. Dreams are creative."

"Dreams are critically connected to one's chi." It's spelled *xi* on his wall diagrams. It's a hot day and I've worn a sleeveless tee. He said to eat beforehand and he'd treat me the first time. He shows me that the acupuncture needles are the size of a sliver of hair, and then inserts about a dozen, with studied gentleness. It's not bad at all. I feel a slight prick once. Then he draws the curtains and leaves the room. The curtains remind me of curtains at the video store that mark the porn videos as off-limits to minors.

"Can you keep the curtains open?" So I can get out of here fast if you come at me. A very handsome man about whom I know very little opens his curtains and leaves me in his secluded house on a secluded street with needles stuck in my right arm and leg.

That night I sleep nine hours; this has not occurred in decades. I am blissfully pain-free. Even if he's Ted Bundy back from the dead, I write in my journal, it works.

## Week 2

I keep sleeping better, seven to eight hours. We settle into twice a week, become first-name friendly, Owen and Kit, even though it's odd. Why is this a problem? So what if he's blindingly handsome? It's a rainy Friday afternoon when he comes on to me.

"Kit, what're you doing when you leave here?"

"My rainy day pleasure. I'm going to the movie, not just one, three for the price of one." He knows the multiplex where I scam my way into three different showings. He's going to see *In the Cut* with Meg Ryan. He gives me a look that on any other person I would translate as, let's go together. Dude, you're my alternative physician. You're in my journal. And you're a dude.

"I'm going after work," he says.

"I'm going as soon as I leave here. You have to freebie at the matinee, when the security is loose." That evening, after one movie, I look for him, but I'm glad he's not next to me during the sex scene. Full frontal male nudity.

On Tuesday, the first thing I get from him, as he's taking my pulse: "I went to the 7:30 *Mystic River*. I looked for you."

He looked for me? "Did you like it?"

He nods. "But I didn't like seeing it alone, sitting next to strangers." His tone is accusatory. What is his problem? If you can't get a date, buddy boy, looking like that, I'm sorry for you.

"Go see *In the Cut*. It's going to video right away." And by yourself, since I don't see Meg Ryan movies twice. I have such smart silent answers in my notebook.

## Week 3

I start telling people about him, that he looks like Clint Eastwood and that the treatment doesn't hurt. It reminds me of my therapist ten years ago, Dr. Gold, and how I started dressing provocatively for his appointments even knowing he was gay. I know about transference, where you project wishes, fantasies, and fears onto an ambiguous figure. I'm not doing that. I'm getting healed. He's a healer. So he's a looker—he can't help that.

Standing over my supine body, he seems so tall. When I get up he's only an inch or so taller than I am. It's an illusion. I tell him he looks like Clint Eastwood in his spaghetti western days.

"I haven't heard that since I was in school."

He knows he looks like a movie star, and it's not a jokey resemblance. He's not an easy equation. I reread the brochure, trying to make sense of what's going on: physiotherapy, the fourth-largest healthcare profession in the world, addresses problems with movement, dysfunction, and pain that can arise from musculoskeletal, neurological, respiratory, and chronic disability conditions, or mental illness and intellectual impairment. Am I impaired or just spellbound?

The next time he looks down to take my pulse, I dare to investigate his face: Ivory-soap skin, unlined except for a faint thread creasing his forehead. But when he inspects my tongue, I notice a thin line of dirt in his fingernails. He's an herbalist—does he grow his own? A health professional with dirty nails?

That keeps infatuation in check for a few visits. This cocky young guy with sideburns. Sideburns, goddammit. My friend Irene with rheumatoid arthritis and ghetto Zen says whenever common mortals approach enlightenment, this devilish function called the Devil of the Sixth Heaven enters the bodies of their relatives or friends to obstruct the light. I tell her about Owen.

"When I leave there I feel like I've been to a male strip club, Irene. The way he rubs my arm from my neck to my fingertips...It's an important meridian he's opening there. Do you think it's sexual harassment the way he touches me, the way he presses his index and forefingers around the perimeter of my right breast? And the back rubs are to die for. The first time he unhooked my bra, I said, Oh no, he's smooth, baby."

"Fuck him already," Irene says. "He's a ho."

"There's something so erotic about him. I think he worked his way through acupuncture school stripping."

"And you keep going?"

"This isn't even half of it."

"He's a ho."

"He does the back rub with a sheet so it's not flesh against flesh. That's professional."

Professional or not, when he finishes the first back rub, the room is so charged erotically, I can't look at him. You're just a punch line, I want to shout, so what if you unhooked my white bra. Thank goodness I didn't have on a black one. Then again, Janet Leigh wore a white bra in *Psycho*.

That night as I drift into sleep, a little guy sits on my leg. He's caressing his head and crying out, "Somebody stole my brain." No, you're just a character in my dream. The theft occurred two weeks ago. That night, I try in earnest to bring Owen into my sexual fantasy, but Dirty Harry comes in me instead. Must be the fingernails.

## Week 4

Ramon, who books me, says the doctor routine worked last night. He's a hound—of course he liked it. But it's progress to be off my sofa babying my arm. I'm back out.

*"I'm paying $367 a month for Blue Cross. Talk about getting screwed* [they laugh]. *Health care fucks over everybody. I'm*

*using up every ounce of this three hundred bucks. I've been going to doctors up the yin yang. Internist. Podiatrist. Physiotherapist. Pain doctor. Chiropractor. Dentist. And, you know, I can't figure if it's written in my health plan. But they're all young, white, healthy specimens* [they laugh hard; I haven't even said the punch line]. *Well, one Asian. They all look like sperm donors. I'm spending my days with these guys. I don't have a guy. I have a medical A-team* [they titter; no laughter]. *Some days one's trimming my toes and rubbing down my feet. So close I can feel his breath on my metatarsal. The next thing I know my gay chiropractor presses his whole body against my torso, body slams me* [they laugh . . . why? The body slam movement or the mention of gay and chiropractor in same breath?], *and says, 'Breathe in, breathe out.' The resident internist at UCSF finishes examining me and says, 'If you want, I'll do your g.y.n. exam* [they crack up]. *That'll save you a trip.' And up he goes, his long bony digits all over, in and around my outstretched pubis. Who says I don't have a guy? I'm promiscuous, the kind of girl you can't bring home to mama. The pain doctor tries to get old-school with me, sings snatches of the Tempts in a bass voice as he goes all over my aching shoulder. I can't believe it. I'm getting screwed, serenaded, prestidigitated, unhinged—who says I'm not getting fucked?"*

Ramon and I haven't talked since I worked Chico State. When the rotator cuff went south, my perpetual motion stopped. The club scene is like Roto-Rooter; the minute you stand still, you go down the drain. When we run out of small talk, Ramon breathes heavily into the receiver. Does he want me to sleep with him too? Is his asthma acting up? Is he reading something on his desk? I start babbling.

"As usual, the black comics were talking about how much pussy they get. And the white guys were talking about how horny they are. Same old same old." Owen's face flashes by. Is he just another horny white guy? Ramon might be a Texas-grown mix of black, Hispanic, and white, but he thinks black, as in hustle-wary. I run it by him.

"What exactly is bothering you about the guy?"

"Like the last appointment, he's wearing a gold chain, his shirt unbuttoned halfway down, and I'm thinking, Whoa, dude, are you Rocky today or what?"

"What makes you think he's dressing for you?"

"Am I being egocentric?"

"Does the dude have chest hair?"

"In abundance and it looks good."

Ramon comes through the receiver like Niagara Falls. "Put this Canadian cracker out of your mind. He ain't nothing but a slim shady."

## Week 5

I try. I really try. I tear up the brochure with his picture. I go in and before treatment, I say what I practiced in the car. "Since I'm feeling and sleeping better, and don't want to do this—you know, doctors and treatments—for the rest of my life, don't you think this is enough?"

We're face to face, standing up. His eyes flash with anger. Being this close removes the handsome from his face. Instead, his face is animal-like, stripped of softness, even of its whiteness. My threat of leaving is bringing out some weird animal aggression.

"You're not ready."

I forgot I used to like only angry men, thinking they were better in bed, with their bang-me-into-the-wall sex.

"It just seems so indulgent." I'm close enough to kiss him goodbye on the mouth. "I feel like it's pretend. I'm hearing myself say: 'On Tuesdays, I do acupuncture; on Thursdays, massage therapy.' That's awful. I'm not some upper-middle-class pampered wife."

I'm not the dentist's wife. When I cleaned $350,000 condos for a stretch there, the one that irked the most was the orthodontist's. He was never there and his blond wife, a post-perky Sandy Duncan, was depressed all the time. I wanted to scream life into her.

Why do I feel fear with him? This is utter bullshit, a situational crush tipped on its side. Meanwhile people are getting blown up in thin air in Israel and Palestine, kids making war with machine guns in Liberia, soldiers with crew cuts and dog tags being blown to smithereens all over, with not even enough left to put in pine boxes; and I'm tripping over this.

"It's not a luxury. And what about your weight?"

He's testy, not concerned. During the session, after he's placed the needles, he picks at a whisker under my chin. He must think it's a piece of lint. He picks at it, oblivious to me.

Hands off my one white whisker, I want to say. I will pluck it, fuck it. But I don't even roll my eyes at him—I have become afraid of him. Compellingly afraid of mighty whitey.

"You need to come regularlarly." He's going on about this, but what I hear is that twice he says "regularlarly." He's flustered. Is this because I'm leaving, or is it the chunk of Blue Cross payments? Or is that the way they say regularly in Canada?

## Week 6

My stepbrother Raj calls and complains about his sprained ankle. When he goes on and on, I tell him about Owen. It's a test. Raj is street-smart. He can spot a hustle a mile off. If Schreib is inappropriate, Raj won't miss it.

Raj misses his first appointment. Schreib says he came on the wrong day.

"Oh well," Schreib says about the missed appointment. It's the first time he cups me. Cupping is a small glass globe fired up, then pressed against the skin and popped off after a few minutes. It pulls up stagnant blood. It leaves ugly bruises all over my arm, which hurt me all day. It gives me something to fuss about when I go back. He acts like it's no big deal. What is he, an alien or something? It's painful, dude.

I manage to put my foot down. "You can't cup me again," I say. "It leaves bruises." They look like hickeys.

My next appointment, Raj pulls up as I leave. It's his second visit. He sings Schreib's praises. "I'm feeling 60 percent less pain." Raj is a cabbie, a smart cabbie who works the airline pilots and ship captains. Numbers are his game. "Your boy is a miracle worker."

I start to put a word in my journal to demystify Schreib, to contraindicate what's happening. *Shapeshifter.* I try to pull away, but the law of gravity works on his behalf.

## Week 7

When I come in now, I'm noticing that Schreib speaks to me in command language: "Take off your top. Get on your back. Turn on your side." Like he's Houdini and I'm the prancing girl. He could be my pimp, for god's sake.

Is bodywork the new jack pimping? He hands me a sheet. I don't know exactly what to do with it. I wrap myself in it and lie face down on the table. After a while, I'm shivering. When he comes back, my teeth are chattering.

"I'm freezing."

He laughs and says in a fiendish voice, "It's called cold therapy."

Is he crazy? I roll my eyes at him. He says, "Just kidding." He turns up the space heater. I'm not even passive-aggressive with him. Am I crazy here? That Saturday, Raj calls me at 8 a.m. He never calls me at that hour.

"I just slept nine hours. That Owen knows his stuff. I haven't slept like that in years. And he has a great bedside manner." Bedside manner? Later in the weekend I talk with Raj's wife, who's amazed. "Raj is pain free." She, who doubts everyone from God to politicians to the greengrocer, raves.

Jesus, this was a test; now they're Dr. Dre and Eminem.

## Week 8

My arm is getting better. My concentration improves. I go online to traffic school for a $384 stop sign ticket (I forgot. Fine tripled. Sue me). Before the treatments, I tried but couldn't sit at the computer for longer than twenty minutes of traffic school. After two months with Schreib, I sit and do the whole test straight through in five hours. I can hardly wait to tell him.

He asks which online traffic school I used and how much I paid. Then he says, "I did it in two hours. What took you so long?"

I'm dumbfounded. He says, "I didn't read each section. I only double backed if I failed the quizzes."

"That means you cheated."

He smiles. "That's not cheating. It's taking a shortcut."

"No it's not. You're a cheater." He's taking great pleasure in this. Ah, another word for him. *Cheat.*

I'm not a one-liner, but like Scheherazade, flat on my back I'm at his mercy. I tell more jokes. *How hard was it to find Saddam, a full grown man buried in the desert under a trap door with an exhaust pipe hooked up to a fig tree?* He laughs, thank goodness. *I went to a singles mixer in Berkeley—first off you see a great mix of Birkenstocks.* I try to refrain from sex stuff, but humor is sex for some of us. *Big breasts are problematic.* He has to tug at my bra to rehook it. *At a party once a man said to me, "You have the nicest breasts in here—can I touch them?"* Like they were a pair of Siberian huskies.

Ramon says I should get a persona and repeat it to myself until it's second nature—that's what successful comics do. So I repeat: I'm an innocent in the whorehouse of life.

## Week 9

There are spiders, a daddy longlegs and a fat black one, on the ceiling. Schreib gets a stepstool and catches them in a tissue and releases them outside. I go into my ants-are-like-a-third-world-country routine. *They have their dictators, their generals and even suicide bombers—the little brown babies they send out for sugar and water.* I stop because he's explaining the black seeds he's taping onto my ears for pain, anxiety, and weight control. Then he starts tripping off my ears. "Your ear opening is unusually large. That signifies a big brain."

Without warning, he speaks very softly, in a sincere tone, right into that outsize opening, "You know, Kit, you're my best client. Always on time. Never miss your appointments. You do everything I tell you to do. So invested in the process of getting well." *Cryptic*. If all that isn't to say I love you, I am a fly on the wall of my own life.

Deep and getting deeper, this treatment. All the people in the world dying meaningful lives while I live this meaningless life with a handsome, pain-inducing Clint Eastwood look-alike who has the feeling capacity of an alien. He's the pebble in my shoe. A moss-agate pebble.

## Week 10

I stretch my hands to the heavens and beg for a sign from God.

Oh, please. Who is God but an overweight schlub who sleeps all the time and never returns your calls? I need this to stop but can't take my foot off the gas. Maybe the Buddhist gods will answer.

I drive to the appointment like a medic with a heart attack victim. I turn right one street too soon. Through the houses on the hill above Schreib's, I see the top of his house. I'm looking between treetops so intently I almost run into a street sign. I stop so close I see the raised metal dots on the mustard-yellow triangle that spell out NOT A THROUGH STREET.

When I park, it's the moment again. I never know what to expect when he opens his front door. His moods are like kegs of dynamite, one day smiling like a Roman candle, the next curt, professional, distant. Today he has a beard, new growth.

"You're growing a beard. Interesting." Covering up something? His hair is a dark lustrous chestnut with no shading, like he's dyeing it. But he couldn't have gotten the beard so precise. *Unreal.*

I've looked up transference. Yes, he's become my poppa, mighty whitey. Irene says he's fresh karma. "You're making causes to be connected to his shit, not to him." She's so blunt with her ghetto-Zen Aries self. I don't listen to Aries women—they have no room in their eye sockets. They only see what they see. I know. I'm Aries.

## Week 12

All the flowers in the garden outside his house have faces. One is a teddy bear. Just before I knock, I see a white gardenia with fuzzy muff-ears for leaves. Intrigue fills the universe between the knock and the opening of the door. What will be there? Welcome, friendliness, irritation, mood indigo? Is he an ordinary guy caught in my web? Have I dragged him into the whorehouse? Maybe this has to do with losing my balance buddy Gina to Hawaii. She was my shock absorber. We e-mail, but nothing takes the place of a close friend who lives close enough for brunch or a movie.

Schreib and I get to chatting about traveling abroad. When I tell him about my trip to France years ago and then to Singapore, he says, "My girlfriend's from Malaysia." It took him three months to tell me he has a lady. Why is this? *Tricky.*

We finish and he comes back in the room as I'm putting my shoe on. The cut of my tank top under my unbuttoned jacket means he gets a bird's eye view of my marilyn monroes. I'm bent over and can't straighten up for a second to say, "You're supposed to look away, doc." Instead I have to put the other shoe on. When I straighten up, I notice he's smiling the grin that makes males look reptilian, or as we say, horny. Another word for my journal. *Lech.*

I put my jacket collar up. He steps over and starts to turn it down. I rear backwards and keep my hand on my collar.

"It's lesbian chic," I say. "I like it up."

Driving off, I think: that was hormonal. Is he more male than healer? My girlie friend, Marisa, who is white and goes with black and Hispanic guys exclusively, says white guys don't have game. Feels like game to me. What does Marisa know? She grew up in Beverly Hills and has the smallest waist and big healthy, white-girl legs, which the boys at B.H. High suggested she reduce by surgery. Men. Oh, that's a totally unique word for the journal. *Male.*

## Week 13

This thing can't be an obsession because I'm not that kind of person. I'm the innocent in the whorehouse. But I'm getting to this touchy point where I can no longer discuss it out loud. I can no longer bring myself to share this. I don't want belittlement. I have lost a marble or two. The next time I go I still wear the tank. After treatment, I button my jacket to my chin like a Victorian lady. He changes focus and asks about my shoes as I lace them.

"What are they?'

"Oxfords." Dude! Plain brown oxfords. "Oh, you mean what kind?"

He nods. Does girlfriend give him enough or what?

"Rockports." I muzzle my mouth. *When I tried them on at the Rockport store in downtown San Francisco, I asked the salesman, "Are these lesbian shoes?" He says, "What do you mean?" I say, "What do you mean, 'what do you mean'? This is San Francisco. Are these lesbian shoes?"* The last thing I want is to dive into the sexual pool here. Ungraceful. I get out of his place by the skin of my teeth.

I feel like I'm slithering out of a lair. Does this princely toad know that each of my precious routines is an ingot, a little brick of moral gold? Hard to birth. I hope as I drive off the hill that I never see him again, or at least not until he's old and chunky and his lips have lost their fullness.

## Week 14

I'm a bunch of scribbled addenda in the margins of my journal where Schreib's become the main attraction.

## Week 15

The crime here is fake seduction and it's all happening inside a journal. I can't blame him for being a distorted mirror inside the whorehouse. I only see clearly when I leave his house and the light of day floods the scene. As self-help, I envision endings to the story:

- Sitting in a Chinese restaurant, Little Shin Shin on Piedmont Avenue, with Gina back from Hawaii on a visit. We're eating our usual—honey walnut prawns and asparagus chicken with oyster sauce. He comes in; he approaches with a goofy alien smile, and I throw ice water in his face. How Hollywood.

- Crying in a courtroom. I send him to prison for life for sexual harassment. As he shuffles away, his ankles already chafing because prison's no place for white men, I realize he's a nice person. I say, Valley-girl style, "Oh my god, I misjudged you."

- Twisting backwards at a yoga class. No longer blindingly handsome, he's gotten pudgy, too pale; the sideburns need clipping. After class, he asks, "Why did you stop coming?" I say, "Too much sexual tension, embarrassing." He smiles because he knows.

- Or show-bizzing my close: *I thought I wasn't fucked up enough to be an entertainer (substitute victim). I thought all entertainers (victims) were either lushes or promiscuous. Then I ventured down Life Street, you know, that road where the bulls come rushing through. And I found out there are many more ways to be fucked up than drinking or whoring. So here I am, fucked up enough.*

I talk therapists and acupuncture with Gina via e-mail. She says, "I had an out-of-body experience with my acupuncturist, who is a Jewish woman, and somebody else said hers did an exorcism." Have I become the orthodontist's wife without the "Dr." on my mailbox?

Schreib and I talk about college. He says he majored in philosophy. "In Logic, I had a professor who flunked a whole class. This triggered such a wave of complaints, including mine, that he changed all the grades."

"An F in Logic for a philosophy major?" This hits my funny bone.

"What's so funny about that?"

It's not a rhetorical question; he wants to know. For a day or two I see the quizzical look on his face like the little man who sat on my knee and said somebody stole his brain. I e-mail him:

Thanks, Schreib. I got 8 and 1/2 hours of sleep last night due to the treatment. I appreciate your help. Very much. I wanted to apologize for laughing inappropriately at your grade. It's nervous laughter. A friend (who has rheumatoid arthritis and related problems) pointed out recently that I make a joke whenever she tells me about her illnesses. I hadn't realized it until she said so.

She and I discussed whether this is cruelty on my part, which she had wondered about. Of course I was horrified that she thought I might be a cruel person. Instead I actually think it's due to the tension and anxiety in my life right now.

Actually I got a D in philosophy and have always felt that my knowledge of that subject is a big hole in my learning. So I admire anyone who majored in it.

See you next appt., Kit

The next appointment I walk in, and he's smiling, teeth bared like a crocodile's, standing as if his knees are braced for attack. He could be a crocodile. Really.

"I got your e-mail."

"The queen of anxiety on the throne again," I say.

"I didn't take it personally," he says with a magnanimity that says he did. Raj and Schreib have a nice unproblematic relationship. They talk about baseball hats. Raj falls asleep during the treatments. Asleep? Oh no, I might wake up with him on top of me. My workless (sounds like worthless) days are spent in a reverie of books, CDs, doctor visits, movies—and cooking, since eating out is too costly. Evenings, the open mikes and showcases where I come alive are a carny world: would-be jokesters, burnt-out jokers coming off the road to work on new stuff, thirty-somethings worried that Robin Williams is going to drop in and steal their joke, or that he won't drop in and won't rip them off. Into this unreal world rides this Schreib thing.

He's real.

I don't do real. I'm comic. I deal with emanations. He's Darwinian. No, he's not. I'm the one trying to evolve, and finding it's a long process.

## Week 16

He has on oversize corduroys, beyond baggy, and a J Crew shirt, XL. Was he fat once? I picture him eighty pounds heavier, with chins and handles. When I take off my pullover, my earrings get tangled. He moves to help me. I jerk away.

"I can do it myself."

He smiles. The face. Today it's Pitiful. The Love-Me face. Next week it'll be Brooding. He does Quizzical very well. I've even seen him do Dedicated. With that much range, he should be a film actor, and out-Clint Clint.

Why do he and Raj get along so well? Maybe this is why: about ten years ago, Raj came over, beside himself with anger. He had gotten a letter from a woman he knew in Viet Nam. She wrote about the child they had. That wasn't the shock. "We all knew what we left behind in Nam." The woman wanted to relocate to Oakland and needed help. Would he send cash and help her, their daughter, and the daughter's baby find a place? "I have no obligation to any of these people. They're from a time capsule. They're not my people. I was in a fucking war. Go to the Red Cross. Go live in London. Go somewhere else. After twenty-five years? You think soldier boy wants to be a sugar daddy?" He never mentioned it again. *Enigmatic*.

I get information online about sexual misconduct and acupuncturists. "Because the healing art of acupuncture requires touching, there is a higher risk that patients will perceive what you do as excessively intrusive, overly intimate, or sexual in nature." I feel relief. There are others like me. I disrobe in private—that's not the problem. And he uses appropriate draping. His flirtatious behavior is the sticking point. I go to the California Acupuncture Board site, which lists a range of sexual misconduct, mapped out by the Medical Council of New Zealand. Like that's going to help. I'm black, not aborigine. The part about sexual transgression, though, hits home: "Inappropriate touching of a patient stopping just short of an overt sexual act may occur with unnecessary breast or genital examinations or trigger point therapy near the breasts or genital areas." He's all over my breasts, copping feels left and right—but it's a turn-on, I'm ashamed to say.

I determine once again to make a graceful exit. Why is this so important, being graceful? It is my last, absolute last day. I have been consumed with him. He's driven me nuts. He opens the door, clean-shaven, more Clint than ever. I do treatment, giving him a song and dance about getting a gig in Sacramento that will keep me on the road. Without his beard, he looks honest and caring, professional. He looks stricken that I won't be coming back.

"You can always come back for a tune-up," he says.

## Week 17

I write him a Dear John. I rewrite it. I hesitate. I stamp it. I keep it for two days. When I send it, that's it. I can't see him again. Ever. I am free at last.

> Schreib, I want to be honest. I really dreaded coming
> to our appointments. You have the healing touch and
> your treatments were effective, perhaps too much so. The

dread came from the uneasy feelings stirred up by all the touching, the erotic nature of our many interchanges—I just couldn't take it ultimately. Sometimes when I left your house in Kensington, I felt like I had been to a strip club. I went online and I understand that the meridian on my right arm stimulates sexuality or is related to it. But again too much! I came for healing, not sexual healing. I also felt very vulnerable and exposed. Maybe it's the home office with nobody around. I will give you a tip. Someone else who feels like I did, even if it's a misperception, might relate this kind of feeling (he touched my breast, he flirted) to a mate. And that mate might not handle it passively. He (or she) may come up to your office and knock your block off. I'm continuing treatment elsewhere. Any problems I had I take as my responsibility.

My best, Kit

This banishes him from the story of my life. I can never think of his porcelain skin or the touch of his fingers on my flesh. I will forget the slightly asthmatic sound of his breathing. I never have to dip into the gray lakes of his eyes and swim back out. It's finished. I mail it on a Tuesday morning. Wednesday night, he e-mails me:

Dear Kit,

I just received what you sent me in the mail. I'm sorry that you felt uncomfortable after some treatments. I would never be unprofessional with anybody, though I realize doing acupuncture can be quite an intimate and invasive treatment. That is its nature, and it stimulates a lot of energies in the person. I appreciate your comments. It would be terrible to lose you as a patient, and I hope you reconsider coming back.

Take care, Owen.

Goodbye, sweet Schreib. It was not meant to be…oh, who's zooming whom? This is a buyers' market. I get a referral and show up at an office in Berkeley. Right away the acupuncturist looks like Barbara Hershey with the dark eyes. Is she kooky or quirky? I sit down and look at her wall charts and let out a long sigh. I love white people, absolutely love them. They make going to the movies so worthwhile.

Alas, she doesn't take Blue Cross.

## Week 20

I get treated now in downtown Oakland's Chinatown with this wizened Chinese woman who must be seventy-five and counting, barely five feet, teeth as brown as peanuts, who cups me all over my back and buttocks. Nothing erotic. She looks like the stock Asian characters that played alongside Woody Strode in his glory days.

> *"The day of my MRI arrives. I go into the city, thinking it'll be like on television, a see-through iron lung. Instead it's closed. I feel like I'm being wheeled into a columbarium. And right before I'm pushed in, the technician gives me a clicker. That's odd, I think, until I'm in there like a sausage with six inches of space above me. My god, a sarcophagus. I'm buried alive for forty-five minutes. What if there had been an earthquake in San Francisco and there I am buried alive in a huge wired magnet, tall buildings crashing around me? At least I know how it feels to be an extra in a coffin on a Hollywood set..."*

And why actors fall for each other on set—because good looks are blinding.

# Husband Hunting,

## or

# The Survival of Indian Arranged Marriage
# in Worcester, Massachusetts

## *SJ Sindu*

---

### For Asha in a Saree

The sequins on the saree made Asha feel like an enormous glittering beetle, or like so many shards of broken glass winking in the sunlight. This saree was a green she had never seen in nature, a stately green with gold thread that darted through the six yards of fabric as she tried to rein it in around her body.

*Wrap it once around and tuck.*

Her mother had taught her how to wear a saree when she bled for the first time, when her fertility first became a prize and everything else mattered less.

*Twice around, and over the shoulder.*

Her hands smelled of henna, an earthy, sharp smell like sweat and cloves. The woman her parents hired to do the henna had insisted on hiding the groom's name in the intricate patterns she laid on Asha's hands. *It's tradition. If he can't find his name on your wedding night then he must give you a prize.*

After the wedding she would have to wear the *mangalsutra* around her neck, and on her feet the toe rings that chimed with each step, just like the ones her mother (her cardiologist-now-housewife mother) and grandmother (who had once reportedly ran wild in the grain fields of India) had agreed to wear.

She pleated the extra saree material and tucked it under her bellybutton.

## For Reena at the Temple

They arrived at the Hindu temple an hour before the appointed time. Reena was sure the reason was to kill her with the stress. The tall piers of the Sri Lakshmi temple greeted them as they turned the corner onto Temple Road. It was set on top of a hill, surrounded by trees to give the illusion that it was set off from the city. The temple had been under construction for years, but they still hadn't painted the outside. It was plaster white, completely unlike the multicolored facades of the temples back home.

The only part about the Hindu temple that Reena liked was watching the women there. Women in glittering sarees and salwars, women in jeans and shirts, short women and tall women, fat and thin. Women whose stomachs were flat and toned, women with stomachs that tumbled out of their sarees with laughter. Women with dark eyes, light eyes, brown, blue, black eyes, black marble eyes, eyes the color of the dark gloomy idols of the gods. Women with carefully painted curry powder lips, women with faces scrubbed clean, women spotted with pimples and warts. Women with bushy eyebrows and mustaches that played shadows on their faces, light women and dark women. White women with their Indian husbands, Indian women with their Korean husbands, women with other women who stood too close. The men there tended to fade into the walls, their dress dark and plain and conservative and their matching haircuts and facial hair too indistinguishable.

They met his sister first, Reena's sister-in-law-to-be. Reena was hopeful. If the guy was half as beautiful as his sister, then he may have a chance.

When he did arrive, it was a disappointing affair. He was short and chubby in his khakis, his hair cut close into little black coils on his skull. He didn't talk much, just stood there brooding while his sister talked about how excited they were to finally get a good match for him, that he had said no to a dozen women but he said yes to Reena's picture and that was huge.

Reena kept her eyes on his sister. She was wearing a stiff maroon saree and as she talked, her lacy black bra peek-a-booed from under her blouse.

She asked Reena about her interests, her studies, her work. She told Reena that the groom was an engineer, that he was a very good boy and Reena wouldn't regret marrying him.

When Reena closed her eyes on the drive back from the temple, she couldn't picture any of the men there, not even her groom or the way he stood with his hands in his pockets. She only remembered his sister, her black bra, the women moving about, circling the shrines and getting down on their hands and knees to pray.

## For Trisha the Feminist

On my twenty-first birthday I was told I was ready for marriage. My parents started their hunt for the perfect Indian boy.

Option 1: an engineer in Toronto. *Exactly like your father, reminds me of your father.* Old and short with a pimped-out car, the one who took me to dinner after I asked to go out for coffee, and ordered for me in the restaurant even though I knew what I wanted.

Option 2: a dentist in Vancouver. *Tall tall tall.* Well, I'm short short short. How do you expect sex to work, and don't you know that dentists have the highest rates of blowing their brains out?

Option 3: an engineer in London (do you see the trend?), a boater who had come from India to finish his master's degree. *He's willing to move to America for you.* Yeah, maybe for my green card.

I like to let the top of my boxers show above the waistband of my saree. Find me a husband who thinks that's hot, who juices at the sight of a woman rocking a saree and a fauxhawk. Find me a husband who will rock me to sleep after I come, even if he hasn't yet, one who likes being tickled in the curve of his back, one with big spilling-forth lips and supple touch-me-hold-me hands. Find me a husband who wants to be held, to be fucked, who cooks and cleans and still wants me to drive even if there's snow on the ground, who doesn't need nasty snot-faced children to prove his potency, who'll sit in the passenger seat and keep his fucking mouth shut.

Let me give you a clue: he won't be a dentist.

# Physics

## *Kim Chinquee*

—⸺❦⸺—

I sat there on the floor, reading about red cells for my thesis. My cat Patches was curled at my feet. My boyfriend, William, had come over, we were trying things again, and now I listened as he talked to my son, Jamie, about his job as a reporter. Jamie nodded, more interested in the TV, where some guy was smacking his guitar and double leaping.

My mother called. It was almost Christmas.

"Eileen," my mother said, "come and see your stepdad."

"What should I say?"

"He loves you, you know."

Patches rubbed my leg. She was calico. I petted her and she started purring. There was silence on my mom's end.

"I'm saying maybe you should come now," she said. "At least think about it."

Her voice began to waver. She started crying, she said she wished it wasn't such a drive for me to see her. I mouthed to William it was my mom. He was making faces at Jamie. Patches scurried to the bedroom.

When I hung up, William told me about a girl he'd known since high school, a girl I'd met in Physics. She was leaving her husband.

"Her problems were that bad?" I said to William.

"One of those marriages that just *look* good," he said.

Miles from next door came over, asking if Jamie could play. He was an older kid who I relied on to babysit. I waved at Jamie as he headed for the door. I sat close to William. He made me feel wanted, just sitting with him.

"Marriage sucks, huh?" he said. He looked at me and started going for something between my teeth with a fingernail.

"It's my stepdad," I said.

"Your mom?" He looked at his watch. He was on his way to a dinner party with this woman. Her name was Anna. He'd just come from the gym, said he should be getting ready.

"Can I come?" I said.

"What about your thesis?" he said.

"I can help," I said. I knew about divorce.

"I guess," he said. "It's your choice."

I called Miles' mother, asked if Miles could stay with Jamie. Then I got dressed and William came and watched, helped me pick an outfit.

I stood there naked, going through my closet. I pulled out a slinky shirt that was falling off a hanger.

"You wearing that?" he said.

I put the shirt back and he got off the bed, rubbing against me. I turned around and let him kiss me but told him the rest could wait. I filtered through my rack, picked out a dress with an embroidered collar.

"You're okay with Shirley Temple?" he said. He took it, put it back, and grabbed the silver top. He told me to show my stuff.

"This one's going to Salvation," I said, taking it from him.

He talked me into my low rider jeans, that top—the whole outfit showed my navel and my cleavage. I wore boots. All the time I was dressing he was touching me. It was hard to keep my mind on my business. I put on hoops, said, "You go for the sleazy look, huh?"

"Whatever," he said. "It's you."

He slapped my butt, said, "Some women would die to carry off this look."

I tapped his cheek. "Hands off until later. You're kind of reminding me of my *dad*."

He put his arms around me and rocked, and though he didn't always say the right things, I felt a little warm there.

As he showered, I found Jamie outside, shooting baskets with Miles and the neighbor boys. I yelled to them that I was going out.

"Man, with that dork?" Miles said. "You must be hard up."

"Just take care of my son," I said. I kissed Jamie and told him to be good. I watched him try a free throw.

In the car, William put in a CD by Madonna, something we listened to when we were fucking.

"Bring back memories?" he said.

We were the first ones at the party. The table was set with fancy silver dishes and candles burning in the center, the lighting to match. It looked nice in a TV soap opera way.

Other guests arrived. There were about ten in all, and I'd met most of them before at other times with William. They were his friends. I sat on the couch, William next to me, and I rubbed my hand along the cushions—soft, covered in velour—as they all laughed about stuff. I took off my boots, left them sitting on the hardwood. I sat on my feet.

When the group broke up, William put his hand on my back and looked at me.

"What're you thinking?" he said.

"I'm going to stay here," I said.

"What, in this apartment?"

"No, I mean in town. I'm not going north to see my stepdad."

"Oh," he said, sipping his wine, looking toward the kitchen where three of the women were laughing loud about something.

When Anna got there, I gave her a hug. "Hard times, huh?" I said.

She took a long swallow.

She went into the kitchen. I returned to the sofa. William edged closer, his hand on my shoulder. He smelled like my shampoo.

"You know," he said, dropping his hand to my leg. "When I was in the shower I promised myself I'm not touching you tonight. You look so hot. It's like sex cheapens our relationship, or something."

"You're *so* sweet," I said, staring down at something.

"You know what I mean," he said. "You want to stop at my place?"

⠶✤⠶

Dinner was all green, lettuce just like grass, and vegetarian lasagna. Red wine to match the green, as if it were Christmas. William looked at my plate. "Two servings," he said.

"Of everything," I said.

"Like you're Ethiopian."

After a while, I excused myself, taking my glass with me to the bathroom.

Everything was pink. I looked at myself in the mirror and dabbed my lipstick. I looked for floss and did my teeth. I arranged my hair. I looked in the cabinet for gel. Then I heard knocking.

"Can I?" said the woman.

I opened the door and found Anna. I told her I was looking for something for my hair. She reached in her purse, gave me this wax thing.

I said, "Like a hair commercial."

She shut the door. "Bill thought you were sick," she said.

"Paranoid?" I said, doing my hair.

"He just cares," she said. She did what she needed, sat. "You two look good together."

After the meal, we all cleared the table. I sat next to William on the sofa. I kept telling him that he looked really tired. He told me he was energetic, thinking of us going back to his place.

"Should we leave?" he said. I told him whenever he was ready.

The hostess was out of wine, and William had more at home, so he decided we should get some. Anna followed in her car, so she could bring the stuff back to the party.

At William's, I sat on the sofa, petting his dog Baby. Anna sat next to me. William went to the kitchen and Anna talked about her husband.

"He'll fight?" I said.

"For everything," she said.

From the kitchen, William called for Baby.

"What about the kids?" I said.

William came back with the bottle. He looked at Anna, asked her what it was now. He sat next to her and put his hand on her, said that she could stay there.

"You don't have to go back," he said. He went back to the kitchen with the wine, returned with three full glasses and some tissues. Baby trailed behind him. He sat between us, handed out the wine and gave Anna his big tissues.

"It's just me," she said. She took off her glasses. We all sipped our wine. Baby got up and sat on the blanket in the corner.

"Is it time?" William said to her. "Are you ready to come out now?"

She put on her glasses, sipped.

I took some of my own wine.

William put his arms around us. "There's something she wants to tell you," he said. He smiled a little.

He leaned over and he kissed her. I didn't really know what to do. They kept on kissing so I nudged him. That wasn't helping.

"Hey," I said, finally getting up then.

I said to them, "Hello?"

They finally stopped and William looked at me, wiping his saliva. His chin was red. "A threesome would be nice," he said.

Baby started barking.

I went to the kitchen to get a glass of water.

As William drove, he told me he'd been waiting to be alone with me. I told him to just shut up about it.

I started thinking of my stepdad. If he was really as sick as my mother made him sound then.

I told William that was a terrible thing to do with Anna. I said, "She's having a hard time already."

We sat there at a stoplight. I talked about my stepdad. I said I had to go there.

"Do what you want," he said. "How much longer does he have now?"

I looked out the window at the streetlights, at a cat that lurked.

William grabbed my hand. "Can you do that thing?" he said.

"Fuck," I said.

"C'mon," he said. "It's fun."

"You have some nerve," I said. "I was bringing up my family."

He said, "Maybe you'll feel better."

I thought about the night we got back together, the night he said he missed me and wanted more than something sexual. I really wanted that, wanted something deep and lasting, although I wasn't desperate.

I undid his belt, unzipped, reached under his boxers. I sucked on all his fingers, moving in the way I knew to tease him.

He told me that he loved me. He said he was sorry. He said he just wanted to be good to me.

"Okay," I said, as if I actually believed him.

He pulled into the lot of my apartment, parked under a streetlight.

It was after midnight. I thought about Jamie. Sometimes he waited up. I imagined him on the sofa, in his jeans and shoes, wearing one of my old Air Force sweatshirts. His leg falling off the cushion, his head leaning crooked on the armrest. An empty carton of milk on the floor next to a box of cereal or something. The TV still on, blaring. Of course, he would be sleeping.

I might nudge him, saying, "Jamie." I might stay there with him, watching.

William had his hand around my neck. I knew what he was up to.

I slid down, moved my mouth over his boxers. He eased the seat back and as I heard him groan, I began to nibble. I took him, moving harder. My eyes watered. My mouth got sore. I kept on, hearing him tell me how much he really liked me. I felt his hand on my head tugging. He yelled for me, saying yes and yes and fuck me. I moved lower, into one thigh, then the other.

He kept calling me his baby, yelling harder, louder, grunting. I bit him, teasing, deeper. He kept asking for more.

I bit again, as if I were a tiger. I heard him scream. He yanked me.

I tasted something salty.

"Jesus fucking Christ," he said.

I sat back and put my hand on my mouth. It was dripping. I opened my door and spit on the concrete. I wiped my face with his jacket.

I took a closer look. "You're bleeding," I said.

There he was, with a wound like a gigantic peanut, the size and color of a plum. I told him it looked like a vagina. He said it wasn't funny.

He sat there with his legs spread.

His blood was bright. I said, "Maybe you're anemic."

I started thinking of the morning. I started thinking of my plans then. I pictured Jamie asleep. I tried not to look back. I thought about tomorrow.

# Discretion

## *Jennifer Baker*

———◦❧◦———

We agreed to be discreet. I remind her of this as we get dressed. My eyes land on the cross tattoo between her breasts. I simultaneously twist the one hanging from my neck.

She was one of the waitresses at our latest fundraiser. It was the cross that struck me, and her chest. Both peeked out from her button-down shirt. I asked if she subscribed to a faith.

"Me?" She scoffed. It seemed she was about to tell me what she really thought before realizing she was at work, that she had an appearance to uphold as well.

"I believe everyone has a right to what they believe," she replied.

"Good answer."

"What about you?"

"I believe that whatever happens behind closed doors should stay behind closed doors." I finished my wine and lay the glass atop her tray. I gestured at her tattoo. "I always wanted one."

"Doesn't hurt," she said.

"The pain is the least of my worries."

Every so often that evening she caught my gaze. It wasn't wise, but by then I knew how to keep my interests hidden.

I was the good wife. Leaning into her husband's embrace. Placing a hand on his chest at just the right moment when the photographer's camera clicked. Our smiles were genuine. Ryan knows me and I him. I married my best friend because that's what people do. It was convenient and it worked in both our favors. We just had to know how to work the game.

I saw Ryan's eyes trail around also. Seeking out the campaign manager who helped him go from councilman to mayor to what we hoped would be the governor's spot.

I looked up at my husband, at the crinkles digging into the side of his lips and eyes as he spoke of our marriage, while his hand trailed from my shoulders to my waist to my backside as he'd done so many times. Gliding from one well-dressed group to another, I listened to Ryan tell reporters and potential donors his ideas for a better state. His hopes for making our municipalities more industrial, so our state would no longer be seen as a backwoods but a budding part of our nation. I watched as he was honest about most of his beliefs.

She runs a hand over her pageboy cut, pushing the bangs out of her eyes. "I know. I know," she mutters.

I came to her place, a studio on the other side of town where the young artists live. It's remote enough for me not to worry about anyone caring who I am.

That's the thing about age, about want, about hiding. Once you set your sights on something there's no hesitation. You dive in, take it, and cover your tracks later. As soon as the door closed my mouth was on hers.

"Why do you hide it?" she asks.

I don't look at her while I go through the list of responses I have ready. Scripted lines that pop out on automatic when you've gone through campaigns and local interviews and forced other people's palms into yours for a quick handshake—just *one* while a camera somewhere is flashing. I don't clear my throat because that denotes indecision, or a cop-out. I don't smile because that may make her feel inferior.

I could tell her she's not yet at that age to understand. She has a mattress but no bedspring. She has a laptop and smartphone but barely any furniture. There's no sense of this place being lived in. This tells me where her priorities are. We stood mostly, looking up at one another, pressed against walls that held the smoke from the crunched butts in her ashtray. What would she know about being middle-aged with triplets and a husband, and a family?

A community as conservative and straight-edged as a spray-starched shirt is something she—a rebel against what, exactly?—couldn't fathom.

I could try to explain that there's a tug between the beliefs I was raised with and what I feel is right. That after mutual heartbreak, Ryan and I thought being together would be a cure-all and in a way it has been, giving me the family I didn't realize I wanted until I felt life tickling then poking me from inside. That encouraging change was supposed to be easier from the inside.

I could attempt to tell her there are pockets of prejudice everywhere. Not just in small towns but in the metropolis, or that Ryan and I being together isn't strange. That when he and I lie in bed we talk for hours without the awkwardness of sex to push a wedge between us. That when I was bedridden in my last trimester, Ryan's face reflected the multitude of fears of my own and there was comfort amidst the tautness of my skin and in my stomach of knowing, again, I wasn't alone. There's so much to it I can't put into words, so I don't.

I turn to her mirror, one of the few items on her wall beside a collage of postcards from various cities around the country. I make sure my hair is slicked down in the right places and my pants have no additional folds. She watches me and I glance at her in the mirror, see her focus on my face, on the glassy eyes and full lips that have been putting people at ease since Ryan took his first oath.

"Sadly, in my line of business, appearances matter."

She rises to show me out, but I encourage her to stay seated or at least put on pants before opening the door. I stand still in the door frame, a polite grin on my face as if we're old friends parting. More plausibly, I'm the kind politician's wife eager to talk to the younger generation and hear their accounts of how things are, encourage them to participate in their community and make a difference. The younger people count. Every vote does.

She stares at me, not hungrily, not attempting to decipher but weighing needs, whether she's weighing mine or her own I'm unsure. When she leans in, it's automatic—my stepping back, my heels clacking against the floor in the hallway ready to go. My head moves either way but the smile doesn't budge, it's iron clad, I've practiced enough.

She steps out, her bare toes adjacent to mine squeezed in taupe pumps.

"Nice meeting you," she says, and gently but swiftly glides a hand across my breasts before stepping back inside and shutting the door.

I hold my breath down each flight of her building, and once I release, I force myself not to discern what type she is. I know. She doesn't just like fucking you, she likes *fucking* you. Before I even start the engine there's a *zing* from the phone in my purse alerting me of a message.

I drive home. I see the bikes splayed out on the lawn and the sprinklers raining on them. I groan at the thought of rust and yell inside the house that the boys better pick up "every item on the lawn or else."

The parade starts down the steps. With mumbles of "Hey, Mom!" they head outside.

The door to Ryan's office is slightly ajar. He and his campaign manager stand side by side. Ryan's finger trails the length of Derrick's shoulder blade. The beginnings of a smile on both their faces.

It's harder for Ryan, but he's managed.

Ryan moves away from Derrick, makes his way out of his office and comes to kiss me on the cheek.

Someone runs into my legs and then another and another, propelling me forward. Our boys grin up at me.

"Hi," I say. Seeing Ryan and me in their cheeks, their eyes, the way they dig into their ears with a pinky.

Derrick doesn't watch our family moment. He's seen enough for a lifetime. I kiss Ryan back and tell him I've missed him.

He asks how my visit with my "friend" was as we walk in a cluster to the dining room. "Is she someone we can count on for a vote?" Another faint sound alerts me of a new message, already a queue in my phone that I hesitate to look at. Right now is family time. Right now I have to be tactful and ready to tap into my arsenal, just in case.

# Runaway Truck Ramp

## *Soniah Kamal*

———❦———

I was in the hospital's chapel when he came in, said, "Excuse me, thought this was the smoking room." I would have left had I not been crying, a million crumpled tissues spilling out of my lap.

"Are you okay?" he asked.

I nodded but he insisted on getting me a cup of water, which I downed.

"I can go…" He sat next to me on the wooden pew, right in front of Mary cradling baby Jesus. I looked up at him to see him clearly. He was one of those exceedingly pretty boys whose features I've sometimes envied for their blemish-free complexions, heavy eyelashes, perfect cheekbones, and a cupid's bow so perfect it can land them a modeling contract. My Mom called them "angel faces." Mom had a bit of a manly face, but when I was younger and hadn't yet learned which face supposedly belonged to which gender, I thought Mom was a beautiful woman. She remains beautiful, if only to me.

"My mother just died." I wiped my cheeks with the back of my hand. "Oh God, just saying it sounds so dreadful."

"I'm so sorry."

From the way his voice had softened, I could tell that he was sorry and wasn't just saying it because it was the polite thing to say. I told him Mom had an unexpected stroke a year ago that had left her all but dead. I was in my sophomore year at college, and I'd taken an extended leave so that I could be by Mom's side even if I was reduced to nothing more than a voice, not that the doctors were sure she was registering even that.

"One year coma-ridden." I tried to focus on Mary's gown, chipped by her little toe. "But once we bury her there's no hope of ever seeing her again."

"Mothers are special." He crossed his long, denim-clad legs. "Even if you don't love them, you love them. In my religion, heaven is said to lie beneath a mother's feet, meaning that you have to respect and love and care for your mother above all else, even above your father, which, honestly, is quite an interesting perspective the older I'm getting, since I would like for both parents to be respected equally."

I did not tell him about my Dad. I did not tell him that my Dad had betrayed my Mom.

"Which religion?" I asked. Mom would have liked to know.

"Islam."

"Moslem, right?"

"Muslim—Moose-Limb. Except the Moose is not so drawn out."

"Moo-slim."

"Good try," he said, smiling kindly.

"Are you Indian?" I squinted. "I love Indian food. Samosas are my thing."

"They're your thing?"

"I had a friend from India back in grade school. Radeeka's Mom would make these little samosas full of potatoes. My Mom said she'd never met a more well-mannered girl than Radeeka."

"It's pronounced Ra-dhi-kaa."

"She used to say Ra-dee-ka and I'm sure she knows how to pronounce her own name."

"Sure," he said, shrugging. "By the way, I'm not from India. I'm from Pakistan."

"Packistan?"

"Paaa-kiss-thaan. It's actually a country next to India. They used to be one."

"My mother's book club read a book set in India. A murder mystery in the Taj Mahal."

"Meh-hell."

"Maa-huhl. My Mom started her neighborhood book club. Books through which they could visit different countries. My Mom didn't like planes, but she wanted to travel. So this was her way." I was babbling. I didn't care. I didn't want to be alone. I pointed to the novel *Memoirs of a Geisha*, sitting on the pew beside me. "It was the latest book club pick. Japan. The book club continued without her. Did I mention she started it? I'm an only child."

He rubbed his thumbs together, as if in deep contemplation, then said, "Me too. Only child."

"Today I hate being an only child."

He sighed. "In an event like this, you're so alone with your memories that you feel as if memory is all, and yet is nothing at all."

"Yes," I said. "That's how I feel—memory is an anchor but it's also setting me adrift."

"Smoke?" He held a pack between his long fingers.

I looked around the chapel, sure we couldn't smoke in here.

"Under the circumstances," I said, lighting up, "my Mom would say, God won't mind."

I wasn't much of a smoker, but I hoped this smoke would calm me. Mom had never smoked. She walked an hour every day. She ate low-fat. She was healthy. The doctors had no idea why this had happened.

Shit happens, Dad said when he came to pick me up from the airport and we hugged each other, trying to get comfortable in the space of two where, previously, our hugs had been a triumvirate of him, me, Mom. Mom and I used to hug a lot, though. Mom was a hugger. She'd adjust my earrings and fix my hair even when nothing needed fixing or adjusting. Shit happens, Dad said. I'd smelled Bitch's drugstore perfume on him even then, but hadn't yet registered it for what it was.

A tear splotched my skirt.

"I don't even know why I'm crying," I said. "I've been preparing for this day ever since the coma."

"My mother passed away seven years ago. I still cry. Mothers die. We have that in common no matter where we are or who we are."

A drop of calm entered me at his reminder that I was not alone.

"How did your mother pass away?" I ashed into the paper cup he'd placed between us.

"Cancer. Aggressive." He took a long drag. The subsequent smoke clouded his face. "What was worse is that she forbade my father, my relatives from telling me she was dying. I'd come out here, to Denver, for college, and had recently graduated, taken a job that had begun sponsoring my green card.

Look," he said suddenly, squatting in front of me, his lovely eyes looking into mine. "I won't say I'm over my mother's passing or that you'll get over your mother's. All I'm saying is that you'll get through it. I can promise you that, okay, you'll get through it with time."

I dropped the cigarette butt into the cup of water, where it gave a last hiss before dying. "By the way"—I extended my hand—"I'm Michelle."

"Sulaiman."

His fingers were long and slim and warm, and I held on a moment longer than I should have just because this was the first person I'd told about Mom's death, and that made contact special. After a second, I let go.

"Nice to meet you, Sulemon."

"Sool-ai-maan."

"Sool-aye-man."

"Just call me Sully. No problem."

"Does it bother you having to change your name so it isn't mispronounced?"

"Bother no, feel sorry yes"—Sully paused, glancing at the altar—"because there are so many names Americans cannot pronounce."

We should have never met again, Sully and I, except that I'd left *Memoirs of a Geisha* in the chapel and the front page was inscribed with my name and address. Sully, being a conscientious individual, decided to return it, though it took him a month to arrive at Dad's house, where I'd moved in after Mom's coma.

"Thank you so much," I said. I'd been kicking myself at having lost the copy of the book that was the last link Mom and I would share.

"You're welcome." Sully handed me the book. "I would have come sooner but I resigned from my job and have been busy with interviews. I did get a chance to read it, though. I thought it was a true story of a geisha until I got to the end and realized it was fiction written by a white guy."

I hugged the book and invited Sully in.

"Arthur Golden must have done a ton of research," Sully said, as he followed me past the small drawing room and into the kitchen overlooking the den, "in order to channel a voice not of his own culture."

"I was more taken by the way he writes from a female perspective. I couldn't tell a guy had written it."

"I think culture is harder." He settled on a bar stool, his long legs dangling on either side, thighs spread wide.

"Anyone can study a culture." I offered him a soda. "But how do you get into the heart of the opposite gender?"

"I truly disagree." He opened the can.

"What if a Japanese male had written the novel?" I said. "It would still be a challenge to channel a woman!"

"Maybe more authentic, though?"

I squinted in confusion. "Isn't every voice authentic?"

Sully glanced at me, then busied himself by taking a sip. He looked taller, much taller than he had in the chapel that day, and he seemed to have gained a little bit of weight. It suited him. He had a slight stubble and a deeper tan and I couldn't help but think how exotic and handsome he looked here in Mom's kitchen, with its birch table and chairs and white linoleum counters flowing over with appliances, and the fridge whose door still held reminders of dates Mom had made: a mammogram appointment, a note to return Blockbuster films, the Book Club reading list a year old. I wouldn't let Dad take Mom's reminders off the fridge.

Although during my year at college I'd dated plenty, and during Mom's coma had hooked up with a guy here or there, I had not brought anyone home, and so, when Dad and Bitch stepped in with leftovers from their Saturday morning breakfast out, Dad looked at me quizzically as he politely shook Sully's hand. Bitch was beaming. As if this were some sign for her that I was getting over Mom. As if that meant I was one step closer to getting into her.

"We were about to leave," I said. To Sully's credit, he played along. He said goodbye to Dad and Bitch and we left the house.

"Sorry about that," I said to Sully in a low voice once we began walking down the drive and toward his car. "You can drop me off at a friend's house."

"Or"—Sully's sleek silver watch caught the sunshine—"would you like to have an early lunch?"

I nodded eagerly, a little too eagerly, I suppose, as I got into Sully's spacious car with temperature-controlled seats. His hair gleamed in the mid-morning sunshine. I wished I'd thought to let down my ponytail, change my T-shirt, put on some lip gloss. I glanced at him again. Angel-faced. There was no other word.

He moved a sheaf of printed papers with red pen scribbles all over them from the passenger seat to the back.

"Are you taking a class?" I asked.

"I'm a writer. In my spare time, I mean. It's a story I'm working on."

"Me too! I'm a writer too!"

When I was young, Mom enrolled me in a writing camp. It was free and she insisted. I had expected to hate it; instead I loved it and had been scribbling something or other since then. I told him that since Mom's coma, I'd filled enough journals to fill a landfill.

"I've published," he said. "A couple of things in journals back home. Short stories mainly."

"Cool." I glanced back at the papers.

"I'm actually working on a short story collection right now."

"What's it about?"

"This and that."

Though he didn't ask me what I might be working on, I told him I was working on a mother-daughter memoir.

"That's interesting."

Perhaps I imagined his indifferent tone. As soon as I said it, I wished I hadn't. It did sound awfully predictable. Even *this and that* seemed to have more gravitas.

"Maybe I will try my hand at a short story collection too," I said in a small voice.

"I dream of writing a novel someday," he said. "No. Scratch that. I *will* write a novel someday." He sounded so sure of himself. "I will write it. It will get published. It will do well. Very well."

I'd allowed Mom to read some of my scribbles and she'd said I had talent. She would have been thrilled if I'd told her I planned to write a novel, whether or not I planned for it to do very well. She would have been so proud of me. Perhaps it was time to get serious. About everything in my life. For starters, I needed to get away from Dad and Bitch.

Sully drove to a pub nearby. We ordered beers. I had not been out like this since Mom's passing, even though my best friend from high school, Erin, who was attending the community college in town, had been trying to get me to leave the house for some fun. But sometimes—often—being with Erin was hard. In the beginning I wanted to be with her because she may as well have been another daughter to Mom, but the fact was, Erin's Mom was vibrantly alive. But Sully and I had a motherless life in common.

Suddenly I was really hungry for the first time after a long time, and we ordered loaded nachos. Sully took out a pack of cigarettes and we lit up. I felt I owed Sully an explanation for the way I'd fled my house. I told him how Dad had decided, three months into Mom's coma, that she was never going to wake up and had begun to date Bitch. That's what I hated Dad for the most, not that he had fallen for someone else but because he made Mom dead even before she was dead.

"What about your Dad?" I asked. "Remarried?"

"No."

I felt a stab in my gut.

"My parents had a happy peaceful marriage, but my father says once is enough."

This time, a stab of joy. How good could a marriage have been if the relationship did not want to be repeated? An ache spread through me. Dad could not repeat what he had with Mom. He could not. Surely.

"What is your father's girlfriend's name?"

"Who cares?" I said.

"Your father cares," Sully said gently.

I ashed into the black plastic ashtray. "Nancy," I said softly. "Her name is Nancy. My mother's name is Sarah. She liked that she was named after the biblical Sarah, Abraham's wife, mother of Isaac and mother of our nation." A waiter came to replace our ashtray with a fresh one. "What's your mother's name?"

Sully glanced at me for a long second before replying. "Hajra."

"What does it mean?"

"Hajra was also Abraham's wife, and the mother of Ismail, and therefore also the mother of a nation."

"That was Hagar."

"In Islam, Hagar is Hajra and Abraham is Ibrahim."

"Oh my God." I stared at him. "That is so cool. Here we are, the descendants of two nations, on a journey to the same destination."

"And what's this destination?" Sully said.

"Happiness, I suppose," I said. "The pursuit of it."

"You are a romantic." Sully smiled tenderly. "Did you just think of your mother?"

"How did you know?"

"Your face," he said. "Breathe. Slow, deep breaths." He leaned over the table and squeezed my hands. "That's what my fiancée tells me to do."

It was the first time I noticed the gold band on his ring finger. It had to have always been there. Encircling his finger in a tight hold. I caught my breath as best as I could before I said,

"Congratulations."

"Thanks." He let go of my hands.

"What's her name?"

"Reema."

"Pretty name."

"Thanks."

"So." I stared at the refried beans. "How long have you been engaged?"

"Since the year I left for America. My mother was insistent. Apparently being engaged is supposed to save you from all the"—he made quotation marks—"bad American girls."

"Bad!"

Sully smiled. "You Americans need to stop exporting *Baywatch* and soap operas like *The Bold and the Beautiful*. In my country, if you don't know any better, that's what America is: one big orgy."

"You can't believe what you see on TV."

"But people do. Don't they?"

"Soaps are stupid anyway. And what idiot watches *Baywatch*?"

Sully shrugged. "My fiancée is addicted."

"Doesn't sound very bright." After a moment I said, "That was not nice. I'm sorry."

"Don't be," Sully said. "She's not very bright."

"Why did you fall in love, then?"

"Who said I fell in love?"

"She's...your fiancée."

"It's an arranged engagement. My mother's wish."

Sully glanced at his watch. He whistled. "It was great hanging out with you, Michelle, but I've got to get back home. I've got some people coming to look at my things in the morning."

"Your things?"

He rolled his eyes playfully. "I'm going to be driving to California. Bay Area. New job. Offer came yesterday. I was packing and wanted to get your book to you without any more delay."

"How long does it take to drive to California?"

"Three days or so."

"When are you leaving?"

"In a week."

So it's Tuesday morning. Bright, sunny, crisp. I pick Sully up. He takes a look at the large moving trailer attached to my used car and claps. I glance at his one bag and clap back. He wants to travel light, fine; I want to take my life along. Mom was part of that life and I wanted to leave behind nothing.

"Surprise," I had told him a few days ago, "I'm moving to California too."

"Crazy, crazy American woman!" Sully's face splintered into a big smile. He'd thought I was crazy enough to have asked him if I could come with him. Dad was severely unhappy at my plan to drive to California with Sully (*"Honey, you barely know the guy"*), but I wanted—needed—to get away from the constant reminder of Dad and Bitch. Dad's face tightened when I said this. Finally Dad made me promise that we would go in my car. Since Sully had been planning to sell his car in California anyway, he had instead sold it in Denver.

We stop for gas and munchies. I get cheese dip, ruffled potato chips, and a Dr. Pepper. Sully indulges in a carton of cigarettes and a bag of assorted mints. He insists on paying for everything. By the time we hit the interstate, the car is smelling minty clean.

"So, I've been meaning to ask you, where's the romance in an arranged marriage." I open up my ruffled potato chips and dill dip. "It's amazing to me how you're so comfortable spending your life with someone you don't love."

"Love is overrated."

"How can you say that?"

"I think compatibility is more important. I prefer *like* over *love*. In fact I respect like over love."

This upsets me. Dad had said something similar. *I loved your mother. I don't love Nancy. But I like her. I like her very much. Can you allow me that, Michelle?*

I turn up the radio dial and try to find a station, but there is nothing I like. I take a Tori Amos cassette out of my backpack and put it into the slot, settle back as the opening bars of a piano flood the car, and then sing along.

"You've got a nice voice," Sully says.

"Thanks." I turn the volume down. I can't stop myself from probing. "What's she like? Reema?"

"My Mom really loved her." Sully rolls the window down and lights a cigarette. The wind ruffles his hair. I hope my loose hair in all its mouse-brown glory is looking just as good windswept. I hope my tinted gloss has not come off.

"And you?"

"She's a kind girl. Doesn't yell at the servants. Doesn't like food going to waste. Doesn't like to see animals mistreated. She reads every book I recommend." He laughs. "Lately, she's recording her favorite passages on tape and mailing them to me. She's into baking. She's learning to bake an orange chiffon cake."

"A chef too? Wow!" It comes out derisively. I flush.

Sully smiles indulgently. "Why do you women always put each other down?"

"I'm not putting her down." I like that he defended her. I don't like that he defended her. "Actually," I say quietly, "she sounds awesome."

"What do you like in a guy?"

"Shit!" I say as we pass a dead, mangled animal in the road.

"Yeah?"

"No, I mean, did you see that roadkill? I couldn't even tell what it was."

Sully looks back for a moment but we've left it far behind, whichever creature had been lying there in the middle of the road, a fat, furry carcass, all jumbled up. Something about the animal, the way it just lay there, helpless, dead, beyond help, like in a coma, as others drove past going on with their lives. Just passing by.

"It just makes me so sad," I say. "A hit and run no one cares about."

"I read an article about taxidermists in L.A. collecting roadkill to be used for film props. Hopefully, it won't go to waste."

"Thanks," I say after a second. "That actually makes me feel better."

I don't tell him that I liked in a man what I'd seen in him: a reminder that even carcasses can be put to use, and so can glasses of water, and books, and writing-with-a-plan, and sewing himself, and his swan-wing fingers, his profile smooth curve after curve, not like some men with protruding foreheads, huge noses, or receding chins.

After the carcass we drive in silence, broken occasionally by a comment or two about how flat the landscape is. I wonder how much Sully would care if Reema died. Or would he just care because she was the girl his mother had chosen for him? For a second, I feel as if, in some weird way, Mom has chosen Sully for me because, had she not died, I might not have met him.

"Do you believe in fate?" I ask.

"Sure," he says. "According to my culture, one's birth, death, and apparently marriage are foreordained. The choices in-between are all free will."

"I can see birth and death, but marriage is totally free will."

"Not where I'm from." He grins.

We banter for a while and, in the pockets of silence, listen to Tori Amos until Sully switches off the tape and says he can't stand Amos's depression any longer. He replaces it with tape from a "back home" band. I listen to the pop melody, to the male singer's soft crooning, to the happy harmony. I pick up the plastic cassette cover: four guys wearing jeans and leather jackets.

"They're Pakistani?"

"Yup. Junaid. Shezad. Salman. Rohail."

"Don't ask me to pronounce their names." When Sully laughs appreciatively at my joke, I can't wait to tell Mom that a cute guy thinks I'm funny. I swallow my pain in my throat and say, "They're so handsome."

"Pakistani guys can be that."

I tap on one of the guys. "He looks white."

"Pakistanis come in all hues."

"So do Americans. We have that in common too. As well as being only children of mothers named after the mothers of nations. As well as mothers who are gone."

"We do. All of that."

I gaze at the cover. The group's name is Vital Signs. "How come they have an English name?"

"English is one of Pakistan's official languages. We used to be a British colony. Like you Americans."

"Oh." I like that this band has an English name even if they sing in Urdu. It is a comforting fusion, a cheerful reminder that languages can be learned and that the distances between people are only as vast as they want them to be.

"Reema loves them. She sent me this album."

I bite my thumbnail and draw blood. I look at the guys on the cover and wonder if they are also engaged to girls their mothers love but they themselves are not too sure of. The fact he shares more tongues with Reema than me upsets me. I wonder if being able to communicate in two languages strengthens or weakens a relationship.

"How come your English accent is so good?" I ask.

"It's an upper-class accent back home." Sully looks pained. "Also, if you wanted to make good with the British colonists, you learned English, but once the colonists left, the Pakistani upper classes continued to distinguish themselves with English and differentiate themselves from the hoi polloi through accents."

"Hoi polloi."

"We're a class-ridden country." Sully shrugs. "It works out for those from the right class."

"Such as yourself?"

"My family used to have money but now we're Broke Nawabs, meaning pedigree rich, but penny poor. That's why I'm here. To make my fortune. Before heading back. That's why I needed a green card."

We don't speak much for a while. I want to say that I don't care about accents or pedigrees or things like that. I wonder what a girl like Reema cares about?

After seven hours of nonstop driving, we stop at a Best Western.

"Two rooms, please," Sully says, smiling at the desk clerk, an elderly woman with a uni-brow. We grab burgers and fries from the diner next door, and return to eat them in Sully's room while we watch *The Newlywed Game*. Sully and I agree that the newlyweds do not know each other too well. He does not mention Reema. Neither do I. On TV the host is asking a husband if he's ever let his wife pick up the tab when they were dating. He says, No, but he wouldn't have minded it once in a while. The audience bursts into laughter.

"It's really unfair for guys to have to pay all the time," I say.

"It's custom," Sully says. "Back home, women are not expected to pay even if they can pay."

"And what if the guy can't pay?"

"Loser."

"That's harsh."

Sully flinches and gives a grim smile. "There's winners. There's losers. That's life, baby. Life is unfair."

"Life's a bitch." My eyes fill up. "I don't want life to be a bitch."

Sully scoots over to me and takes my hand. I lay my head on his shoulder and he strokes my hair. I shut my eyes. When I open them next, Sully is curled up on the couch, his head in my lap. I rise gently and drag the quilt off the bed and put it over him. I turn off the lights and, in the sliver of moon from the window, he looks truly angelic. I leave his room and enter mine.

We breakfast on burgers at the diner because Sully says it might be the rule but it is not the law in America that breakfast has to be cereal or eggs. I'm up for adventure so okay, I order a burger, but also coffee and pancakes. I go to the pay phone to make a quick phone call to Dad to let him know I'm still alive. I call Erin and tell her that Sully is *the one*. She sighs and reminds me that in *Not Without My Daughter*, Sally Field's character also fell for a Middle Eastern *the one* and if I could please remember the kidnapping etc. that followed. He's not Middle Eastern, I say, he's South Asian. She says, same difference, and I tell her that that's like saying the crazy white husband from *Sleeping with the Enemy* is every white guy. She tells me not to be dumb. *You* don't be dumb, I say. Old friends can be a problem, I think as I hang up.

When the check comes, I grab it and say it's on me. Sully tries to argue about why he cannot let that be. Suddenly I'm begging to be allowed to pay, "Please, please," and he frowns as he gives me permission, adding benevolently, that he's only going to indulge me this one time. As I begin to calculate the exact tip, Sully takes out a wad of dollars and plonks them on the table.

"Tip is on me," he says.

"But that's way too much," I say.

"I can afford it."

"That's not the point."

"It is for me. These people work hard. A few extra dollars won't kill me."

My heart swells until I can barely contain it. I want to lean over and kiss him to death. But I'm shy, and then there's the small matter of the ring on his finger. As we leave the diner for the parking lot, Sully adds,

"And also I might be the only brown person the waitress ever waits on, and so I must leave a good impression." He holds the car door open for me. "We are nothing if not mini-cultural ambassadors 24/7."

I climb into the passenger seat, my heart deflating a little at this premeditated national narrative-building.

Sully gets into the car behind the wheel. I twine my hands around the headrest, yawn and stretch. He whistles, looking at my straining shirt and denim skirt riding up over the tan lines on my thighs.

"Hey," I say, whacking him on his upper arm. "What would Reema say!"

"That I'm engaged to her but not blind. Anyway, what she doesn't know won't hurt her. Ignorance is bliss."

I whack him again, allowing my fingers to caress his forearm for a moment too long, and think that what he's saying is right: Ms. Reema won't know. Ignorance *is* bliss. Immediately I feel sick. Mom was ignorant the whole time about Dad's newfound bliss. I clasp my hands in my lap.

Sully switches Vital Signs on again.

"Hey," I say as a song comes on, "is that 'Red Red Wine'? My parents loved the UB40 song and this tune is identical."

"Homage."

"Is that authentic?" I tease him.

"Isn't every homage authentic?" He winks back.

I start belting out the original song until this one is drowned out. I'm swaying from side to side. I look heavenwards and know that if Mom is looking down at me, she's happy. A car passes by and honks at us. The family inside waves to me. I wave back as if waving is going out of style. I'm feeling happy. Restless, but happy.

"Have you always been so uninhibited?" Sully's voice is pinched.

"Have you always had a stick up your ass?" I ask.

Sully flushes. "I was giving you a compliment."

"It didn't sound like one." After I second, "So Reema would not sing out loud?"

"Reema is so demure I'm going to ravish her behind and she won't know why the hell she's not getting pregnant."

"Sully!" I punch his arm. "That is *so* rude."

But he's laughing and I laugh too because of course he's joking, joking about demure being so important, and behinds, and all the American girls, two a week if possible, he's going to have sunny side up. But between the laughter there's a savageness that speaks of a fiancée being blind and deaf because what she can't see or isn't told never happened.

"You're not very demure," I say, "are you?"

"I'm a man." He grunts like a caveman.

We're still laughing when we enter Utah. Still laughing when flatlands turn greener and greener and the bushes turn into trees, laughing when we stop at a gas station to use the unisex restroom, separately, the seat piss-splattered, despite a urinal, and stinking. Laughing as he buys turkey-cheddar sandwiches for us, laughing, coming out to the car surrounded by seagulls, five, ten, fifteen large creatures pecking the tarmac, the others swooping so close they could land on my hair. Shrieking, I rush into the car, glad the windows are up, and, for a second imagine myself a damsel in distress and Sully a gallant prince.

"See," Sully says through the crack in the window, "you are demure after all, just like a girl should be."

"Oh fuck you," I say. "I just happened to have watched this film called *The Birds* at an age I should not have watched it."

"That was a horror film. This is life, and they just want to be fed."

He walks amidst them boldly. I think of Mom lying in that hospital bed on linen we'd brought her from home, a fusion of who she once was and who she had become in sickness and in health, and before I surrender to a full-blown panic attack, I open the car door and walk tall among the birds.

Sully grabs me and twirls me round and round and round and the gulls flap faster and faster.

I caress his lips. I hadn't planned to. Or maybe I had. He does not push me away. His lips stay against my fingers. The gulls begin to take flight, a great flutter as if they are late to another party. We break free. But I can feel the press of his lips and I know that he can feel the press of my fingertips, and I know something unspoken has been understood.

We laugh and get back into the car and we laugh some more. We are still laughing when we get to Salt Lake City. Laughing as we drive on sprawling spider leg flyovers and guess which exit to take. Laughing when we take a wrong one and laughing when we take the right one and get to Holiday Inn.

We park, enter the lobby, there are rooms available, Sully asks for one room, and we laugh. We are giddy over nothing in particular and everything in general, over demure and bold and everything in between, but when we get to the room the curtains are drawn and the bed beckons. For a second I feel bad for a fiancée waiting for orange chiffon cakes to rise, and then decide that she's not my problem, she's his, and that I can take her place and, because I won't be busy baking, will make sure no one takes mine. We find ourselves naked, on the bed, in it, off it, back on, and now he's on, I'm off, my knees pinned against the rough carpet and when I look up for a moment, in the mirror adjacent to us, I see Sully's head cradled in his hands, eyes shut, mouth pursed, and I finish it off, *swallow, swallow,* he orders, and so I do, and then come up and say, "My turn," and sit up, brusquely, when he says, "No, no, I can't do that."

And he doesn't. He gags at the thought of it.

"I know it's not fair," he says. "I know and I'm sorry. It's just so... unclean."

"Then why did you let me? You told me to swallow."

He looks at me as if that was my choice, which it was, I suppose, but then I'd thought he was going to reciprocate like every other guy I'd been with. Sully looks at me as if that's what I get for being uninhibited, for not being demure, or maybe I'm reading too much into this thick shame that is welling up in my throat.

"I didn't think you'd expect me to reciprocate," he says.

"Why would you think that?"

"No one else has ever expected me to," he says.

"Well you lucked out, then. What if your wife expects you to?"

"She won't."

"You don't know that for sure."

"She won't," he repeats, "but if she does, and I have to, well then I will."

I stare at him.

"I'm really sorry."

His angel face looks genuinely apologetic. So he's never gone down before. Not a crime. And there's time to change that. I start to laugh.

"Don't laugh at me," he snaps.

"I'm not laughing *at* you!" I lean over to kiss him.

He rears back. "Um, can you wash your mouth first?"

The shame I'd thought was gone comes back in a great spurt. I can understand that he might be hesitant about oral sex, but kissing me? I feel so dirty.

"You might not have commanded me to give you a blow job—"

He flinches.

"—but you *did* tell me to swallow. It's you in my mouth, asshole, and now you can't kiss me."

When I leave to get a different room, he doesn't follow.

The next morning we drive out of Utah with the radio on at the first audible frequency. The DJ is announcing a contest to win free Bette Midler concert tickets. It's my day to drive and I drive upon a straight highway with a lake on both sides, which increasingly becomes whiter and whiter until finally the lakes are nothing but vast stretches of salt, which I'd swear was snow if I didn't know better.

"I am really sorry," Sully says. His arms are crossed, his hands tucked into his armpits. He looks tired. As if he hasn't slept. "What can I do to make up?"

I don't answer him. I've never felt so *used* before, but I'm not sure why I'm feeling this way. The radio station is coming on garbled. I turn it off. Sully turns on his tape. "Red Red Wine" spills throughout the car. Today it's not sounding so hot. Today the band does not sound like the epitome of fusion but like copycats. My chest begins to hurt. What am I going to do in San Fran? What sort of an idiot was I to have packed up with no planning? Why had I thought I had the goods to make Sully fall in *like* with me? When the hell had like become more important than love? Was I insane? Was I just a crazy American?

I switch off Vital Signs, eject the cassette, and toss it into the back seat. Sully sighs.

I want silence. I want peace. I want my Mom.

When we get to Reno I ask for separate rooms but it is Sully who shakes his head, says, "Just wait," and as soon as we enter the suite in La Quinta Inn, tumbles me onto the queen-size bed.

"Are you sure?" His ferocity alarms me. "Are you sure?"

Without an answer he dives down; he's clueless. Twice he gags, but before I can say anything he takes a deep breath and is back to jabbing away. I'm getting a bit sore. I wonder if helping him out would be the complete opposite of demure. His fingers uselessly clutch the beige bedspread on either side of me.

I grimace and wait, because of course he'll get better. He's a novice and there is no such thing as a natural. But for now I fake and do a great job because he comes up beaming, gasping for air, and I lean over to kiss him, to let him know I appreciate what he's done. He shoves me aside and hurtles into the bathroom and I can hear him gargle. He gargles for a while.

When he comes out, we share a cigarette. I keep smiling and he keeps saying, "What? What?" and not looking me in the eye. After the smoke, I spread him out on the bed. I'm sitting on top of him, stretching, triumphant, my fingers locked, arms thrown back, proud, arching my lower back, breasts, and belly button—one smart, continuous treble clef.

"I thought you were only going to do that with your wife," I say.

He says, quite matter of fact, "I was practicing."

I lower my arms, slide off him, try to still my trembling. It stings— *practice*. It stings. I. Am. A. Cheap. Trashy. Whore. For. Someone. Who. Will. Marry. A. Virgin. And. Do. Her. Backside. Until. He. Decides. To. Flip. Her. Over.

"Hey," Sully says, sitting up on one elbow, "what's wrong? I was just kidding."

I bury my head in my knees.

"Wasn't I any good?" Sully says. "Is that it?"

I look up. It comes out, moments later, because I can't keep it in, no matter how humiliating. "I didn't like being *practiced* upon."

"I told you I was kidding."

"*You* were playing mind games. *You* were being a jerk."

Sully stares at me. He lights a cigarette and smokes it silently. When he's done, he sticks the butt in a Dr. Pepper can. The room smells of wet smoke, a maggot-infested carcass slowly burning.

"*You* were playing mind games, Michelle, when you taunted me about only doing it with my wife."

Now I stare at him.

"We're supposed to be having fun, right?" Sully waves at the motel room. In the dim lamplight his fingers look like old, discolored wooden chopsticks. "This is hardly love."

"Believe me," I say, my heart constricting, "I would not fall in love with you even if you paid me. I might be just a practice session for you and Orange Chiffon the real deal, but you don't have to tell me that. You don't have to call a fuck a fuck."

"It's not just…a fuck. We're friends."

Friends. I wish he'd said that I was the real deal and that Orange Chiffon would have to go. I wish he wasn't so handsome. I wish he'd stop smiling like that. I wish I didn't feel trapped between languages that I could understand one minute but were undecipherable the next. Like. Love. Weren't they supposed to be the same thing? Mom would have translated for me. Mom would have picked the alphabets apart. Mom would have restored a word order that made sense.

In Reno and not going to a casino. I feign sleep while Sully gets ready for a night on the town and leaves. I go to the in-room phone to call Dad. There's a small black address book lying face down by the phone. I turn it around. It is open to R. An international area code followed by her number. What sort of a man does not remember his fiancée's telephone number by heart? When did he call her? While I was taking a shower? What did he say to her? I wonder what language they'd spoken in. English. The language they took for their own, although if they were going to malign colonists, shouldn't the language have been the first thing gone? Hypocrites. I rip out the page. I decide not to call Dad. I talk to God. I talk to Mom for much longer. For the first time, I'm relieved she's gone so she will never know how disappointed I am in myself.

I despise Sully for making me glad that she's gone.

I want to get a separate room—this room doesn't even have a couch—but there is a Bette Midler concert going on and, apparently, we are lucky to get any room at all.

When Sully comes back from his night on the town, I am watching a *Beverly Hills 90210* rerun. He crawls in next to me, and when his fingers creep up my knee I stiffen, swat them away, and turn my back to him. What does he know about me: that I like cheese dip with ruffled potato chips, that I only drink Dr. Pepper, that my mother is dead, that my father had an affair. What do I know about him: nothing I care to recall.

Sully's voice cuts through my thoughts. "Do you mind if I change the channel?"

I don't answer. After a second, he flips through channels, finally settling on Leno. I hear Leno taking digs at Kevin Eubanks, mocking Donald Trump, and then making a fool out of a couple in the audience on account of them dressed in identical overalls, T-shirts, and hats. Sully's tickled. The bed's shaking. He's laughing like his life depends on it. He's laughing and I wish we'd respect ourselves, us Americans—all of us and each other—and quit thinking that pointing out our mistakes is healthy and will endear us to the world, because here is this man come for an American education and planning to stay for an American job and making room in his plans to fuck an American girl or two pér week, but first confuse her about demure or no demure, confuse this naïve American who thinks she's bold and brave and going about the world on her own terms.

When I leave, he's in deep sleep, his eyelids jerking in the way that used to scare the life out of me when I was a kid. I leave between the middle of the night and the early morning. I wonder what he'll think with me gone, my car gone, and I hope he knows that this is me screwing him up his butt. I leave the check for the room to him. He'll appreciate that.

⚜

I returned to Denver. Dad couldn't get out of me what had happened, and neither could Nancy. When I told Erin, I could see she was longing to say "I told you so," but she settled for reminding me that she knew he wasn't *the one*. After a month of feeling like misery, I returned to college and to my life pre-Mom as best I could. Those two days I'd spent with Sully seemed unreal at times, but at other times, when I saw an angel face around campus, or passed by an international student with their similar clipped English accent, those two days would became all too real. I thought about him often those first few days, weeks, months, and it kept coming down to "practice, practice, practice."

I called Reema one day. I surprised myself. Just fished out the scrap of paper from my bag and dialed.

"Hello?"

"Is this Reema?"

"Speaking."

Her voice was nothing special.

"Who is this?" she asked.

Who was I?

"This is the girl that…umm, look I just wanted to tell you, one woman to another, that your fiancé, Sully, Soolaimon, he's—he's cheating on you."

There's a sharp intake of breath.

"Who is this? How do you know this? Why are you calling me?"

"We drove to California together. We had sex."

I felt like shit but also relieved to have done the right thing.

"Why are you calling me?"

"Excuse me?" I said.

"You had sex with Sully. So what? That's what men do with girls they are not going to marry. Girls they marry, they respect too much to treat this way."

In her elite accent she sounded like an expert on BBC explaining some universal truth that had escaped me, or perhaps she was reminding herself.

"I expected as much when he left for America. But once we are married, the leash is no longer loose and it will be a different story. And listen, don't dare call me again, bitch."

Then she hung up on me. *Bitch*. I hung my head in shame.

I tore up the paper with her phone number lest temptation to get the last word, the last hang-up, proved too much. There was only so much humiliation I could take. *Practice Respect Bitch* began to go hand-in-hand. Both man and woman had left me tongue-tied. I should never have called her. I did not tell Erin. I knew what she would say. She would say I'd been trying to be a bitch and Reema had out-bitched me. She would say I was a cheater, in my own right. She would also say it was a bad episode but not the end of the world.

I told the therapist I was seeing that it was more than the end of the world. It was as if I were trapped in a never-ending conversation I hadn't known I was having, in a language I could not speak. I began to frequent ethnic restaurants, engaging with the wait staff in order to hear non-English speakers speak English the way, according to me, they should: halting and with risible accents. I would always leave a massive tip so they would know exactly how benevolent an American could be. It took me forever before I could listen to Tori again. I chose not to sing along. I asked the therapist to decode what world Reema was living in and what world I was living in and whether I was the bitch or she was the bitch. The therapist told me to push these matters into a cabinet, right into a corner at the back, and move forward, onward, to let go.

I tried.

One day, as I was browsing through a new stock of journals at the bookstore, I came across an anthology someone had discarded atop the leather-covered red journals. *Stories in the Stepmother Tongue*. I turned the book around and spoke the contributors' names to myself, not caring if I bungled them. There was no one to reprimand me. To correct me. To laugh at me. To frown at me. I could pronounce them as I pleased in whichever accent I pleased. And I did:

Alvarez. Codrescu. Cofer. Danticat. Duarte.
Ho. Jin. Lam. Lim.
Manrique. Mukherjee.
Ortiz. Palkeel. Rachlin. Uchido. Upadhyay.

I bought the book. I read it slowly over the next many weeks, a sentence here, a paragraph there, coming to the end of one story, beginning the next, reading again and again the notes the writers had written about their relationship with the English language, how they learned it, why they learned, why it was a good and valid language to know.

I felt as if Mom had somehow guided this book to end up in the wrong place in the bookstore just so that I would find it. Mom had translated for me. She had picked the alphabets apart. In restoring a word order that made sense, my mother was trying to restore me to myself.

I reread *Memoirs of a Geisha*, pushing through, not letting any memory mar the pages, and slowly, slowly, the bruise of *practice respect bitch* began to fade like all insults, hurts, wounds do—slowly, slowy, slowly.

I started to read foreign voices, foreign stories, until I started to lose interest in them because they began to sound, simply, humans stuck in the same old bullshit, merely in another place. Alvarez to Upadhyay. So ordinary.

By the time I graduated and began working in dental insurance and, two years later, met Daniel, a dentist, Sully was barely a story I cared to tell anyone, except that I did tell Daniel, and afterwards, he told me how he was going to kick the shit out of the road trip asshole if he ever got his hands on him. Mom would have liked Daniel. He was angel-faced enough, and gave me hugs that I sank into. He thought I was pretty beautiful too and he was forever telling me, in his corn-fed accent, that he loved me.

Daniel and I married one autumn day. Once our twin daughters came along, a couple of years later, we decided that we were the sort of parents who wanted one parent to be at home. Daniel's dental practice took off. Ten years later, I was a full-time Mom who shopped at farmers' markets, lunched at the club, and indulged our Dalmatian, Bundt, with long hikes in hilly parks. I do write, yes, I contribute regularly to our community newsletter, usually about the benefits of keeping a journal, and I had a story about a lost dog published in the *Four Walls*, a journal that sent me one complimentary copy. And then there was my writing group. I was the member of a close-knit writers' group, and we'd been meeting at a Tattered Cover bookstore every Sunday evening for the past ten years.

This Sunday night, after workshop was over, we lingered over our goodbyes until finally, one of us broke free and headed toward the doors. I was on my way out of the giant independent bookstore when I saw the poster. There was no trick of the light upon the eye. I recognized him. And—how could I have missed it—his novel was stacked in a tower as tall as me. I stared at it. It was like going on a perfectly normal journey, only to run over an animal going on its way, too, and then leaving it there.

It took me a while, but finally I snatched up a copy. The title: *Crazy*. The cover: nighttime, a motel, a car with a trailer. A very important author had blurbed that Sully's novel was the "most important debut of the year."

The most important debut of the year was about a female foreign student from Pakistan and a white guy, their chance meeting that leads to a cross-country trip, and love—or something like it—and hate too, definitely hate.

My chest constricted. My novel was about a guy who leaves a girl asleep and car-less in a motel after she inadvertently says something terribly offensive to him, but here was my book, my idea, *my life* stolen right from under me, and I was still incomplete and he was all done.

When I returned home, the twins were in their pajamas and, though they should have been in bed, they were still watching TV with Daniel's arms around them. I yelled at the girls. I yelled at Daniel. I would have yelled anyway at this laxity of bedtime rules, Sully's novel or no Sully's novel. Once the girls had escaped upstairs and banged their door shut, Daniel turned to me with a concerned look.

"What's wrong?" he asked. "Bad workshop?"

"No. Nothing."

I accepted the glass of wine Daniel handed me as we snuggled on the oversized couch to watch *ER*. Then there was always sex on Sunday night to keep ignited the eternal flame as well as combat Monday blues. This Sunday night, though, I was not the wonder woman I usually was in bed and, after faking, I stared up at the ceiling while Daniel snored away. The fact was, nothing had made me feel guiltier than the fact that I'd told Sully that I hated

Dad. I felt that in confessing to Sully, I had somehow betrayed Dad, because the fact also was that I had not hated my Dad at all. I had been angry and disappointed, and anger and disappointment are not hate. There Sully had been loving his father no matter how much sex the man had, while there I'd been maligning my father when all he'd wanted was a person to hold because Mom had held him so well. I imagined Sully's reading the next evening. At the podium. The audience filling row upon row of foldable chairs. The congratulations. The clapping. I jumped out of bed. I was not going to let his life derail my life.

Mom, I called out, help me. Daniel turned in his sleep and hugged me.

It took me a while to decide what to wear. Daniel was not thrilled about me going out two nights in a row, but I told him this was important. This was the guy I'd gone on that road trip with twenty years ago.

"*Road trip asshole?*" Daniel said.

I nodded.

"I'm coming too."

I said yes, then no, then yes, and then finally settled on no. I wanted to face this alone. Daniel kissed me and held me close and told me to take my time with whatever it was I needed to do. I left home knowing that pizza was going to be ordered yet again and that the twins would not keep their bedtime and that I'd return to find Daniel and the girls dozing in front of the TV. It didn't matter. Sometimes predictable was good. Sometimes predictable was preferable. Sometimes, predictable was another word for happy.

When I got to the Tattered Cover I loitered in the car, pretending to fix my lipstick. Last time I ran away from Sully and eventually from life as I'd envisioned it, I'd turned into a runaway truck up a dead-end ramp, at an incomplete stop. But the past cannot be tucked into a cabinet behind the files of one's present. A snide remark, a betrayal, a mistake, an unrequited love, an insult: these are the one-night stands that can determine the future of the rest of our nights.

I reached for his novel. He had dedicated it to his mother: *To my late mother, who always put my well-being before hers.* I turned to the bio. He had been to Bread Loaf. He had studied with hotshots. He had won grants and fellowships. I had applied to all these and been turned down. The last line said that he lived with his wife, the acclaimed poet Rebecca Adelgren, and their two sons in Lahore, Pakistan. I blinked. Rebecca. No matter which accent

I employed, I could not translate-interpret-transcribe-twist-or-turn Reema into Rebecca or Rebecca into Reema. I flipped to the acknowledgments: Rebecca Adelgren. Their sons' names were Adam and Harris. Then I saw the next sentence, as if it were seeking out my eyes: *To hotel rooms and crazy Americans.*

For a moment I returned to the suffocating expanse of a car, to sun streaming in through the windows, to flatlands, to music keeping us busy, even as Sully tells me about the real cost of his green card. I return to a glass of water, to being twirled round in a storm of gulls, to having my hand held, to a guarantee that it was just a matter of time and I would survive my mother's death. And then I was hurt. I was humiliated. I had thought we were equals. But I saw now that it was not race but an even older division that had come between us: man-woman.

I stood at the back of the bookstore, half hidden in the crowd of people come to hear his talk. I had not seen him for the last twenty years, and the last time I had, I'd fled. He had stolen my story. There was that. But that wasn't the only theft. I'd stolen from him too. It was his story too. Our story. His. Mine. I looked at him closely and I saw that the man whose angel-faced beauty had devastated me two decades ago was now just a short, skinny, half-balding guy. He was not the devil. There was nothing to be scared of. I straightened my shoulders. I took a breath. I took a deep, deep breath. When Sully began to read, I shut my eyes and I concentrated on his accent. Ordinary, really, and extraordinary, the descendants of two nations on a journey to the same destination, the place between like and love.

# The Star of the North

## Cathleen Calbert

———◦✦◦———

W hat would happen," I mused aloud.

"God," my husband said.

Simon hated *What Would Happen*. I think he feared this game would incriminate him for fantasized infidelities. Actually, I'd only gone that route a few times. *What would happen if you ran into your old girlfriend? What if you ran into her and I were dead? What if I'd never been born?* I also had asked him to consider the consequences of avalanches and wind tunnels, cliffs and broken legs. I don't know why I worried then about disasters and their aftermath. When an earthquake rolled me out of bed as a child, I loved the surprise of it, the promise of something different.

"What if I put my bare foot in the snow at fifteen below?" I said, gazing at the crooked Christmas tree as I waited for Simon to quit tapping his keyboard. Rows of lit red peppers and green cows encircled the tree, which wouldn't stand up straight. Still, the red and green looked festive. Watching my neighbors, I'd figured out that you had to have something bright and cheerful to look at once the snow descended. Strings of white lights framed the windows and circled the shrubs of the bungalows surrounding our flat. Inside, lamps glowed pink, gold, or yellow, as if staying inside were a matter of choice, as if doing so had nothing to do with the car not turning over and the garage door no longer opening.

"Why wouldn't you have your boots on?" Simon said, finally.

"What if I got locked out of the house without any clothes?"

"Why wouldn't you have clothes on?"

That's how Simon always responded to *What Would Happen*. He'd point out that his ex-fiancée was happily married and probably inclined to remain so whether I lived or died and that I never went camping so was not likely to backpack twenty miles into Yosemite, lose both contacts and glasses, then have to be led back to civilization *virtually blind*.

"Well." I drew out the word. "What do you think would happen if we threw boiling water into the air *right now*? Would it actually turn into snow?" The six o'clock news had highlighted such tricks: how you could use a frozen banana as a hammer, crack an egg onto the icy sidewalk and see it petrify, create your own snowfall at home.

That got the laptop off his crotch and Simon off the couch. When not at the college, he lived on that couch, his long legs taking over the striped pillows, his eyes on the computer screen. But I'd managed to pique his interest: he wanted to make snow. We both watched the pot of water come to a boil as if waiting for a mother's homemade pudding. Together, we trotted down the stairs to carry out our experiment. Cringing, Simon swung the pot upward. Hot water shot out and came down as a miniature snow shower.

"Wow," we both said.

"I can't believe I live here," I stuttered because my lips had frozen.

"Here" was St. Paul, where people were nicer and taller and grayer than in San Francisco. Whenever I mentioned that we'd come from California, I received a thoughtful wrinkling of the Minnesotan brow. I saw longing in people's faces as well as concern, which I took to mean that they wondered two things: Was I a crazy Californian? Did I look down on them? St. Paulies are touchy about the film *Fargo*, the lilt of their accents, and the fact that they live in the middle of the country. They're protective of the bland Canadian Walleye that shows up on every restaurant menu, even Mexican or Thai, and defensive about F. Scott Fitzgerald, who hated this city.

Personally, I was happy to come to St. Paul, to try somewhere different, and amused to be a "faculty wife," which conjured images to me of 1950s martinis and homemade sugar cookies, of sherry and cubes of cheese at the dean's. I pictured myself wearing a frilly apron over gold lamé. Simon and I did go to an opening reception at the Chair's house, all walnut wood and leather books, where we were plied with sweet wine along with an array of local cheeses, but no one seemed to regard the party as ironic or to understand that I was only playing the role of faculty wife.

"Yep, I'm at home, making curtains and babies," I told one of Simon's new colleagues, a man who looked like a shy but smiling Freud.

Simon broke in, "Laura's an artist. She's had several shows in the Bay Area."

"You must meet some of the other spouses, Laura," Freud said, still smiling benignly as if Simon had commented on my collection of commemorative spoons. "Everyone's done such interesting things." He left it at that. Simon and I left the party early.

Throughout the fall, which was brisk and fresh and not frightening, I tried to think of myself as an artist even though I wasn't making any art. I was an artist taking in the Walker, an artist taking a walk, an artist gazing up at the clouds passing over Summit Avenue—for several hours at a stretch. But I never opened up a sketchbook.

"I'm absorbing," I told Simon over watery Indian takeout. "This afternoon I went to Camp Snoopy. At the Mall of America. It's the largest mall in the country."

"Is that right," Simon said, a model of neutrality.

This was the sort of conversation we'd begun having over dinner.

Then winter hit.

The screen went red on the weather channel. *Winter Warning Advisory. Winter Storm Watch. Snow Alert. Snow Emergency.* We received automated phone calls telling us to stay off the roads. You'd think Minnesotans would be unfazed by heavy snowfalls, yet they didn't take winter lightly. The schedule for contra dancing at the college remained constant, and new posters went up advertising "curling," which involved ice and brooms. But my neighbors also bought enormous bottles of water and snowblowers as loud as Volkswagens. They had deerskin gloves, and thick, knitted hats that they wore under the hoods of their down parkas. Even our apartment stood at the ready, with eight coat hooks in the front hall and six in the stairwell.

In response to the concern expressed by our adopted town and rented digs, I stopped wandering haphazardly around town and concentrated on the inside of the apartment. We squeezed our queen-sized bed into the second bedroom, and I made the master bedroom my studio. Simon encouraged me to do so, shrugging his husbandly shoulders over the sacrifice, but I felt as though I'd accepted a bribe. He was busy professing—grading, meeting students, meeting colleagues, meeting students, grading—and wanted his wife to occupy herself in some way that didn't intrude on any of this. At least, that's how it seemed to me.

When I met him, I found Simon unusually beautiful—his skin a rich olive, his hair the color of chocolate—and dreamy for a historian. Everyone connected to the College of Arts and Crafts thought of grad students at Cal as stiffs, little better than the business majors down at Stanford. Yet Simon spent whole mornings at Mama's Royal Café in North Oakland, an open book before his faraway eyes. I had to pass by his table several times before I got his attention.

After we hooked up, he still spent mornings at Mama's, watching me contentedly over cups of heart-jolting coffee. He finished his program on time even though he leisurely picked out coffee beans with me at Peets, picked out tomatoes with me at the farmers' market, and fell in love with me. But in his first year as a Visiting Assistant Professor, he developed a ferocious energy, devoting himself to the job as if he never had wanted to do anything else.

Once I commandeered our bedroom, I also felt compelled to do something. At first, I considered giving the walls a fresh coat of lemon cream, but that smacked too much of feminine nesting. Carefully, I prepared six square canvases instead.

Then Simon surprised me, whirling me into a kiss. "There's my girl," he said.

I laughed, spinning free. "Don't you have a class?"

"Yep, I've only got a minute, but I wanted to tell you, I talked to my Chair," he said breathlessly. "The department just got approval for this line to become tenure-track."

"Tenure-track," I repeated after him. I thought of a long line of railroad tracks. Johnny Cash echoed in my head, "Folsom Prison Blues" and a train coming 'round the bend. "As in permanent?"

"As in, it could be permanent in seven years."

"Seven years?"

Simon furrowed his brow. "Why are you repeating everything I say, Laura? That's what my students do when they don't know the answer to something."

"I'm not your fucking student," I said, reaching for my coat.

"Sweetie, stop. What's up?"

At that, I whirled to face him. "What happened to 'We'll be academic nomads'?"

"Well, now I could have a job for life."

"Who wants a job for life!"

For a minute, we stared at each other. Then I ran down the stairs and slammed the door behind me.

The following morning, Simon and I drank our coffee separately, but he kissed me before he left for the college.

That day, I painted white on white, white with a shading of blue, with a shading of gray, more white. I did a whole series of these as snow fell steadily outside our windows.

"What do you think?" I asked Simon as soon as he came home.

He blinked at me as though trying to adjust his focus, then turned to the paintings. "They're nice, Laura," he said. "Maybe they could use something... but what do I know. You're the artist."

After Simon left for his Pagans and Christians class, *You're the artist* stayed with me as I rinsed brushes, as I did the dishes, as I scoured pans. His comment didn't sound like an acknowledgment so much as an accusation. *You're the artist.*

I was an artist when I met him in San Francisco. Passionate. Unpredictable. I could laze with my lover the whole of a morning, then stay up all night, painting like mad, my clothes flecked with color, music crashing off the walls. But since we'd come to the "Star of the North," I had only done those six white squares in the living room. What if I weren't an artist anymore? Would that make me a bona fide faculty wife? Did all faculty wives imagine they were artistic in some way? *Doing lots of interesting things.*

By the time I clanked the last pot into its cupboard below the kitchen sink, I felt ready to jump out of my skin, so I put on Green Day and let their fast beat bounce off the walls. Then I unrolled all my tampons, and stuck each one into the thick, wet paint on White Painting #6. Afterwards, I added gashes of red. The tampons formed a halo in the middle of the painting, and the red cheered me up.

"Is it some sort of feminist statement?" Flicking snowflakes from his nose, Simon stood in front of my areole.

"It's the sun," I told him. "The sun above an uninhabitable tundra."

Maybe I had a moment of prescience, because I wouldn't be needing those tampons for a while. Mid-December, I took myself out to breakfast at the Coffee News and slipped runny eggs down my throat as I perused classifieds in the local alternative paper. Those ads cracked me up: the man looking for a lactating woman, the man who called himself "an anal-yst," the woman in need of a golden shower. They made me happy to be with Simon instead of dating someone new, someone who might want to pee on me. They also unveiled another side of the granola intellectuals and orange-clad huntsmen: lonely souls in the market for spankings and diaper-changes.

Wrapping my scarf over my mouth, I trudged back to the apartment, only a five-minute walk. By the time I got inside, my face had numbed and the earrings I'd stupidly put on made my head ring. As I struggled out of my boots, coat, hat, and gloves, dripping water in the entryway, a wave of sickness rolled over me. I threw up on the floor of the bathroom before I could raise the toilet seat.

This was what we wanted.

It made sense, we had said on the drive east. Both of us through with school. Simon with a job and insurance for the year. Besides, we said. Making a baby might take a while. Some of our friends had had unreproductive sex for years. Couples we knew, straight and gay, struggled with their bodies and the bureaucracy of babies. But when winter descended, Simon's sperm must have gotten moving, despite the constant baking of them with his laptop. Or my egg had frozen in place.

The afternoon after I spewed Coffee News eggs all over the bathroom, I took half a dozen pregnancy tests. First, I watched for a red line, and my urine magically conjured a red line. I knew I was pregnant then, but I couldn't resist trying the rest. They rewarded me with pink stains, blue squares, and purple triangles. I painted the wands onto a new canvas, creating another halo. Apparently, all I could come up with was circles.

"Great," Simon said when I told him the news that night. *Great.* As if I said I'd ordered Chinese and he was eyeing the moo-shoo chicken. He sounded pleased but not surprised—as though he had gotten exactly what he'd ordered. Wangled a job for life, check. Knocked up the wife, check. After a few kisses and a hand to my stomach, he sat on the couch and slid the silver rectangle of his computer back onto his lap. I thought for a minute that he wanted to look up information related to the pregnancy—about the formation of little fins or how to pleasure a hugely pregnant woman—but Simon returned to an article he'd been hammering out about Sumerians and sodomy or something like that. I called up T'ang Dynasty and ordered ten dishes, with extra fried rice.

Simon must have figured out that anyone who emptied that many greasy white cartons really was hungry for something else, because the next day he brought me home a clear, beaded necklace that looked like a string of diamonds and long-stemmed roses, which made me feel like I'd won something. *There she goes, Miss America.* Pleased, I put the roses into cut glass, a wedding present, and placed the vase on the windowsill. I liked the contrast of blood-red petals against the falling snow, though the flowers chilled within a day, and the petals chipped when I touched them as if they were made of glass.

I received more accolades at the doctor's a week later. My new ob/ gyn, a blond Viking in clogs, congratulated me. How often does a doc do that? His nurse and the receptionist gave me toothy smiles, a prescription for prenatal vitamins, and a palm-sized blue and pink bear wearing a tiny diaper. "Congratulations," they chimed. "Congratulations." No copayment for any prenatal visits, the receptionist assured me as she booked four more appointments on the spot. I gave them my winning wave as I left the office.

With nothing in my stomach, I spent the morning after my exam at the kitchen table, leaning my chin into my palms and snorting over the personals. I didn't always understand the ads even though I'm from a city of drag cabarets and shops filled with lesbian sex toys. *Big-bottomed Baby. Bad boy. Tantric massage for women: focused, free-flowing, personal.*

I thought of the "impersonal" massage Simon had arranged for me at a spa in Napa before we left California. The dim lighting, the Middle Eastern rhythms, and the curling smoke from a stick of incense made me feel like I was back in high school and about to be seduced by the local stoner. Still, I stripped, then lay between a pair of sheets waiting for the return of Wanda, the handsome young woman whose handshake had assured me of her strength. "Close your eyes and let go," she told me. Wanda circled her fingertips on my forehead, let the circles move into my scalp, then took my neck in her hands. When she reached my left hand, rolling each of my fingers in her oily palms, I murmured, "I love you." Flushing, I corrected myself. "I mean, I love this." She laughed as if she heard that all the time and moved onto my thigh. But I felt shy with Simon that night, as if he'd caught me flirting with another guy at a party. Of course, it was a slip of the tongue, that

*I love you*, but half of me meant what I'd said. How could I not love someone who touched my body like that? How could she not be half in love with me?

I tossed the paper and gathered all the sheets and towels into a ball, which I held in front of me as if it were my nine-month belly—how would that feel?—and huffed to the Laundromat on Grand. As our stuff sloshed, making satisfying *shug, shug* sounds, I watched other launderers. A girl who looked as wholesome as a milkmaid—big-boned and red-cheeked—washed her sweatshirts and jogging pants. A large Indian family acted as if this were a day of celebration, chatting animatedly as they folded bright squares of color. A thin, shallowly bearded guy, young and delicately good-looking, tacked up a flyer on the community bulletin board. He lacked the height and the breadth of most Minnesota men, so was able to fit himself easily between me and the youngest of the Indian girls, who whispered endearments to her long-haired pink pony. I smiled at him because that's what people do in St. Paul. They smile and look away. He smiled back, then dipped his head in the direction of the notice he'd put up.

"Tantric massage," he told me.

I was surprised into saying, "Free-flowing and personal?"

"Have you seen my ads?"

"No," I said, not wanting to admit my daily intake of others' fetishes. "I think my husband mentioned it."

"Did he think something like that might interest you?" he asked, pressing his palms together. He had the hands of an artist—long, thin fingers.

"No, he just thought it was…funny." I shook off the words, not liking how my pretend-husband sounded—oafish and guffawing. Of course, I was the one who snickered over the classifieds. Simon never found things like that amusing.

"Do you know anything about tantric?" he asked me.

"Is it anything like tandoori?"

He widened his eyes, a pure green, the color of grapes. "Tandoori? No—"

"I'm teasing," I assured him.

No one in the Midwest bantered, but I hadn't gotten used to that yet. At bookstores and community centers, St. Paulies spoke seriously about important things—noise pollution, recycling, how to reignite the Democratic Party—but did so without jokes or innuendos. Lawns in our neighborhood proclaimed homeowners' allegiances to worthwhile organizations and pleas to insensitive transients: *We live here. Please don't speed. World peace.* At any gathering, I was the only one with a smirk or lipstick. "I've heard of tantric," I told him. "Woody Harrelson and Sting, right?" The Indian girl eyed me, then swung one brown arm in the air. Her pony flew around the Laundromat. Suddenly, I felt wonderful. My stomach had stopped jumping. I couldn't even tell I was pregnant.

He stroked the smooth cheek above his hopeful beard. "Tantric's a whole philosophy," he said. "Not just something celebrities do. It involves feeling one's self within one's body. Women especially get out of touch with this. They forget to feel. That's what I help with."

I laughed. "You sound Californian."

"People have bodies even in Minnesota." He gave me an uneven grin. "Some of them even enjoy them."

"But aren't you really talking about sex for money? Isn't that a form—"

"It's so much more than that," he said, as earnest as any other Minnesotan. "You just have to open your mind."

At his plea to open my mind, I got up: conversation finished, time to dry.

He put his hand in mine from behind. I twisted around to get another look at him.

"Jesse," he said, pressing a softened business card in my hand. "Call me."

I saluted him with the card, then stuck it into the front pocket of my jeans, so I could plunge both arms into the wet linens and pull them up.

The afternoon that I spoke with Jesse, Master of Tantric Massage, was the last time I felt free of the pregnancy. As the days accumulated, my breasts tightened; so did my belly. Simon and I opted to stay "home" for the holidays, not going back to the snow-free streets of San Francisco, where Christmas meant cool rain and dim sum. Instead of indulging in shrimp puffs and spare ribs and tiny custard pies that dissolve on your tongue, we made snow and watched TV. Those custard pies didn't do much for me anyway. I still couldn't keep much down except saltines and milk, which I'd begun mashing together as though I were my own baby. I stopped painting again after I had circled the living room with white squares, leaning the canvases against all four walls. I liked the bloody sun, but the rest looked blank to me, empty.

"I'm incubating," I said, having spent New Year's Day lying on the couch, Simon's couch. Without complaint, he had moved his computer and his books to the kitchen table. "Do you suppose that makes me poultry?"

"I love you, Laura," Simon responded as if this were an answer to my question.

Those days, he left the couch to me, spending more time at his office. "Better for networking," he said. He brought me whatever I wanted— usually hot cross buns and the *City Pages*—then thunked back down the stairs, his boots muffled once he hit the snow on our stoop.

When his lecture on homosocial bonding and the beginnings of the nuclear family was cancelled because of burst pipes, Simon did spend a dark morning kissing me before he parted my legs and pressed his face between them. I stretched my arms up under the pillows, ready to be swept out to sea. After a minute, he pulled away.

"You taste different," he said.

"Bad?"

"Just different. Like you've been eating dandelions."

I drew the comforter over my waist. "What if—"

"Sweetie," he cut me off.

"I'm never the same? What if from now on I'll taste like ... motherhood?"

"Does motherhood taste like dandelions?" He squinted as if trying to determine the answer to his own question.

I said that he probably should leave the room before I vomited on him, and he did, scooting into his pants as if I meant what I said. It was no big deal, the dandelion comment. Simon had wanted to make love to me. He'd admired the small swells of my breasts. But I lay in bed for the rest of the day, weeping as if bereaved under the billows of down.

That Monday, I went to Planned Parenthood for an "initial consultation." I told the "counselor" I was poor, single, and uninsured. "It's not the right time," I said. "It's a terrible time. A terrible place."

"A terrible place?"

"I'm in a terrible place," I corrected myself.

"Okay," she said. "Sure, okay."

She scheduled me for Thursday. Over the next three days, I lived on a whole new moral plane. I was doing the most awful thing I'd ever done, something unimaginable, unforgivable, divorceable. Because I didn't plan to tell Simon I no longer wanted to have a child. I planned on lying. Miscarriages happened all the time. My husband would come home to a pale and bleeding wife understandably consoling herself with a glass of wine. He'd be nice to me for weeks—take me out to dinner, for drinks, maybe even dancing. This deception seemed better than confessing that I didn't want to be trapped in St. Paul, where winter lasted more than half a year, that I didn't want to be saddled with a child, this Minnesotan inside me. Minnesota had nothing to do with my art or my life. I was nothing here. But I'd become something: the worst woman I knew.

It took my breath away, to be that woman. I felt like I did when an art school friend turned me on to a few lines of coke: stronger, taller, grander. I had my first cup of coffee in weeks, relishing the smoky aroma as well as the burn when it went down my throat. I stretched a new canvas, laid down a base coat, and spread out what I'd bought. Humming, I stuck each object onto the surface of white waves: rubber nipples, pacifiers, and inch-long, plastic babies. At the center of this circle, I painted an eye, my left eye. Wide open.

On Thursday morning, the cab I'd ordered pulled up in front. Our old Civic had started up and the electric garage door had opened, but the driveway was ice. After I'd slipped forward and backward half a dozen times, I finally had slid the car back in its place, then made the calls.

"Seventh Avenue, Miss?" the driver said, smiling.

I peered down at the address. "Lyndale," I told him.

I was operating by instinct then and sure of myself. This certainty stayed with me even as Jesse, wearing a white t-shirt and madras pants, led me through a string of red beads into a room filled with a sweet scent—cinnamon rolls or incense—that made me hungry.

"You haven't made a mistake," Jesse said, wet licks of hair around his ears; he must have just showered. "I promise."

I nodded without saying anything.

*What Would Happen*, I began, but didn't go any further than that. *What if, what if, what if* circled pleasantly in my head as if it were a complete idea on its own. Jesse left me to step out of my clothes. I shook off the wet coat, pulled off my black boots with their white rime. I unwound and unbuttoned, peeling away layers until I stood in the middle of my things. Stepping free of them, I lay face down on the massage table, my breasts full and firm, my belly round and hard. *What if, what if, what if* I said to myself as Jesse lifted the sheet that covered my body, as he poured warm oil over me, encircled my shoulders, my soles, with his hands, even as he parted my legs.

# And the Wisdom to Know the Difference
## *Hilary Zaid*

I sought the women's locker room at the West Campus pool only for relief of the most unbearable urges. Deep in the tile-slick vault of lockers and benches, I might twist the towel, wimple-like, into my hair, I might bend over my pale, shaved legs and rub them smooth as relics, I might pull my suit and goggles from my bag and lay them out like a holy veil across the bench, while all the time I was prowling, spying a young woman with sidelong eyes as she stripped off her skirt and tugged herself into a black and narrow spandex suit and disappeared into the chlorine haze beyond the double doors. Then I would glide across the tiles to the woman's locker, fish out her cell phone, and double-thumb a sharp and witty text message of mind-fuckery and small revenge to Phillipa Rush, my former lover. While I gripped the phone, my face became flushed and my fingers trembled, but when I pressed "Send," with the whooshing of the words away, fear and trembling and hatred left me, and I pulled on my clothes, relieved, and went back home. I had done it dozens of times.

The campus gym offered bins of small, white towels I thought of as something like communion wafers—they were that tiny and brittle and white. I liked to be poised naked at the bench in front of my locker, staring in a distracted way into its depths, clutching one of these white towels, as I lay in wait for the Sunday swimmers, one by one, to kneel against the benches, to bow into the darkness of their narrow cubbies, to strip down for their ablutions. It was an idea of Catholicism I'd gotten from the movies.

I wanted to feel the agonies of simple suffering, a world of good and evil. Sin, guilt, confession. They would have served me better than all my agnostic, Jewish questioning. They would have pointed a clear way straight to heaven and hell.

Film critic Phillipa Rush, known by everyone on the small California liberal arts school campus as Pippa, had seduced me with the world's oldest line—"My wife is a brilliant woman, but she won't touch me"—and a soft, pained look that nearly wrinkled her strangely baby-smooth skin. The problem was that, though I was thirty-five, life had not loaned me its concordance of seduction lines. I had been married since I was twenty-one to a very kind man named Mike. Mike wasn't the type to use a line, and if he ever had been, I'd forgotten what. I no longer touched Mike either.

Also a cliché: I was Pippa's grad student. A decade after having children, I had gone back to school to get that film degree I had sacrificed for marriage, children, job. At thirty-five, there was something burning a hole in my heart, a void that needed to be filled. How long had it taken Pippa to convince me that the burning void was the one between my thighs? Pitifully, not long. The fact that she was a woman had made it feel so much like love.

These were truths I could see only in retrospect: the smooth professor with her dark hair (dyed black) and baby face (acid-peeled and Botoxed), her practiced interest, her rehearsed torment.

She could be so penetrating in her glances, so intent, so kind. I was exotic, she whispered, so passionate, so intellectual. Who, at thirty-five, would not want to be a phenomenon, a mystery? I was a woman: how couldn't I notice that she was articulate, self-confident, sexy? And I was a mother: couldn't I see the places where she had been hurt, the places she needed to be touched? I wished I could rewind my life to the moment in her office hours when Pippa leaned across her book-strewn desk and murmured, "Dahlia, you're a very, very dangerous woman for me to meet." I wished I could reach back in time and slap myself in the face.

Mike loved me unconditionally. But at a certain stage of life, you want conditions. You want to feel like you're still good enough to pass a test. Pippa was an academic, a film critic without a column or a TV show. Her fame extended only to the borders of a world that was too small for her ego, and so, often, after a lunch date on which she'd slid her hand inside my bra in the darkness of the theater, she would call me and scream at me about the little-mindedness of women who had children. Any woman in her right mind would know this was abusive. But I was no longer in my right mind. Pippa's steamy texts, her forbidden glances, her showings of Cocteau: she had done something to my brain.

Afterwards, I'd miraculously crawled from the ashes back into the quiet, trying, ordinary life with children. For that—the blessing of a life without a Pippa in it—I resolved to shout hosannas, to count out peaceful rosaries of days. I resolved, like the martyrs and the saints who seemed to give Mike's mother so much comfort, to brutalize myself. Only, every now and then, I felt a stray surge of powerless rage and I had to let it out. I had to punish Pippa, who had done so much to punish me.

I stood at my usual locker, number 1157, the one with the Hurley sticker slapped across the vents, waiting for a woman to show up, strip down, and leave behind her phone. (This was one of the truths I loved and feared about women: we trusted each other dangerously; we didn't lock our locker doors.) I was naked, sharpening the phrasing of a text in my head. Early on in her seduction, Pippa had warned me, "Watch out for me. I'm a real asshole." Another line. What I realized now: she wasn't warning me; she was bragging. So I couldn't text her: *You're a philandering bitch.* I had to goose her at her blind spot: Pippa had a nasty little habit of "forgetting" her sources in her lectures and her research papers. I had actually heard Pippa repeat my own comments about the female form in *Metropolis* and claim them as her own. Like the habit of seduction, plagiarism was probably pathological with her. An assimilation of everything around her into her own devouring ego. But, unlike seduction, not something she was proud of.

*Do they know u steal?*

Best to keep it general, I thought, and simple. Just enough to stoke Pippa's slow-burning paranoia. (Pippa loved wind-bagging about her frenetic social scene of semi-famous academics, especially in the Ivy Leagues; the faculty in her own department, Pippa suspected, had it in for her, professional jealousies. More likely, I thought, it was that she was derivative and fucking their wives.)

*Do they know u steal?*

I imagined Pippa frantically thumbing her iPhone: *Who is this?* She would never mistake the sender of that message for one of her many conquests.

A young woman glided into the locker room, a graduate student or young faculty type, yoga pants and a college sweatshirt. I smiled at her. *Thank you for letting me borrow your phone,* I whispered to the woman inside my secret mind. *You are doing a good, good thing.* And the young woman smiled back, a deep, warm, brown-eyed smile that made me feel an even deeper gush of gratitude. You could tell in a glance: she was a good person; her iPhone password was going to be 1234. I waited for the brown-eyed girl to snap on her suit and goggles. Afterwards, she trailed behind her the scent of jasmine and cedar. A sweet smell that reminded me of my children.

No one ever swam for under twenty minutes, minimum. I didn't hurry as I lifted the latch, sifted through the gym bag, and found the telephone. I made sure not to disturb the young woman's bra or panties.

It always made me nervous, this part, the phone in hand, not because I was afraid of getting caught, but because I feared that, once I typed Pippa's number into the text message app, the closed channel between us would open up again like Hell's gate, Pippa would reach out her fingers and grab me by the throat. She was still that powerful, still that terrifying in my mind. A leg-shaking dread and terror: it was the residual echo of the fear that had plagued me, when I knew Pippa, every time my phone would buzz. Yes, I knew this vengeance texting was a bad thing. I knew a future version of myself would want to reach back into this moment and shriek. But the present version of myself saw it as exposure therapy, the kind they used for phobias, the repeated stimulus that would cure me, so I would no longer feel afraid.

Pippa had been a lens through which my husband and my children, and myself beside them, had appeared weirdly, weirdly small. The thing about a lens, though, was that you could turn it around. Or smash it.

I typed in the message first, then the phone number I wished I didn't know by heart. When the number began to auto-fill, and then Pippa's name popped up by itself, I ran into a toilet stall and felt my liquid bowels rush into the toilet bowl.

Inside the locked stall, a wet confessional, I scrolled through the string of text messages between Pippa and the Brown-Eyed Girl and waited for the rising tide of jealousy to flood me. Pippa had loved to whip me into frantic fits with the mention of other women, took pleasure in the act of manipulation: *Marta M. was scintillating,* she'd text. *Best watch out, my dark Dahlia.* But as I read through Pippa's luring messages to the Brown-Eyed Girl, messages very, very much like the messages she had once texted me (a script!), I felt myself overcome not by jealousy, but by a terrible, terrible sadness. Sadness for the poor idiot I had been, and sadness for the cedar-smelling Brown-Eyed Girl. The towel perched on my head tilted off toward the wall like the fallen statue of a saint. *I am evil*, Pippa texted me/the Brown-Eyed Girl, *and you are so very good*. The eagerness with which I had lapped up this woman's filth was a crime that needed to be expiated. Now it spun into a web of protective anger for the Brown-Eyed Girl. I flushed until the water beneath me ran clear as a baptismal font.

My thumbs ventriloquized: *Don't call me anymore. Don't text. Or I'll contact your department head*. I assumed that disciplinary action was a real threat that might call Professor Pippa off. But what about the Brown-Eyed Girl? Pippa's sudden absence would hit her like so many of her punishing silences had struck me, astonishing icebergs of silence and withholding. Distances to be overcome. I rubbed the screen blank, and went back to the lockers, thinking.

I could befriend the Brown-Eyed Girl. Casually. Over weeks. I could show up in the locker room, and chat about laps and school, until the Brown-Eyed Girl revealed her heartache. With Pippa, there could only, ever be heartache. I pulled the towel off my head and peered into the dark of the Brown-Eyed Girl's locker, looking for clues. Befriending her was a nice idea, but if I knew anything about the way Pippa preyed on women, I knew that this girl would keep Pippa hidden. I knew the pleasure and the searing pain of Pippa Rush: the Brown-Eyed Girl would protect the wounded place where Pippa made her feel like less than nothing; she would feel too much shame not to protect her.

The smell of cedar wafted up from the dark locker, the warm human smell of the Brown-Eyed Girl's blue jeans. What would I have wanted someone to tell me when I was wound up in Pippa's snares? ("If only I had met you years ago.") What would I have listened to? The only one I had told, my sister in Boulder, had handled me so gently: "She's not necessarily a bad person, honey. Just bad for you. Very, very bad for you." But that would be a lie. Pippa was a bad person, a broken person, a brittle person, a toxic and destructive person. And the Brown-Eyed Girl would never believe that, not yet.

Worse, if I tried to warn this girl, Pippa would tell her what she'd told me about the last one: that she was being stalked by a woman she'd rejected, a woman who'd never gotten over her. A woman full of pent-up bitterness and rage. "This is different," Pippa would reassure the Brown-Eyed Girl, as she'd once reassured me: "You are different from anyone I've ever met." I blinked at the iPhone glowing in my hand. Should I just delete Pippa's name and number? There was nothing I could tell Brown Eyes that Pippa wouldn't turn into something else. That's what happened when one person controlled the entire conversation.

I picked up the Brown-Eyed Girl's soft T-shirt and inhaled the innocence. I wanted to take this young woman in my arms, press her brown eyes into my breast and coo, "You poor, poor thing." I wanted to tell the Brown-Eyed Girl that Pippa fucked like a teenage boy. *Thirty seconds!*

I remembered the words from the Sinead O' Connor record Mike and I had listened to over and over in our senior spring at college. Cat-eyed, bald Sinead, before she tore up her picture of the Pope. Back then, I thought the opening words of the record were part of the catechism: *Grant me the serenity to accept the things I cannot change; the courage to change the things I can; and the wisdom to know the difference.* Then I slid the phone back into the woman's pool bag, the bag back into the locker and shut the door. There was nothing I could do.

"Johanna's mother died."

"Pardon?" Still naked except for my skimpy gym towel, I swiveled toward the voice, a woman in a black and red tank suit who seemed to be speaking to me. I recognized her as a swimmer whose phone I had borrowed to text Pippa a couple months ago. Password: 0000. "Johanna?"

The swimmer peeled her cap away from her head like a robber tearing off a rubber face. I wondered if Pippa had ever texted this woman back. Broad-shouldered and tall, the swimmer looked sturdy and practical, like someone who would have replied to Pippa: *Wrong number.* I wondered if it had sent Pippa off into one of her fits of paranoia. I devoutly hoped so.

"Small, dark-haired woman, big ankh tattoo?" the swimmer prompted me.

This woman assumed I was a Sunday regular, that I knew the other regulars. Come to think of it, I could place the ankh tattoo. I had seen Johanna, who always showed up with a lively-looking older woman, dress and undress.

"Her mother?" I watched the swimmer strip her black straps from her shoulders. Their white ghosts traced her scapulas like wings.

"Mmm. Johanna's inviting all her mother's pool friends to the wake." The swimmer pulled on a pair of black panties, turned and fished around her bag. Then she pulled out a Xerox showing a photo of Johanna and her mother—I recognized her merry blue eyes—and a fringe of strips giving the address, and tacked it to the post between the lockers.

To lose a mother, a champion and life's companion! I fingered the paper fringe.

My destructive addiction to Pippa had felt like mortal tragedy. I had wanted what I'd wanted, and I hadn't cared whose life I destroyed, even when it turned out to be my own. But Pippa was gone. My life had, mercifully, returned to its garden patch of mundane losses: the tiny plot of dirt in the front yard where I dropped the children's curled goldfish. I was still breathing.

"Could I have one?" I asked. These swimmers, I saw now, looked after their own. This was something Pippa, who thrived on women's backbiting, their horrible, sordid dramas, could never understand. Love, mutuality. Transcendence. I had used to be a part of that. I wanted to be a part of it still. I watched the angel-backed swimmer as she dressed, then pulled out my own unused white one-piece from my gym bag.

I never really wanted to become a Catholic. I'd just wanted an iconography that made a virtue out of suffering. But there was no virtue in pain. Or punishment. Just the firmness of holding on, the relief of letting go.

The cool and purifying air washed my bare shoulders as I stepped onto the deck. I felt like a pilgrim in my tight swim costume and my bare, chilled feet; I tiptoed with care along the slippery tiles like a sinner along a bed of nails, a sinner renouncing sin. I would never text Pippa again.

Inside the locker room, tacked to the wall under the poster for Johanna's mother like the fragment of the shroud torn from a martyred saint, the second poster fluttered in the breeze of the closing door. I had flipped it over and, on the back, I'd Sharpied my confession: *The Lies I Let Myself Believe* and tacked it next to Brown Eyes' locker. "You are a dangerous woman for me to meet," I'd written. "You are different than anyone I've ever met." The Brown-Eyed Girl would have to draw her own conclusions. I'd drawn mine: none of us is that special, not in love, not in suffering; and whatever you believed about an angry or a compassionate God, no one should be. To be merely human: Wasn't that really the point?

Out on the deck, I plunged into the clear, blue water and washed myself clean.

# Game, Set, Match

## *Janis Butler Holm*

The matchmaker meets me at the café and asks for my I.D. She studies my picture, frowns a little, and hands it back to me.

"No," she says. "I don't think you're what we're looking for."

"What do you mean?" I say. "I thought you wanted this meeting so you could check me out, and all you've done is look at my driver's license."

"A driver's license can be enough," she says.

"I don't understand," I say, beginning to feel angry.

"The people on the show have to be attractive," she says. "You're not photogenic."

"It's a driver's license photo!" I'm getting really pissed off.

"Look," she says, "this isn't personal. I just don't think the camera likes you very much."

"But what about my other photos? If you'd told me the camera stuff was so goddamn important, I'd have brought you plenty of good pictures."

"The driver's license tells me all I need to know," she says, picking up her purse and scooting back her chair.

"You're not giving me a chance!" My voice is loud now. I try to grab her arm.

"Actually, I did give you a chance," she says, moving out of reach. "The driver's license test isn't about the picture."

And the bitch walks away, just like that.

# Part IV

# Mother Figures

# Yatri

## *Jay O'Shea*

After Mom died, I went to India. I flew to Mumbai, the only ticket I could afford on my student loan money. I didn't qualify for a bereavement fare, since I was flying away from a death, not toward one.

Nalini Auntie had been at the funeral. Grief rendered her fragile as her daughters flanked her in their brand-new Western clothes. But when she held me, she became a mass of strength and warmth. I had forgotten how an Indian woman hugs, with a tight embrace that ought to be reserved for the parting of lovers or the reunion of estranged siblings. "Come home," she said. Indian people say that when they mean, visit me. I knew that. My eyes burned anyway.

Mom called India home. No matter how long she lived in America, no matter how many months or years passed between visits, she always called it home.

After she got sick, Dad refused to go. He buried himself in Sanskrit texts and meetings with grad students. India faded and I was just a teenager with olive skin, a faintly exotic name, and the lingering sense I belonged nowhere.

In Shivaji Airport, I followed signs in Hindi and English through an institutional green glow. I could make out the Devanagari script, moving my lips when I read. The word for passenger is *yatri*, from the Sanskrit *yatra*, or journey. A man in gray polyester took a long look at my visa, multicolored and stiff. He frowned.

Eyes sticky with interrupted sleep, I left the terminal, thanking god and the Lonely Planet for my prepaid taxi ticket. It was a few hours after midnight and exhaust choked the air. Humidity wrapped itself around me. Boys with short, slick hair jostled behind a railing, a gauntlet my ticket let me avoid. A tall man in a red turban stepped forward. Idle men looked on as I handed him the paper and tried to act unfazed. I waved away the mosquitoes that circled my head. The driver disappeared into a row of cars. He returned with an old Ambassador, black and crumbling. I repeated the name of my hotel although I saw him write it down.

For three days, I drifted through the city in a jet-lagged dream. I made my way into Victoria Terminus, only to be swept up in the crush of bodies leaving the train platforms. In Crawford market, I found myself in a lonely corner where cats fought over the entrails of slaughtered chickens while humans fried up the rest. At Chowpatty Beach, vendors cluttered the sidewalk and multicolored lights decked the horizon like costume jewelry. I stuck to the shadows to avoid the dull stares that seemed to follow me everywhere.

These places were new. My parents never took me to Bombay. We flew into Madras and spent our days with relatives, seeing little of a vast country. Yet I found traces of my mother everywhere. In the brisk accent of the bank teller who exchanged my money. In the Carnatic music that played out the window of a dance school. In the train station, on the face of a woman, aging gracefully in a way my mother never would. This was what remained: snapshots layered on each other. A jerky progression of stills, as in a silent film. We think of death as stealing the whole of someone. But fragments remain as bones do, long after flesh is gone. Death robs us of continuity, fluidity, the in-between moments.

On a side street I found a yellow storefront with black lettering in English: Standard Trunk Dialing, Local Call, Fax, Xerox. A skinny boy—he couldn't have been more than ten—sat in a booth, watching a cricket game on a small TV. He gestured me toward a heavy plastic phone. I called Nalini Auntie and tried to speak Tamil with her maid. The words caught in my throat; I couldn't tell if it was dust or sorrow or just a failure of memory. Nalini Auntie picked up. Tears pricked my eyes as she said it again: come home.

The next day, I was on my way to Chennai. A breeze wafted in as the train started to move. I imitated the ladies around me and slipped off my sandals, tucking my bare feet under me on the black plastic seat. The family next to me carried food in shiny stainless steel boxes. They offered me fried snacks I didn't recognize. When we stopped in a dusty little town, I bought sugary tea, passing rupee bills out the window to a vendor walking the platform. Dislocated sounds poured in from sunbaked land: car horns, snippets of *filmi* songs, the clatter of metal.

We pulled into Chennai Central as evening began to soak up the heat. The train station loomed, its red and white Victorian arches cluttered by a rank of motorbikes. Nalini Auntie pulled me from the press of passengers, her driver following in silence. Nalini has never been a beautiful woman. Her face is long, nose heavy, complexion darker than a middle-class Indian lady's skin is supposed to be. But when twilight blended with the dust in the air, it cast her in a warm glow, softening her features. Her makeup was fresh and recently applied, black braid thick and crisp. She wore an orange and red sari that was polyester but looked expensive nonetheless.

For a moment, it was a different time, a different arrival. The heat and bustle of the train station faded and I saw a younger Nalini, waiting behind the barrier at the airport. I could picture the arrival sign, in English and Tamil; the city was called Madras then. I sensed my mother by my side. I turned and, for an instant, I saw her: softer-featured than Nalini Auntie, with the big brown eyes celebrated in Sanskrit poetry and Bollywood songs alike. By all accounts, Indian and American, she was the prettier sister. But my mother always pinned her sari to her blouse. Its hem twisted around her feet.

Nalini Auntie's arms encircled me, returning me to the train station, the porters with suitcases on their heads, the touts kept at bay by my aunt's darting eyes. Her fingers sank into my shoulders and she patted my cheek before taking my arm and walking me to the car. I smelled jasmine in her hair. Sometimes my mother wore flowers. The smell of America was all wrong, she said: clean and synthetic. Even the fragrances smelled sharp instead of rich. She brought back bottles of essential oil and bars of Mysore sandalwood soap, talismans against homesickness.

"Madras is not as you remember," Nalini Auntie was saying. "But my driver is here. He'll take you where you need to go."

Annoyance rushed through me. It came on fast and cut through the comfort I got from the scent of her French cologne and the way the end of her sari draped across my jeans as we sat.

"I live in Los Angeles."

That meant nothing to her. I remembered the times she visited my parents' home. She stayed in the spare bedroom. We showed her the Indian markets and the Tamil cinema in town. When we ventured farther afield, we brought her to Disneyland and the Asian Art Museum.

"I hear gunshots from my bedroom," I said. "I'm so used to them sometimes I forget to call the police."

"You Americans are very innocent," she said.

Buses, heavy black taxis, and bicycles jostled over lanes that didn't exist. Cows wandered between vehicles and goats sat on the embankment, oblivious to honking horns and the spill of exhaust. The ocean appeared on our left, its blue-gray deepening as the sun set. The beach came alive as warmth faded and the city poured out to celebrate the departure of the day's heat, an inverse of the retreat from a California beach at sunset. Vendors sold bottles of soda from tiny stalls. Men fried *chat* in huge woks. Families walked along the sand and groups of boys hung out by the seawall. I fought the urge to open the car door and step out into the swell. I couldn't help but feel caught, trapped in this car, in this traffic, in this life.

We turned off the main road. The route looked familiar even as I saw how much had changed: new apartment buildings, ads for cell phones, boutique shops. And how much hadn't: garbage in rough piles on the street, beggars with bandaged hands. The road narrowed, flanked by scrub. A slum appeared, dirt paths and huts with roofs of thatch and corrugated iron. A teenage boy, dark and leanly muscled, dumped a bucket of water over his head. Soapy liquid plastered his hair and shrunk his shorts around his thighs. A girl in a pink sari pumped a well handle.

Nalini Auntie looked out the window too.

"When are you getting married?" she asked.

Where did she get the idea I was about to marry? Had my father mentioned Martin to her? I didn't introduce him at the funeral. A boyfriend, a love too turbulent to last—that was beyond her understanding. Besides, I knew she pictured me with an Indian boy, not the sandy-haired Jewish guy I lived with. I didn't answer. Just before she spoke again, I understood. She meant it in the Indian way: everyone gets married, so when would the inevitable happen?

"You're so pretty," she said. "And fair. But you can't wait forever."

When we got home, the other aunties were there and I entered a relational world: Saraswati is not just Saraswati, she is someone's cousin, linked to my mother through someone; her daughter was studying abroad and I should be sure to meet her when I went back. I tried to remember whose sister taught biology in Pennsylvania and whose son just took his new wife back to Dubai. But as soon as the information came in, it dissolved.

The girls clustered together, Nalini Auntie's daughters among them. The younger ones wore floor-length skirt and blouse sets straight out of a fairy tale. The older ones flicked their *dupattas* over their shoulders, turning *salwar kameez* into catwalk fashion. For a long stretch, half an hour or more, I didn't think about my mother. I was surrounded by Indian ladies. None of them was the one I wanted beside me, but for a time it didn't matter. What mattered was this exchange. We saw ourselves as connected; we enacted it and felt comforted by it.

Am I still studying, the aunties asked? They looked uneasy when I said yes, but I smiled anyway. After a while, they talked about me as if I weren't there. So fair but so skinny, no wonder she's not married. I stared at my plate, feigning fascination with ruined piles of rice and *sambar*. The ceiling fan whirred above the table. The heaviness of the outside air encroached, even now, well after sundown.

A ghost twin appeared next to me. I recognized her. Girls like her danced at the *melas* my mother took us to in spurts of nostalgia. At our suburban Hindu temple, they knew which direction to walk and where to place their baskets of flowers and coconuts. They sat next to me in college classes, arriving at 9:00 a.m. with blow-dried hair and eye shadow. My attempts at friendship glanced off their shiny surfaces.

Like me, Ghost Twin is in graduate school. But she chose a practical subject that yields a steady job at its end. She's American so she won't let her parents fix up a marriage for her. She doesn't need to. She found a guy who is both a nice Indian boy and an all-American beefcake at once, someone who brings gifts for the aunties and goes to *pujas* and weddings but spends his weekends playing baseball with the guys from Alpha Kappa Epsilon. Ghost Twin radiates with him beside her, knowing she'll look just as lovely in that red wedding sari as she does in her DKNY sportswear.

The aunties don't know my ghost twin well. They wouldn't approve of the frat parties she went to in college and her live-in fiancé, even if he is Indian. Still, Ghost Twin shares something with them. Despite her American ways, the time she spends at barbecues and nightclubs, she, like everyone here, knows what to be when.

Nalini Auntie said there was a marriage in the family. Hundreds of people would attend; I didn't need an invitation. She gave me a silk sari and a matching blouse that was too tight. The length of the fabric billowed, unmanageable, until Nalini switched off the fan. A murky heat filled the room. Sweat stood out on my face, my back, even on my legs, sticking the petticoat to my knees. Nalini's daughter helped me wrap the cloth, folding the pleats and tucking them in place. Nalini Auntie tried to draw my hair into a braid. She gave up and handed me a clump of jasmine to cover the bump at the nape of my neck.

Outside, the sunlight had a weight to it, a force. I had managed to forget this: how hot South India is. I was born and raised in California. I've spent time in the desert. But nowhere have I felt heat like this, a living thing, with determination and drive, wrapping me up and refusing to let me go, refusing to let me think about anything else, even.

We entered the hall through an awning painted gold and decorated with flowers. The drone of an instrument my mother must have told me about insinuated itself into the space, punctuated by the sharp ring of a drum. The bride and groom sat on a dais, wearing brocaded silk, red for her, cream for him. A shirtless man in a white cotton *dhoti* performed a ritual we could barely see. The dozen people around the celebrants looked on. Everyone else mingled, paying no attention to what happened onstage.

I was shunted around, introduced, and ignored. Conversations slipped back into Tamil and I smiled tightly, hands clasped in front of me with no pockets to jam them into. For a while, I tagged after Nalini's daughter as she milled around with the other teenagers. They spoke in English of deliberately banal things. I tried to catch the currents of air created by the ceiling fans. But in this crowded space, it was impossible. The air wafted unpredictably, the undertow of a roiling sea. No matter where I stood, I was fixed in a pocket of heat.

We sat on the floor to eat, cross-legged, with banana leaves in front of us. No one showed me what to do. I watched Nalini and her daughters as they tilted forward, scooping up sauce-covered rice with their right hands. The folds of my sari dipped toward the spreading liquid. I pictured turmeric stains on purple silk.

Ghost Twin did fine. She knew who to talk to and what to say. Her hair stayed pinned back, even if she refused a braid. She was as comfortable eating on the floor as she would be squeezed into a booth at a diner.

I was reminded of other gatherings, ones back home. Here I was in India and my thoughts kept returning to America. As if my mother were not dead, but lost, in the true sense. As if I might find her someplace I hadn't checked yet. I remembered her, dressed in a black turtleneck and neat slacks, long hair loose. She held a flute of sparkling wine, circulating at a Christmas party my parents threw before she got sick. The other faculty wives were charmed and disappointed by her. They had hoped she would wear a sari. They didn't think of her as just another high-school English teacher; they wanted her to tell stories of mountain ashrams and desert palaces, of elephants and camels, not of a city where she bicycled to college and went to the movies. But they ended up captivated by her bright laugh and the attentive look that told you she wanted to hear what you had to say.

Tears stood out in my eyes. I forced them back into my throat like a bad-tasting liquid everyone says is good for you. Even here, where people cry, sing, and shout freely, no one expected me to sob in the midst of hundreds of loosely connected strangers.

A woman entered the room. Conversation didn't exactly stop and heads didn't exactly turn. But they would have if their owners allowed themselves the indulgence. She was short, even by Indian standards, and dark-skinned. Her strong jaw and bright eyes put the lie to the cherished notion that an Indian woman must be fair to be beautiful. What really got me was her hair, cropped and standing up in eccentric points. And her sari. It was the only cotton one in the room, forest green and black in blocky print.

Nalini Auntie introduced her. Her name was Leela. No complicated Tamil name. Just Leela. I wondered why but I didn't ask. Nalini turned away, expecting me to follow.

"You've come, just like this?" Leela's English was brisk, its inflection light. "After eight years?"

Everyone else assumed I'd returned to the family. As they knew I would. No one commented on the passage of time or what the trip had to do with my mother's death.

"I'm here because of my mother," I said.

"Malati and I were friends." Her eyes glistened. She hesitated but she wasn't mournful, not exactly. "We were alike. Both black sheep," she added, relishing the feel of the foreign phrase.

Black sheep? My mother was a diligent daughter, a good sister. A woman who left America in jeans and put on a sari in the airplane bathroom. A parent who sent her children to learn Tamil and Carnatic music, albeit inconsistently.

"In university, we really struggled," Leela said. "It's not like in your place. Here everyone is serious. They read one subject and study so hard. They're well behaved. Or they are not but they pretend. Malati and I were different. We weren't wild. At least an American wouldn't find us so." She laughed, taking the edge off what could have been an accusation. "But we had love affairs. Broken hearts. When it came to marriage, she was braver than I. Leaving with an American. I let them fix up my marriage. They said the boy was modern and wouldn't mind my previous relationships, as you would call them. In any case, Malati is no more. And I am divorced."

I knew there were women like this in India. I'd read about them. Read things by them, even. But I had no idea I was related to one.

"Yes," she said. "We do have divorce in India. It was tough. I suppose it is everywhere. But here there are expectations. Your home turns cold, then others reject you. I suspect I like it cold, however. I moved to Delhi. No warmth there. I run an art gallery and answer to no one."

The crowd shifted and a space opened around us. Air rushed through, prickling the sweat on my skin. I filled my lungs as though this was the first breath I had taken for hours. The hem of the blouse pressed against my ribs.

"What about you?" she asked. "Do you have someone back home?" Her smile revealed raised eyeteeth.

"I have a boyfriend," I said. "We lived together."

"Yet you are here," Leela said. "He must be very understanding."

"I put my stuff in storage when I left." Until I spoke, I hadn't thought about what that meant. Instead, I made excuses: what if I decided to stay in India? What if Martin needed to move?

Leela took my hand. Her grasp felt less like an Indian lady's solid grip and more like the touch of an old friend. I was still thinking about her when Nalini Auntie decided it was time to go.

I thought about her a lot over the next few days.

My mother, a rebel? She came from another country, but that's everyone story in America. If not them, then their parents or grandparents. Mom was a middle-class lady, with a regular job and a family, an Indian who wove herself into the fabric of American life. It never occurred to me to question my parents' marriage. I liked the romance of it. An American professor falls in love with his Indian research assistant; she leaves to follow him. I never thought about the kind of woman who would make such a momentous move in the first place.

I argued with my mother not long before she died. She took issue with me going back to school. Not because it was impractical. Because it was too practical. Are you sure you want this, she asked? I have to do something, I said.

I thought of her last visit to India. She spent hours under the ceiling fan in Nalini Auntie's house as ferocious old ladies, some orthodox enough to wear widow's white, offered opinions in dense Tamil. They shifted from sofa to floor and back again while my father sat in a chair. Mom took us out with the cousins, pretty, plump girls in colorful *salwar kameez*, to Dasaprakash for ice cream and to my grandmother's favorite sari shops, where cold air spun in the foyer like an indoor snowstorm. After a few days, my mother grew restless and words ran dry. Nalini Auntie looked wounded. Malati's going out alone, she said. Even though we went as a family. But mother, father, child, that's not family. Family is the people my father called relatives. Why come home, they asked, to roam around like a dog in the street? Why go to the beach in the blazing sun? Why take an autorickshaw when we have a driver?

A few days later, I sat with the aunties in Nalini's living room. Several of the women rested on the floor, leaning their backs against the couch. I perched at the edge of a straight-back chair. The ceiling fan creaked. Nalini Auntie served coffee in metal cups, thick, sweet, and strong, with Indian confections so sandy with sugar they hurt my teeth. My plate rested on my knees, cup balanced on it. Ghost Twin sat next to me. But my shy smiles were gone.

Nalini Auntie's friend Ranjana asked again about marriage. I didn't avoid the question this time. Words tumbled out of me. Nalini's mouth twisted. She glanced at her daughters to see if they were listening. I wondered if she was going to ask them to leave. Ranjana was more forgiving.

"You've met your prince charming," she said.

"Maybe," I said.

"You Americans are career girls," said one of the other aunties, a sharp-faced woman with glasses. "So many of you delay marriage."

"I'm taking time off," I said. "I have an open-ended ticket."

A stillness settled on the room, the only sound the fan's drone and the distant blare of car horns outside.

"My mother would have wanted me to," I said.

Ghost Twin shifted. I avoided looking at her. She stood, stepped back from our seat, and circled the aunties, facing in on them like in one of those dance performances from so long ago. She hovered in the doorway, then eased back over the threshold. I had to stop myself from waving to her. My eyes ached with tears.

With my mother here, I could be something I wasn't and it cost me nothing. She pretended so I didn't have to. With her gone, I had to decide for myself who to be. Here and everywhere else. The grief I braced myself for didn't arrive.

It took only a few minutes to pack. I left on foot. Nalini hugged me and patted my cheek. She didn't send for her driver. An autorickshaw waited by the gate.

She turned to her daughter when she thought I was out of earshot.

"A strange girl," she said.

I thought she was done.

"So much like her mother," she added.

# How to Save a Child from Choking
## Maureen O'Leary

Eddie wanted children all of a sudden. Beth thought it was classic water sign behavior. Eddie was a Cancer born in late June. His mind changed with the force of a river whose weirs have been lifted after a heavy rain.

But Beth was an earth sign born in April. This made her very good at her job. Not everybody was cut out to be a nurse at a children's hospital. The human body had enormous potential for infection and injury, pain and stink. Every day at work she tended to the broken, invaded, and diseased of other people's children. Earth signs gave comfort. She did the job.

But Beth knew this for a grounded certainty: She did not want her own children.

Eddie wanted to talk about it in the car on the way to his parents' house for Christmas. Eddie's sweet begging was too much. Beth looked out the window as they wound down the Pacific Coast Highway. At least the ocean was on her side.

"You can't say you'll never want kids, Beth. You can't say that. You don't know."

"I do know."

"You know for now," Eddie said. "But you don't know a year from now."

"I do know."

"And I respect that you feel that way *now*," he said. "But at some point we are going to want to make a family."

Beth turned to study his profile. He looked like Richard Gere in the *American Gigolo* years. His looks still surprised her sometimes. In the mirror they were mismatched. She wanted to be home lying on top of him with the top of her head wedged beneath his round chin. Mostly she wanted him to stop talking so that their marriage would quit shifting around like watery landfill in a seismic event.

"You'll make a great mom," he said. "That's what *I* know."

Dread flipped in Beth's stomach. He didn't look at her at all but kept his eyes on the traffic.

Within a half hour of their arrival Eddie's mother asked straight out, "When are you going to start having babies?"

She spoke with the usual authority but with a sly smile too. The woman never smiled. Beth ached to return it. How nice it would be to be able to feel that her mother-in-law liked her and had an interest in her, maybe even loved her a little bit just because she was part of the family. But Beth caught Eddie's eyes and saw their hopeful shine. She couldn't play games. Not even for a second.

"We're not having children, Alma. We never planned to."

The old mother's face fell and she looked over at her son. Eddie wrapped his arm around her thin shoulder and muttered in Spanish. Alma nodded and glared as if Beth had just bared her teeth.

All evening Eddie's parents welcomed a never-ending stream of guests Beth did not know. She stuck by her husband's side, smiling and meeting all of the relatives and family associates. They were handsome, silver-haired people, burnished by the sun even in winter. The oldsters were interspersed with a few exhausted but well-groomed cousins Eddie and Beth's age who also had driven a far distance for the party. Eddie's sister, Carmen, worked the crowd. She talked and smiled as though she were happy and kind, holding her two-year-old daughter, Nadia, on one hip. She'd done the child up in white lace, ankle socks, shiny black patent shoes. Nadia stared at everyone with enormous brown eyes and clutched her mother's blouse.

Eddie's relatives came from Bolivia. They were Yugoslav expats whose families had emigrated to South America after World War II before making their way to California later on. They were bankers, car dealers, jewelry store owners. They comported themselves with the elegance and remove of banished royalty.

Before lapsing into conversations in Spanish, several of the older generation remarked aloud that Beth and Eddie had no children. In the eyes of these tan and silver relatives, this was an error to be fixed, like the hole in the knee of her pants that she'd only just noticed. Beth ended up by herself in the corner by the sliding glass door with a glass of wine. She considered hiding behind the curtain with it so that she could drink alone.

Eddie approached with another old woman on his arm. His aunt. She raised her spider-leg eyebrows and asked a question in rapid Spanish. Beth chuckled and turned to her husband.

"In translation." Eddie cleared his throat. "Are you pregnant now?"

He left Beth to answer. He watched her answer.

"No. Why? Do I look fat?" She laughed again, but nobody else did.

Eddie's mother didn't speak to Beth the whole night of the party, nor later when they helped clean up. She still did not speak to her in the morning when Beth got up early and made breakfast for the whole family.

Carmen wouldn't even look at Beth. During the breakfast, she spoke only to her mother, and then mostly in clipped Bolivian Spanish. The old woman responded in a tired voice. She did not sit down to eat. She hovered while Beth cooked. She elbowed in to wash the pans Beth used the minute Eddie announced breakfast was ready.

"We'll do that, Mama," Eddie said, but he did not fight his mother. She scrubbed at the dishes with steel wool. Her forearms flexed. Eddie took a seat across from his father, who read the newspaper and ignored everybody.

"I don't like breakfast food," Carmen said to no one in particular. She had scraped back her sleek hair into a bun. She looked like an angry ballerina. Baby Nadia threw an apple slice across the table, but nobody paid attention.

Eddie and Beth ate baked peach pancakes and sausage in silence and looked at one another. He: Are you angry? She: Don't talk to me.

Nadia sat in a wooden high chair. It was the one Eddie sat in as a baby and Carmen before him. Eddie's baby butt must have suffered in that hard chair. It was an absurd and archaic piece of furniture. Beth hated it while she cut sausage into much daintier pieces than she would have if they were alone. Eddie's family made her feel like a troll.

Carmen wouldn't give her daughter any of the breakfast. She had prepared Nadia's food herself and it was red apple slices and skinned grapes. Nadia was a different kid from the clinger at the party. She laughed and was the only one talking to everybody. She had a lot of commentary in a mix of English and Spanish, the nouns rounded in the tumbler of her baby mouth.

"Appoh," she said and dropped an apple slice on the floor. Beth reached down to get it but Carmen moved faster. Carmen scooped it up, her curved acrylic fingernails clicking against the linoleum like stilettos.

"Manzana," Carmen said.

Nadia laughed, showing off a row of gapped teeth. Carmen's own smile escaped. Her eyes flashed softness as she wiped the baby's mouth.

At the final blessed end of the meal, Eddie took plates to the sink to be sucked into the storm of his mother's washing.

"It's time for us to go, Ma," Eddie said. "We have to hit the road."

His father rattled the newspaper. "The traffic is going to be bad," he said.

Carmen screamed. Her chair toppled backwards. Nadia's eyes widened in a mottled purple face. Her arms and legs flopped while Carmen grabbed her and drummed at her narrow back with a futile open hand. The grandfather began to bark directions in Spanish, jabbing the air with his knobby finger.

The grandmother rushed over and pulled on Nadia's legs. Eddie's mother and sister made a tug-of-war with the dying, choking child between them.

Beth moved in. She shoved Eddie's mother aside and took the baby. She hefted Nadia face-down across the length of her arm. Carmen flapped at Beth's back like a crow, but Beth just squeezed Nadia's little face between thumb and forefinger, folding the baby's cheeks and mouth in one hand. She struck the space between the baby's shoulders and did it again and then the baby coughed. An apple wedge fell from her mouth and she cried the loud long breathless wail of a child in true pain and fear.

Beth righted her child-laden arm and gathered Nadia into her chest. She kissed her firm, wet cheek and whispered in her ear. Only then did she hand the baby over to Carmen, who stood weeping with her hard knuckled fists opening and closing.

Eddie slumped at the table and put his head in his hands. His mother made the sign of the cross.

Carmen turned away from them all and went into the living room. Nadia's crumpled but now pink face looked over her mother's shoulder and with one tired starfish hand waved Beth good-bye.

Sixteen years later, Nadia missed the late-night Greyhound to Oroville out of San Jose because they changed the lines without bothering to change the schedule.

"You missed it," the ticket lady said. "Next one, 6:00 a.m."

Nadia dropped into a plastic chair in the empty station. The hostile engines of an unmanned NASCAR arcade game droned by the soda machine. She could have been the last person in the world, or else stuck in a very lonely and frustrating level of Hell.

The thought of getting on a bus back to the dorms in Santa Cruz hurt like a hammer upside the head. Nadia wanted to be at Dani's house in Oroville. She wanted Dani's bedroom with its candles and incense. She wanted Dani with her butterscotch arms and cornsilk hair.

A person who wanted another person as much as Nadia wanted Dani should have that person. She should be able to get to her. It shouldn't be so fucking difficult.

The Greyhound meandered from Santa Cruz to Oroville on a string of nowherevilles: Vacaville, Roseville. She didn't have to disembark and transfer but one time. San Jose. Now the bus chugged up Highway 680 with an empty seat that she'd already paid for.

Nadia meant to roll into Oroville at four in the morning and crawl into bed with Dani while she slept. She meant to be there earlier than expected as a surprise. Now Nadia had to go back to the dorms at UCSC. Try again tomorrow. It was so stupid. The disappointment got hard in her stomach and rolled around in there. She felt like puking.

"Santa Cruz," Nadia said, back at the ticket window.

"There's no more lines tonight." The lady turned away as Nadia cursed and then a security guard grabbed her elbow. He shoved her out onto the street and locked the glass door between them.

Nadia spun around. The building across the street stood dark and boarded-up. Nothing up the street looked open either. She pounded on the station door, but someone inside turned off the lights. She was left in the hazy yellow halo of the streetlamp.

She didn't know anyone in San Jose at all. There was nobody back at school with a car that she knew well enough to call for help. She couldn't pay for a cab back over the mountain. She only had what was left of the tips from a week of waiting tables, and that money came too hard anyway to spend on a damn cab.

Her abuela and mother lived four hours away, in Los Osos. They lived too far away to help. Even if she did call them, they would only yell and scream and ask questions she could never answer.

Tío Eddie and his wife, Risa, lived in San Luis. Not helpful. Too far away. Plus, they'd tell.

That left Tío Eddie's ex-wife, Beth Martin, in Los Gatos. Beth sent a birthday card every year along with twenty bucks even though Nadia never saw her. After her thirteenth birthday Nadia asked how come she never had to write a thank you note to Beth. For other relatives she had to write notes if they so much as said bless you after she sneezed.

"She's not even your aunt anymore," Mama said.

"Then why does she send me money?"

Abuela made the sign of the cross. Mama didn't answer. She only looked out the window.

Nadia began writing secret thank you notes to her ex-aunt and sending them without telling anybody. She remembered liking Beth. Tío Eddie and Beth divorced when Nadia was five. Mama said Beth was no good. She said Beth told stories at family parties about working as a nurse in a children's hospital. She dealt with the worst cancers, dog maulings, kids with intestinal parasites. She didn't notice everyone losing their appetites when she talked about it over the paella.

Nadia would have liked the stories. A lady like Beth would never flinch no matter what a kid had wrong with her. Anyway, it was worth it to try because if she stayed here she would get killed or raped or maybe both. She stepped out of the light and ticked away at her phone in the dark. She found the number of Beth Martin in Los Gatos. Beth's voice was cool as water. She promised to hurry. She ordered Nadia to stay put and to stay out of sight.

Nadia leaned against the wall. She closed her eyes and conjured Dani. Dani wore long feathered earrings that she let Nadia remove with her teeth. Dani's neck smelled like warm cloves and the smoke from a woodburning stove.

The last time she'd visited Oroville was in September. Dani's soft belly from just the summer before was gone. Her hipbones jutted beyond her stomach and Nadia's were getting like that too. They lay smoking in Dani's bed. Their hips touched. Their elbows too. "We'll be knocking together like old ladies pretty soon," Dani said. "We'll be a couple of bags of bones." If Dani were caught out in the cold in a bad part of a city, she would laugh and say fuck it and anybody who tried to mess with her would end up with her boot in his mouth. Nadia huffed into her hands and tried to conjure that level of courage. She was exhausted. The long bus ride was when she was finally supposed to get some sleep. She'd timed it on purpose.

A Subaru pulled up and a red-haired woman inside popped open the passenger door. Nadia bounded out of the shadows and jumped into the car.

"That is an awful place," Beth said, heading toward the freeway. "Totally unsafe. I'm glad you called. Where can I take you?"

"Can I sleep on your couch tonight? You can just drop me at a Greyhound station on your way to work or whatever." Nadia felt out of breath.

"Where are you going on the bus?"

"Visiting somebody."

"Boyfriend?"

"Nope." Nadia held her fingers to the heater vent and played with the hot air and tried to breathe regular.

"Aren't you in school? Won't you be missing class?"

"Are you going to call my mother?"

Beth's mouth clamped into a line. She shook her head. "You're eighteen."

On the way, Nadia dozed off without meaning to and woke up when they stopped.

Beth's house smelled like vanilla. "Are your kids asleep?" Nadia whispered.

"I don't have kids," she said.

Nadia was surprised. She knew that Beth and Eddie hadn't had children together, but Beth seemed like she'd be somebody's mother. She led Nadia to a yellow room with a bed covered in a fat quilt.

"That's Don across the hall in my room," she said. "He's a big guy. If you meet him on the way to the toilet in the middle of the night, don't be scared."

Nadia nodded and eyed the bed. "I guess I'll get some sleep now," she said.

Beth stood there for a second, then took Nadia's hand like they were about to cross a street or something. She pulled her into the bathroom and flipped on the overhead light. With iron hands she grabbed Nadia's shoulders and forced her to face the mirror. The rim of the sink dug into Nadia's stomach. It felt like it would cut her in half.

"You might want to look at yourself," Beth said. "I don't know if you've done that in a while."

Nadia squinted. Bruisey purple half moons underscored her eyes. Her cheekbones cut long grooves into her face.

She twisted free and fled back into the guest bedroom with its cheery lemonade walls and fluffy pillows.

She should leave. Run out of the house and not come back.

Beth strode in after her—chased her, really—and stopped on the other side of the bed. Nadia just wanted to lie down. If she didn't, her head would crack open and all of the brains would spill out, ending the impasse right there.

A man emerged behind Beth. He was a tall black man in pajamas. He whispered something and Beth sighed but didn't say another thing to Nadia. She followed the man into the other bedroom and closed the door.

Nadia took off her jeans and slipped in between the cool white sheets and fell asleep.

Afternoon winter light sliced through Nadia's eyelids. She blinked awake and pawed the floor for her jeans and her phone to look at the time.

It was after one o'clock in the afternoon. Her jaw ached and her teeth were killing her. She threw a pillow at the wall and cursed.

Beth knew she needed a ride to the bus in the morning but didn't bother to wake her up. She should have known better than to trust her.

Nadia yanked her jeans back on and laced up her boots. She stomped into the empty kitchen. A note on the table from Beth said that she would be home by four. It said help yourself to anything. *Help yourself.*

Nadia looked out the window. There was a car in the driveway, not the Subaru, a Volkswagen bug. It was yellow and shiny in the sunny afternoon. It was cheerful and winking.

She took a hit from the stuff she had in her bag and then went into the bathroom. A hot shower washed away the smells of the twelve hours straight of work in a greasy restaurant and the hopeless bus station. Nadia used Beth's honey and vanilla-smelling soap and lotion. When Nadia and Dani were rich, they would never ride the bus. They would work in law firms or run their own businesses. They would be through waitressing in the cheapo old people restaurants that served calamari steak specials that sat on the plate like beige shoe leather. They would drive around in a beautiful car and eat in fine places and leave grand tips for their waitresses because they would know how it felt.

Nadia found the keys in a ceramic frog's mouth on the mantel above the fireplace. Nadia's own high school graduation photo stood beside it in a frame. It startled her. Her shiny chubby face grinned between curtains of long hair. That was how she used to look. Nadia knocked it down.

She wrote Beth a note in return. *I'll be back in three days.* She added a smiley face to lighten the mood.

The air was cool on her wet head. She buzzed with energy and fresh purpose. The miles between Los Gatos and Dani stretched and contracted ahead of her. She headed north to the faceless town of Oroville, that dirt-colored shell that held Dani, who was like a beautiful pearl and the only thing she cared about in the world.

North and east she headed. She would face only north and east until she made it to the lair of the source of the northeastern wind, her northeastern goddess, her witch, her sweetheart, her best and only friend.

The next morning in the tiny apartment bathroom, Dani pushed Nadia with hands like claws. Her hard palms slammed against Nadia's breastbone. Dani's face contorted with rage Nadia recognized but also an emptiness that she didn't. She begged Dani to move with her to Santa Cruz and apply for financial aid and go to school. Dani sang back the idea in a mean singsong that stung like a whip.

"We'll graduate together. We'll live in a big house by the sea," Dani said. She sneered and cursed. She tore at her own hair and pulled at her own uniform work skirt. She was a brown gingham nightmare shadow of Dani, shrieking, "This is me. This is how it is."

Nadia's head still buzzed a little from the leftover crystal they smoked the night before. She shoved her things into her bag while Dani brushed her teeth in hard jabs and muttered around the toothbrush that she had to go to work. She worked for a living and if she didn't work then she didn't get paid. She didn't have time for bullshit.

Dani spit and let the water glass fall to the hard tiles beneath her bare feet. It shattered as Nadia walked out the door.

For five hours Nadia drove straight through. No stops, not even to pee. She pulled into Beth's driveway.

She left her bag on the porch and knocked and waited.

Beth opened the door and stepped back. She went into the kitchen and sat down.

Nadia followed and handed over the keys. It seemed pointless to speak, though she understood some things were expected when you took someone's car without asking.

"Thanks for not calling the police," she said.

"I didn't do you any favors by not."

Nadia felt too hollow to be embarrassed. She was on the downside of a high that was weak to begin with. She was rolling down and picking up velocity toward a steel hammer headache and a leaden soul.

"You're a mess," Beth said. The late winter camellias in the front yard brushed against the window glass in the wind.

"It would have been nice if you woke me up. I wouldn't have taken your car then."

"I tried. You might as well have been dead. Methamphetamines, I'm guessing."

Nadia didn't answer. She couldn't explain that the meth wasn't the point. It was just a way to be with Dani. In high school they would go to clubs together high and powerful as queens, dancing until their bodies moved together like one beautiful, four-armed creature. What she used back in Santa Cruz was only to help through the monster work shifts she needed to raise money to see Dani, to give to Dani. Dani made the days in the crowded and noisy dorms and boring lecture halls have a reason. Nadia had no problem writing papers and gutting out exams when she knew that someday at the end of it Dani would be her family. The big house by the sea had been more than just an idea for Nadia. It had been the land she was swimming toward.

Now her future stretched out like a dead body.

She ached for some coffee but didn't want to ask Beth for another thing.

"I saved your life once before," Beth said, her voice calm and pleasant like the beginning of a bedtime story. "You were two. You almost died, choking on an apple slice. It's amazing, what will take a child. You keep the poisons up high, then she chokes to death on breakfast." Beth filled a pot with water, scooped out coffee, ground up beans.

"We were at the table and suddenly you turned blue. Nobody knew what to do. Your grandmother, of course, with her prayers." Beth shook her head. "I picked you up and did what you do when a baby chokes. And you turned pink again."

Nadia felt relieved that it ended well. It was good news that once she was rescued.

"But what do you do," Beth asked, "when a young woman chokes?"

She came forward and took Nadia's face in between her finger and thumb. She clutched Nadia's chin in the web of her strong hand and squeezed her cheeks until her lips puckered. It hurt, but Nadia let her do it.

"I must have been a fool," Beth said. "Leaving a teenage drug addict alone in my house. And you're a fire sign on top of it, with tendencies toward passion and spontaneous travel."

Nadia's tears spilled into Beth's palm. "I don't know what you're talking about," she said. Her voice sounded funny from out of a scrunched-up mouth.

"In translation," Beth said. "Stay here. Let me help you. We are family, after all. In a way." She let Nadia's face go and went to pour the coffee.

Nadia turned to the window by her chair. She rested her forehead against a cold pane. Her breath steamed up the glass as she exhaled through air passages constricted by fear.

She'd stay for at least a night or two. For that chunk of time she might live.

She took another breath.

# Dear Juana of God
### *Beth Alvarado*

*In which Jillian makes a pilgrimage to Magdalena, Mexico, encounters Juana of God, and thus brings Marisol home to Bella.*

## 1

It is not surprising, given the state of her world, that Angie O'Malley would look to Oprah for guidance. Of course, she doesn't actually turn to Oprah, not personally, but all the same she gives Oprah credit for inspiration, Oprah via Angie's daughter, Jillian.

This is how it happened: Jillian was sitting on her Aunt Glenda's hospital bed in the living room—Glenda was asleep, earphones in, Mozart playing quietly on her iPod so the sonatas could rearrange her brain cells—and on the TV, this little Mexican woman was shoving nasal probes up a man's nostrils to rid him of a brain tumor. Jillian let out a noise, a grunt maybe, but the closest she'd ever come in her thirteen years of life to a word. And Angie—hoping for a miracle—rushed in from the kitchen and saw Jillian, dear mute Jillian, pointing at Juana of God. She took it for a sign.

Not that Angie wants anyone to shove anything up Glenda's nose, but there are other ways of performing miracles, she's sure, and there was a very handsome medical doctor—an American, Ivy League—on the show who showed a scar on his chest just below his ribs where he had spontaneously started bleeding after witnessing the near lobotomy. The doctor went on to tell Oprah that the experience had turned his life upside down. Upside down! Because, for one, the near lobotomy had made the guy's tumor shrink and then disappear. And for another, he, the doctor, now had to question everything, *everything*. His entire worldview.

The doctor shrugged. "Sure, maybe there's a logical, a medical, explanation. Maybe it stimulated the pituitary gland, maybe not. Maybe we will never know. But the tumor is gone. That I do know."

Here, a short film of the doctor and the man whose nostrils had been probed walking away from the healing. The man looked dizzy, woozy, as if he couldn't believe he'd just allowed someone to shove steel rods like knitting needles up his nose. The doctor lifted his shirt and streaming from a hole in his side, blood. He touched it. He touched it again, amazed.

"There are things we don't understand," the doctor went on, seated next to Oprah in front of her studio audience. "All things are mysteriously connected, this is what I learned. Empiricism is not the be-all and end-all."

Here, a panning of the audience, to whom Oprah nodded and smiled, Oprah as solemn as she always is on occasions involving transformation.

Angie sat down and watched the rest of the show. What else could they do, but seek a miracle? The doctors here in San Francisco were offering nothing, *nada*, no hope for Glenda. Marisol, the woman who had been taking care of Glenda, had been deported. Angie had been helping her mother, Lois, take care of Glenda, and they were both utterly exhausted. Utterly. So in spite of the 10,000 deaths in Mexico in the last year due to the warring drug cartels, in spite of the stories about American women and Mexican babies being abducted and killed by drug dealers, their corpses being hollowed out and used as containers to transport drugs, in spite of all that, Angie decided they would risk it. After all, lots of people live in Mexico and don't get beheaded or stuffed with drugs or shot execution-style and dumped in pits of lime, and it's only a fifty-mile drive from Tucson to Magdalena along a four-lane highway, and the Angels in Green rove that stretch of road and stop to help stranded motorists. They don't do that here in the States, she thought. *¡No angeles verdes aquí!* She popped a Xanax.

*Dear Juana of God*, she wrote at the top of the letter she would send ahead of them, and then she described Glenda's maladies of the mind and body and heart.

## 2

Magdalena de Kino, Sonora, Mexico: brown hills squatting in the distance, then ranches and fields of green, and at the center lies the town and the lovely Plaza Monumental with the Temple of Santa María de Magdalena and the white igloo-shaped crypt in which lie, in a glass case, the bones of the town's founding father, Father Eusebio Kino. When Angie sets out from Tucson, with Glenda and Jillian, she doesn't realize that it's the Festival of San Francisco Xavier, a time when people make pilgrimages to Magdalena, walking sometimes one hundred miles or more as they have done for years, centuries, maybe, and she wonders if their devotion has thus charged the ions in the air and if maybe that's how Juana of God is able to perform her miracles.

Do you have to believe in God or Christ, she wonders, for Juana to cure you? She thinks not. After all, that handsome doctor didn't seem to be religious. Even though his wound was exactly where Christ's was, he didn't say anything about God, not God the Father, not God the Son, nor God the Holy Ghost. Neither did Oprah. She didn't even ask the obvious Oprah questions.

Angie is a more-than-lapsed Catholic, but even she could see it: looking at that wound was like looking at the stigmata and saying nothing. Curious. Christ as the elephant in the room. Angie has heard of cathedrals in Mexico where the stone floors have grooves worn in them from people crawling on their knees to the altar. Even if you don't believe in God, she thinks, there must be something to believe in—even if it's only the faith of others. But for now, she just drives carefully, hoping that no pedestrian or pilgrim will decide to test God by stepping in front of her car.

## 3

They come into the café every morning for *desayuno*, the woman with her hair as if it is on fire, *la rubia* in the wheelchair, and the girl who does not talk. They did not know it was the festival and so the woman, she was very upset at the streets full of people. She had hoped, she said, for *más cálmate*, by which I think she was *not* telling me "more you calm down," but saying instead that she wished the town was more quiet, not so noisy with the bands and the dancing in the streets. So I set a table aside for them in the corner and every morning, it's the same thing. *La rubia* in the wheelchair gets a quesadilla because, no matter how much her hand shakes, she can bring it to her mouth. The mother of the girl, she gets *huevos rancheros*, and the girl, when she points to *tacos de lengua* on the menu, the mother shrugs and says, *a ella le gusta la carne*. Every morning. Evidently the mother does not see the irony that we see—those of us busy in the kitchen—a girl who cannot speak eating *lengua*.

"Tell me," the mother of the girl says to me on the third morning, "what do you know of this Juana of God? And why is it we have to wait so long for an appointment?"

Of course, it is a coincidence for right at that moment, Juana and her assistant, Nardo, are sitting at their table, which is set aside for them in the other corner of the restaurant. But I say nothing. Because. Who knows if Juana wants to see them?

"All I know," I say, "is that Juana has taken away my toothaches. With one touch of her fingers, she lifts away the pain. She has even taken away the dreams of my teeth crumbling in my mouth. Perhaps that is worth waiting for."

The mother tilts her head as though considering this, and just then the silent girl lifts her face and I know she recognizes Juana of God—who could forget her?—the thick eyebrows that meet in a line like Frida's, the snow-white hair piled high on her head, the huge hoop earrings, the heavy turquoise rings on her fingers and the hundreds of jangling bracelets. Juana is a striking woman. With her full breasts and haunches, she looks like one of those goddesses before *la virgen* ever showed herself to Juan Diego.

Right now, Juana is eating a breakfast of pastries that I make especially for her in the old French way, butter, *crema*, eggs, all the things she is not supposed to have because of her heart disease. It is like the painter whose house needs painting, the healer who needs a cure. What can I say?

When I go over to her table to tell her that she has visitors, she pats the chair next to her. "*Siéntate*, Jorge. Let me tell you what those American doctors did to me. They pumped my veins full of radioactivity and I could feel myself begin to glow. All through my veins, up my right arm, into my armpit, into my lungs and heart, even into my brain, I could feel it. The warmth like scorpion venom. It was moving all through me, down into my legs, up into my other arm, lighting me up like thousands of stars. There it was flowing through me. I knew they could see it even without their machines and it scared them."

"And so what did they say?"

"*Nada*," Nardo says, "*nada que ya no sabemos*."

"Pfft!" Juana waves her hand as if she is swishing away a fly. "But as if that is not bad enough! They make you run on this treadmill as if you are a rat, a rat with wires all taped to you. You are full of their poison and you have wires taped to you and they watch the computer as you run. They do not watch you. You could fall off and hit your head and die and they would not notice until their computer told them to look. And then, while you are running as fast as you can, they pump still more poison into you and it burns like hell and no matter if you say it burns, they do not listen. All of this just so they can see inside you because, without their machines and their poisons, they cannot see inside."

The mother rises and begins to push *la rubia* toward the door, and right then Juana's little Chihuahua begins to growl deep in his throat.

"Watch out for the dog!" Nardo warns them. "He bites!"

But the silent girl, she comes over to our table and puts her hand on Juana's shoulder and Junie, I swear, he stops growling. He does not bite. It's the only time he has ever let a stranger touch Juana of God.

"Ah," Juana belches, a deep one, from her whole body. She studies the girl's pale face. "You have a gift, *mi'ja*. That was just what I needed."

4

White is not in the palette of Jillian's wardrobe. Nor is it in her mother's or in Glenda's, but after much grumbling about the commercialism of the Juana of God enterprise and how it supports the whole goddamned town, her mother buys peasant blouses for the three of them from a store on the Plaza Monumental. They are thin white cotton with bright embroidered flowers all along the top and the edges. On Glenda's, even the flowers are white since she is the patient, which makes Jillian think she is like a nun or a bride or an angel. Even *La Casa*, which is what the people call Juana of God's *hacienda*, is white. White walls, white floors, white domed roof, white ceilings, white curtains. Has color been erased? Have they died and gone to a bland heaven? These questions enter Jillian's mind.

In the courtyard of *La Casa Blanca*, as Jillian now thinks of it, rows and rows of white plastic lawn chairs filled with rows and rows of supplicants dressed in white clothing. Jillian and her mother wheel Glenda in front of them, take two chairs on the aisle next to her. A red flash of the wings of a cardinal, green leaves of huge plants sway in terra cotta pots, fronds of the palms above them rustle. Junie, the Chihuahua, struts across the stage. And then Juana appears in a white pantsuit and is standing in the center of the stage where the visible healing takes place, where she gets inhabited by a saint or by an old German doctor or by Florence Nightingale, maybe, or by Oswaldo Cruz, or maybe by several entities in succession, depending on what the patients need.

There is the visible healing, where people go up on to the stage and get healed because the entity enters Juana of God and she goes into a trance and the entity operates—not Juana, Juana does not operate for, as even she will tell you, she has no medical training and, besides, as her assistants will tell you, the sight of blood makes her swoon—Jillian knows this from Oprah—and then there is the *in*visible healing, which happens when people in the audience sit and quietly focus on their own inner need for healing, and then the spirit entities move among them and even inside them and leave invisible sutures.

Jillian, of course, can't wait to see blood spurting from people's noses or to see the part where Juana sticks her hand inside someone's body, right through the skin!

But, until then: all around Jillian, the rising hum of everyone's desires for wholeness, and she has to say, some of their desires are a little crass. Even her mother's. Since she is closest to Jillian, Jillian can hear her mother's desire for money. Her mother believes that if only she could win the lottery, she would have enough money to take care of everything else herself. She wouldn't need Juana of God or even God, although, as a more-than-lapsed Catholic, she doesn't dare think this for more than one nanosecond. (Of course, she needs God.) But she *could*. Take care of everything. The Lord helps those who help themselves, after all. If she had money, she could quit her job and take care of Glenda and take care of her mother and Jillian and even Stevie Jr., whom they've had to leave behind with her mother. (Poor Stevie Jr., Jillian suddenly thinks, imagining her fierce grandmother yanking the remote out of Stevie Jr.'s hand so she can watch *Wheel! of! Fortune!*) Meanwhile her mother is almost in a frenzy of anxiety, revising her monetary needs up and up and up, more and more and more zeroes, because she'll need help, won't she? For years. No, for decades. With her mother's declining health as well as Glenda's, she'll need two Marisols, at least, and if she takes in two Marisols, then she'll have to take in Marisol One's granddaughter, Bella, and probably another Bella for the other Marisol, for she doesn't want to exploit anyone, and she'll need a bigger house for all of them to live together and she'll have to put the Bellas through college as well as Stevie Jr. and Jillian. And Stevie Jr. will probably want to go to graduate school, for he is one smart cookie, and Jillian, if Jillian wants to go to art school, Angie is determined that she will. Why, oh why, had she bought the white blouses? They didn't really need them, did they, to come here? And why did she buy that expensive face lotion and that expensive wine the other night and why had she put the airline tickets on her card instead of letting her mother pay for them? And what if she has to sell the house to take care of Glenda? The more Angie thinks about everyone who needs her and how little money she has saved and how much she wastes—one of her cards is at 19.99%!—and how little she earns from her job and how she's run out of sick leave and vacation time— although everyone tells her she should be thankful she even had that!—and how little Jillian's father, Bobby, sends and how little Stevie Sr. sends for Stevie Jr., the more and more oppressed she feels and the more and more money she thinks she needs and the more she wishes she just had something simple wrong with her, even a tumor, say, so that Juana of God could just shove something up her nose and cure it once and for all. Yes, if her money woes could be over, if she could quit the nightly tossing and turning that started as soon as she heard about Glenda's accident, she would let someone shove knitting needles up her nose. She would. She would let someone stab her in the stomach and give her the stigmata. Let the bleeding begin!

At this, Jillian takes her mother's hand and strokes it. She presses her other hand against her mother's cheek. *Shhh*, Jillian thinks to her mother, and to all the others whose needs are rising in them, whose knots of anxiety are twisting and twisting.

Does Juana of God hear them, too?

## 5

*El perrito*, nightmare of my existence, the way he nips at my heels. If he were a bigger dog, he would be dead already. He barks, and it is a signal that Juana is about to begin. Juana, whose *Casa Blanca* I have been cleaning. *¿Juana es de Dios? No sé.* Anything is possible, *pues*, but when you clean a person's toilet, you know things about her no one else should know. Juana is of the flesh and God is ineffable. Of this, I have no doubt. Perhaps God works through her in the way He works through all of us. An act of kindness here, you give money there, a crust of bread, a tortilla, whatever you can because the beggar at your door may be the Savior— *¿quién sabe?* —who knows, you never know—but does this mean Juana is any closer to God than the rest of us? *Je ne sais pas!* as the French would say.

She is a *curandera*, okay, of this I am sure—and a good one, maybe, one hopes she does no harm—it's just that she's found her market, and a *curandera*, she is not supposed to have a market. She is supposed to give her gifts freely for they came to her freely—but such is the free market system and its power to corrupt. After years of living on the other side, of this I can testify. *¡Ay, Dios mío! Los norteamericanos*, they are the only ones in the world who think that God proves Himself by granting wishes.

And so Junie barks and so I see them, *my norteamericanos*, Angie and Glenda and Jillian, they are sitting a few rows in front of me. At first, my heart skips a beat, for I am hoping and also not hoping that they have brought my Bella, *mi nieta*, who got left behind in the States when I got deported. *Mi vida.* Oh, I wonder how she is doing without me and if she knows I am cleaning *baños* as fast as I can to get back to her, working my way north, for even in Mexico there are those who don't like to clean their own bathrooms.

Angie stands up and pushes her sister forward, up the ramp, on to the stage. Jillian, *pobrecita*, is left by herself and so I move up and sit next to her. She is a strange one, I know, but sweet. She touches my hand without even looking at me, as if she were expecting me, Marisol, to come and sit next to her, as if to say "Hi!" She is looking at the dog as if she expects him to change into a much larger, a mythical creature. This is something I also expect of him, and so I remind him, often, to keep him in his place, that my ancestors ate his ancestors. You exist only because your ancestors were raised for food, I tell him, and then he slinks away like the little hairless dog that he is.

On stage, Juana has gone into one of her trances and the voice that comes out of her mouth, *y eso es la verdad*, I swear, is the voice of a very old man who is stuck in a tunnel. It is not a voice I have heard before. It is speaking a language other than Spanish or English or French and I look down and the girl, Jillian, is drawing in a notebook and in the drawing, there is a small creature with wings and with the face of *el perrito*, Junie. *El perrito*, he is pierced with small arrows and his bug-eyes roll up in his head like the eyes of a saint. And now she is drawing, I see it, Juana holding out her hand for the knife and, around Juana, like a shadow, the larger shape of a man, a man in old-fashioned clothing. And now another shadow and now another, until all over the page there are shadows, what is left of those who have gone before us, maybe, gathered there on the stage hearing our sad prayers. And so I think, maybe these *norteamericanos* are on to something. Maybe we, *los pobres*, are behind the times, thinking we're supposed to serve God and not the other way around.

*Entonces. ¿Quién sabe?* Maybe God will grant our wishes. Can it hurt to try? And so I do, I try, and even as I try, I know, I can feel it, there is a difference between praying and wishing because with praying, your whole soul rises and expands and becomes filled with light, but with wishing, it is only half of your soul, not enough light to share with others. I can feel part of my heart holding back and this, I know, is my own lack. *Me falta* not faith in God but the belief that prayers are for wishing. This is a lack that is in me and not God's fault. Still, I try to wish, like the others seated around me, and I wish not to be Mexican.

I want to be cured of being Mexican? Oh, no, that is not what I intend. *Soy mexicana, siempre.* By this I mean I want to go back to where is my home now, the area of the bay, San Francisco. I want a claim to my own life. I want to be free to belong where I belong. My blood will always be here in this soil, but the heart that pumps my blood is in *el otro lado*, with my *nieta* Bella, where I am needed. Here, I will come back here to die.

6

Even before Marisol sits next to her, Jillian has been drawing what she sees. She has drawn a brown cloud coming out of the dog's mouth like a puff of earthy dust or smoke and, as it materialized, it became a man in a brown suit, and then another cloud floated forward and it was a woman in a long black gown, and then another and another and another, too many for Jillian to draw all at once. Then Junie the dog sprouted wings and then arrows pierced him as if he were a small deer being hunted by invisible archers, and when his eyes rolled back in his head, the head of Juana of God snapped back and snapped forward and when she opened her mouth, a gravelly voice, the voice of an old man, came out. The voice said *unters messen kommen* and because Jillian, in her few moments of omniscience when she was being born, was granted a limited vocabulary in many languages—a particularly ironic gift since she would never be able to speak any of them—she understood that the voice was saying something about undergoing the knife and it must have been true because when Juana of God held out her hand—although she was no longer all there and so to say she held out her hand seems to imply a volition that she did not, in actuality, seem to have—an assistant, who was also dressed all in white, slapped a dinner knife in her palm. Slapped, as if she needed to be sure that Juana could feel it.

Just then, as Marisol sits next to her, Jillian watches as Juana of God steps up to a man with a goatee, the first supplicant, and he puts both his hands over his heart, and Juana is mumbling something, perhaps praying, Jillian thinks, although she is now drawing so quickly, all of her consciousness focused on her hand moving across the page, that she isn't really paying attention to sound. All is vision. Juana has stretched the man's eyelids apart and she has begun to scrape his eyeball with the dinner knife. The man seems to feel no pain. He doesn't say a word, he doesn't lift his hands from his chest, he doesn't even seem to resist by pulling his head back. Jillian can see a glowing red spot on the man's left lung, it is glowing through his skin, and so she wonders *why the eyeball when he has a growth on his lung?* But now Juana of God is moving toward her mother and her aunt.

Later, much later, Jillian will wonder why it did not surprise her when Juana of God went directly to her mother, as if Angie were the patient and not Glenda, but, of course, because Juana was in a trance, not seeing the world as it existed in front of her eyes but seeing, instead, some version of it painted inside her own mind, Juana of God moved toward Angie and she put her hand on Angie's shoulder and Angie put her hands over her heart, as if she were, indeed, the supplicant, the person who was in need of healing. The voice that came out of Juana of God's mouth this time was in an ancient language, so ancient that none of her assistants understood her, it was a language of trees growing or of magma from deep in the earth or of ancient water, a language without words, but Juana seemed to understand it and Jillian, as she drew, understood it in her muscles and bones, for she could draw as quickly as if she were drawing a movie, as if the drawing were causing the events to happen and not merely recording them.

Juana of God lifted Angie's shirt and there was Angie's smooth white stomach with one dark mole right below her left breast, and Juana plunged her hand into Angie's stomach, right through the skin, no need for a knife, no need for an incision, even the assistants gasped, even the shadows on the stage gasped, and the spirits who were moving among the supplicants seated for invisible healing, they all gasped, and Juana drew out of Angie's stomach a large black stone, like a river stone, pure black, heavy, worn smooth by millennia and millennia of water running over it, and she handed the stone to Glenda, who took it in her hands and pressed it to her cheek, and then Juana pulled stone after stone out of Angie's stomach until there were seven stones and, after each stone, she handed it to Glenda and Glenda held it first to her cheek and then cradled it in her lap. No one could believe that seven such large stones had been housed in such a thin body. After the last stone, Juana of God seemed to look at her own hand, for she held it to the sky and turned it back and forth, and then she waved her hand over Angie's stomach and the skin was smooth, healed, as if it had never been broken.

Jillian continues to draw and, in her drawing, her mother floats up above the stage, she seems very happy, and Jillian draws a large house below her and, in the house, she draws her grandmother and Stevie Jr. watching TV. She draws Bella knocking at the front door. She draws the handsome American doctor, the one from the Ivy League who was on *Oprah*. He comes up on the stage to help Angie with Glenda. He loves the smooth rocks, he holds them to his own cheek, one by one, and then he takes Glenda's face in his hands and she whispers—what, Jillian cannot hear for her head is bent over her drawing—but they are the first words Glenda has uttered since her accident and, although Jillian does not believe in fairy tales, she knows what kind of woman her aunt is, a woman who is only happy when she is with a man, and so Jillian draws her floating up out of the chair and she and the doctor are flying slant-wise over the stage as if they are the bride and groom in the painting by Chagall. They have left the stones that burdened Angie below. The stones are below. Angie begins to sing, a song like a lullaby, and everyone, including the spirits, including Juana of God, including Junie, the chanelling Chihuahua, feel as if someone invisible is cradling them. Sutures, visible and invisible, anywhere within fifty miles, melt and leave no marks.

## 7

Jillian draws a sunny day for their departure. When they pack up the car, they will leave the stones behind, because now that the doctor and Marisol are traveling with them, there is no room for the stones and, besides, Juana of God wants to use them in her herb garden. She will swap them for payment because she is sure they will help her grow the most marvelous herbs. She is sad to see the doctor go, primarily because he was such good publicity, but *c'est la vie, que será será*, and all that.

Even Junie, for all his growling at Marisol, wishes her the best, hopes she won't be deposited again in the middle of the burning desert. Goodbye, he barks. Goodbye! Good luck! Marisol, remembering when he bit her finger, gives him the evil eye, but Jillian waves. Junie, she knows, contains multitudes, and so it's not surprising that he's a little schizophrenic.

As they approach the border, Jillian feels overwhelmed with the lines and lines of cars, their hulking bodies, their exhaust rising in gray ghost clouds. Likewise, she is overwhelmed by the little girls wilting like paper flowers, *chicle for sale* melting in the palms of their hands, and the grubby boys who clamor at the windows and climb on the hoods of cars, waving their spray bottles and squeegees. Not to mention: on the periphery of her vision, the shadows of teenagers who were shot for throwing rocks at the border patrol on the other side or for trying to climb the fence back into this country, or who were hit by stray bullets as they walked along the street across from the wall, head down, eyes averted, hunched shoulders. José Antonio Elena Rodríguez. Seven bullets in the back, that's how the *corrido* will go. One day, there should be a song remembering, Jillian thinks.

She looks down at her drawing. She hopes the guards won't notice Marisol—Marisol, who at this moment, is doing her best to vanish and so is becoming thinner and thinner to the point of near translucence, almost melting into the upholstery between Jillian and her mother. Jillian scoots closer as if to hide her. She hopes the guards will be too mesmerized by her mother's singing and too busy looking at the lovebirds in the backseat and at the light that emanates from the car itself to notice Marisol. The light, which is the light of concentrated prayers, will blind them, Jillian decides. It will be a laser-beam light, a light so bright that the car can rise above all the other cars and float over the border in a bubble—this is how Jillian draws the car—in a blue bubble with tongues of light all around, just like *la virgen de Guadalupe* in those paintings on velvet. For it's true, *la virgen* can go anywhere. Borders never stop her. Maybe, Jillian thinks, Marisol's escape will count as the miracle they've been hoping for.

# Away

## *Ellie Knightsbridge*

———◦⸝⸎⸜◦———

They tell you it's one of the hardest things you'll ever have to do. The ultimate sacrifice, as if ruining your vagina in the first place wasn't enough.

They spout clichés about leaving the nest and about loving someone enough to let them go. There are even self-help books about it: *Mum Done: How to Live for You!* and *Empty House, Full Life*.

My friends seem to glue themselves back together with evening ceramics classes and salsa dancing in the middle of the day at clubs with sticky floors. But I'm a slippery, slimy eel and I've always been able to wriggle my way through "life events."

I don't miss Jake like they seem to miss their kids who've gone off to university.

I feel real. Like I have an identity and if I committed a crime an image of my actual face would be on the news. I exist. I'm a person, not a parasite feeding off the nutrients of my family. For so many years I felt like the smudged, blurred text under a sweaty thumb that holds the edge of the newspaper, a fuzzy, replaceable blot on the periphery. A casualty of use.

Now I have sex with my husband on the kitchen table. I let the fridge get empty and then eat a Dairy Milk for lunch, and I fall asleep on the L-shaped cream sofa in the middle of the day if I want to.

When Jake calls I sit on one of our solid oak stools at our solid oak breakfast bar in the kitchen, and I try to ask the right questions about whether he has enough socks while I paint my nails in lurid hot pink shiny polish.

I don't want to lie to him, so when he asks in his self-assured jokey tone whether I miss him, I say I'm looking forward to seeing him during the next holidays or some variation on that. I don't want him to think of me differently now, not when everything else is already so different for him in his new life.

Do I feel bad about this? That I'm so happy? No. At least I don't think I do, but when my friends talk about their kids' permanently closed bedroom doors and their withdrawn, emotionally illiterate husbands' DIY projects, I make up stories about going up in the loft to find Jake's baby shoes. I tell them I keep making too much spaghetti or that I drove all the way to see him in the middle of the night because I had a nightmare that he was being bullied.

I suppose that this deceit implies that on some level I must feel ashamed, but I wriggle myself out of that—I note it is society and convention and expectation that pricks the solid surface of my conscience. It's the other women whispering at me to cry at preposterous Pampers adverts or run a bath so hot it burns my skin.

# Miss Emily Gray

*Theodora Goss*

## I. A Lane in Albion

It was April in Albion. To the south, in the civilized counties, farmers were already putting their lambs out to pasture, and lakeshores were covered with the daffodils beloved of the Poet. The daffodils were plucked by tourists, who photographed the lambs, or each other with bunches of daffodils, or the cottage of the Poet, who had not been particularly revered until after his death. But this was the north of Albion, where sea winds blew from one side of the island to the other, so that even in the pastures a farmer could smell salt, and in that place April was not the month of lambs or daffodils or tourists, but of rain.

In the north of Albion, it was raining. It was not raining steadily. The night before had wrung most of the water out of the sky, and morning was now scattering its last drops, like the final sobs after a fit of weeping. The wind blew the drops of water here and there, into a web that a spider had, earlier that morning, carefully arranged between two slats of a fence, and over the leaves, dried by the previous autumn, that still hung from the branches of an oak tree. The branches of the oak, which had stood on that spot since William the Conqueror had added words like mutton and testament to the language, stretched over the fence and the lane that ran beside it. The lane was still sodden from the night's rains, and covered by a low gray mist.

Along this lane came a sudden gust of wind, detaching an oak leaf from its branch, detaching the spiderweb from its fence, sweeping them along with puffs of mist so that they tumbled together, like something one might find under a bureau: a tattered collection of gray fluff, brown paper, and string. As this collection tumbled down the lane, it began to extend upward like a whirlwind, and then to solidify. Soon, where there had been a leaf and a spiderweb speckled with rain, there was now a plain but neat gray dress with white collar and cuffs, and brown hair pulled back in a neat but very plain bun, and a small white nose, and a pair of serious but very clear gray eyes. Beneath the dress, held up by small white hands so that its hem would not touch the sodden lane, were a pair of plain brown boots. And as they stepped carefully among the puddles, sending the mist swirling before them, they gathered not a single speck of mud.

## II. Genevieve in a Mood

When Genevieve was in a "mood," she went to the nursery, to sulk among the rocking horses and decapitated dolls. That was where Nanny finally found her, sitting on a settee with broken springs, reading *Pilgrim's Progress.*

"There you are, Miss Genevieve," she said. She puffed and patted a hand against her ample bosom. She had been climbing up and down stairs for the last half hour, and she was a short, stout woman, with an untidy bun of hair held together by hairpins that dropped out at intervals, leaving a trail behind her.

"Evidently," said Genevieve. Nanny was the only person with authority who would not send her to her room for using "that" tone of voice. Therefore, she used it with Nanny as often as possible.

"Supper's almost over. Didn't you hear the bell? Sir Edward is having a fit. One of these days he'll fall down dead from apoplexy, and you'll be to blame."

Genevieve had no doubt he would. She could imagine her father's face growing red and redder, until it looked like a slice of rare roast beef. He would shout, "Where have you been, young lady?" followed by "Don't use that tone of voice with me!" followed by "Up to your room, Miss!" Then she would have brown bread and water for supper. Genevieve rather liked brown bread, and liked even better imagining herself as a prisoner, a modern Mary, Queen of Scots.

"And what will Miss Gray think?"

"I don't care," said Genevieve. "I didn't ask for a bloody governess."

"Genevieve!" said Nanny. She did not believe in girls cursing, riding bicycles, or—heaven forbid—smoking cigarettes.

"Do you know who's going away to school? Amelia Thwaite. You know, Farmer Thwaite's daughter. Who used to milk our cows. Whose grandfather was our butler. She's going to Paris, to study art!" Genevieve shut *Pilgrim's Progress* with a bang and tossed it on the settee, where it landed in a cloud of dust.

"I know, my dear," said Nanny, smoothing her skirt, which Genevieve and occasionally Roland had spotted with tears when their father had refused them something they particularly wanted: in Roland's case, a brown pony and riding crop that Farmer Thwaite was selling at what seemed a ridiculously low price. "Sir Edward doesn't believe in girls going away to school, and I quite agree with him. Now come down and make your apologies to Miss Gray. How do you think she feels, just arrived from—well, wherever she arrived from—without a pupil to greet her?"

Genevieve did not much care, but the habit of obedience was strong, particularly to Nanny's comfortable voice, so she rose from the settee, kicking aside *Pilgrim's Progress*. This, although unintentional, sufficiently expressed her attitude toward the book, which Old Thwaite had read to her and Roland every Sunday afternoon, after church, while her father slept on the sofa with a handkerchief over his face. When she read the book herself, which was not often, she imagined him snoring. More often, when she was in a "mood," she would simply hold it open on her lap at the picture of Christian in the Slough of Despond, imagining interesting ways to keep him from reaching the Celestial City, which she believed must be the most boring place in the universe.

As she clattered down the stairs after Nanny, speculating that her father would not shout or send her to her room in front of the new governess, she began to imagine a marsh with green weeds that looked like solid ground. From it would rise seven women, nude and strategically covered with mud, with names like Desire and Foolishness. They would twine their arms around Christian and drag him downward into the muddy depths, where they would subject him to unspeakable pleasures. She did not think he would escape their clutches.

## III. The Book in the Chimney

It was not what she was, exactly. She was not anything, exactly. Genevieve could see her now, through the library window, sitting in a garden chair, embroidering something. Once, Genevieve had crept up behind her and seen that she was embroidering on white linen with white thread so fine that the pattern was barely perceptible.

Her gray dress was always neat, her white face was always solemn. Her irregular verbs, as far as Genevieve could judge, were always correct. She knew the principal exports of Byzantium. When Genevieve did particularly well on her botany or geography, she smiled a placid smile.

It was not, then, anything in particular, except that her hands were so small, and moved so quickly over the piano keys, like jumping spiders. She preferred to play Chopin.

No, it was something more mysterious, something missing. Genevieve reached into the back of the fireplace and carefully pulled out a loose brick. Behind it was an opening just large enough for a cigar box filled with dead beetles, which was what Roland had kept there, or a book, which was what she had kept there since Roland had left for Harrow and then the university. No fire had been lit in the library since her mother's death, when Genevieve was still young enough to be carried around in Nanny's arms. Her mother, who had liked books, had left her *Pilgrim's Progress* and a copy of *Clarissa* in one volume, which Genevieve read every night until she fell asleep. She never remembered what she had read the night before, so she always started again at the beginning. She had never made it past the first letter.

Out of the opening behind the brick, she pulled a book with a red leather cover, faded and sooty from its hiding place. On the cover, in gold lettering, Genevieve could still read the words *Practical Divination*. On the first page was written,

*Practical Divination for the Adept or Amateur*
*By the Right Reverend Alice Widdicomb*
*Endorsed by the Theosophical Society*

She brought the book to the library table, where she had set the basin and a bottle of ink. She was out of black ink, so it would have to be purple. Her father would shout at her when he discovered that she was out of ink again, but this time she could blame it on Miss Gray and irregular verbs.

She poured purple ink into the basin, then blew on it and repeated the words the Right Reverend Alice Widdicomb recommended, which sounded so much like a nonsense rhyme that she always wondered if they were strictly necessary. But she repeated them anyway. Then she stared at the purple ink until her eyes crossed, and said to the basin, as solemnly as though she were purchasing a railway ticket, "Miss Gray, please."

First, the purple ink showed her Miss Gray sitting in the garden, looking faintly violet. Sir Edward came up from behind and leaned over her shoulder, admiring her violet embroidery. Then it showed a lane covered with purple mud, by a field whose fence needed considerable repair, over which grew a purple oak tree. Rain came down from the lavender sky. Genevieve waited, but the scene remained the same.

"Perfectly useless," she said with disgust. It was probably the purple ink. Magic was like Bach. If you didn't play the right notes in the right order, it never came out right. She turned to the back of the book, where she had tucked in a piece of paper covered with spidery handwriting. On one side it said "To Biddy, from Alice. A Sovereign Remedy for the Catarrh." On the other side was "A Spell to Make Come True Your Heart's Desire." That had not worked either, although Genevieve had gathered the ingredients carefully, even clipping the whiskers from the taxidermed fox in the front hall. She read it over again, wondering where she had made a mistake. Perhaps it needed to be a live fox?

In the basin, Miss Gray was once again working on her violet embroidery. Genevieve frowned, rubbing a streak of purple ink across her cheek. What was it, exactly? She would have to find out another way.

## IV. A Wedding on the Lawn

How, and this was the important question, had she done it? The tulle, floating behind her over the clipped lawn like foam. The satin, like spilled milk. The orange flowers brought from London.

Roland was drunk, which was only to be expected. He was standing beside the tea table, itself set beside the yew hedge, looking glum. Genevieve found it in her heart to sympathize.

"Oh, what a day," said Nanny, who was serving tea. She was upholstered in brown. A lace shawl that looked as though it had been yellowing in the attic was pinned to her bodice by a brooch handpainted, entirely unnecessarily, thought Genevieve, with daffodils. Genevieve was "helping."

"The Romans," said Roland.

Genevieve waited for him to say something further, but he merely took another mouthful of punch.

"To think," said Nanny. "Like the woman who nursed a serpent, until it bit her bosom so that she died. My mother told me that story, and never did she say a truer word. And she so plain and respectable."

Miss Gray, the plain and respectable, was now walking around the garden in satin and tulle, on Sir Edward's arm, nodding placidly to the farmers and gentry. In spite of her finery, she looked as neat and ordinary as a pin.

"The Romans," said Roland, "had a special room where they could go to vomit. It was called the vomitorium." He lurched forward and almost fell on the tea table.

"Take him away, won't you, Nanny," said Genevieve. "Lay him down before he gives his best imitation of a Roman." That would get rid of them both, leaving her to ponder the mystery that was Miss Gray, holding orange blossoms.

When Nanny had taken Roland into the library—she could hear through the window that he had developed a case of hiccups—Genevieve circled behind the hedge, to an overgrown holly that she had once discovered in a game of hide and seek with Roland. From the outside, the tree looked like a mass of leaves edged with needles that would prick anyone who ventured too close. If you pushed your way carefully inside, however, you found that the inner branches were sparse and bare. It was the perfect place to hide. And if you pushed a branch aside just slightly, you could see through the outer leaves without being seen. Roland had never found her, and in a fit of anger had decapitated her dolls. But she had never liked dolls anyway.

Miss Gray was listening to Farmer Thwaite, who was addressing her as Lady Trefusis. She was nodding and giving him one of her placid smiles. Sir Edward was looking particularly satisfied, which turned his face particularly red.

The old fool, thought Genevieve. She wondered what Miss Gray had up those capacious sleeves, which were in the latest fashion. Was it money she wanted?

That did not, to Genevieve's disappointment, seem to fit the Miss Gray who knew the parts of the flower and the principal rivers of Cathay.

Security? thought Genevieve. People often married for security. Nanny had said so, and in this at least she was willing to concede that Nanny might be right. The security of never again having to teach irregular verbs.

Genevieve pushed the holly leaves farther to one side. Miss Gray turned her head, with yards of tulle floating behind it. She looked directly at Genevieve, as though she could see through the holly leaves, and—she winked.

I must have imagined it, thought Genevieve a moment later. Miss Gray was smiling placidly at Amelia Thwaite, who looked like she had stepped out of a French fashion magazine.

She couldn't have seen me, thought Genevieve. And then, I wonder if she will expect me to call her mother?

## V. A Meeting by Moonlight

Genevieve was on page four of *Clarissa* when she heard the voices.

First voice: "Angel, darling, you can't mean it."

Second voice: Inaudible murmur.

First voice, which obviously and unfortunately belonged to Roland: "If you only knew how I felt. Put your hand on my heart. Can you feel it? Beating and burning for you."

How embarrassing, having one's brother under one's bedroom window, mouthing banalities to a kitchenmaid.

Second voice, presumably the maid: Inaudible murmur.

Roland: "But you can't, you just can't. I would die without you. Don't you see what you've done to me? Emily, my own. Let me kiss this white neck, these little hands. Tell me you don't love him, tell me you'll run away with me. Tell me anything, but don't tell me to leave you. I can't do it any more than a moth can leave a flame." A convincing sob.

How was she supposed to read *Clarissa*? At this rate, she would never finish the first letter. Of course, she had never finished it on any other night, but it was the principle that mattered.

Genevieve put *Clarissa* down on the coverlet, open in a way that would eventually crack the spine, and picked up the pitcher, still full of tepid water, from her nightstand. She walked to the window. It was lucky that Nanny insisted on fresh air. She leaned out over the sill. Below, she could see the top of Roland's head. Beside him, her neck and shoulders white in the moonlight, stood Emily the kitchenmaid.

Except, thought Genevieve suddenly, that none of the maids was named Emily. The woman with the white shoulders looked up.

This time it was unmistakable. Miss Gray had winked at her. Genevieve lay on her bed for a long time, with *Clarissa* at an uncomfortable angle beneath her, staring at the ceiling.

## VI. The Burial of the Dead

"I am the resurrection and the life, saith the Lord."

"He was so handsome," whispered Amelia Thwaite to the farmer's daughter standing beside her, whose attention was absorbed in studying the pattern of the clocks on Amelia's stockings. "I let him kiss me once, before he went to Oxford. He asked me not to fall in love with anyone else while he was away, and I wouldn't promise, and he must have been so angry because when I saw him again this summer, he would barely speak to me. And I'm just sick with guilt. Because I really did think, in my heart, that I could love only him, and now I will never, ever have the chance to tell him so."

"Blessed are the dead who die in the Lord; even so saith the Spirit, for they rest from their labors."

"There's something behind it," whispered Farmer Thwaite to the farmer standing beside him, who had been up the night before with a sick ewe and was trying, with some success, not to fall asleep. "You mark my words." His neighbor marked them with a stifled yawn. "A gun doesn't go off, not just like that, not by itself. They say he was drunk, but he must've been pointing it at the old man for a reason. A strict enough landlord he was, and I'm not sorry to be rid of him, I tell you. The question is, whether our Ladyship will hold the reins as tightly. She's a pretty little thing in black satin, like a cat that's got into the pantry and is sitting looking at you, all innocent with the cream on its chin. But there's something behind it, you mark my words." His neighbor dutifully marked them.

"Why art thou so full of heaviness, O my soul? and why art thou so disquiet within me?"

It was inexplicable. Genevieve could hear the rustle of dresses, the shuffle of boots, the drone of the minister filling the chapel. Each window with its stained-glass saint was dedicated to a Trefusis. A Trefusis lay under each stone knight in his stone armor, each stone lady folding her hands over stone drapery. A plaque beside the altar commemorated Sir Roland Trefusis, who had come across the channel with William the Conqueror—some ungenerously whispered, as his cook.

"We must believe it was an accident," Mr. Herbert had said. "In that moment of confusion, he must have turned the pistol toward himself, examining it, unable to imagine how it could have gone off in his hands. And we have evidence, gentlemen," this to the constable and the magistrate of the county, "that the young man was intoxicated. What is the use, I put it to you, of calling it suicide under these circumstances? You have a son yourself," to the magistrate. "Would you want any earthly power denying him the right to rest in sacred ground?"

Nanny sniffed loudly into her handkerchief, which had a broad black border. "If it wasn't for that woman, that wicked, wicked woman, your dear father and that dear, dear boy would still be alive. I don't know how she done it, but she done it somehow, and if the good Lord don't smite her like he smote the witch of Endor, I'll become a Mahometan."

"By his last will and testament, signed and witnessed two weeks before the unfortunate—accident," Mr. Herbert had said, "your father left you to the guardianship of your stepmother, Lady Emily Trefusis. You will, of course, come into your own money when you reach the age of majority—or marry, with your guardian's permission. I don't suppose, Genevieve, that you've discussed any of this with your stepmother?"

Miss Gray turned, as though she had heard Nanny's angry whisper. For a moment she looked at Genevieve and then, inexplicably, she smiled, as though the two of them shared an amusing secret.

"There is a river, the streams whereof make glad the city of God, the holy place of the tabernacle of the Most High."

"I am quite certain it was an accident," the minister had said, patting Genevieve's hand. His palm was damp. "I knew young Roland when he was a boy. Oh, he would steal eggs from under a chicken for mischief, but there was no malice in his heart. Be comforted, my dear. They are in the Celestial City, singing hymns with the angels of the Lord."

Genevieve wondered. She was inclined, herself, to believe that Roland at least was most likely in Hell. It seemed, remembering Old Thwaite's Sunday lessons, an appropriate penalty for patricide.

She sniffed. She could not help it, fiercely as she was trying to hold whatever it was inside her so that it would not come out, like a wail. Because, as often as she thought of Mary, Queen of Scots, who had gone to her execution without hesitation or tears, she had to admit that she was very much afraid.

"For so thou didst ordain when thou createdst me, saying, dust thou art, and unto dust shalt thou return. All we go down to the dust; yet even at the grave we make our song: Alleluia."

It must, of course, be explicable. But she had hidden and watched and followed, and she was no closer to an explanation than that day on which, in a bowl of purple ink, she had watched violet clouds floating against a lavender sky.

For a moment she leaned her head against Nanny's arm, but found no comfort there. She would have, she realized, to confront the spider in its web. She would have to talk with Miss Gray.

## VII. A Conversation with Miss Gray

"...and this prayer I make,
Knowing that Nature never did betray
The heart that loved her; 'tis her privilege,
Through all the years of this our life, to lead
From joy to joy: for she can so inform
The mind that is within us, so impress
With quietness and beauty, and so feed
With lofty thoughts, that neither evil tongues,
Rash judgments, nor the sneers of selfish men,
Nor greetings where no kindness is, nor all
The dreary intercourse of daily life,
Shall e'er prevail against us, or disturb
Our cheerful faith, that all which we behold
Is full of blessings."

Miss Gray shut her book. "Hello, Genevieve. Can you tell me what I have been reading?"

"Wordsworth," said Genevieve. Miss Gray always read Wordsworth.

She was sitting on a stone bench beside the yew hedge, dressed in black with a white collar and cuffs, looking plain but very neat. The holly was now covered with red berries.

"In these lines, the Poet is telling us that if we pray to Nature, our great mother, she will answer us, not by transporting us to a literal heaven, but by making a heaven for us here upon earth, in our minds and hearts. I'm afraid, my dear, that you don't read enough poetry."

Genevieve stood, not knowing what to say. It had rained the night before, and she could feel a dampness around her ankles, where her stockings had brushed again wet grass.

"Have you been studying your irregular verbs?"

Genevieve said, in a voice that to her dismay sounded hoarse and uncertain, "This won't do, you know. Talking about irregular verbs. We must have it out sometime." How, if Miss Gray said whatever do you mean Genevieve, would she respond? Her hands trembled, and she clasped them in front of her.

But Miss Gray said only, "I do apologize. I assumed it was perfectly clear."

Genevieve spread her hands in a silent question.

"I was sent to make come true your heart's desire."

"That's impossible," said Genevieve, and "I don't understand."

Miss Gray smiled placidly, mysteriously, like a respectable Mona Lisa. "You wanted to go to school, like Amelia Thwaite, and wear fine clothes, and be rid of your father."

"You're lying," said Genevieve. "It's not true," and "I didn't mean it." Then she fell on her knees, in the wet grass. Her head fell forward, until it almost, but not quite, touched Miss Gray's unwrinkled lap.

"Hush, my dear," said Miss Gray, stroking Genevieve's hair and brushing away the tears that were beginning to fall on her dress. "You will go to school in Paris, and we will go together to Worth's, to find you an appropriate wardrobe. And we will go to the galleries and the Academy of Art..."

There was sobbing now, and tears soaking through to her knees, but she continued to stroke Genevieve's hair and said, in the soothing voice of a hospital nurse, "And my dear, although you have suffered a great loss, I hope you will someday come to think of me as your mother."

In the north of Albion, rain once again began to fall, which was no surprise, since it was autumn.

# Part V

# Transformation

# Heart Like a Drum

## *Alison Newall*

———◦✢∫ß✢◦———

When she first noticed the faint brown stain on the back of her hand, it was a strangely bright November afternoon. The supper was in the oven, the last shirt ironed, and now she leaned dazed elbows on the battered table, in a kitchen that smelled of crisp laundry and pot roast. Her tea steamed before her, evoking distant jungles. She drank the tea and conjured up green leaves brushing her skin, unexpected pools to slip her tired body into, oddly familiar noises and the scent of hidden flowers. The stain glistened on her left hand like a sheen of dark water. She touched it gingerly, thinking of age and liver spots, and resigned herself to decline.

The stain did not go away. Instead, it grew insistently larger. She visited the drugstore to consult an embarrassed pharmacist. He was somewhat deaf, and spoke condescendingly of age and laser treatments. Cowed, she filled her basket and went home to anoint the stain with creams. She began rubbing at it absentmindedly, but it refused to disappear. In fact, it began to develop an almost invisible velvet down.

December came, dark and rainy. Christmas loomed, and she girded her loins to the task of making everybody happy. This year, the burden of the season was hard to bear. She had started the pies in late November, and they glowed quietly in the basement freezer. Early in December, she began rolling cookies and planning presents from the children's growing lists. She was chopping stale bread for the eventual stuffing when the heavy knife ricocheted off the hard crust and plunged into the brown stain.

Blood pulsed out. The cut was deep, yet almost a relief. She grabbed a tea towel, pressed hard upon the stain, and a growl seemed to come from it. She lifted the towel to look. The cut's edges gaped, yet around the wound, the brown stain pulsed vigorously.

At the emergency room, she waited patiently until she was called.

"What happened?" the intern asked.

She withdrew the towel, stained beyond rescue now with her blood. She explained sheepishly, and the doctor gazed at her. "Are you all right?" she asked with so much sympathy that tears leapt into the woman's eyes.

"It hurts," she said.

"Yes," said the intern. She gently froze the skin and sewed her back together with neat small stitches.

"I feel quilted," commented the woman. The doctor laughed. "That's how I learned to sew," she said. "My grandmother showed me."

They nodded together companionably. The doctor looked at the injured skin. "It shouldn't scar too badly. It will be hidden by this stain." She looked closer, and saw the faint down gleaming on the surface. "Were you injured here before?" she asked.

"No," replied the woman.

"I've never seen anything like this mark. It's lovely, don't you think?"

The woman gaped, surprised. "Really? I thought I was just getting old."

"This isn't part of that. It makes me want to stroke it."

"Me too," said the woman. They stared at each other, uncomprehending.

The doctor wound gauze firmly over the cut and around the woman's wrist, stilling her hand. "Rest it," she said.

"But it's Christmas!" the woman exclaimed.

"Christmas or not, it needs rest."

It was past four when she got home, and the children were already waiting on the doorstep, hungry, cold, and discontented. She began an apology, and the oldest boy growled at her.

"Where were you!" he insisted as she fumbled with the key. "I've been waiting!"

"I was at the hospital," she explained gently.

"You could have told me," he said, stomping in.

The youngest boy gasped. "What happened?" She showed him her hand, swathed in gauze. "Does it hurt?" he asked.

"Yes."

"Can I kiss it better?" He dropped a soft kiss upon the bandages, and behind the painful throb, the stain pulsed with pleasure.

She began to touch it whenever she needed strength. During difficult conversations with her husband and school principals, its iridescence exuded a subtle force. She would stroke it with delight, and it thrived under her loving touch, grew deeper and richer until a warm dark glow emanated from it.

Still she baked and nurtured, shepherding often reluctant husband and children through the predictable parade of days. It was almost Christmas when a second spot joined the first, appearing on the back of her other hand. She had carted home the requisite pine giant, and braved its needles to decorate it with as much love as she could muster. The house was spotless and adorned; the aroma of mince pie permeated every corner; and snow provided the final perfect touch.

The second spot covered the sculpture of knotted muscles and veins that time and labour had made of her hands. This spot grew faster, and soon its velvet down competed with the other in beauty. More spots arrived with alacrity, until by late January she had begun to resemble a leopard in woman's clothing. She was only a little frightened, which surprised her. Until now, she thought, her existence had been so utterly unspectacular that perhaps it was some cosmic joke. It seemed comparable to the tabloid headlines she'd read on her way out of the supermarket, which blared about aliens and other unlikely happenings.

One day, the spots became so obvious that her husband noticed them, and asked her, as subtly as he could, if she really shouldn't shave. She hesitated only for a second between his pleasure and her own, reluctant to offend her newfound spots. Really, she preferred to offend him, she discovered. Duly offended, he promptly retired to the guest room.

She didn't really mind, much. His conversation was dull, and the sex only occasionally great. Lately, she'd begun to feel like a duty to him, fulfilled absentmindedly at best. When he was in bed beside her, his breathing invaded her dreams until they became his. And her breasts had tired of his unconscious suckling.

In the spring, she began to grow her nails, and to paint them in different colours, sometimes even in stripes. Her oldest son begged her to cover the spots with makeup. His friends were starting to laugh, to cover their own astonishment and fear. Secretly, of course, they went home at night and examined their own mothers for the telltale signs, but he was too young to know that, and too old to forgive her for her difference.

Her youngest son sat on her lap and stroked the spots. He invented endless nicknames for them, and her. Each day after school he ran into the kitchen to find out if there were any more, and would tell her the new stories he'd made up about how they got there.

Only the family dog was alarmed when her fangs began to grow. Bewildered though they were, her children understood that she would never devour them. The daughter took over some of the burdens of womanhood her mother had relinquished and began to check her father every morning for teeth marks. He didn't seem to appreciate it, so she gave up and, shortly afterward, began to wish for spots of her own.

At night, dreams of the jungle coursed through the woman like a pounding drum. Her heartbeat sounded imperiously in her ears, insisting on a message she couldn't understand, though her hearing, like her teeth, had begun to sharpen. The unnecessary noises of the city began to irritate her, the motorcycles with disabled mufflers, the backfire of trucks, the incessant hissing of thousands of TVs and telephone wires. When some unruly young men moved into the neighbourhood and began to violate the air still further with their blaring music, her patience lasted for a while. But when they started racing their truck up and down the street, and jostling elderly neighbours on the sidewalk, a newborn rage lit her. She began to stare fixedly at them as they passed, and refuse to move aside. When one of them brushed past her with the words "old bitch," a long growl emerged from her throat. Her eyes changed to a flaming green, and she pinned him with her gaze as all the others fled. That night, they quietly moved away, consoling themselves with promises of more noise in some other part of town.

Other husbands in the neighbourhood were unnerved by the changes in that household. Gossip about the spots spread quickly down the street, whose trees and neat flowerbeds had seemed so respectable when they'd staked their down payments. Now, the air itself smelled mildly foreign to them, an odour they couldn't quite pin down. It frightened them. In the spring, when mittens and coats were shed like outgrown skins, everyone could see the woman's dappled arms. The women murmured to each other, or made sarcastic jokes at the local bar after dinner. One, with perfect nails and legs, made no secret of her disdain. Others, though, were less categorical.

Spring brought the woman's dreams closer. The smell of new grass, the damp of the air, made the drums louder until her skin pulsed and tingled with their rhythm, and her spots deepened and shone. She spoke less now, and only after a resonant pause, as if her words emerged from a deep well. She no longer rushed. She baked not at all, and gave up the P.T.A. entirely, saying only, when reproached, that she'd done her time. She threw away her recipe books, and began to eat her food nearly raw, red juices running wantonly out of her steak where she pierced it with her knife.

Her husband, who liked everything well done, reacted with disgust. She gazed at him and, after a considerable pause, asked if something was wrong with his food, and whether he would like to try cooking it himself.

Her stillness unnerved him, and for one fantastic moment he thought he saw a long tail behind her, twitching relentlessly. He was a practical man, who believed in nothing he couldn't see, but he began dining in restaurants and entering the house stealthily at the end of the evening, though he could never have said why, and preferred not to think about it.

Summer came. The heat and noise of the city kindled an anger in her that she'd never known before. She'd borne it all in a ladylike manner, she supposed, the confinement and restrictions, the routine and schedules laid down for her by others, the years of labour without reward in the service of something she could not name. She had done it only because it seemed to be expected of her. The ceaseless scrambling to be on time, to see the homework done, were, in her new skin, stripped of all but a rudiment of meaning. The rage grew at the irrelevance of it all, the incoherence. What was one brownie or bake sale more or less, she thought. Or bedtime, or even Scouts, although she'd religiously driven children to and fro for years.

She took to prowling when the longing seized her to be out. The walls of her kitchen now seemed too close in summer's heat, and the cool night air called to her with its sweet scent, its dark tranquility. After midnight, the streets lost their bustle, and the moon's gleam beckoned to her. Sometimes it was daybreak before she came in.

By August, her husband was gone. He moved in with a sweet young waitress who was delighted to take care of him, for he seemed steady, if unhappy. She thought she would understand him better than his wife did, not realizing until far too late that there was nothing more to understand.

The eldest son soon followed, but her daughter and youngest son stayed.

Now her spots were deep and luminescent, covering her lithe and weathered body. Strangers would stare as she passed, or fall back a little. Sometimes a man would move toward her, his hand reaching out involuntarily to touch her, longing caught in his throat. Then she would pause, gazing back out of green eyes like tranquil pools. Once, she was even followed home by a tall thin man with a body like a cat's. He seemed to see a tail flicking behind her, and she watched him until he turned and left.

By fall, the woman knew. All this time, she'd felt it moving within her, beneath the chaos and confusion, like a voice too distant to hear. She put the house up for sale, and closed before the first snow fell. The children packed only their most loved things, and gave the rest away. They sent the trinkets and heirlooms to the new wife, who needed them, and the next morning they were gone. Sighs of relief echoed among the respectable, along with questions about where exactly they had gone. No postcards ever arrived to enlighten them.

# What Do You Call a Monster?

## *Laura Hart*

—◦❦◦—

He lived in my closet until I was five. Or maybe under my bed. Or some variation of the two, depending on where my mom was least likely to check. When I was five I finally stopped taking a running start to jump into my bed; I stopped making my dad look in the closet with my brother's bat. In that moment, I became what I had considered then the noblest of all qualities: a big kid. Now, I sat adjacent to my monster at the bar.

My monster had not aged well—or perhaps he had, by monsters' standards. His eyes sunk into deep crevices, waves of purpled skin dripping like oil down his face; two saber-like teeth protruding from his bottom lip and climbing upwards.

I waved a ten in the air, my hand swiveling on my wrist motioning to the bartender. I ordered my monster another drink, as his claws began to echo against the emptiness of his glass.

He was sad to see me, to see that even without him I still existed in this realm. I faked a polite smile and he reciprocated, dejected by the emotion that had put him out of business. We ate handfuls of peanuts, like I had before we retired to my room when I was young, and we caught up on other things we no longer believed in.

Let's call me Kinsey.

I was seven when I last saw my parents kiss. My dad pulled my mom under his heavy arm as she tilted her head back and whispered something that I was too young to understand. Their ankles lost in a sea of ribbon and tissue paper, cards signed under a mystical name. This was simultaneously the moment I knew Santa wasn't real. I watched as my mother danced around our tree, stringing candy canes along the pine branches, while my dad strategically placed my presents and my brother's in meticulous piles. My parents didn't know I was watching, my trust in magic dissolving. I didn't know my parents were crying, their love for each other decomposing. When I was eight, I had to pick where I wanted to spend Christmas, I had to watch my mom's heart shatter in her eyes. When I was eight, I told my five-year-old brother to grow up, because all big kids knew Santa wasn't real. When I was eight, I became my brother's monster.

When I was ten, my dad took my friend, let's call her Hannah, and me to our first magic show. I trained myself not to blink, no matter how dry my eyes felt, as the magician picked a totally-and-completely-random person from the audience and made him float. And another person who-he-had-never-met-before-ever and cut her into three pieces. Hannah and I watched him eat fire and pull animals from small, dark places. Fireworks shot from his sleeves, each one erupting in the reflection of my corneas. When we got home my dad taught me my first magic trick. Something involving bunnies made out of yellow sponges and quick hand movements that my thumbs were too clumsy to keep up with. He made magic an illusion that I could hold and understand. Magic became something I could explain. He had pulled back the curtain and revealed the trickery of the monster with quick hands and see-through strings.

By the time I was thirteen Hannah was my only friend whose parents were still together, so I never felt like I deserved the apologies adults gave me when I told them my parents were divorced. I had two moms because my dad remarried and I felt nothing less than blessed. When I was sixteen I didn't tell my mom I was in love because I didn't want her to laugh. I didn't think I could handle having such a strong feeling dismissed by my age. I told my step-mom because she was farther removed, because if she disparaged my feelings, at least I knew my dad had been in love before her. My step-mom's cheeks opened when I told her, the little limbs of her smile opening up to cradle me within it. She asked for details and made me coffee that warmed me alongside the lovesick giddiness and appreciation for having someone to talk to. She asked questions that made it feel real, that made me feel wise and right to be in love.

My boyfriend was older and expected me to do things that older girls did, which was fine by me because I craved anything that made us closer. When it hurt more than I expected and he forgot to call me to say good night, Hannah was the only person there for me to talk to. She patted my hand and I don't remember her saying much, but the presence of someone who had always been around was comforting. We made popcorn in her kitchen, I remember watching the starlight tear through her window and land on the basket of fresh apples that her mother had picked with us earlier in the week. One of the apples was bruised from when I dropped it while carrying it in. I picked up the tarnished apple and felt naked, thinking that I knew what it was like to be kicked out of somewhere.

Later that year my boyfriend, let's call him Jim, hit me for the first time. I didn't tell my mom, my step-mom, or Hannah this, because my mom still didn't know about Jim and I didn't want my step-mom or Hannah to tell me that I was wrong about what I felt. I didn't stop believing in love and that I was meant to stay with Jim by a plan something bigger than me had made. I wish I had told my step-mom, though, because I found out later that someone she used to love hit her too. Let's call him Jim for categorization's sake. That she kept on loving her Jim and thought it was her fault. When I was seventeen, my step-mom took her life and I stopped believing in divine plans. I hated to admit it, but I think this was because my dad stopped believing too.

My monster put down his drink hard enough for me to hear it was empty, as I again began to motion to the bartender, this time for shots. I saw my monster's fangs release momentarily from his upper lip, as if he was about to speak, before clamping his jaws back together on a second thought. I could see his hesitance in approaching my rejection of the divine for a reason that usually brings people closer with the idea of an afterlife.

"Listen," I started as I slapped the money down onto the bar, ignoring the bartender's scowl at my lack of tip, "I'm not saying I'm a good person."

I felt my monster raise his eyes lazily. I could tell they were becoming as heavy as my own.

"I'm not implying some karmic reaction wasn't the cause of those heartaches."

Other people at the bar were ogling us, looks of confusion and disgust swarmed together into a kaleidoscope of things I didn't want to put up with.

"I'm just saying, since that heartache, I know for a fact boys cry too."

At eighteen, Jim had broken up with me because he thought I was too emotional. In retrospect, I think that's what made me seem the most weak; that I endured every blow, literal and metaphorical, from the relationship. In retrospect, it didn't ever really matter. At eighteen, I had a fake ID and met a boy in a bar that was too warm and required night-vision goggles to be in. He was the first person I had perceived as better than me, and allowed into my life since Jim. Let's call him Patrick. Despite my mother's warnings, the first time Patrick and I kissed was in that bar, and it became something of a sacred ground for me. Hannah had watched the kiss, and I could have sworn she said she was happy for me, but I guess everyone slurs their words when they're drunk.

Commitment was always fleeting after my parents. After the Jims. Buttery silk on a hot skillet. No matter how he felt, I still flirted. I still wore low-cut shirts and touched other boys' faces in soft ways. Jealousy was the only emotion that satiated my thirst for attention. I only felt something when emotion pulsed in a heat so blue that the whiteness of his skin was punctuated by the graffiti of veins. I only felt love when love was intensely returned.

For two and a half years Patrick and I danced around the musical chairs of being in a relationship with each other or sleeping with other people. This stopped when I saw Hannah kiss him in the same bar, when the speeches began to mix together about just being drunk, about not being able to help who you care for. All things Patrick stopped when I remembered that the weaker person sticks around for the blows. All things Hannah stopped when I realized that most things good are an illusion.

When I was twenty, my heart had been broken two and a half times by boys I had loved, which was probably average, I thought. When I was twenty-one, I stopped believing anyone was capable of feeling love the way it was described in movies. I stopped believing in infinity and thought even the old couples who walked together in the produce section of the grocery store on Sundays were faking the magic out of tradition.

My monster interrupted my story with a small *hmph* of disagreement.

"I've learned to trust no one," I countered.

"Have you ever thought maybe the world isn't all bad, that if you bettered yourself other people may notice and mimic just that?" He wasn't accusing, he was considering.

"No, see, I've tried that. And it's not that I'm saying I'm a great person or even a wholly trustworthy one. No, I know that I'm not in any way better than anyone. I'm just saying that I know how I think, and feel, and I know how that makes me treat people, and that's the scariest part."

My monster shook his head at my stories, and when he laughed I couldn't help but think that he meant it. He laughed and so did I; our laughter raining around us like a sad song we still enjoyed singing. I didn't know if we were laughing because he thought I was too dumb or too ignorant or too something to understand what real monsters are. I didn't know if he was laughing because I could never be a monster like him, or if it was because he thought I was a better monster than he ever was. This was the saddest thing I had ever found pleasure in, but then I thought that was how it always seemed to go.

There were two kinds of monsters, I thought, as I looked into the drooping eyes of my own monster. There was a type of monster who existed in his world, who was just doing his job. And then there was the type of monster who existed in mine. Real monsters put twigs in the spines of rabbits at a young age and didn't care. It wasn't until now that I realized the harm didn't have to be physical to make you a monster. I realized that anytime I made someone hurt and didn't care, I became the kid with the pocket knife and the class pet at recess. I realized the worst kind of monster put a car on the road while their vision was blurry, and saw potential lives leaking out from the warm nuggets behind every other wheel, and the first thing that came to mind was the thought: I can get away with this.

My monster and I hooked our seatbelts with a simultaneous click, but only because I could never stand the beeping persistence of the car when I didn't. My monster and I were still laughing, wiping tears from our eyes as his antennae-like poles arched backwards like spines against the wind that began to intrude from the moon-roof.

"Did you know that one-third of all traffic accidents are alcohol-related?" my monster asked. I swear, it wasn't in an accusatory tone, as his words were broken with bits of a residual laugh.

"I'm fine."

"Shit, that's a lot. You think they make those statistics up?"

"You're fine."

"Isn't that how it always goes?" He echoed my earlier thoughts. I kept my eyes trained on the road as whirs of lights flickered by like a rollercoaster.

"You never think it will happen to you," I continued his thought, our minds flowing together into one cohesive being. "You never think you're the monster."

My monster hesitates as the divots on the side of the road shake the inside of the car, causing our jaw to quiver.

"Wouldn't it be nice," he began, watching the passing lights as well, they illumined all the potential things that could go wrong, "if we were the only monsters the other ever had to worry about?"

# Accessories Extra
## *Elizabeth Kerlikowske*
———⊸❦⊸———

A woman willed her unwanted hair to grow from a single follicle. Where to place the follicle was the question; the hair grew between three and five feet a day. She wouldn't want it on her chin, for example, or even on her head, though that seemed the most logical place. She considered her armpit, but that could get bunchy under winter layers. Locating the follicle in her pubic hair, which she was keeping, made the most sense. She always carried little golden scissors in a smart case. She was often seen with them, and when asked what they were for, would only smile enigmatically.

One night after the opera or a karaoke session, she brought home a young man who fell asleep with his leg across her body. He woke affixed to her by hair. His struggling caused her a great deal of pain, as you can imagine, yet she reached her scissors on the nightstand and cut him free. "What are you, some kind of freakin' spider?" he cried as he scrambled into his clothes.

When angered, she was a thrower.

They removed the golden scissors from his back easily in the emergency room. "She's a spider or something, man. I woke up, like, encased in hair." He failed the tox screen, though, and there were a couple of outstanding warrants. The woman never found another pair of scissors quite as perfect as those she had wasted on the man's back. She never let a man spend an entire night with her again, carefully wrapping herself in extravagant negligees to disguise what were becoming spinnerets.

# Reading Maps

## Elizabeth Kerlikowske

Back when my fingers were crayons, eating was like a party that no one came home from happy. They didn't bend unless it was hot; I couldn't keep my hands in my pockets, and summer was a time of anxiety. Once I fell asleep in a car and lost a pinkie to the sunlight. It pooled and hardened like a tiny record album. My dad carved it into the shape of a real finger.

When grown-ups shook my hand, some crayons just snapped. The points had worn down long ago. By the time I married, most of the fingers on my right hand were nubbins. The left I was saving for middle age. My new husband called me Nubbins.

"Nubbins," he said, "which way is New York?" I made a red line on the map with what was left of my thumb. "I'm going to go there when I leave you," he said.

I drew a black X over our town. It was my best finger, generous with itself.

"Why did you do that?

"I'm taking it away. Our town is gone. Now you're free to go. Go."

He packed alone; I'm not allowed to touch his clothes: rainbows. The cab came.

"Nubbins, you'll miss me, you freak, but I won't miss you."

I shut the door and spread my hands out to look at them. Something was missing on the left; no place to wear my wedding ring. It's hard to say when he unpacks if he'll understand about me giving him the finger.

# The Mirror

### *Teresa Milbrodt*

———⚬⚭❀⚭⚬———

Later I called it a fight. He said it was an extended discussion conducted at high volume. We couldn't agree on much anymore.

This time we'd been yelling about whether or not it made sense for me to get a job. He said I should do volunteer work a few hours every week, perhaps knit scarves for orphans, but nothing too taxing. He liked coming home to a hot dinner and a tidy house.

"Housekeeping and daily chores take a lot of work," he said.

"Not so much that I don't have time for anything else," I said. "I don't want cooking and cleaning to be the focus of my life."

He bristled when I said that, like making sure we had a comfortable home should have been more than enough for me. Cooking and cleaning had been more than enough when I was still living with the dwarfs, but there were seven of them plus me, and the dwarfs were happy to do the dishes and scrub pots after supper. I didn't bring this up to him, though I considered it.

"We'll talk about this tomorrow," he said, which is when I threw the plate at him. We'd had this discussion before, several times actually, and "tomorrow" never came.

"You're impossible," he yelled before storming out the door, probably going down to the tavern for a pint.

I was still breathing heavily. "That felt good," I told the ghostly green face in the mirror.

It nodded sagely. "A little cathartic plate smashing can be good for the soul, but best not make it a habit."

"I know, I know," I sighed. But I didn't particularly like our dishes, anyway. They had gold edging, too fancy for my tastes. My husband had picked them out.

He didn't know about the mirror's face or past history, just that it hung in the living room. I'd inherited it after the death of my stepmother, though I didn't consult it for the same reasons she had. I knew I was pretty, and who cared if I was the prettiest in the land? I needed a therapist, not a beauty consultant, which is where the mirror came in. My husband never listened to me, making me wonder if he'd ever listened in the first place. When we'd been king and queen, it hadn't mattered so much.

We'd been lucky to escape the castle with the mirror and our lives after the raid. As fiery arrows arced over the walls and a battering ram was rolled to the gate, we donned heavy gray cloaks and left through a secret entrance that dumped us into the woods. It had been a year and a half since then, and he hadn't recovered from the insult of being shoved off the throne.

"I didn't spend enough money to equip the army," he lamented at dinner the next evening. I'd made bangers and mash, his new favorite supper, but even that didn't put him in a good mood when he was determined to be sore. Our subjects had liked him so he assumed his reign was secure, but he hadn't counted on outside foes. "With a larger militia, we wouldn't have needed to flee."

I forked another bite of mashed potato and resisted the urge to shrug. We'd had to get new identities and a new cottage, but he'd never forget that he'd been a prince and then a king. I wished he could. He was much more stressed and less charming than he'd been when we were first married. My husband wanted to assume the usual man's role and take care of me, but I wanted to help care for us both.

"I could clean the homes of wealthy people," I said, but he balked at that.

"You were a queen," he said. "You can't lower yourself to tidying up after others."

I muttered that I'd cleaned up after seven dwarfs for a number of months and been just fine, thank you very much. He grimaced at his plate and asked for more sausages. I resisted the urge to tell him he could get them himself if he didn't want me serving other people.

I didn't mind life as a commoner, but after the plate incident I was surprised that breaking things felt as good as it did. I'd been sweet and mild-mannered before, like a *princess*, so it was satisfying to do something a little bad. As king he'd maintained a calm and idealistic demeanor, taking jaunts around the kingdom on horseback to distribute bread and wave beneficently to peasants. But he didn't understand what it was like to live in the village and be a normal person. Now he had to figure that out, and I thought it was good for him. Educational.

But life was bad for those who still resided in our old kingdom. The new ruler was an awful tyrant, my mirror confirmed. I didn't tell my husband. He'd go crazy, try to raise an army, and probably get himself killed. It was far better for him to stay at his current job as a bookkeeper, since he was good with figures. Ten years of private tutoring had assured that.

I was awfully bored of cooking and cleaning and doing laundry, which is why I asked the mirror to teach me a few of my stepmother's transformation spells. The mirror went into great detail, explaining spells I could use to make myself older or younger, or even the opposite gender. I tried the crone spell first, and found it was particularly amusing to see myself as a gray-haired old lady.

"Can't I be a little plumper?" I asked the mirror. "Plump old ladies are cute, and they look more trustworthy. The skinny ones look like they're up to something."

"As you wish," said the mirror, teaching me a few extra words to fill out my cheeks, waist, and bosom so I looked more like someone's kindly great-aunt. That was the guise I used to get a part-time job with a seamstress.

People figured that cute old ladies were good at things like sewing and doling out wisdom. The women who frequented the shop where I worked were all too willing to confide in me and ask for advice with their children, marriages, and aging parents.

"You're always so helpful, Auntie," they said, hugging my soft shoulders.

"Happy to help, my dears," I said, patting my gray curls.

The not-quite-a-crone spell was the best thing that had ever happened to me. No one was willing to spill their guts in front of me when I'd been queen. Then they had to be fake cheery, assuming I was pretty and clueless and didn't understand real people. But sometimes winning others' trust was based on how you looked, a sad fact I used to my advantage.

I turned into an old man when I wanted to have a beer and spy on my husband in the local tavern. I found him wet-eyed in front of his ale, bemoaning his situation to the bartender, who nodded while he polished a glass.

"My boss wants me to work faster," my husband groused. "I made two miscalculations in the books today, and when he found out I thought he'd give me a thrashing."

My husband wasn't accustomed to being yelled at. Before, he'd done the yelling. I sat at a table in the corner and watched him, pleased that he was telling his problems to *someone*, but upset that he put on a mask for me, his wife. I wanted to know these things, too.

I sipped my beer and shook my head. I'd survived three attempts on my life in the past, so certainly I could listen to my husband's problems without breaking down in tears. I took on another part-time job as a bookkeeper for the tavern so I could keep a curious eye on him and listen to his laments while doing figures. Maybe it was the fact that I'd been walking around as an old woman for a while, but I was starting to feel more maternal toward him. But he'd been trying to care for me ever since we'd moved, which was something I didn't particularly like.

Maybe we were better parents than lovers.

I was busier and happier than I'd ever been, and thought it was a shame that my stepmother hadn't used the mirror in more interesting ways. Being pretty was a pain. You had to waste all that energy on staying pretty, and that could make you strange and obsessive. It was much more fun to turn myself into someone who could have an interesting life.

The mirror gave me sober updates on how the situation in the old kingdom was going from bad to worse. I pondered the problem while adjusting the hem on velvet dresses. For several afternoons in a row I daydreamed plots, wondering if I could return to the castle as my old-lady self, covertly spy on the new ruler, and see if there were any plans for a revolt.

I didn't want my husband back in power. He was a kind man, but I quietly enjoyed seeing his frustration in the evening, hearing him rant that he wasn't being paid enough for the work he did. He'd grown up in gilded rooms and never had to toil so hard or endure criticism.

But I loved my former kingdom and its inhabitants too much to let them suffer if I thought I could do something. My subjects were enduring the usual cruel tyranny—baseless arrests, imprisonment for anyone who spoke against the king, and all the pretty young girls were being recruited for jobs as ladies-in-waiting. At least that's what they were told.

When I launched my plan, I explained to my husband that I was going to visit my friends the dwarfs, as it had been forever since I'd seen them. Instead, I shrouded myself in the old woman's skin and took a job in the castle kitchen. A month of kneading bread dough and listening closely to conversations was just enough to understand the new political machinations—who supported the regime and who was launching a resistance movement and trying to organize everyone else.

I attending meetings in darkened cottages, listened to their plans, and supplied detailed maps of the castle's hidden passages and secret rooms with extra ammunition.

"How did you ever come by these, Grandmother?" said Artin, one of the revolt's leaders.

"You'd be surprised what kind of information an old woman can glean if she keeps her ears open," I said, tapping on the side of my head. No one doubted my honesty or my identity, and I relished the evenings spent with my former subjects. They were intelligent men and women, excellent storytellers, and didn't give themselves airs. They had the same work ethic as my dear dwarfs, who I did need to visit at some point, but not until this crisis was resolved.

I loved Artin's children to bits, brought them toys and sweet buns and told them stories about a princess who just wanted to live like everyone else.

"Castle life gets boring," I explained. "You can't run around or make noise. You get to wear pretty dresses, but if one of them gets ripped in the garden, you get yelled at for an hour."

"You speak as though from experience, Grandmother," Artin's wife, Lela, teased me.

"No," I said, "just a good imagination."

I'd never had the opportunity to chat with my subjects like this. Now they weren't people under my rule. They were friends. After the children went to bed, Artin and I reviewed castle maps, and I suggested the best ways for outside forces to enter.

"You're an angel and a general," Artin said. I blushed. My husband didn't know I'd read his books on military tactics in the library when I was bored. The more I thought about it, there were entirely too many sides of me he didn't know, but so many of them could emerge when I was freed of my young body and nestled into an older one.

The mirror had warned I needed to change back into a young woman nightly or risk the transformation spell becoming permanent. In my small cook's chambers, it wasn't hard to manage the metamorphosis and giggle a little behind my cupped hands. I hadn't thought fooling everyone would be so much fun. The strange thing was, after a few weeks, changing back into my younger self felt strange. Almost unnatural. It was how I'd looked when I'd been a princess and a queen and ultimately ignored by anyone who was making important decisions. As an old woman I (allegedly) had age and experience on my side.

All this masquerading had made me hone my talents for concealment and stealth, so it was simple to hide a packet of poison in my apron pocket and slip a few grains in the soup and bread dough. When the new king slumped over at the dinner table, our attack began.

Even as arrows started to fly, I was calm and controlled, unafraid of dying in battle. My stepmother had tried to kill me many times, but now I'd taken hold of my fate. I was tempted to pick up a dagger—if I were killed it would be for a good reason—but I made myself duck out of the castle through the same passage I'd used when we had to flee the first time.

It was hard to leave the new kingdom, since I was more invested in it and its people than I'd been before. I couldn't forget Artin and his children and my other friends, but I had to return home to my husband, who still needed me. I had been gone for eight weeks, but hid the details of our insurrection and said I'd had a lovely time with the dwarfs.

"I missed you," my husband said, giving me a hug like he really meant it. I squeezed him back. Now that I was home I realized how much I'd missed him, too. I also understood more about his investment in the kingdom, even if I didn't think he'd really connected with its people. Neither had I, before now, but every day I found myself aching to return and see everyone.

I consulted the mirror daily for reports on the kingdom's new governing council. Artin was its leader, but his vote counted the same as everyone else's. They made some good decisions and some not-so-good ones in the rebuilding process. I wished I could join them and be an extra voice of caution. They needed to invest more money in fortifications and reconstruction, or risk another takeover, but I reassured myself daily that they had everything under control.

Two months later, my husband heard about the uprising and formation of a new government. Of course he wanted to return to the old kingdom.

"Just imagine the parades they'll have in my honor," he said.

"I don't think they want a king again," I said.

"But they loved me."

"I want to stay here," I said. "I got sick of all those satin and velvet dresses. I like our cottage and this village and I'm perfectly happy." I knew I wouldn't survive if I couldn't put on the skin of an old woman and go to the seamstress shop every day for the usual chatter.

My husband pouted for a day, then quit his job at the bookkeepers and left without me. I found the note on the kitchen table when I returned from marketing. He said he would love for me to join him if I changed my mind. I made bangers and mash for dinner and sulked. I'd left the kingdom and returned for him, but he cared more about that stupid old crown than he did about me.

"Maybe we've grown too far apart," I sulked to the mirror.

"Or maybe your hearts are close to the same place," it said.

It took one more day before I broke down and started the journey back to our kingdom. I went as my old-lady self, though the mirror reminded me again that spending too long under any transformation spell meant it would stick. I was willing to accept the consequences.

When I returned to Artin's cottage, the governing council was having a meeting. They'd declared his home to be their new headquarters until they could build a new town hall.

The discussion stopped when I arrived. All of the council members stood up and embraced me, saying, "Grandmother, we wondered where you'd gone." I claimed weakness, saying I'd needed to recuperate for some weeks since I was exhausted.

"You're welcome to join the meeting as an advisor on the council," Artin told me, then the council members resumed what they'd been doing when I entered.

Berating my husband. I assumed this had been going on for some time, as he had his hands folded in his lap and looked quite beaten down.

"Waltzing in here and telling us you should be king again," Artin said. "Have you no humility?"

"I still say we should tar and feather you for even setting foot in town," said another council member.

"Or at least for expecting to be the ruler again," a third man sniffed.

"Come now," said Bertam, who was more soft-spoken than the rest. "We could allow him to advise the council on occasion. He has experience he could lend to our discussions."

"He'll want his vote to count for three people," said the first man.

"His voice will count for none," I said, surprised to hear myself speak so suddenly. "I agree that he may have wisdom to share, just as I do. You don't have to listen to us, though."

My husband flashed a meek smile of thanks. In the end, the council allowed that we could both act as non-voting advisors. I assumed he'd burned a few bridges before I arrived, but I was certain this exercise in democracy had shrunken his ego, which was a good thing. I shook his hand as I left the meeting and wished him well.

"Thank you for speaking for me," he said. "I didn't think things would be so different upon my return. My wife warned me about that."

"It will be a pleasure to act as an advisor with you," I said, giving him a nod before I ventured into the darkening streets to find a boarding house for the night.

The next day I would secure work as a seamstress and more steady accommodations. It felt good to be back in the old body. Maybe I'd always been an old woman disguised as a young one and never realized it before. The skin was warm and pleasantly wrinkled, like a comfortable shirt. In only a matter of weeks it would be my own. I didn't mind that at all.

# Test Group 4
## Womanhood and Other Failures

### *SJ Sindu*

———⚬⚭⚭⚬———

My love affair with women started when I learned about the female suicide bombers in Sri Lanka. I was five. It blew my mind that women—the make-upped, dark-eyed beauty queens of the Indian Bollywood movies—could be dangerous enough to strap on explosives beneath the folds of their sarees.

My lover's scar is crocheted across his chest with baby-pink yarn by someone who was just learning. The scar runs through like a tiny mountain range, stretching from armpit to armpit along the line of his pectoral muscles but never syncing with the contours of his body. When the surgeon scooped out the breast tissue, he left my lover's chest flat.

The scar is pink like his nipples, soft and spongy where it bubbled up from the stitches and healed around them. Sometimes he's afraid he'll catch his nipples on something and rip them off. He has nightmares about being nipple-less.

There is a dark spot where his nipples used to be, a sunset gradation of color into the scar. Dark hairs sprout, tall and curly, around the scar line. They weren't there before the testosterone. They grow a forest over his chest and down his stomach.

The outer edges of his scar bulge out in dog-ears, a side effect of having had large breasts.

His lovers, the ones before me, wouldn't look at his chest. They would turn away, mumble into their coffee, tuck their hair behind their ears. They wouldn't touch him there, their fingers cringing from the ridges of the scar, their bodies shivering at the absence. He can't feel his chest anymore. Numbness reaches up from his scar, a vacancy of nerves, hollow when he pushes on the skin. His lungs underneath can discern the pressure, but the message of touch is lost between the skin and his insides.

My mother keeps a leather-bound album of my baby pictures tucked away in the recesses of her closet. These pictures are few, and it took years—decades—to collect them in one volume. Most were lost to late-night flights from our family home in Sri Lanka, where we always kept bags packed. The bags had to be light enough to carry for days, spare enough to unpack and repack at the Army checkpoints. Photo albums were treasured but bulky, and my baby pictures won out over my parents' wedding album. We were ready to leave as soon as we heard that the battle line was nearing our town.

Now the pictures sleep peacefully in my mother's closet. I've stolen a few photos of my own. I need to remember.

It's tempting to retell my childhood veiled in virginity, a chaste Hindu girl's strict upbringing. But it's a little boy who stands in these pictures, one who was given too much freedom and adored to the point of exhaustion by extended family before they remembered that he would bleed every month.

I had short curly hair and wore boy's clothes. In beach pictures I wear only my panties. I mourn the loss of that flat chest that allowed me to be rambunctious. Wild.

At six years of age my best friend and I pretended to be Americans on vacation at a beach. We walked around in our panties inside locked rooms, windows shut for modesty. We played at being American women—smoking, drinking, kissing—unconstrained by sarees and rules.

To Emily Dickinson: I once met you—but you were dead—

To the middle-aged white lady who pretended to be Emily Dickinson at the library, whom I believed and loved until I told my friends and they made fun of me for not knowing that Emily Dickinson was dead and this lady was a fake: You were too pretty to play the part of a lonely writer. I should've known. Even the Americans like their smart women ugly.

The dusty, blue linoleum feels warm even though it snows outside. The tip of my nose is cold from the air. I lie against the warm floor, and the heat seeps in through the frilly cotton pajamas my mother made for me. My little brother laughs in the living room; his toddler voice hiccups around the walls as my dad plays with him. My mother types her thesis at the computer.

I am drawing. Today I'm practicing lips, diligently consulting a three-ring binder of tutorials I have printed out from the Internet. I fill my papers with lips like the ones the tutorials demonstrate, the round curves of women's lips that bite down on secrets and the flat plains of men's lips that don't smile.

I am in love with a man who doesn't believe in God but believes that English majors and hippies are the fussy frou-frou in an otherwise functioning society. He teaches me how to catch and throw a softball, and he buys me fountain pens and leather-bound journals. He tries to train our cat, and when he can't, he maintains that our cat overgeneralizes. He lets me run my hands and lips along his chest scar, asks me to give him testosterone shots. I take pictures of the hairs that explode slowly on his jaw. Together we celebrate the dissolving curves of his body, my insides squirming at the woman slowly dying.

To my lover: Do you know, *kanna*, I learned about life from the female soldiers who patrolled my hometown. And about love, too. Those women had things figured out, their wisdoms wrapped away in the tight braids of their hair.

I see my best friend when I visit Sri Lanka after high school. We have seen eighteen from two different oceans. I wear makeup and short skirts in the Sri Lankan heat. She has hair braided down her back and makes tea for everyone. I wonder why she won't look me in the eye. I wonder if she remembers the pretend cigarettes and booze.

She doesn't talk. I talk too much.

When I bled for the first time, on New Year's Day of 1999, my parents threw a party. We drove from Boston to Canada and rented a reception hall that specialized in Hindu celebrations. *Manjal neerattu vizha* loses its poetry when it spells "puberty ceremony" in English.

My parents hired a makeup lady, who pulled and tugged my unruly hair into a bun, added extensions so that my flowered braid hung down to my butt. My chubby body wrestled into a saree. The blouse was tight and I could barely breathe. The makeup lady pinned jewelry to my head and brushed powder on my face, and when she was done, someone pretty looked back at me from the mirror. As a last touch she pressed a jeweled, fake nose ring into my septum. It dangled in front of my mouth. All day long I suppressed violent urges to sneeze.

I watch my mother kill mice. I kneel on an office chair, pumped up to its full height so I can see the frigid steel of the lab table from my fourth-grade height. The mice are a white that matches my mother's lab coat. She pulls them one by one out of their cage labeled "Test Group 4." They have to die, she says, because they are sick.

She presses a black sharpie to their necks, and they are dead, just like that, *tuk*.

# Devil Take the Hindmost

## *Rosalie Morales Kearns*

———⋯⋆⋇⋆⋯———

## I.

Whoever takes his place in the beginning will know the end, and will not taste death.

—*Gospel of Thomas* (1st-century Christian gospel, banned as heretical in the 4th century)

## A Lime-Green Shelter Door

Goddammit, you'd think she'd get it right by now. They'd had the bio-chem drills since grade school. You hear the alarm, drop everything, run like hell. Somehow Pilar was always the last to show up.

Twenty years later, wouldn't you know it: grade school all over again.

From the ridge on White Mountain it takes an hour to scramble down to where her car's parked, and then for miles she bounces along the dirt-and-gravel ribbon that's labeled a "drivable trail" on the State Forest map. "It's a drill," she says out loud. But they stopped the drills years ago. Or it's a mistake. Or something local, a toxic spill on the interstate. Gravel turns into blacktop and she's on the access road, then Rt. 235, still not another car in sight.

She tries to remember the protocol for the alarms. After so many hours the alarm sound gets shorter, intervals between, longer. The lime-green posters were meant to be soothing: *Proceed in a calm, orderly fashion to the designated meeting place.* Right.

She brakes and pulls up in front of the smallest bio-chem shelter sign she's ever seen. Nasty-looking place, electrified fence with razor wire on top.

The gates are still ajar. Someone must have tried to close them and then stopped, like the power went out just then. She throws a stick against the wire to make sure the juice isn't still on, squeezes between the gates, and runs down a gravel path toward the regulation lime-green shelter door. Presses the intercom buzzer. Nothing.

Come on, come on, answer. If it's not a drill what is it—biological, chemical, localized, airborne, ingested epidermally, inhaled? Is she breathing it in right now?

She'd be safe back in D.C., working quietly in her lab. Reading news reports about some minor incident in the middle of nowhere.

She presses the buzzer again, slaps at it with her open palm. She's about to kick at the door when the intercom erupts in static. A blurry face swims out of the darkness, presses itself against the high-density plastic window. Other faces crowd in, then recede.

The intercom spits out: "Password!"

She can't be hearing right. She's hit with a wave of dizziness and nausea and, what's worse, what's much worse, an overwhelming sense that she's been through all of this before.

# Washington, D.C.

The Reassignment Memo lists no phone number, no name of a human person amid the small-print instructions on filing an appeal.

"A lateral move," a supervisor tells her. "An opportunity."

Pilar grips the memo tights as she reads. And rereads. As if maybe she'll discover the tiny print, faint as a watermark, that explains how the U.S. Budget Office could have jurisdiction over the National Academy of Sciences.

"Bald Eagle State Forest," she reads in a monotone.

"Pretty countryside," someone else says. "Or used to be. Pennsylvania. Lots of farms way back when."

There are meetings with middle managers. They're indistinguishable to Pilar, they look alike, they say the same things:

"You brought this on yourself, Pilar.'"

"That last little stunt, nothing but a provocation."

"I'm a scientist," she says. "I do research. I make my findings available to the public."

"You should have known better."

"I should have known better coming in here. I was hoping to speak to a live human."

"This is what we mean, Pilar. You need to work on your interpersonal skills."

Reassignment. Take one geologist specializing in erosion control. Turn her into a fire safety officer in the U.S. Forest Service. What do you get? *I work in a state-of-the-art lab*, she writes in her appeal. *I go to conferences all over the world. The only fieldwork I do is in agricultural extensions and botanical gardens.* In case that isn't clear enough, she adds, *What do I know from forests?*

Her only other such correspondence has been forever unanswered. *Dear Government*, she'd written when she was ten, *if you keep using lime-green paint for the bioterror shelter doors, people will start to hate limes.*

U.S. BUDGET OFFICE is etched into the bronze plaque, but the burnished metal doors are locked. A small sign in fluorescent yellow cardboard directs Pilar around the corner to the east entrance, where smoked glass doors are also locked, this time no sign, no buzzer, no guard. Is it even the same building? Maybe she's walked past the right entrance. She rounds a corner to another side, then a fourth, then what seems to be a fifth because the metal doors aren't there, but how could the unimaginative granite blocks that make up the Budget Office be in anything but rectangular form?

She asks for so little: an office, a desk, a name with a person attached to it, and she'll hand over her appeal letter and all of this will be cleared up. The Reassignment Memo listed only a P.O. box and she's received no answer, she's had to pack up her office at the Academy, turn over her lab space, reassign her research assistants, store her samples, her data. They must not have read the letter yet. Tomorrow she'll put her belongings in storage. This is all a silly mistake. She'll laugh about it someday.

She looks up at the granite-faced cube. Seven stories she counts. There must be people in there, bureaucrats making their calculations, inputs and yields, cost-benefit, risk assessment, and the corresponding Reassignment Memos that will make the numbers jump back into the right columns. She thinks she sees their small pale faces looking out. She steps back for a better look, but the tall narrow windows reflect back only gray sky.

## Bald Eagle State Forest

A forest ranger with a face as impassive as stone gives Pilar her new assignment:

Fire safety.

Could he elaborate? He shrugs. Why do they need someone from federal for a state-level agency? He shrugs. Where are Pilar's quarters? He digs out a sheet of paper, points to a yellow X. Can she read a trail map?

She can, but the map, it turns out, is inaccurate. By the time she finds the ranger substation it's almost dark. She feels her way into the cabin, finds a table, sets up the battery-powered camp lantern that brilliantly illuminates layers of dust, cobwebs, dead bodies of insects, dried leaves blown in under doors and through window cracks.

She spends hours cleaning, and by the time she's finished she's too tired and grimy to fall asleep. She steps out into the nighttime forest.

You can do this, Pilar.

She'll keep writing letters of appeal. She's going to get out of here. And in the meantime, why should she care whether the damn place catches fire?

She has the sense that the forest hears her: fingers wagging, murmurs of disapproval. "OK," she says out loud. "I'll be a damn fire safety officer."

Not a good sign. Here one day and she's talking to the forest.

She looks at the trail map showing nonexistent paths, logical impossibilities like a creek running along the top of a ridge.

She'll make an accurate map. It'll give her something to do.

Breathing hard already, not even a steep incline but it's humid and she's out of shape, yet another reason she's unsuited for this damn job.

("Transfer," they called it.)

(Demotion. Banishment.)

("And consider yourself lucky.")

Every few yards another enormous fallen hemlock or beech in the way. Pilar has to hoist herself over or slither under. When a new path veers off to the left, she squats down to read the fallen trail sign, faded letters barely visible: TOWER TRAIL.

She takes out one of the maps, creased and sweaty and it was a blurry photocopy to begin with. No trail.

The page torn from a road atlas is the closest she's got to a topographical map now that they disbanded the U.S. Geological Survey (no need to show the enemy our terrain, they said). That one shows the trail, so does the State Forest brochure, but never with a name. Shouldn't someone have *told* her there were still firetowers here?

Tower Trail takes her down the steep slope of Strong Mountain and across the stream. She knows it's Swift Run, but at this point it's covered with slabs of rock. She hears the water rushing beneath her, and an odd echoing sound as if someone nearby is stomping on it, a rock-and-water drum, but she can see up and down the stream and the only living creatures in sight are birds, spiders, slugs.

The path on the other side turns sharply up. It must zigzag further up, she decides, or veer through some gap she can't see from here. Can't be that steep anyway, these mountains are low, old, smoothed down by weather and trees and time.

She starts up the path. Her calves hurt intensely for five minutes and then the pain disappears, but her heart is knocking against her ribcage. She has to stop every few minutes, tries to recall the heights shown on the park district map in faint gray ink. No more than a thousand feet, was it?

Possibly two thousand. She tries to get her mind around that number, it's like walking up twenty flights of stairs, which she's never done in her life, and that could explain why she's dry-heaving, staggering at the top, and of course there's no firetower here. Of course.

Whatever it was made of, wood, brick, it's gone now, except for a crumbling cement foundation.

She lies face up, looking at the patch of sky fringed by trees all round. She is unconcerned about all the dangers of bare skin against forest floor. Ant bites, poison ivy, Lyme disease. Skinned elbows. Tetanus. She remembers learning about the presence of bacteria in soil and rocks, it made her laugh, how anyone could think innocent rocks were so dangerous. She picks up a small stone and nuzzles it against her cheek. There, there. *What?*

Not so different, flesh and stone: same elements, carbon, iron, oxygen. Skeleton turns to stone in the right conditions, perfect fate for a geologist.

This is the worst place for fossilization, though, moist forest soil. The whole mountain would have to slide on top of her, and stay on top, for Pilar to ever end up in the fossil record.

She stands up, brushes herself off. She has a schedule to stick to. Every morning she makes a plan for the day, and she knows that if she can hold on to that, she can hold on.

She pulls up to the Smokey Bear sign at the entrance to Hairy John's Picnic Area. Written across Smokey's chest in large white letters is

RISK OF FOREST FIRES TODAY:

Beneath is a space for a sliding panel. She slides out yesterday's sign, HIGH, and considers her options.

HIGH.

LOW.

She looks around, senses the wind direction, weighs the variables: (1) it's going to be over 90 degrees today, but (2) there's been plenty of rainfall, and furthermore, (3) the humidity can plaster you to the floor; moreover, (4) she has no idea how to determine the risk of forest fires. She slides in HIGH.

Of course she can't do this every day of the year. Some random hunter could come across it on a cold snowy morning; it could breed cynicism.

Seems like someone's watching her, but there's no other car around, and besides she doesn't have that crawly feeling at the back of her neck. *Hairy John*, she feels like saying, *is that you?* only because the name sounds pornographic and she still finds it funny, and she knows she's being immature because no one else around here seems to find it odd at all. A legend is attached to him, he must have done something impressive to merit a picnic area. She could get like that herself someday, if she stays away from civilization long enough. Grumpy Pilar. A shaggy woman who lived in a hut in the mountains all by herself. They'll name a trail after her.

At the post office she checks her mailbox for a response to her latest letter of appeal. Nothing.

Pilar is prepared for this, she has another letter ready to go. But instead of putting it in the mail slot, she walks round to the counter. She needs human contact even if she doesn't want it. The fact that she doesn't want it is already cause for alarm.

The postmistress takes the envelope Pilar hands her.

"Any anthrax in here?" she rasps.

Above her, a sign says it's a violation of federal regulations to joke about mail tampering.

Pilar hasn't spoken all day and her voice comes out in squeaks.

"Couldn't get my hands on any this time," she says, and the postmistress cackles.

In her cabin Pilar lights the kerosene lamp and begins the next appeal letter.

*It has come to my attention*, she writes, *that fire prevention may not be the best method of forest management.*

The things she's learning.

*Fire rids the forest of weaker trees, slows the growth of certain less-desired understory plants, and promotes forest diversity.*

Someone, one of her predecessors in this ranger substation, has left an old issue of the *Journal of Forestry*. She had almost thrown it out, in the cleaning frenzy when she first got here. The journal and a few other books, dust-covered and brittle, had almost gone into the woodburning stove.

Now she's glad she spared them. She reads them slowly, to make them last—who else keeps her company every evening? From the *Annals of Snyder County* she's learned that Hairy John was a recluse in these mountains, no human contact except in a diphtheria epidemic, when he showed up carrying fresh water to people. They remember him for that, the hundred-year-old book says, even to this day. The Forest Service manual was written back when the ruined firetower on Thick Mountain was new and whole. Pilar has learned how often she is supposed to go there, how often to turn to face different parts of the compass. *Scan the horizon for smoke*, it tells her. *If you see flames, the conflagration is already in full force.* You have failed, in other words. The mountain is on fire.

*In short, the duties to which I have been arbitrarily reassigned by your office are not only outside the purview of my expertise, they are counterproductive to optimal forest health.*

She looks at what she's written, crosses out the last sentence.

*Fire cleans*, she writes. *Fire heals.*

A spider dangles from a ceiling beam, climbs back up. Pilar notices the webs in the corners, but she's given up on trying to oust the spiders. They're quiet, nonjudgmental. Pilar appreciates their company.

She tries to recall a law, simple and elegant, from college physics, something that would be easily understandable to whatever person in the Budget Office opens her letters and tosses them in the trash.

*For every destruction,* she writes, *there is an equal and opposite creation.*

The path up White Mountain narrows, and Pilar stubs her toe on a tree root that she can't even see. Mountain laurel bushes are waist high and she's wading through and a branch is grabbing at her ankle, she has to stop and disentangle her foot. Once she gets to a clear part of the path she sits down. Forest up here mostly hemlock and white pine, the soil hard and dry and the small stones along the path are pinkish white, silicate tinged with iron. She picks up a chunk and sniffs it. *What am I doing?*

Tiny flurry of movement on the path and she sees a toad skitter away, which makes her smile, but then she stands up, gets her face smacked by a low-hanging hemlock branch, goddammit. A wind shakes the tops of the trees, she smells leaf rot and pine needles on the air currents.

She hears something rustling nearby, maybe a deer. She can't remember which wolves they used to have here, gray or timber, but they're extinct now, same with the mountain lions, though the locals insist they still see them, and she knows for sure there's black bears around. No time for any of that because just ahead off the path a diamondback rattlesnake is sunning itself on flat rocks and it's so beautiful she can only stand and stare. The snake uncoils itself, esses away in sidewinding curves, and here she is at the edge of a steep drop—she knew it was here no matter what the map said.

She sits down on the rock ledge, puts out one foot to test her weight on the part where it juts out into space, yes, it'll hold. She lies on her belly and looks down, 1,300 feet to Penns Creek below, and out to ridge after forest-covered ridge. Formed by plate tectonics 300 million years ago. It makes her giddy to imagine herself back then, witnessing.

And the thing about trees that grow on craggy mountains: loggers can't get at them, plus hemlock's no good for timbering, shatters when you try to cut it. She's been wandering all over the last undisturbed soil in the whole mid-Atlantic.

From far off a sound wafts in, a throaty wailing bullhorn sound that ends on high sharp notes like brakes squealing. She waits, she can't believe, doesn't want to believe, hasn't heard the sound in a long time since they gave up on the mandatory drills.

And here again. The bioterror siren.

## The Lime-Green Shelter Door

She presses the buzzer again, slaps at it with her open palm. She's about to kick at the door when the intercom erupts in static. A blurry face swims out of the darkness, presses itself against the high-density plastic window. Other faces crowd in, then recede. The intercom spits out: "Password!"

"What the fuck?" *No, Pilar, this is not the right approach.*

She holds up her Forest Service I.D. "My radio's not working. Have you heard yet whether it's a drill?"

The answer makes no sense, something about President Ashfield, and end times.

"I don't know what kind of research you're doing here, I'm not trying to spy on you. Can you just let me in?"

The intercom ekes out staticky fragments of voices: "...back to the reservation!" ...back to Mexico!" ("I'm from Wilmington, Delaware," she says. Fucking rednecks, she's about to say—*Keep your mouth shut, Pilar.*) "Look at that short hair—she's one of *those.*" "That's what's wrong with this country."

Pilar is getting more and more nervous. What's beyond this door has become everything she could ever imagine wanting. She stares in horror at the intercom, like it's a grisly accident she can't look away from.

Faintly, almost at the bottom of this pile of voices: "We should help her." "Help one of *those?*" "Enough with your nonsense about Mud People. There's no Mud People in the Bible." "My point exactly."

Finally Pilar looks, really looks, at the sign that she'd taken to be just an abbreviation for some organization or research lab. SOLS, the sign says in large letters, then, in smaller letters along the bottom:

SOLDIERS OF OUR LORD AND SAVIOR.

"Oh Jesus," she says.

"Is she praying?"

"That didn't sound like a prayer."

One last try. "If you were true Christians," she shouts, "you'd let me in."

She doesn't wait for the answer, but hears it anyway as she runs back up the gravel path.

"If the Lord chose you to be saved, you'd be in here already."

The car won't start, solar capacity disrupted somehow, she has to switch to ethanol backup, but that should be enough to get her to the Agro-Chem Biosphere. They know her there.

A haze of reddish dust hangs in the air. Pilar coughs once, a deep-down spasm that seems to rip through her lungs. Power of suggestion, she tells herself. It's only a drill.

## Washington, D.C.

The breeze off the Potomac makes her shiver, riffles the pages of the report she's holding.

"Part One," she reads, but her voice comes out hoarse. She clears her throat. "Soil Depletion."

Behind her, the flags surrounding the Washington Monument snap and strain at their moorings. A few people stop to listen, but the section on erosion statistics makes their eyes glaze over, and they move on. Someone else wants directions to the Natural History Museum. Pilar points west, loses her place in the report, and starts over again. New people show up and she has to recap quickly:

"That big panel, you've heard about it probably, on soil regeneration? The Agriculture Division? Their final report came out last week."

She holds up one of her visual aids, a large square of posterboard on which she's drawn a map of the East Coast, using red marker to indicate the abandoned farmland all along the Atlantic seaboard.

"First they talked about terraforming the soil," she says. "It was all hush-hush, that plan, but they were ignoring the kind of ecosystem damage you can get when you introduce Amazonian microbes into a completely different context. So, well, when the environmentalists heard about it…" She never did admit to being the leak, but the higher-ups figured it out and she was kicked off the panel.

"And then the final report, it's everything agro-biz wants to hear."

She holds up chart #2, she's used black marker to scrawl a picture of the final report with a cartoon balloon issuing from where its mouth might be: *Apply petrochemicals liberally.*

She's especially proud of visual aid #3, an organizational chart showing Ag shrinking and then whooshing into the gaping maw of Homeland Security. "Agriculture used to be its own department. Of course, if these were planets it would make sense—larger bodies with stronger gravity pull smaller bodies into their orbit." You're off on a tangent, Pilar, you need to focus. "But we're not talking about planets here, these are government agencies, and it's like, animals on the food chain, a whale gobbling up plankton. Not that the Agriculture Department is like plankton..."

People think her Five-Hundred-Year Plan is performance art. The *Washington Post* calls her "wittily subversive."

And then come the Reassignment Memo, the blank-faced bureaucrats, the hulking granite Budget Office with no doors that she can discover, no windows. The exile to Bald Eagle, the forest with its muddy paths and slugs and unmarked trails and she gets to the top of White Mountain and she is lying on the rock outcrops looking down and it's a moment of grace so beautiful and dangerous and fragile. And then the siren.

## Wilmington, Delaware

She's out by the football field smoking a cigarette. She's cut study hall, she wants to look mysterious and daring, but the older boys, football players, are standing in a clump smoking pot and sneering at her.

They start running when the alarm sounds, she can't believe how fast a muscle-bound guy can move, and she's out of breath by the time she makes it to the side door. Damn drills. The vice principal ignores the star athletes filing past her and focuses on Pilar. "You're tempting fate, young lady. Do you know what happens to stragglers?"

It's recess and she's bored with the jump rope games the other girls are playing. She wanders three blocks down the street to their old elementary school, condemned for safety violations. In a few weeks it'll be torn down. Pilar looks up at the worn yellow-brick building, feels sorry for it. She's in the presence of something that's going to die, something that was part of her life.

She climbs the rickety metal jungle gym, wraps her knees around the rusty top bar and hangs deliciously suspended high above concrete pavement, everything hard and dangerous, you slip and you have broken bones, a cracked skull.

The alarm starts up.

## Another Shelter Door

She thinks about her parents, her nieces, everyone else. They must be safe. Focus, Pilar. Compartmentalize. Deny. Useful skills. She'll believe they're safe, and that's it. They were with a whole crowd of people when the alarm started. They weren't off somewhere daydreaming, they didn't straggle.

The car's ethanol tank is empty but the last quarter-mile is on a gentle downhill slope. She coasts past abandoned farmland bought up by Agro-Chem and into the driveway of the Agro-Chem compound.

It isn't a drill. That much she learns at the lime-green shelter door.

A droning voice at the intercom informs her about regulations and threat levels and she realizes he isn't going to open the door. A wind is kicking up the red dust. She wonders if it's clinging to her hair, her eyebrows.

"The regulations are clear."

"Guidelines," Pilar says, "not regulations."

"The risk is too great."

"Based on what? What data? What calculus?"

"Precisely. The risk is unknown."

She keeps her voice calm. "Follow my logic here. I'm obviously still alive." She winces, doubles over as a coughing spasm hits. She straightens up, bracing herself against the door. "OK, I grant you there's some kind of airborne irritant I'm reacting to. That's no reason for hysteria. I'm still alive, therefore—are you following me?—whatever toxins are in the air haven't reached a lethal—"

"The regulations are clear."

"You're not making any sense! You've decided on some arbitrary time frame, whoever hears the alarm within that time is safe, and to hell with everyone else."

"The risk is too great."

"I'd like to speak to a live human."

"You know, you need to work on your interpersonal skills."

She stomps back up to the main road and starts walking, no idea of a destination, just away. Any kind of shelter is better than nothing, there has to be some farmhouse or barn not yet torn down by Agro-Chem wrecking crews.

She breaks into a run. Not because there's any building in sight, but for the sake of running, while her body still works, while her muscles are still strong. If death is going to get her, it will have to tackle her at a full gallop, not find her cringing by a locked door, begging to be let in.

And what if someone *had* opened the door? Hell of a choice, redneck fundamentalists or rule-abiding cowards, and she'd have been stuck with them for who knows how long, years, maybe decades. She would have gone insane.

What the hell, Pilar, there's a bright side.

She laughs.

She runs faster, pumping her arms, lowering her head against the wind that keeps getting stronger, the dust stings her skin and flies in her eyes. Soon it's so thick she can hardly see the road, but she keeps running, long, fast strides that start to seem like leaps, until she takes a leap and doesn't land, she's in the air, and she feels hands reaching for her, strong, kind hands, many hands, breaking her fall, cradling her to the warm, soft earth.

## II.

> The name of the Devil . . . is nothing else than a corruption of *deva*, the Sanskrit name for God.
> —John Fiske, *Myths and Myth-Makers*

She wakes up hearing the voice. A low, rumbling sound that seems like her own blood pulsing through her veins. Slowly she realizes the voice is forming words.

"So," it says, "you must have done something pretty bad to get shut out like that."

"My hair's too short."

Laughter, almost below hearing, like the ground trembling when trains pass.

She falls asleep, smiling at the voice.

## III.

Whoever dances belongs to the whole.
—*Round Dance of the Cross* (2nd-century Christian
gospel, banned as heretical in the 4th century)

They dance in the clearing. Sun filters through lacy hemlock branches, and in the shafts of light they shuffle and hop, they sway, they spin around, giggle when they bump together. No one minds that Pilar looks dazed, red dust clinging to her fine black hair, her thick eyebrows. She'll snap out of it.

They move faster and laugh more, they bounce, they leap and fling their arms out.

The red-tailed hawk riding the air currents far above them sees shapes and colors, jerky elbows and knees in faded velvet, deerskin, soccer jersey and jeans, shimmy and bop, nothing that looks like plump pheasant or juicy chipmunk. She flies on.

The dance breaks apart as easily as it comes together. People scramble up the rock face on the other side of Swift Run, they scale a flank of the mountain, grabbing on to witch hazel branches and knobby roots of white pine. Or they run downstream, to where Rock Springs plunges down over sandstone slabs and a cool mist rises on the hottest summer day. Or they scurry upstream, where Swift Run goes underground and you can stomp out a drumbeat, hear your feet echo on hollow rock and rushing water while far off a bull elk in a frisky mood is grunting and bugling.

On the bank of Swift Run, a giant hairy naked man stands still and lets Pilar walk slowly around him, looking at him from all angles.

He can tell she's confused, she's been out there again, the siren, the road, blah de blah. Poor child, all those locked doors.

The more she scowls the wider he grins. He takes a slow step forward, lunge, then a leap back.

"You don't have horns and a tail," she says.

"I don't torment souls either, but who can control the rumor mill?"

Hands on hips, he squats deeply, kicks up one foot and then the other. He raises a hand and does the squat-kick while spinning around.

"You can call me Dev," he says.

The answer to every question:

Why is there a wide blue sky?

What's the reason for grass?

Why do we sing?

To dance under. To dance on. So that we can dance.

The Devil's Catechism, Pilar calls it.

She climbs a tall pine tree and no matter how high she climbs and how delicate the branches, they still hold her weight. Dev's there ahead of her, on an impossibly tiny branch, hanging upside down by his knees the way she used to do on jungle gyms when she was a kid.

"It's an arrangement we have, he and I," Dev says. "The other guy— some people like to think of him as my rival—" he wants to point at the sky, but he's upside down and his finger points to the ground. "Oops," he says, "other way around." He swings up and sits cross-legged on the branch. "He gets the winners, I get—well, you all."

Pilar clings to the top of the pine as it sways in the breeze. "I never paid attention to churchy stuff," she says, "but this isn't like anything I've ever heard about."

"I hate to criticize a colleague, but he's a bit harsh. You hear all this lip service about blessed are the poor, the meek are slated to inherit the earth someday, but in the meantime—well, anyone who watches the way things go can tell you, it's clear who he prefers. He doesn't have a lot of sympathy for life's losers."

"So I'm a loser. Thanks a lot."

"Let's dance."

She presses the buzzer again, slaps at it. They want a password, they talk about the Bible, tell her go back to Mexico.

She kicks at the lime-green door, shakes her fist at the high-density plastic window.

"Listen, you stupid rednecks—"

*I'll never get this right.*

She sits by a forest stream, water rushing over her bare feet. Kneeling before her on a rock is a white man wearing yards of burlap, belted around with a frayed rope. He has light brown hair and a short beard, his skin is pitted and weathered, his eyes have a hint of blue or green, but are mostly glittering gray. At one time she knew his kind, knew what the robe meant, the rope belt, the sandals.

He cradles Pilar's foot in his hand, caresses her arch with his thumb.

"That's much better now, isn't it?" he says. "Those things you wore, like hobnail boots…"

He speaks a language she doesn't know, German-sounding, yet she understands him. His voice soothes her.

He looks up at her and his eyes cloud over.

"I'm Brother Wulfstan," he says gently. "You've been out there, haven't you, alone on that road. Dear heart, you must forget it. You're here with us now."

"He's coaxed you out of socks and shoes again," Dev says. "Wulfstan's afraid you'll stomp him with your boots. He's the least wolf-like man I know."

She laughs. Wulfstan smiles as she leans toward him and cups his chin in her hand.

You could get lost in that other life, your life before, there's a jump in time and suddenly you're *there*, pounding on a locked door and you turn around and face soldiers with bayonets raised, or airborne plague, slave traders, armed mercenaries, radiation, villagers with torches and pitchforks. But then you hear laughter, someone touches your arm and calls you back to *now*:

What do we believe in?

The dance.

How did we come into being?

We danced ourselves into existence.

Why are we here?

To dance.

Elemental cloud swirling, our atoms, our molecules. Gases and dust, yes, the same soft motes that float onto your desk, the same stuff to which you will return, turn, we swirl, we collide, explode and rejoin, we cling together and our molten iron heart shouts and throbs. Rockmelt, call it rock broth, bubbles and steams. Molecules grip molecules, form lattice of crystals, yes, connection, jump, grab hands. Chunks of the rock puree cool and it's a stew, then all of it crusts over. Rock islands float on rock sea, collide and rift apart, mountains push up, crumble, rain drizzles through soil and gushes out in streams, callused feet stomp and skip and kick up clouds of dust.

Look at her, disgruntled geologist in a virgin forest, she comes huffing and puffing, clomps along in her hiking boots, that nonstop interior monologue, *I've been wronged, I've been wronged*. The trees are exhaling oxygen for her, she's not even grateful. This is one angry public servant. We swat her in the face and laugh when she curses.

Pilar lies face-down sniffing the soil, laughing, iron ore's like perfume, silicon and potassium have a bitter tang, magnesium's spicy-sweet. The magnetic field reverberates up her legs, out the top of her head.

She and the others watch the stars, or sit around bonfires, or gather to watch a sunset like a crowd at a sporting event, finding the perfect word, carmine? vermillion? Anything you think would be good to eat, is: honeysuckle blossoms, pinecones, hay. No thirst of any kind goes unsatisfied.

Wulfstan hardly ever talks about himself. Pilar gathers his story from stray comments. She guesses thirteenth century, central Europe, though he has no sense of years, of places.

He didn't read or write, wasn't interested in that. Learning was for the monks of noble birth, the beautiful illuminated manuscripts he wouldn't have dared touch. He swept out the barns, milked the cows, made butter and cheese. He didn't begrudge the other monks their refusal to help when he set up a hospital, a few straw pallets in an outlying grain barn, for the villagers who were showing up with symptoms of an unknown disease that was soon becoming a plague. The abbot fretted over the declining tribute from bedridden peasants while Wulfstan tried to ease their last days, holding their hands, wiping their feverish skin and murmuring prayers. The monks turned him out when he started showing symptoms himself.

Pilar craves a cigarette. She finds a tobacco plant, hangs some leaves up to dry for a few days and then lights them on a campfire. The smell reminds her of cigars.

"It's a stress reliever," she tells an old wreck of a white man. He nods.

People's symptoms reappear sometimes: a rash, sores from bubonic plague or hemorrhagic fever, Pilar's lung-ripping cough.

The old man, Marlin, sits next to her on a log, breathing in the cigar-tinged air.

"Who *is* Dev?" Pilar says, and Marlin thinks about it for a while.

"He knows a lot. I think he's the mayor."

Marlin tells her how he used to spend his days sitting by the railroad tracks, how the summer sun made the metal give off a shiny smell. "The railway cars, you know, in the old days, they used to hook one up with another like this"—he holds up his index finger and with the other hand makes a loop around it. "So I gets to thinking, wouldn't they be stronger if they linked up like this"—he holds up one hand, palm-down, fingers gripping the upturned fingers of the other hand—"and wouldn't you know, them railroad people did what I said. Do you remember railroads? Do y'know what I mean?"

"Sounds familiar," Pilar says. "I'm not sure."

He looks around for something he can compare to steel. He hardly remembers, either. He has flashes of people somewhere laughing at him and calling him simple. Nights spent sleeping in the county jail when the winter wind blew through the gaps in his cabin walls. "What was I saying?"

Pilar shrugs.

"Patents," he says, "ever hear of them? I'm waiting on the paperwork."

Paperwork. Pilar sits at her desk reading a memo and she's aware of her cells, the way they vibrate, metabolize energy. Her blood is pumping and her cells are soft and squashy, no protective bark, and what are these vertical things all around her, like cliff faces but naked and smooth, and this thing that stretches above her head, not a rock ledge, no. What? *What?*

Words like *past* and *future* lose their meaning. She'll be in what she thinks is the present, and then realizes it's the past, and then fast-forward to a later time that still feels like the present. One moment she's waking up under the trees after a night of dancing, cushioned by pine needles. Another moment she's with the others, a crowd of them, running quickly, bearing down on Wulfstan as he stumbles around dazed and feverish, they grab him, carry him off without slowing down or breaking stride.

Time is circular.

"I think it's spiral," Wulfstan says, tracing the whorls of her earlobe with his finger.

"Like the dance," she says, or maybe he says it, or they both think it at the same time.

"Who do *you* think he is?" Pilar asks Dorothea, a Black woman with neatly braided graying hair and eyes that are bright and severe until she smiles. She wears an old-fashioned button-up dress of some iridescent dark material that reminds Pilar of feathers.

"A circuit preacher," Dorothea says. Pilar always asks this question. She gives her a different answer each time.

"To everything there is a season," Dev says. "A time to dance, a time to embrace, a time to love."

"You're leaving out entire sentences," Dorothea tells him. At one time she knew the whole book by heart. She doesn't know what's happening to her memory.

"Did I mention a time to dance?" Dev grips her waist, lifts her till she's eye-level with him. "You're priceless," he says.

A pearl of great price. People with a price on their heads, sad dark people showing up at Dorothea's house for food and money and shelter on their way—where? North? God bless you, they told her. She made speeches, raised money. You're an angel, they told her. May the Lord bless and keep you, but she's not sure anymore what "bless" means, or who the Lord is, sounds too much like a boss-man.

"Go thy way," Dev says, "eat thy bread with joy, and drink thy wine with a merry heart."

They dance in the clearing, crowded around Dev, a jumble of movements and rhythms. Pilar sways, waves her arms above her head, dodges out of the way of elbows and knees. Wulfstan spins around, face tilted up, eyes closed, arms flung out like he's about to hug them all. Slowly the dancers move outward away from Dev, he's in the middle and they're circling round him. They speed up, slow down, speed up, crash into each other and jump away. Dev is heat and light at the center, someday he'll swell up and engulf them and that's another turn of the dance.

"Truly the light is sweet," he says, "and a pleasant thing it is to behold the sun. So behold the sun!"

Sunny day, she can get out of the office, have lunch in the park. She sits on a rock and it looks delicious, her fingers reach greedily, she'll break it up and eat the little pieces through her skin. *What?*

"Lots of things you're forgetting," Dev says as they sit under a pine tree. Pilar digs her toes into loose soil and pine needles and leans against him while he massages her neck. "Remember all those rules you people used to have for coupling," he says. "Contracts to sign, vows to take."

"What were we thinking?"

He kisses the back of her neck, lets his breath cascade along her skin. "It's beautifully simple," he says. "When you're thirsty, drink from the stream."

"Do you remember," Wulfstan says, "those troupes that travel around the countryside, they sing, do performances. I think that's what we are, though we never do any plays, do we, and I've never seen our horse and caravan."

Pilar considers organizing a performance of *Godspell*. "Excellent suggestion," Dev says, and launches into "All Good Gifts" in a fine bass-baritone.

"I don't know," Pilar says. "It might confuse people." The cast of characters, the whole story line are things she no longer understands.

She stands still, watching wild turkey pick their way through beech and hickory trees. A young black bear walks up to her, puts a forepaw on her shoulder and with a hind paw tries to find a foothold on her knee. Pilar topples over and he walks off, disappointed. She looks up at the sky, she is not magnificent like the bear, even a small one, with its thick fur and lumbering rolling walk, in fact she's the opposite, she gets more shambly by the minute. She sees Dev's face loom over her.

"Pilar Quiñones?" he gasps. "*The* Pilar Quiñones, author of the Five-Hundred-Year Plan for Soil Regeneration?" Yes, she starts to say, flattered, and then she's confused, he's said this before, right, or is this the first time again?

The breeze off the Potomac makes her shiver, riffles the pages of the report she's holding. Behind her, the flags surrounding the Washington Monument snap and strain at their moorings.

"Part One," she reads, but her voice comes out hoarse. She clears her throat. "Soil Depletion."

The controversy, the banishment: just a way to get to the forest.

In the cabin she uses an old-fashioned, fire-heated iron to press her Forest Service uniform. It's a way to keep up her morale, but why would she think this? She loves it here, what more could she ask than to be in service to the forest?

"Who do you think he is?" she asks Wulfstan, and it makes him sad, he's heard this question before. Who do they say that I am? Voices of his brother monks resound around him, they used to sing to greet the morning, sing to the evening, where are they now?

"Are you a heathen?" he asks Pilar hopefully. He's never seen one.

"Just like you now," she says, "you old sinner, you," and he laughs even though she hasn't answered his question.

People sit by the campfire and listen to Pilar try to explain where mountains come from. "You've got your basic sandstone," she says. "It metamorphoses, changes, into quartzite. What we've got here. The hardest mineral on earth."

"Why?"

"Why does it change? From pressure and heat in the mantle."

"Why?"

"Okay," she says. "Think of a core. Down in the middle of a ball, and layers over it. Those layers are always on the move, like vegetables in a broth."

"I think you're mixing your metaphors," Dorothea says.

"Good point. So this stuff churns around, some stuff sinks, some rises to the surface. These mountains here, they're hundreds of millions of years old. The glaciers are just yesterday, in comparison, they receded only ten thousand years ago."

Marlin raises his hand. "Ten thousand years before what?"

"Good question," Pilar says.

Dev hugs him.

"You've got my vote, sir," Marlin says.

Ten thousand years before the lime-green shelter door, of course, because time is anchored to place, doesn't everyone know that?

She's lying under a pine tree, head cradled on Dev's lap. She digs her toes into loose soil and pine needles.

"You have to forget it," Dev says, "if you want to move on."

"Forget the shelter door? My memories make me who I am. What would I be if not for that?"

"What would you like to be?"

She pounds her fist against the lime-green door, kicks at it. "Fanatics! Fucking cowards!"

One day, she knows, she'll knock on that door and just laugh, just lean on it and laugh and go straight to the dancing in the clearing and then hum and quiver her branches at the memory of it all.

"Blessed are those who tell the truth," Dev says. "They shall dance."

"Blessed are those who laugh in the face of death. They shall have their heart's desire."

Wulfstan hardly remembers the monastery, the whole drama of the plague time, being turned out by the monks when he fell ill. What stands out in his memory is the beauty of that last night wandering in the forest. The moon was just past full but still bright enough to cast shadows. He had the sense that wild animals were nearby; out of pity they were keeping him company, their breathing timed to his own labored breaths, in, out, in.

"After intense suffering," Dev says, "intense joy."

They give each other looks: *Dev. Inscrutable as always.*

"What does 'after' mean?" they say.

"Breath of breaths," Wulfstan says, "everything is breath." He grows more and more distant from his old life. "Long ago," he says, "I was with...others...another troupe, maybe. They thought the act of love was, I don't remember the word...wrong, somehow."

He struggles to think of the term. The woman he's with, she can't remember it either.

Dev's mistaken about Wulfstan, Pilar thinks. She can see the graceful, intelligent wolf he's in the process of becoming. One day he'll leave altogether, he'll drop down on all fours and go loping away up the mountain, and the Pilar of the before time will be there with clipboard and backpack and neatly pressed Forest Service uniform, and she'll catch a glimpse of him, there'll be a whiff of cigar smoke, she'll see a flurry of movement out of the corner of her eye, a ragged sleeve, a wisp of uncombed hair, her own self dancing past.

# ACKNOWLEDGMENTS

"Bringing Down the Clouds" copyright © 2000 by Kathleen Alcalá. Previously published in *Treasures in Heaven* (Chronicle, 2000).

"Dear Juana of God" copyright © 2015 by Beth Alvarado. Previously published in *Drunken Boat*, Librotraficante issue, spring 2014.

"Discretion" copyright © 2015 by Jennifer Baker.

"Silted Castle Walls" copyright © 2015 by Megan Rahija Bush.

"The Star of the North" copyright © 2014 by Cathleen Calbert.

"Noelia and Amparo" copyright © 2013 by Glendaliz Camacho. Previously published in *Southern Pacific Review,* July 2013, and *All About Skin: Short Fiction by Women of Color* (University of Wisconsin Press, 2014).

"Physics" copyright © 2010 by Kim Chinquee. Previously published in *New World Writing*, Spring 2010.

"The Conversion of Sister Terence" copyright © 2015 by Liz Dougherty Dolan.

"Your Giraffe Is Burning" copyright © 2015 by E. A. Fow.

"A Big Girl Has a Good Time with Small Men" copyright © 2013 by Heather Fowler. Previously published in *This Time, While We're Awake* (Aqueous, 2013).

"Accident" copyright © 2013 by Tracy Gold. Previously published in *YARN*, October 2013.

"Miss Emily Gray" copyright © 2004 by Theodora Goss. Previously published in *Alchemy 2*, August 2004.

"What Do You Call a Monster?" copyright © 2015 by Laura Hart.

"Test Group 4: Womanhood and Other Failures" copyright © 2011 by SJ Sindu. Previously published in *Water~Stone Review*, Fall 2011.

"The Last Man on Earth" copyright © 2008 by Karen Stromberg. Previously published in *qarrtsiluni*, November 2008.

"Our Lady of the Artichokes" copyright © 2004 by Katherine Vaz. Previously published in *Pleiades*, 24.1 (2004) and *Our Lady of the Artichokes and Other Portuguese-American Stories* (University of Nebraska Press, 2007).

"And the Wisdom to Know the Difference" copyright © 2015 by Hilary Zaid.

# CONTRIBUTORS

**Kathleen Alcalá** is the author of five books set in the Southwest and Mexico. A founding editor of the *Raven Chronicles*, she teaches fiction at the Northwest Institute of Literary Arts in Washington State. More at www.kathleenalcala. com.

"Dear Juana of God" is from **Beth Alvarado**'s story-cycle *Jillian in the Borderlands*. Recent stories and essays have been published in *The Sun*, *Southern Review, Western Humanities Review, Drunken Boat*'s Librotraficante Portfolio, *Eleven Eleven*, and *The Collagist*. She is the author of two books, *Anthropologies* (University of Iowa, 2011) and *Not a Matter of Love* (New Rivers, 2006). She is the fiction editor of *Cutthroat: A Journal of the Arts*.

**Jennifer Baker** is a native New Yorker and writer of fiction and nonfiction, creator of the Minorities in Publishing podcast, and social media manager for We Need Diverse Books. Her writing has appeared in *Newtown Literary, Boston Literary Magazine, Eclectic Flash*, and *Poets & Writers* magazine. Her website is www.jennifernbaker.com.

**Megan Rahija Bush** has just completed her MFA in Creative Nonfiction from the University of Alaska–Fairbanks. She currently lives in a wall tent in Gustavus, Alaska, which is the cheapest, most freeing way to complete her memoir about her family's experience with schizophrenia. Bush has recently been published in *Tidal Echoes, Cactus Heart Press*, and *If and Only If Journal*.

**Cathleen Calbert**'s poetry and prose have appeared in many publications, including the *New Republic*, the *New York Times*, and *Paris Review*. She has published three books of poems: *Lessons in Space, Bad Judgment,* and *Sleeping* *with a Famous Poet.* Her fourth, *The Afflicted Girls,* is forthcoming from Little Red Tree. She has been awarded the Nation Discovery Award, a Pushcart Prize, and the Mary Tucker Thorp Award from Rhode Island College, where she is a professor of English.

**Glendaliz Camacho** was born and raised in the Washington Heights neighborhood of New York City. Her writing has appeared in *All About Skin: An Anthology of Short Fiction by Award-Winning Women Writers of Color* (University of Wisconsin Press, 2014), *Saraba Magazine,* and *Kweli Journal,* among others. She was a 2013 Pushcart Prize nominee and is currently working on a short story collection.

**Kim Chinquee** is the author of the collections *Pistol, Pretty,* and *Oh Baby.* She lives in Buffalo, New York. Her website is www.kimchinquee.com.

**Liz Dougherty Dolan**'s poetry collection, *A Secret of Long Life,* nominated for both the Robert McGovern Prize, Ashville University, and a Pushcart, has been published by Cave Moon Press. Her first poetry collection, *They Abide,* was published by March Street. An eight-time Pushcart nominee and winner of *Best of the Web,* she was a finalist for *Best of the Net 2014.* She won the Nassau Prize for Nonfiction 2011, and the same prize for fiction, 2015. She has received fellowships from the Delaware Division of the Arts, the Atlantic Center for the Arts, and Martha's Vineyard. Dolan serves on the poetry board of *Philadelphia Stories.* She is most grateful for her ten grandchildren, who pepper her life and who live on the next block.

**E. A. Fow** was born and raised in New Zealand but has lived in Brooklyn, New York, for the past twenty-five years. When not writing fiction, she is teaching college or working on inclusive approaches to Joseph Campbell's monomyth.

**Heather Fowler** is the author of the story collections *Suspended Heart* (Aqueous, 2010), *People with Holes* (Pink Narcissus, 2012), *This Time, While We're Awake* (Aqueous, 2013), and *Elegantly Naked in My Sexy Mental Illness* (Queen's Ferry, 2014). She is poetry editor at *Corium Magazine.* Please visit www.heatherfowler.com.

**Tracy Gold** is a writer, editor, marketer, and teacher. Her writing is published or forthcoming in *YARN, Stoneslide Corrective, Refractions,* and several other journals. Gold is an MFA candidate at the University of Baltimore. When she's not working, she's hanging out with her rescued horse and dog.

**Theodora Goss**'s publications include the short story collection *In the Forest of Forgetting* (2006); *Interfictions* (2007), a short story anthology coedited with Delia Sherman; *Voices from Fairyland* (2008), a poetry anthology with critical essays and a selection of her own poems; *The Thorn and the Blossom* (2012), a novella in a two-sided accordion format; and the poetry collection *Songs for Ophelia* (2014). Her work has been translated into ten languages, including French, Japanese, and Turkish. She has been a finalist for the Nebula, Crawford, Locus, Seiun, and Mythopoeic Awards, and on the Tiptree Award Honor List. Her short story "Singing of Mount Abora" (2007) won the World Fantasy Award. She teaches literature and writing at Boston University and in the Stonecoast MFA Program.

**Laura Hart** is a marketing manager in New York City, but prefers to just say she's a writer. She is a cat fanatic, an extroverted introvert, and a lover of beautiful things and beautiful words and beautiful people. Her work has also appeared in *Lake Region Review*. In the spring of 2014, Hart graduated from SUNY Fredonia with a degree in English and moved to Brooklyn with her kitten and her best friend.

**Catherine Haustein** is the author of *Natural Attraction* (Penner, 2015). She's a mother, grandmother, and analytical chemist. She likes kids and dogs, has a messy desk, and dislikes mansplaining.

**Janis Butler Holm** lives in Athens, Ohio, where she has served as associate editor for *Wide Angle*, the film journal. Her prose, poems, and performance pieces have appeared in small-press, national, and international magazines. Her sound poems have been featured in the inaugural edition of *Best American Experimental Writing*, edited by Cole Swensen.

**Judy Juanita**'s novel *Virgin Soul* (Viking, 2013) tells of a naive student in the San Francisco Bay Area who becomes radicalized and joins the Black Panther Party in the 1960s. Juanita's plays, poetry, and fiction are published widely.

**Soniah Kamal**'s novel *An Isolated Incident* was a finalist for the KLF French Fiction Prize. Kamal is a Paul Bowles Fiction Fellow at Georgia State University (MFA) and the recipient of the Susan B. Irene Award from St.

Johns College for her thesis "Arranged versus Love Marriages." Kamal curated and edited "No Place Like Home: Borders, Boundaries and Identity in South Asia and Diaspora" (*Sugar Mule*, issue 43). Her essays, book reviews, author interviews, and short stories have appeared in *Scroll. in*, *Huffington Post*, *Bengal Lights*, *The Rumpus*, *Arts ATL*, *Akashic Thursdaze*, and more, and are included in critically acclaimed anthologies. For more, visit Kamal at www.soniahkamal.com.

**Rosalie Morales Kearns** is a writer of Puerto Rican and Pennsylvania Dutch descent and author of the feminist magic-realist story collection *Virgins and Tricksters* (Aqueous, 2012). Her stories, poems, essays, and book reviews have appeared in *Witness*, *Drunken Boat*, *The Nervous Breakdown*, and other journals. She is also the founder of Shade Mountain Press.

**Elizabeth Kerlikowske** is the author of eight books/chapbooks, most recently *Last Hula*, winner of the Standing Rock Cultural Arts Chapbook Contest, 2013. She is president of Friends of Poetry, a nonprofit dedicated to putting people and poetry together. Her visual art has appeared in several juried shows. She is a professor emeritus of Kellogg Community College.

**Ellie Knightsbridge** is from London and enjoys such things as peeling stickers off fruit and binging on TV box sets. Her work has featured in print and online and her next story will appear in *Dreams from the Witch House: Female Voices of Lovecraftian Horror* in late 2015.

**Dawn Knox** is married with one son and has been writing fiction for several years. She has had several short horror, sci-fi, speculative fiction, and romance stories published, and her first novel, *Daffodil and the Thin Place*, was published in 2014. Also in 2014, she wrote a script that was performed as part of her town's commemoration of World War I.

**Joanna Lesher** is a freelance writer from suburban Detroit. She spent a year in Hiroshima after college and speaks passable Japanese. She is a member of Mid Michigan Poetry and Prose and contributes to that organization's blog, as well as her personal website, www.joannalesher.com.

**Sharanya Manivannan**'s first book, *Witchcraft*, was described in the *Straits Times* (Singapore) as "sensuous and spiritual, delicate and dangerous and as full as the moon reflected in a knife." She was specially commissioned to write and perform a poem at the 2015 Commonwealth Day Observance at

Westminster Abbey, London, in front of an audience including the British royal family. Her next book of poems will be published by HarperCollins India in 2016.

**Teresa Milbrodt** has published a short story collection, *Bearded Women: Stories* (ChiZine); a novel, *The Patron Saint of Unattractive People* (Boxfire); and a flash fiction collection, *Larissa Takes Flight: Stories* (Pressgang). Her stories have appeared in numerous literary magazines, and her work has been nominated for a Pushcart Prize. She received her MFA in Creative Writing from Bowling Green State University.

**Alison Newall** is a Montreal-based writer and translator whose work has appeared in *Hejira, Canadian Woman Studies*, and *Carte Blanche*, and short-listed for *This Magazine* and Writer's Union of Canada competitions.

**Gina Ochsner** lives in Keizer, Oregon, and teaches writing and literature at Corban University and with Seattle Pacific's low-residency MFA program. She is the author of the short story collections *The Necessary Grace to Fall* and *People I Wanted to Be* and the novel *The Russian Dreambook of Color and Flight*, which was long-listed for the Orange Award. A novel set in eastern Latvia and featuring a boy with enormous ears is forthcoming.

**Maureen O'Leary** is a writer and educator from Sacramento, California. She is an award-winning poet and author of the novels *How to Be Manly, The Arrow,* and *The Ghost Daughter*. Her short stories and poems appear in *Esopus, Night Train Journal, Revolution John, Brackish, Prick of the Spindle, Gold Man Review*, and other publications. O'Leary loves writing, reading, West African dance and drumming, working out in old-school gyms, and swimming in the ocean.

Award-winning author, vegan warrior, and amateur neuroscientist **Jay O'Shea** lives and works in Los Angeles. A professor at UCLA, she is currently studying the cognitive benefits of hard-style martial arts training. She has written and edited several books on dance; her essays have been published in three languages and six countries. Her short fiction has appeared in *Bartleby Snopes, Toasted Cheese*, and in the anthologies *Bloody Knuckles* and *Death's Realm*. She is currently completing a novel titled *The Alchemy of Loss*. Website: www.jayoshea.com. Twitter: @jayboshea.

**Sarah Marian Seltzer** is a journalist and fiction writer based out of New York City who currently serves as the editor-at-large at *Flavorwire.com*. Her work has appeared in dozens of online and print publications and earned her several fellowships. She graduated from the MFA program at Vermont College of Fine Arts in 2012. Find out more at www.sarahmseltzer.com.

**Enid Shomer** is the author of four books of poetry and three of fiction. *Imaginary Men* (University of Iowa Press) won the Iowa Prize in Fiction as well as the LSU/*Southern Review* Prize. *Tourist Season: Stories* (Random House, 2007) won the Gold Medal in Fiction from the State of Florida. *The Twelve Rooms of the Nile* (Simon & Schuster, 2012) was selected by NPR as one of the top six historical novels of the year. In 2013, Shomer received the Lifetime Achievement Award in Writing from the Florida Humanities Council.

**SJ Sindu** is a Tamil Sri Lankan American writer interested in intersections of marginalized identities and violence. Sindu was a 2013 Lambda Literary Fellow, and received a fellowship from the Skidmore Summer Writers' Conference in 2012. Sindu is a PhD student at Florida State University, and has published in *Brevity, Water~Stone Review, Harpur Palate, The MacGuffin, Sinister Wisdom*, and elsewhere.

**Karen Stromberg**'s poetry and flash fiction appear in *qarrtsiluni, Red River Review, wordgathering, Right Hand Pointing, Pedestal Magazine, A Year in Ink* (vols. 5 and 6), the *San Diego Poetry Annual*, and elsewhere. She also has work included in two anthologies: *Bigger Than They Appear: Anthology of Very Short Poems* (Accents Publishing, 2011); and *Forgetting Home: Poems about Alzheimer's* (CreateSpace, 2013). Stromberg has an MA in Creative Writing–Fiction from San Diego State University and has been nominated twice for the Pushcart Prize.

**Katherine Vaz** has been a Briggs-Copeland Fellow in Fiction at Harvard University and Fellow of the Radcliffe Institute for Advanced Study. She's the author of two novels, *Saudade* (a Barnes and Noble Discover Great New Writers selection) and *Mariana*, published in six languages and picked by the Library of Congress as one of the Top 30 International Books of 1998. Her collection *Fado & Other Stories* won a Drue Heinz Literature Prize, and *Our Lady of the Artichokes* won a *Prairie Schooner* Award. Her children's stories have appeared in anthologies by Viking, Penguin, and Simon and Schuster, and her short fiction has appeared in many magazines. She won a New

York Film Academy and Writer's Store national contest for a screenplay idea based on one of her stories. She lives in New York City. She's the first Portuguese-American to have her work recorded by the Library of Congress (Hispanic Division). Other honors include a National Endowment for the Arts Fellowship, a citation as a Portuguese-American Woman of the Year, and an appointment to the six-person Presidential Delegation (Clinton) to the World's Fair/Expo 98 in Lisbon.

**Hilary Zaid** is an alumna of the 2013 Tin House Writers Workshop and the 2012 James D. Houston Scholar at the Squaw Valley Community of Writers. Her short fiction has appeared in numerous publications, including *Lilith Magazine, Utne Reader, Southwest Review*, and (forthcoming) *CALYX*. Her story "The Darkness between the Stars" is the 2014 *BLOOM* Chapbook Prize winner in fiction (Judge: Lucy Jane Bledsoe).

# ALSO FROM SHADE MOUNTAIN PRESS

### WHITE LIGHT
**Vanessa Garcia**

*Novel*

A young Cuban-American artist distills her grief, rage, and love onto the canvas.

"Lyrical"—Wole Soyinka
"A lush, vibrant portrayal"—*Kirkus* (starred)

Paperback, 284 pages, $28.00, September 2015

### HER OWN VIETNAM
**Lynn Kanter**

*Novel*

Decades after serving as a U.S. Army nurse in Vietnam, a woman confronts buried wartime memories and unresolved family issues.

"Compassionate and perceptively told"
—*Foreword Reviews*
Silver Award, Indiefab Book of the Year,
War & Military Fiction

Paperback, 211 pages, $18.95, November 2014

### EGG HEAVEN: STORIES
**Robin Parks**

*Short Stories*

Lyrical tales of diner waitresses and their customers, living the un-glamorous life in Southern California.

"A skilled and elegiac storyteller"—René Steinke
"Illuminates a world entirely its own"—*Kenyon Review*

Paperback, 150 pages, $16.95, October 2014

Shade Mountain Press
www.ShadeMountainPress.com